A Daughter of the Land

A Daughter of the Land
by Gene Stratton Porter

Wilder Publications, LLC.
PO Box 3005
Radford VA 24143-3005

ISBN 10: 1-60459-475-6
ISBN 13: 978-1-60459-475-1

The Wings of Morning

"Take the wings of Morning."

Kate Bates followed the narrow footpath rounding the corner of the small country church, as the old minister raised his voice slowly and impressively to repeat the command he had selected for his text. Fearing that her head would be level with the windows, she bent and walked swiftly past the church; but the words went with her, iterating and reiterating themselves in her brain. Once she paused to glance back toward the church, wondering what the minister would say in expounding that text. She had a fleeting thought of slipping in, taking the back seat and listening to the sermon. The remembrance that she had not dressed for church deterred her; then her face twisted grimly as she again turned to the path, for it occurred to her that she had nothing else to wear if she had started to attend church instead of going to see her brother.

As usual, she had left her bed at four o'clock; for seven hours she had cooked, washed dishes, made beds, swept, dusted, milked, churned, following the usual routine of a big family in the country. Then she had gone upstairs, dressed in clean gingham and confronted her mother.

"I think I have done my share for to-day," she said. "Suppose you call on our lady school-mistress for help with dinner. I'm going to Adam's."

Mrs. Bates lifted her gaunt form to very close six feet of height, looking narrowly at her daughter.

"Well, what the nation are you going to Adam's at this time a- Sunday for?" she demanded.

"Oh, I have a curiosity to learn if there is one of the eighteen members of this family who gives a cent what becomes of me!" answered Kate, her eyes meeting and looking clearly into her mother's.

"You are not letting yourself think he would 'give a cent' to send you to that fool normal-thing, are you?"

"I am not! But it wasn't a 'fool thing' when Mary and Nancy Ellen, and the older girls wanted to go. You even let Mary go to college two years."

"Mary had exceptional ability," said Mrs. Bates.

"I wonder how she convinced you of it. None of the rest of us can discover it," said Kate.

"What you need is a good strapping, Miss."

"I know it; but considering the facts that I am larger than you, and was eighteen in September, I shouldn't advise you to attempt it. What is the difference whether I was born in '62 or '42? Give me the chance you gave Mary, and I'll prove to you that I can do anything she has done, without having 'exceptional ability!'"

"The difference is that I am past sixty now. I was stout as an ox when Mary wanted to go to school. It is your duty and your job to stay here and do this work."

"To pay for having been born last? Not a bit more than if I had been born first. Any girl in the family owes you as much for life as I do; it is up to the others to pay back in service, after they are of age, if it is to me. I have done my share. If Father were not the richest farmer in the county, and one of the richest men, it would be different. He can afford to hire help for you, quite as well as he can for himself."

"Hire help! Who would I get to do the work here?"

"You'd have to double your assistants. You could not hire two women who would come here and do so much work as I do in a day. That is why I decline to give up teaching, and stay here to slave at your option, for gingham dresses and cowhide shoes, of your selection. If I were a boy, I'd work three years more and then I would be given two hundred acres of land, have a house and barn built for me, and a start of stock given me, as every boy in this family has had at twenty-one."

"A man is a man! He founds a family, he runs the Government! It is a different matter," said Mrs. Bates.

"It surely is; in this family. But I think, even with us, a man would have rather a difficult proposition on his hands to found a family without a woman; or to run the Government either."

"All right! Go on to Adam and see what you get."

"I'll have the satisfaction of knowing that Nancy Ellen gets dinner, anyway," said Kate as she passed through the door and followed the long path to the gate, from there walking beside the road in the direction of her brother's home. There were many horses in the pasture and single and double buggies in the barn; but it never occurred to Kate that she might ride: it was Sunday and the horses were resting. So she followed the path beside the fences, rounded the corner of the church and went on her way with the text from which the pastor was preaching, hammering in her brain. She became so absorbed in thought that she scarcely saw the footpath she followed, while June flowered, and perfumed, and sang all around her.

She was so intent upon the words she had heard that her feet unconsciously followed a well-defined branch from the main path leading into the woods, from the bridge, where she sat on a log, and for the unnumbered time, reviewed her problem. She had worked ever since she could remember. Never in her life had she gotten to school before noon on Monday, because of the large washings. After the other work was finished she had spent nights and mornings ironing, when she longed to study, seldom finishing before Saturday. Summer brought an endless round of harvesting, canning, drying; winter brought butchering, heaps of sewing, and postponed summer work. School began late in the fall and closed early in spring, with teachers often inefficient; yet because she was a close student and kept her books where she could take a peep and memorize and think as she washed dishes and cooked, she had thoroughly mastered all the country school near her home could teach her. With six weeks of a summer Normal course she would be as well prepared to teach as any of her sisters were, with the exception of Mary, who had been able to convince her parents that she possessed two college years' worth of "ability."

Kate laid no claim to "ability," herself; but she knew she was as strong as most men, had an ordinary brain that could be trained, and while she was far from beautiful she was equally as far from being ugly, for her skin was smooth and pink, her eyes large and blue-gray, her teeth even and white. She missed beauty because her cheekbones were high, her mouth large, her nose barely escaping a pug; but she had a real "crown of glory" in her hair, which was silken fine, long and heavy, of sunshine-gold in colour, curling naturally around her face and neck. Given pure blood to paint such a skin with varying emotions, enough wind to ravel out a few locks of such hair, the proportions of a Venus and perfect health, any girl could rest very well assured of being looked at twice, if not oftener.

Kate sat on a log, a most unusual occurrence for her, for she was familiar only with bare, hot houses, furnished with meagre necessities; reeking stables, barnyards and vegetable gardens. She knew less of the woods than the average city girl; but there was a soothing wind, a sweet perfume, a calming silence that quieted her tense mood and enabled her to think clearly; so the review went on over years of work and petty economies, amounting to one grand aggregate that gave to each of seven sons house, stock, and land at twenty-one; and to each of nine daughters a bolt of muslin and a fairly decent dress when she married, as the seven older ones did speedily, for they were fine, large, upstanding girls, some having real beauty, all exceptionally well-trained economists and workers. Because her mother had the younger daughters to help in the absence of the elder, each girl had been allowed the time and money to prepare herself to teach a country school; all of them had taught until they married. Nancy Ellen, the beauty of the family, the girl next older than Kate, had taken the home school for the second winter. Going to school to Nancy Ellen had been the greatest trial of Kate's life, until the possibility of not going to Normal had confronted her.

Nancy Ellen was almost as large as Kate, quite as pink, her features assembled in a manner that made all the difference, her jet-black hair as curly as Kate's, her eyes big and dark, her lips red. As for looking at Kate twice, no one ever looked at her at all if Nancy Ellen happened to be walking beside her. Kate bore that without protest; it would have wounded her pride to rebel openly; she did Nancy Ellen's share of the work to allow her to study and have her Normal course; she remained at home plainly clothed to loan Nancy Ellen her best dress when she attended Normal; but when she found that she was doomed to finish her last year at school under Nancy Ellen, to work double so that her sister might go to school early and remain late, coming home tired and with lessons to prepare for the morrow, some of the spontaneity left Kate's efforts.

She had a worse grievance when Nancy Ellen hung several new dresses and a wrapper on her side of the closet after her first pay-day, and furnished her end of the bureau with a white hair brush and a brass box filled with pink powder, with a swan's-down puff for its application. For three months Kate had waited and hoped that at least "thank you" would be vouchsafed her; when it failed for that length of time she did two things: she studied so diligently that her father called her into the barn and told her that if before the school, she asked Nancy Ellen another question she could not answer, he would use the buggy whip on her to within an inch of her life. The buggy whip always had been a familiar implement to Kate, so she stopped asking slippery questions, worked harder than ever, and spent her spare time planning what she would hang in the closet and put on her end of the bureau when she had finished her Normal course, and was teaching her first term of school.

Now she had learned all that Nancy Ellen could teach her, and much that Nancy Ellen never knew: it was time for Kate to be starting away to school. Because it was so self-evident that she should have what the others had had, she said nothing about it until the time came; then she found her father determined that she should remain at home to do the housework, for no compensation other than her board and such clothes as she always had worn, her mother wholly in accord with him, and marvel of all, Nancy Ellen quite enthusiastic on the subject.

Her father always had driven himself and his family like slaves, while her mother had ably seconded his efforts. Money from the sale of chickens, turkeys, butter, eggs, and garden truck that other women of the neighbourhood used for extra clothing for themselves and their daughters and to prettify their homes, Mrs. Bates handed to her husband to increase the amount necessary to purchase the two hundred acres of land for each son when he came of age. The youngest son had farmed his land with comfortable profit and started a bank account, while his parents and two sisters were still saving and working to finish the last payment. Kate thought with bitterness that if this final payment had been made possibly there would have been money to spare for her; but with that thought came the knowledge that her father had numerous investments on which he could have realized and made the payments had he not preferred that they should be a burden on his family.

"Take the wings of morning," repeated Kate, with all the emphasis the old minister had used. "Hummm! I wonder what kind of wings. Those of a peewee would scarcely do for me; I'd need the wings of an eagle to get me anywhere, and anyway it wasn't the wings of a bird I was to take, it was the wings of morning. I wonder what the wings of morning are, and how I go about taking them. God knows where my wings come in; by the ache in my feet I seem to have walked, mostly. Oh, what ARE the wings of morning?"

Kate stared straight before her, sitting absorbed and motionless. Close in front of her a little white moth fluttered over the twigs and grasses. A kingbird sailed into view and perched on a brush- heap preparatory to darting after the moth. While the bird measured the distance and waited for the moth to rise above the entangling grasses, with a sweep and a snap a smaller bird, very similar in shape and colouring, flashed down, catching the moth and flying high among the branches of a big tree.

"Aha! You missed your opportunity!" said Kate to the kingbird.

She sat straighter suddenly. "Opportunity," she repeated. "Here is where I am threatened with missing mine. Opportunity! I wonder now if that might not be another name for 'the wings of morning.' Morning is winging its way past me, the question is: do I sit still and let it pass, or do I take its wings and fly away?"

Kate brooded on that awhile, then her thought formulated into words again.

"It isn't as if Mother were sick or poor, she is perfectly well and stronger than nine women out of ten of her age; Father can afford to hire all the help she needs; there is nothing cruel or unkind in leaving her; and as for Nancy Ellen, why does the fact that I am a few years younger than she, make me her servant? Why do I cook for her, and make her bed, and wash her clothes, while she earns money to spend on herself? And she is doing everything in her power to keep me at it, because she likes what she is doing and what it brings her, and she doesn't give a tinker whether I like what I am doing or not; or whether I get anything I want out of it or not; or whether I miss getting off to Normal on time or not. She is blame selfish, that's what she is, so she won't like the jolt she's going to get; but it will benefit her soul, her soul that her pretty face keeps her from developing, so I shall give her a little valuable assistance. Mother will be furious and Father will have the buggy whip convenient; but I am going! I don't know how, or when, but I am *going*.

"Who has a thirst for knowledge, in Helicon may slake it,
    If he has still, the Roman will, to find a way, or make it."

Kate arose tall and straight and addressed the surrounding woods. "Now you just watch me 'find a way or make it,'" she said. "I am 'taking the wings of morning,' observe my flight! See me cut curves and circles and sail and soar around all the other Bates girls the Lord ever made, one named Nancy Ellen in particular. It must be far past noon, and I've much to do to get ready. I fly!"

Kate walked back to the highway, but instead of going on she turned toward home. When she reached the gate she saw Nancy Ellen, dressed her prettiest, sitting beneath a cherry tree reading a book, in very plain view from the road. As Kate came up the path: "Hello!" said Nancy Ellen. "Wasn't Adam at home?"

"I don't know," answered Kate. "I was not there."

"You weren't? Why, where were you?" asked Nancy Ellen.

"Oh, I just took a walk!" answered Kate.

"Right at dinner time on Sunday? Well, I'll be switched!" cried Nancy Ellen.

"Pity you weren't oftener, when you most needed it," said Kate, passing up the walk and entering the door. Her mother asked the same questions so Kate answered them.

"Well, I am glad you came home," said Mrs. Bates. "There was no use tagging to Adam with a sorry story, when your father said flatly that you couldn't go."

"But I must go!" urged Kate. "I have as good a right to my chance as the others. If you put your foot down and say so, Mother, Father will let me go. Why shouldn't I have the same chance as Nancy Ellen? Please Mother, let me go!"

"You stay right where you are. There is an awful summer's work before us," said Mrs. Bates.

"There always is," answered Kate. "But now is just my chance while you have Nancy Ellen here to help you."

"She has some special studying to do, and you very well know that she has to attend the County Institute, and take the summer course of training for teachers."

"So do I," said Kate, stubbornly. "You really will not help me, Mother?"

"I've said my say! Your place is here! Here you stay!" answered her mother.

"All right," said Kate, "I'll cross you off the docket of my hopes, and try Father."

"Well, I warn you, you had better not! He has been nagged until his patience is lost," said Mrs. Bates.

Kate closed her lips and started in search of her father. She found him leaning on the pig pen watching pigs grow into money, one of his most favoured occupations. He scowled at her, drawing his huge frame to full height.

"I don't want to hear a word you have to say," he said. "You are the youngest, and your place is in the kitchen helping your mother. We have got the last installment to pay on Hiram's land this summer. March back to the house and busy yourself with something useful!"

Kate looked at him, from his big-boned, weather-beaten face, to his heavy shoes, then turned without a word and went back toward the house. She went around it to the cherry tree and with no preliminaries said to her sister: "Nancy Ellen, I want you to lend me enough money to fix my clothes a little and pay my way to Normal this summer. I can pay it all back this winter. I'll pay every cent with interest, before I spend any on anything else."

"Why, you must be crazy!" said Nancy Ellen.

"Would I be any crazier than you, when you wanted to go?" asked Kate.

"But you were here to help Mother," said Nancy Ellen.

"And you are here to help her now," persisted Kate.

"But I've got to fix up my clothes for the County Institute," said Nancy Ellen, "I'll be gone most of the summer."

"I have just as much right to go as you had," said Kate.

"Father and Mother both say you shall not go," answered her sister.

"I suppose there is no use to remind you that I did all in my power to help you to your chance."

"You did no more than you should have done," said Nancy Ellen.

"And this is no more than you should do for me, in the circumstances," said Kate.

"You very well know I can't! Father and Mother would turn me out of the house," said Nancy Ellen.

"I'd be only too glad if they would turn me out," said Kate. "You can let me have the money if you like. Mother wouldn't do anything but talk; and Father would not strike you, or make you go, he always favours you."

"He does nothing of the sort! I can't, and I won't, so there!" cried Nancy Ellen.

"'Won't,' is the real answer, 'so there,'" said Kate.

She went into the cellar and ate some cold food from the cupboard and drank a cup of milk. Then she went to her room and looked over all of her scanty stock of clothing, laying in a heap the pieces that needed mending. She took the clothes basket to the wash room, which was the front of the woodhouse, in summer; built a fire, heated water, and while making it appear that she was putting the clothes to soak, as usual, she washed everything she had that was fit to use, hanging the pieces to dry in the building.

"Watch me fly!" muttered Kate. "I don't seem to be cutting those curves so very fast; but I'm moving. I believe now, having exhausted all home resources, that Adam is my next objective. He is the only one in the family who ever paid the slightest attention to me, maybe he cares a trifle what becomes of me, but Oh, how I dread Agatha! However, watch me take wing! If Adam fails me I have six remaining prospects among my loving brothers, and if none of them has any feeling for me or faith in me there yet remain my seven dear brothers-in-law, before I appeal to the tender mercies of the neighbours; but how I dread Agatha! Yet I fly!"

An Embryo Mind Reader

Kate was far from physical flight as she pounded the indignation of her soul into the path with her substantial feet. Baffled and angry, she kept reviewing the situation as she went swiftly on her way, regardless of dust and heat. She could see no justice in being forced into a position that promised to end in further humiliation and defeat of her hopes. If she only could find Adam at the stable, as she passed, and talk with him alone! Secretly, she well knew that the chief source of her dread of meeting her sister-in-law was that to her Agatha was so funny that ridiculing her had been regarded as perfectly legitimate pastime. For Agatha *was* funny; but she had no idea of it, and could no more avoid it than a bee could avoid being buzzy, so the manner in which her sisters-in-law imitated her and laughed at her, none too secretly, was far from kind. While she never guessed what was going on, she realized the antagonism in their attitude and stoutly resented it.

Adam was his father's favourite son, a stalwart, fine-appearing, big man, silent, honest, and forceful; the son most after the desires of the father's heart, yet Adam was the one son of the seven who had ignored his father's law that all of his boys were to marry strong, healthy young women, poor women, working women. Each of the others at coming of age had contracted this prescribed marriage as speedily as possible, first asking father Bates, the girl afterward. If father Bates disapproved, the girl was never asked at all. And the reason for this docility on the part of these big, matured men, lay wholly in the methods of father Bates. He gave those two hundred acres of land to each of them on coming of age, and the same sum to each for the building of a house and barn and the purchase of stock; gave it to them in words, and with the fullest assurance that it was theirs to improve, to live on, to add to. Each of them had seen and handled his deed, each had to admit he never had known his father to tell a lie or deviate the least from fairness in a deal of any kind, each had been compelled to go in the way indicated by his father for years; but not a man of them held his own deed. These precious bits of paper remained locked in the big wooden chest beside the father's bed, while the land stood on the records in his name; the taxes they paid him each year he, himself, carried to the county clerk; so that he was the largest landholder in the county and one of the very richest men. It must have been extreme unction to his soul to enter the county office and ask for the assessment on those "little parcels of land of mine." Men treated him very deferentially, and so did his sons. Those documents carefully locked away had the effect of obtaining ever-ready help to harvest his hay and wheat whenever he desired, to make his least wish quickly deferred to, to give him authority and the power for which he lived and worked earlier, later, and harder than any other man of his day and locality.

Adam was like him as possible up to the time he married, yet Adam was the only one of his sons who disobeyed him; but there was a redeeming feature. Adam married a slender tall slip of a woman, four years his senior, who had been teaching in the Hartley schools when he began courting her. She was a prim, fussy woman, born of a prim father and a fussy mother, so what was to be expected? Her face was narrow and set, her body and her movements almost rigid, her hair, always parted, lifted from each side and tied on the crown, fell in stiff little curls, the back part hanging free. Her speech, as precise as her movements, was formed into set habit through long study of the dictionary. She was born antagonistic to whatever existed, no matter what it was. So surely as every other woman agreed on a dress, a recipe, a house, anything whatever, so surely Agatha thought out and followed a different method, the disconcerting thing about her being that she usually finished any undertaking with less exertion, ahead of time, and having saved considerable money.

She could have written a fine book of synonyms, for as certainly as any one said anything in her presence that she had occasion to repeat, she changed the wording to six-syllabled mouthfuls, delivered with ponderous circumlocution. She subscribed to papers and magazines, which she read and remembered. And she danced! When other women thought even a waltz immoral and shocking; perfectly stiff, her curls exactly in place, Agatha could be seen, and frequently was seen, waltzing on the front porch in the arms of, and to a tune whistled by young Adam, whose full name was Adam Alcibiades Bates. In his younger days, when discipline had been required, Kate once had heard her say to the little fellow: "Adam Alcibiades ascend these steps and proceed immediately to your maternal ancestor."

Kate thought of this with a dry smile as she plodded on toward Agatha's home hoping she could see her brother at the barn, but she knew that most probably she would "ascend the steps and proceed to the maternal ancestor," of Adam Bates 3d. Then she would be forced to explain her visit and combat both Adam and his wife; for Agatha was not a nonentity like her collection of healthful, hard-working sisters-in-law. Agatha worked if she chose, and she did not work if she did not choose. Mostly she worked and worked harder than any one ever thought. She had a habit of keeping her house always immaculate, finishing her cleaning very early and then reading in a conspicuous spot on the veranda when other women were busy with their most tiresome tasks. Such was Agatha, whom Kate dreaded meeting, with every reason, for Agatha, despite curls, bony structure, language, and dance, was the most powerful factor in the whole Bates family with her father-in-law; and all because when he purchased the original two hundred acres for Adam, and made the first allowance for buildings and stock, Agatha slipped the money from Adam's fingers in some inexplainable way, and spent it all for stock; because forsooth! Agatha was an only child, and her prim father endowed her, she said so herself, with three hundred acres of land, better in location and more fertile than that given to Adam, land having on it a roomy and comfortable brick house, completely furnished, a large barn and also stock;

so that her place could be used to live on and farm, while Adam's could be given over to grazing herds of cattle which he bought cheaply, fattened and sold at the top of the market.

If each had brought such a farm into the family with her, father Bates could have endured six more prim, angular, becurled daughters-in-law, very well indeed, for land was his one and only God. His respect for Agatha was markedly very high, for in addition to her farm he secretly admired her independence of thought and action, and was amazed by the fact that she was about her work when several of the blooming girls he had selected for wives for his sons were confined to the sofa with a pain, while not one of them schemed, planned, connived with her husband and piled up the money as Agatha did, therefore she stood at the head of the women of the Bates family; while she was considered to have worked miracles in the heart of Adam Bates, for with his exception no man of the family ever had been seen to touch a woman, either publicly or privately, to offer the slightest form of endearment, assistance or courtesy. "Women are to work and to bear children," said the elder Bates. "Put them at the first job when they are born, and at the second at eighteen, and keep them hard at it."

At their rate of progression several of the Bates sons and daughters would produce families that, with a couple of pairs of twins, would equal the sixteen of the elder Bates; but not so Agatha. She had one son of fifteen and one daughter of ten, and she said that was all she intended to have, certainly it was all she did have; but she further aggravated matters by announcing that she had had them because she wanted them; at such times as she intended to; and that she had the boy first and five years the older, so that he could look after his sister when they went into company. Also she walked up and sat upon Adam's lap whenever she chose, ruffled his hair, pulled his ears, and kissed him squarely on the mouth, with every appearance of having help, while the dance on the front porch with her son or daughter was of daily occurrence. And anything funnier than Agatha, prim and angular with never a hair out of place, stiffly hopping "Money Musk" and "Turkey In The Straw," or the "Blue Danube" waltz, anything funnier than that, never happened. But the two Adams, Jr. and 3d, watched with reverent and adoring eyes, for she was *Mother*, and no one else on earth rested so high in their respect as the inflexible woman they lived with. That she was different from all the other women of her time and location was hard on the other women. Had they been exactly right, they would have been exactly like her.

So Kate, thinking all these things over, her own problem acutely "advanced and proceeded." She advanced past the closed barn, and stock in the pasture, past the garden flaming June, past the dooryard, up the steps, down the hall, into the screened back porch dining room and "proceeded" to take a chair, while the family finished the Sunday night supper, at which they were seated. Kate was not hungry and she did not wish to trouble her sister-in-law to set another place, so she took the remaining chair, against the wall, behind Agatha, facing Adam, 3d, across the table, and with Adam Jr., in profile at the head, and little Susan at the foot. Then she waited her chance. Being tired and aggressive she did not wait long.

"I might as well tell you why I came," she said bluntly. "Father won't give me money to go to Normal, as he has all the others. He says I have got to stay at home and help Mother."

"Well, Mother is getting so old she needs help," said Adam, Jr., as he continued his supper.

"Of course she is," said Kate. "We all know that. But what is the matter with Nancy Ellen helping her, while I take my turn at Normal? There wasn't a thing I could do last summer to help her off that I didn't do, even to lending her my best dress and staying at home for six Sundays because I had nothing else fit to wear where I'd be seen."

No one said a word. Kate continued: "Then Father secured our home school for her and I had to spend the winter going to school to her, when you very well know that I always studied harder, and was ahead of her, even after she'd been to Normal. And I got up early and worked late, and cooked, and washed, and waited on her, while she got her lessons and reports ready, and fixed up her nice new clothes, and now she won't touch the work, and she is doing all she can to help Father keep me from going."

"I never knew Father to need much help on anything he made up his mind to," said Adam.

Kate sat very tense. She looked steadily at her brother, but he looked quite as steadily at his plate. The back of her sister-in- law was fully as expressive as her face. Her head was very erect, her shoulders stiff and still, not a curl moved as she poured Adam's tea and Susan's milk. Only Adam, 3d, looked at Kate with companionable eyes, as if he might feel a slight degree of interest or sympathy, so she found herself explaining directly to him.

"Things are blame unfair in our family, anyway!" she said, bitterly. "You have got to be born a boy to have any chance worth while; if you are a girl it is mighty small, and if you are the youngest, by any mischance, you have none at all. I don't want to harp things over; but I wish you would explain to me why having been born a few years after Nancy Ellen makes me her slave, and cuts me out of my chance to teach, and to have some freedom and clothes. They might as well have told Hiram he was not to have any land and stay at home and help Father because he was the youngest boy; it would have been quite as fair; but nothing like that happens to the boys of this family, it is always the girls who get left. I have worked for years, knowing every cent I saved and earned above barely enough to cover me, would go to help pay for Hiram's land and house and stock; but he wouldn't turn a hand to help me, neither will any of the rest of you."

"Then what are you here for?" asked Adam.

"Because I am going to give you, and every other brother and sister I have, the chance to *refuse* to loan me enough to buy a few clothes and pay my way to Normal, so I can pass the examinations, and teach this fall. And when you have all refused, I am going to the neighbours, until I find someone who will loan me the money I need. A hundred dollars would be plenty. I could pay it back with two months' teaching, with any interest you say."

Kate paused, short of breath, her eyes blazing, her cheeks red. Adam went steadily on with his supper. Agatha appeared stiffer and more uncompromising in the back than before, which Kate had not thought possible. But the same dull red on the girl's cheeks had begun to burn on the face of young Adam. Suddenly he broke into a clear laugh.

"Oh, Ma, you're too funny!" he cried. "I can read your face like a book. I bet you ten dollars I can tell you just word for word what you are going to say. I dare you let me! You know I can!" Still laughing, his eyes dancing, a picture to see, he stretched his arm across the table toward her, and his mother adored him, however she strove to conceal the fact from him.

"Ten dollars!" she scoffed. "When did we become so wealthy? I'll give you one dollar if you tell me exactly what I was going to say."

The boy glanced at his father. "Oh this is too easy!" he cried. "It's like robbing the baby's bank!" And then to his mother: "You were just opening your lips to say: 'Give it to her! If you don't, I will!' And you are even a little bit more of a brick than usual to do it. It's a darned shame the way all of them impose on Kate."

There was a complete change in Agatha's back. Adam, Jr., laid down his fork and stared at his wife in deep amazement. Adam, 3d, stretched his hand farther toward his mother. "Give me that dollar!" he cajoled.

"Well, I am not concealing it in the sleeve of my garments," she said. "If I have one, it is reposing in my purse, in juxtaposition to the other articles that belong there, and if you receive it, it will be bestowed upon you when I deem the occasion suitable."

Young Adam's fist came down with a smash. "I get the dollar!" he triumphed. "I *told* you so! I *knew* she was going to say it! Ain't I a dandy mind reader though? But it is bully for you, Father, because of course, if Mother wouldn't let Kate have it, you'd *have* to; but if you *did* it might make trouble with your paternal land-grabber, and endanger your precious deed that you hope to get in the sweet by-and-by. But if Mother loans the money, Grandfather can't say a word, because it is her very own, and didn't cost him anything, and he always agrees with her anyway! Hurrah for hurrah, Kate! Nancy Ellen may wash her own petticoat in the morning, while I take you to the train. You'll let me, Father? You did let me go to Hartley alone, once. I'll be careful! I won't let a thing happen. I'll come straight home. And oh, my dollar, you and me; I'll put you in the bank and let you grow to three!"

"You may go," said his father, promptly.

"You shall proceed according to your Aunt Katherine's instructions," said his mother, at the same time.

"Katie, get your carpet-sack! When do we start?" demanded young Adam.

"Morning will be all right with me, you blessed youngun," said Kate, "but I don't own a telescope or anything to put what little I have in, and Nancy Ellen never would spare hers; she will want to go to County Institute before I get back."

"You may have mine," said Agatha. "You are perfectly welcome to take it wherever your peregrinations lead you, and return it when you please. I shall proceed to my chamber and formulate your check immediately. You are also welcome to my best hat and cape, and any of my clothing or personal adornments you can use to advantage."

"Oh, Agatha, I wish you were as big as a house, like me," said Kate, joyfully. "I couldn't possibly crowd into anything you wear, but it would almost tickle me to death to have Nancy Ellen know you let me take your things, when she won't even offer me a dud of her old stuff; I never remotely hoped for any of the new."

"You shall have my cape and hat, anyway. The cape is new and very fashionable. Come upstairs and try the hat," said Agatha.

The cape was new and fashionable as Agatha had said; it would not fasten at the neck, but there would be no necessity that it should during July and August, while it would improve any dress it was worn with on a cool evening. The hat Kate could not possibly use with her large, broad face and mass of hair, but she was almost as pleased with the offer as if the hat had been most becoming. Then Agatha brought out her telescope, in which Kate laid the cape while Agatha wrote her a check for one hundred and twenty dollars, and told her where and how to cash it. The extra twenty was to buy a pair of new walking shoes, some hose, and a hat, before she went to her train. When they went downstairs Adam, Jr., had a horse hitched and Adam, 3d, drove her to her home, where, at the foot of the garden, they took one long survey of the landscape and hid the telescope behind the privet bush. Then Adam drove away quietly, Kate entered the dooryard from the garden, and soon afterward went to the wash room and hastily ironed her clothing.

Nancy Ellen had gone to visit a neighbour girl, so Kate risked her remaining until after church in the evening. She hurried to their room and mended all her own clothing she had laid out. Then she deliberately went over Nancy Ellen's and helped herself to a pair of pretty nightdresses, such as she had never owned, a white embroidered petticoat, the second best white dress, and a most becoming sailor hat. These she made into a parcel and carried to the wash room, brought in the telescope and packed it, hiding it under a workbench and covering it with shavings. After that she went to her room and wrote a note, and then slept deeply until the morning call. She arose at once and went to the wash room but instead of washing the family clothing, she took a bath in the largest tub, and washed her hair to a state resembling spun gold. During breakfast she kept sharp watch down the road. When she saw Adam, 3d, coming she stuck her note under the hook on which she had seen her father hang his hat all her life, and carrying the telescope in the clothes basket covered with a rumpled sheet, she passed across the yard and handed it over the fence to Adam, climbed that same fence, and they started toward Hartley.

Kate put the sailor hat on her head, and sat very straight, an anxious line crossing her forehead. She was running away, and if discovered, there was the barest chance that her father might follow, and make a most disagreeable scene, before the train pulled out. He had gone to a far field to plow corn and Kate fervently hoped he would plow until noon, which he did. Nancy Ellen washed the dishes, and went into the front room to study, while Mrs. Bates put on her sunbonnet and began hoeing the potatoes. Not one of the family noticed that Monday's wash was not on the clothes line as usual. Kate and Adam drove as fast as they dared, and on reaching town, cashed the check, decided that Nancy Ellen's hat would serve, thus saving the price of a new one for emergencies that might arise, bought the shoes, and went to the depot, where they had an anxious hour to wait.

"I expect Grandpa will be pretty mad," said Adam.

"I am sure there is not the slightest chance but that he will be," said Kate.

"Dare you go back home when school is over?" he asked.

"Probably not," she answered.

"What will you do?" he questioned.

"When I investigated sister Nancy Ellen's bureau I found a list of the School Supervisors of the county, so I am going to put in my spare time writing them about my qualifications to teach their schools this winter. All the other girls did well and taught first-class schools, I shall also. I am not a bit afraid but that I may take my choice of several. When I finish it will be only a few days until school begins, so I can go hunt my boarding place and stay there."

"Mother would let you stay at our house," said Adam.

"Yes, I think she would, after yesterday; but I don't want to make trouble that might extend to Father and your father. I had better keep away."

"Yes, I guess you had," said Adam. "If Grandfather rows, he raises a racket. But maybe he won't!"

"Maybe! Wouldn't you like to see what happens when Mother come in from the potatoes and Nancy Ellen comes out from the living room, and Father comes to dinner, all about the same time?"

Adam laughed appreciatively.

"Wouldn't I just!" he cried. "Kate, you like my mother, don't you?"

"I certainly do! She has been splendid. I never dreamed of such a thing as getting the money from her."

"I didn't either," said Adam, "until – I became a mind reader."

Kate looked straight into his eyes.

"How about that, Adam?" she asked.

Adam chuckled. "She didn't intend to say a word. She was going to let the Bateses fight it out among themselves. Her mouth was shut so tight it didn't look as if she could open it if she wanted to. I thought it would be better for you to borrow the money from her, so Father wouldn't get into a mess, and I knew how fine she was, so I just *suggested* it to her. That's all!"

"Adam, you're a dandy!" cried Kate.

"I am having a whole buggy load of fun, and you ought to go," said he. "It's all right! Don't you worry! I'll take care of you."

"Why, thank you, Adam!" said Kate. "That is the first time any one ever offered to take care of me in my life. With me it always has been pretty much of a 'go-it-alone' proposition."

"What of Nancy Ellen's did you take?" he asked. "Why didn't you get some gloves? Your hands are so red and work-worn. Mother's never look that way."

"Your mother never has done the rough field work I do, and I haven't taken time to be careful. They do look badly. I wish I had taken a pair of the lady's gloves; but I doubt if she would have survived that. I understand that one of the unpardonable sins is putting on gloves belonging to any one else."

Then the train came and Kate climbed aboard with Adam's parting injunction in her ears: "Sit beside an open window on this side!"

So she looked for and found the window and as she seated herself she saw Adam on the outside and leaned to speak to him again. Just as the train started he thrust his hand inside, dropped his dollar on her lap, and in a tense whisper commanded her: "Get yourself some gloves!" Then he ran.

Kate picked up the dollar, while her eyes dimmed with tears.

"Why, the fine youngster!" she said. "The Jim-dandy fine youngster!"

Adam could not remember when he ever had been so happy as he was driving home. He found his mother singing, his father in a genial mood, so he concluded that the greatest thing in the world to make a whole family happy was to do something kind for someone else. But he reflected that there would be far from a happy family at his grandfather's; and he was right. Grandmother Bates came in from her hoeing at eleven o'clock tired and hungry, expecting to find the wash dry and dinner almost ready. There was no wash and no odour of food. She went to the wood-shed and stared unbelievingly at the cold stove, the tubs of soaking clothes.

She turned and went into the kitchen, where she saw no signs of Kate or of dinner, then she lifted up her voice and shouted: "Nancy Ellen!"

Nancy Ellen came in a hurry. "Why, Mother, what is the matter?" she cried.

"Matter, yourself!" exclaimed Mrs. Bates. "Look in the wash room! Why aren't the clothes on the line? Where is that good-for- nothing Kate?"

Nancy Ellen went to the wash room and looked. She came back pale and amazed. "Maybe she is sick," she ventured. "She never has been; but she might be! Maybe she has lain down."

"On Monday morning! And the wash not out! You simpleton!" cried Mrs. Bates.

Nancy Ellen hurried upstairs and came back with bulging eyes.

"Every scrap of her clothing is gone, and half of mine!"

"She's gone to that fool Normal-thing! Where did she get the money?" cried Mrs. Bates.

"I don't know!" said Nancy Ellen. "She asked me yesterday, but of course I told her that so long as you and Father decided she was not to go, I couldn't possibly lend her the money."

"Did you look if she had taken it?"

Nancy Ellen straightened. "Mother! I didn't need do that!"

"You said she took your clothes," said Mrs. Bates.

"I had hers this time last year. She'll bring back clothes."

"Not here, she won't! Father will see that she never darkens these doors again. This is the first time in his life that a child of his has disobeyed him."

"Except Adam, when he married Agatha; and he strutted like a fighting cock about that."

"Well, he won't 'strut' about this, and you won't either, even if you are showing signs of standing up for her. Go at that wash, while I get dinner."

Dinner was on the table when Adam Bates hung his hat on its hook and saw the note for him. He took it down and read:

FATHER: I have gone to Normal. I borrowed the money of a woman who was willing to trust me to pay it back as soon as I earned it. Not Nancy Ellen, of course. She would not even loan me a pocket handkerchief, though you remember I stayed at home six weeks last summer to let her take what she wanted of mine. Mother: I think you can get Sally Whistler to help you as cheaply as any one and that she will do very well. Nancy Ellen: I have taken your second best hat and a few of your things, but not half so many as I loaned you. I hope it makes you mad enough to burst. I hope you get as mad and stay as mad as I have been most of this year while you taught me things you didn't know yourself; and I cooked and washed for you so you could wear fine clothes and play the lady. KATE

Adam Bates read that note to himself, stretching every inch of his six feet six, his face a dull red, his eyes glaring. Then he turned to his wife and daughter.

"Is Kate gone? Without proper clothing and on borrowed money," he demanded.

"I don't know," said Mrs. Bates. "I was hoeing potatoes all forenoon."

"Listen to this," he thundered. Then he slowly read the note aloud. But someway the spoken words did not have the same effect as when he read them mentally in the first shock of anger. When he heard his own voice read off the line, "I hope it makes you mad enough to burst," there was a catch and a queer gurgle in his throat. Mrs. Bates gazed at him anxiously. Was he so surprised and angry he was choking? Might it be a stroke? It was! It was a master stroke. He got no farther than "taught me things you didn't know yourself," when he lowered the sheet, threw back his head and laughed as none of his family ever had seen him laugh in his life; laughed and laughed until his frame was shaken and the tears rolled. Finally he looked at the dazed Nancy Ellen. "Get Sally Whistler, nothing!" he said. "You hustle your stumps and do for your mother what Kate did while you were away last summer. And if you have any common decency send your sister as many of your best things as you had of hers, at least. Do you hear me?"

Peregrinations

"*Peregrinations*," laughed Kate, turning to the window to hide her face. "Oh, Agatha, you are a dear, but you are too funny! Even a Fourth of July orator would not have used that word. I never heard it before in all of my life outside spelling-school."

Then she looked at the dollar she was gripping and ceased to laugh.

"The dear lad," she whispered. "He did the whole thing. She was going to let us 'fight it out'; I could tell by her back, and Adam wouldn't have helped me a cent, quite as much because he didn't want to as because Father wouldn't have liked it. Fancy the little chap knowing he can wheedle his mother into anything, and exactly how to go about it! I won't spend a penny on myself until she is paid, and then I'll make her a present of something nice, just to let her and Nancy Ellen see that I appreciate being helped to my chance, for I had reached that point where I would have walked to school and worked in somebody's kitchen, before I'd have missed my opportunity. I could have done it; but this will be far pleasanter and give me a much better showing."

Then Kate began watching the people in the car with eager curiosity, for she had been on a train only twice before in her life. She decided that she was in a company of young people and some even of middle age, going to Normal. She also noticed that most of them were looking at her with probably the same interest she found in them. Then at one of the stations a girl asked to sit with her and explained that she was going to Normal, so Kate said she was also. The girl seemed to have several acquaintances on the car, for she left her seat to speak with them and when the train stopped at a very pleasant city and the car began to empty itself, on the platform Kate was introduced by this girl to several young women and men near her age. A party of four, going to board close the school, with a woman they knew about, invited Kate to go with them and because she was strange and shaken by her experiences she agreed. All of them piled their luggage on a wagon to be delivered, so Kate let hers go also. Then they walked down a long shady street, and entered a dainty and comfortable residence, a place that seemed to Kate to be the home of people of wealth. She was assigned a room with another girl, such a pleasant girl; but a vague uneasiness had begun to make itself felt, so before she unpacked she went back to the sitting room and learned that the price of board was eight dollars a week. Forty- eight dollars for six weeks! She would not have enough for books and tuition. Besides, Nancy Ellen had boarded with a family on Butler Street whose charge was only five-fifty. Kate was eager to stay where these very agreeable young people did, she imagined herself going to classes with them and having association that to her would be a great treat, but she never would dare ask for more money. She thought swiftly a minute, and then made her first mistake.

Instead of going to the other girls and frankly confessing that she could not afford the prices they were paying, she watched her chance, picked up her telescope and hurried down the street, walking swiftly until she was out of sight of the house. Then she began inquiring her way to Butler Street and after a long, hot walk, found the place. The rooms and board were very poor, but Kate felt that she could endure whatever Nancy Ellen had, so she unpacked, and went to the Normal School to register and learn what she would need. On coming from the building she saw that she would be forced to pass close by the group of girls she had deserted and this was made doubly difficult because she could see that they were talking about her. Then she understood how foolish she had been and as she was struggling to summon courage to explain to them she caught these words plainly:

"Who is going to ask her for it?"

"I am," said the girl who had sat beside Kate on the train. "I don't propose to pay it myself!"

Then she came directly to Kate and said briefly: "Fifty cents, please!"

"For what?" stammered Kate.

"Your luggage. You changed your boarding place in such a hurry you forgot to settle, and as I made the arrangement, I had to pay it."

"Do please excuse me," said Kate. "I was so bewildered, I forgot."

"Certainly!" said the girl and Kate dropped the money into the extended hand and hurried past, her face scorched red with shame, for one of them had said: "That's a good one! I wouldn't have thought it of her."

Kate went back to her hot, stuffy room and tried to study, but she succeeded only in being miserable, for she realized that she had lost her second chance to have either companions or friends, by not saying the few words of explanation that would have righted her in the opinion of those she would meet each day for six weeks. It was not a good beginning, while the end was what might have been expected. A young man from her neighbourhood spoke to her and the girls seeing, asked him about Kate, learning thereby that her father was worth more money than all of theirs put together. Some of them had accepted the explanation that Kate was "bewildered" and had acted hastily; but when the young man finished Bates history, they merely thought her mean, and left her severely to herself, so her only recourse was to study so diligently, and recite so perfectly that none of them could equal her, and this she did.

In acute discomfort and with a sore heart, Kate passed her first six weeks away from home. She wrote to each man on the list of school directors she had taken from Nancy Ellen's desk. Some answered that they had their teachers already engaged, others made no reply. One bright spot was the receipt of a letter from Nancy Ellen saying she was sending her best dress, to be very careful of it, and if Kate would let her know the day she would be home she would meet her at the station. Kate sent her thanks, wore the dress to two lectures, and wrote the letter telling when she would return.

As the time drew nearer she became sickeningly anxious about a school. What if she failed in securing one? What if she could not pay back Agatha's money? What if she had taken "the wings of morning," and fallen in her flight? In desperation she went to the Superintendent of the Normal and told him her trouble. He wrote her a fine letter of recommendation and she sent it to one of the men from whom she had not heard, the director of a school in the village of Walden, seven miles east of Hartley, being seventeen miles from her home, thus seeming to Kate a desirable location, also she knew the village to be pretty and the school one that paid well. Then she finished her work the best she could, and disappointed and anxious, entered the train for home.

When the engine whistled at the bridge outside Hartley Kate arose, lifted her telescope from the rack overhead, and made her way to the door, so that she was the first person to leave the car when it stopped. As she stepped to the platform she had a distinct shock, for her father reached for the telescope, while his greeting and his face were decidedly friendly, for him. As they walked down the street Kate was trying wildly to think of the best thing to say when he asked if she had a school. But he did not ask. Then she saw in the pocket of his light summer coat a packet of letters folded inside a newspaper, and there was one long, official-looking envelope that stood above the others far enough that she could see "Miss K–" of the address. Instantly she decided that it was her answer from the School Director of Walden and she was tremblingly eager to see it. She thought an instant and then asked: "Have you been to the post office?"

"Yes, I got the mail," he answered.

"Will you please see if there are any letters for me?" she asked.

"When we get home," he said. "I am in a hurry now. Here's a list of things Ma wants, and don't be all day about getting them."

Kate's lips closed to a thin line and her eyes began to grow steel coloured and big. She dragged back a step and looked at the loosely swaying pocket again. She thought intently a second. As they passed several people on the walk she stepped back of her father and gently raised the letter enough to see that the address was to her. Instantly she lifted it from the others, slipped it up her dress sleeve, and again took her place beside her father until they reached the store where her mother did her shopping. Then he waited outside while Kate hurried in, and ripping open the letter, found a contract ready for her to sign for the Walden school. The salary was twenty dollars a month more than Nancy Ellen had received for their country school the previous winter and the term four months longer.

Kate was so delighted she could have shouted. Instead she went with all speed to the stationery counter and bought an envelope to fit the contract, which she signed, and writing a hasty note of thanks she mailed the letter in the store mail box, then began her mother's purchases. This took so much time that her father came into the store before she had finished, demanding that she hurry, so in feverish haste she bought what was wanted and followed to the buggy. On the road home she began to study her father; she could see that he was well pleased over something but she had no idea what could have happened; she had expected anything from verbal wrath to the buggy whip, so she was surprised, but so happy over having secured such a good school, at higher wages than Nancy Ellen's, that she spent most of her time thinking of herself and planning as to when she would go to Walden, where she would stay, how she would teach, and Oh, bliss unspeakable, what she would do with so much money; for two month's pay would more than wipe out her indebtedness to Agatha, and by getting the very cheapest board she could endure, after that she would have over three fourths of her money to spend each month for books and clothes. She was intently engaged with her side of the closet and her end of the bureau, when she had her first glimpse of home; even preoccupied as she was, she saw a difference. Several loose pickets in the fence had been nailed in place. The lilac beside the door and the cabbage roses had been trimmed, so that they did not drag over the walk, while the yard had been gone over with a lawn-mower.

Kate turned to her father. "Well, for land's sake!" she said. "I wanted a lawn-mower all last summer, and you wouldn't buy it for me. I wonder why you got it the minute I was gone."

"I got it because Nancy Ellen especially wanted it, and she has been a mighty good girl all summer," he said.

"If that is the case, then she should be rewarded with the privilege of running a lawn-mower," said Kate.

Her father looked at her sharply; but her face was so pleasant he decided she did not intend to be saucy, so he said: "No doubt she will be willing to let you help her all you want to."

"Not the ghost of a doubt about that," laughed Kate, "and I always wanted to try running one, too. They look so nice in pictures, and how one improves a place! I hardly know this is home. Now if we only had a fresh coat of white paint we could line up with the neighbours."

"I have been thinking about that," said Mr. Bates, and Kate glanced at him, doubting her hearing.

He noticed her surprise and added in explanation: "Paint every so often saves a building. It's good economy."

"Then let's economize immediately," said Kate. "And on the barn, too. It is even more weather-beaten than the house."

"I'll see about it the next time I go to town," said Mr. Bates; so Kate entered the house prepared for anything and wondering what it all meant for wherever she looked everything was shining the brightest that scrubbing and scouring could make it shine, the best of everything was out and in use; not that it was much, but it made a noticeable difference. Her mother greeted her pleasantly, with a new tone of voice, while Nancy Ellen was transformed. Kate noticed that, immediately. She always had been a pretty girl, now she was beautiful, radiantly beautiful, with a new shining beauty that dazzled Kate as she looked at her. No one offered any explanation while Kate could see none. At last she asked: "What on earth has happened? I don't understand."

"Of course you don't," laughed Nancy Ellen. "You thought you ran the whole place and did everything yourself, so I thought I'd just show you how things look when I run them."

"You are a top-notcher," said Kate. "Figuratively and literally, I offer you the palm. Let the good work go on! I highly approve; but I don't see how you found time to do all this and go to Institute."

"I didn't go to Institute," said Nancy Ellen.

"You didn't! But you must!" cried Kate.

"Oh must I? Well, since you have decided to run your affairs as you please, in spite of all of us, just suppose you let me run mine the same way. Only, I rather enjoy having Father and Mother approve of what I do."

Kate climbed the stairs with this to digest as she went; so while she put away her clothing she thought things over, but saw no light. She would go to Adam's to return the telescope to-morrow, possibly he could tell her. As she hung her dresses in the closet and returned Nancy Ellen's to their places she was still more amazed, for there hung three pretty new wash dresses, one of a rosy pink that would make Nancy Ellen appear very lovely.

What was the reason, Kate wondered. The Bates family never did anything unless there was some purpose in it, what was the purpose in this? And Nancy Ellen had not gone to Institute. She evidently had worked constantly and hard, yet she was in much sweeter frame of mind than usual. She must have spent almost all she had saved from her school on new clothes. Kate could not solve the problem, so she decided to watch and wait. She also waited for someone to say something about her plans, but no one said a word, so after waiting all evening Kate decided that they would ask before they learned anything from her. She took her place as usual, and the work went on as if she had not been away; but she was happy, even in her bewilderment.

If her father noticed the absence of the letter she had slipped from his pocket he said nothing about it as he drew the paper and letters forth and laid them on the table. Kate had a few bad minutes while this was going on, she was sure he hesitated an instant and looked closely at the letters he sorted; but when he said nothing, she breathed deeply in relief and went on being joyous. It seemed to her that never had the family been in such a good-natured state since Adam had married Agatha and her three hundred acres with house, furniture, and stock. She went on in ignorance of what had happened until after Sunday dinner the following day. Then she had planned to visit Agatha and Adam. It was very probable that it was because she was dressing for this visit that Nancy Ellen decided on Kate's enlightenment, for she could not have helped seeing that her sister was almost stunned at times.

Kate gave her a fine opening. As she stood brushing her wealth of gold with full-length sweeps of her arm, she was at an angle that brought her facing the mirror before which Nancy Ellen sat training waves and pinning up loose braids. Her hair was beautiful and she slowly smiled at her image as she tried different effects of wave, loose curl, braids high piled or flat. Across her bed lay a dress that was a reproduction of one that she had worn for three years, but a glorified reproduction. The original dress had been Nancy Ellen's first departure from the brown and gray gingham which her mother always had purchased because it would wear well, and when from constant washing it faded to an exact dirt colour it had the advantage of providing a background that did not show the dirt. Nancy Ellen had earned the money for a new dress by raising turkeys, so when the turkeys went to town to be sold, for the first time in her life Nancy Ellen went along to select the dress. No one told her what kind of dress to get, because no one imagined that she would dare buy any startling variation from what always had been provided for her.

But Nancy Ellen had stood facing a narrow mirror when she reached the gingham counter and the clerk, taking one look at her fresh, beautiful face with its sharp contrasts of black eyes and hair, rose-tinted skin that refused to tan, and red cheeks and lips, began shaking out delicate blues, pale pinks, golden yellows. He called them chambray; insisted that they wore for ever, and were fadeless, which was practically the truth. On the day that dress was like to burst its waist seams, it was the same warm rosy pink that transformed Nancy Ellen from the disfiguration of dirt-brown to apple and peach bloom, wild roses and swamp mallow, a girl quite as pretty as a girl ever grows, and much prettier than any girl ever has any business to be. The instant Nancy Ellen held the chambray under her chin and in an oblique glance saw the face of the clerk, the material was hers no matter what the cost, which does not refer to the price, by any means. Knowing that the dress would be an innovation that would set her mother storming and fill Kate with envy, which would probably culminate in the demand that the goods be returned and exchanged for dirt-brown, when she reached home Nancy Ellen climbed from the wagon and told her father that she was going on to Adam's to have Agatha cut out her dress so that she could begin to sew on it that night. Such commendable industry met his hearty approval, so he told her to go and he would see that Kate did her share of the work. Wise Nancy Ellen came home and sat her down to sew on her gorgeous frock, while the storm she had feared raged in all its fury; but the goods was cut, and could not be returned. Yet, through it, a miracle happened: Nancy Ellen so appreciated herself in pink that the extreme care she used with that dress saved it from half the trips of a dirt-brown one to the wash board and the ironing table; while, marvel of marvels, it did not shrink, it did not fade, also it wore like buckskin. The result was that before the season had passed Kate was allowed to purchase a pale blue, which improved her appearance quite as much in proportion as pink had Nancy Ellen's; neither did the blue fade nor shrink nor require so much washing, for the same reason. Three years the pink dress had been Nancy Ellen's *piece de resistance*; now she had a new one, much the same, yet conspicuously different. This was a daring rose colour, full and wide, peeping white embroidery trimming, and big pearl buttons, really a beautiful dress, made in a becoming manner. Kate looked at it in cheerful envy. Never mind! The coming summer she would have a blue that would make that pink look silly. From the dress she turned to Nancy Ellen, barely in time to see her bend her head and smirk, broadly, smilingly, approvingly, at her reflection in the glass.

"For mercy sake, what IS the matter with you?" demanded Kate, ripping a strand of hair in sudden irritation.

"Oh, something lovely!" answered her sister, knowing that this was her chance to impart the glad tidings herself; if she lost it, Agatha would get the thrill of Kate's surprise. So Nancy Ellen opened her drawer and slowly produced and set upon her bureau a cabinet photograph of a remarkably strong-featured, handsome young man. Then she turned to Kate and smiled a slow, challenging smile. Kate walked over and picked up the picture, studying it intently but in growing amazement.

"Who is he?" she asked finally.

"My man!" answered Nancy Ellen, possessively, triumphantly.

Kate stared at her. "Honest to God?" she cried in wonderment.

"Honest!" said Nancy Ellen.

"Where on earth did you find him?" demanded Kate.

"Picked him out of the blackberry patch," said Nancy Ellen.

"Those darn blackberries are always late," said Kate, throwing the picture back on the bureau. "Ain't that just my luck! You wouldn't touch the raspberries. I had to pick them every one myself. But the minute I turn my back, you go pick a man like that, out of the blackberry patch. I bet a cow you wore your pink chambray, and carried grandmother's old blue bowl."

"Certainly," said Nancy Ellen, "and my pink sun-bonnet. I think maybe the bonnet started it."

Kate sat down limply on the first chair and studied the toes of her shoes. At last she roused and looked at Nancy Ellen, waiting in smiling complaisance as she returned the picture to her end of the bureau.

"Well, why don't you go ahead?" cried Kate in a thick, rasping voice. "Empty yourself! Who is he? Where did he come from? *Why* was he *in* our blackberry patch? Has he really been to see you, and is he courting you in earnest? – But of *course* he is! There's the lilac bush, the lawn-mower, the house to be painted, and a humdinger dress. Is he a millionaire? For Heaven's sake tell me–"

"Give me some chance! I did meet him in the blackberry patch. He's a nephew of Henry Lang and his name is Robert Gray. He has just finished a medical course and he came here to rest and look at Hartley for a location, because Lang thinks it would be such a good one. And since we met he has decided to take an office in Hartley, and he has money to furnish it, and to buy and furnish a nice house."

"Great Jehoshaphat!" cried Kate. "And I bet he's got wings, too! I do have the rottenest luck!"

"You act for all the world as if it were a foregone conclusion that if you had been here, you'd have won him!"

Nancy Ellen glanced in the mirror and smiled, while Kate saw the smile. She picked up her comb and drew herself to full height.

"If anything ever was a 'foregone conclusion,'" she said, "it is a 'foregone conclusion' that if I *had* been here, I'd have picked the blackberries, and so I'd have had the first chance at him, at least."

"Much good it would have done you!" cried Nancy Ellen. "Wait until he comes, and you see him!"

"You may do your mushing in private," said Kate. "I don't need a demonstration to convince me. He looks from the picture like a man who would be as soft as a frosted pawpaw."

Nancy Ellen's face flamed crimson. "You hateful spite-cat!" she cried.

Then she picked up the picture and laid it face down in her drawer, while two big tears ran down her cheeks. Kate saw those also. Instantly she relented.

"You big silly goose!" she said. "Can't you tell when any one is teasing? I think I never saw a finer face than the one in that picture. I'm jealous because I never left home a day before in all my life, and the minute I do, here you go and have such luck. Are you really sure of him, Nancy Ellen?"

"Well, he asked Father and Mother, and I've been to visit his folks, and he told them; and I've been with him to Hartley hunting a house; and I'm not to teach this winter, so I can have all my time to make my clothes and bedding. Father likes him fine, so he is going to give me money to get all I need. He offered to, himself."

Kate finished her braid, pulled the combings from the comb and slowly wrapped the end of her hair as she digested these convincing facts. She swung the heavy braid around her head, placed a few pins, then crossed to her sister and laid a shaking hand on her shoulder. Her face was working strongly.

"Nancy Ellen, I didn't mean one ugly word I said. You gave me an awful surprise, and that was just my bald, ugly Bates way of taking it. I think you are one of the most beautiful women I ever have seen, alive or pictured. I have always thought you would make a fine marriage, and I am sure you will. I haven't a doubt that Robert Gray is all you think him, and I am as glad for you as I can be. You can keep house in Hartley for two with scarcely any work at all, and you can have all the pretty clothes you want, and time to wear them. Doctors always get rich if they are good ones, and he is sure to be a good one, once he gets a start. If only we weren't so beastly healthy there are enough Bates and Langs to support you for the first year. And I'll help you sew, and do all I can for you. Now wipe up and look your handsomest!"

Nancy Ellen arose and put her arms around Kate's neck, a stunningly unusual proceeding. "Thank you," she said. "That is big and fine of you. But I always have shirked and put my work on you; I guess now I'll quit, and do my sewing myself."

Then she slipped the pink dress over her head and stood slowly fastening it as Kate started to leave the room. Seeing her go: "I wish you would wait and meet Robert," she said. "I have told him about what a nice sister I have."

"I think I'll go on to Adam's now," said Kate. "I don't want to wait until they go some place, and I miss them. I'll do better to meet your man after I become more accustomed to bare facts, anyway. By the way, is he as tall as you?"

"Yes," said Nancy Ellen, laughing. "He is an inch and a half taller. Why?"

"Oh, I hate seeing a woman taller than her husband and I've always wondered where we'd find men to reach our shoulders. But if they can be picked at random from the berry patch–"

So Kate went on her way laughing, lifting her white skirts high from the late August dust. She took a short cut through the woods and at a small stream, with sure foot, crossed the log to within a few steps of the opposite bank. There she stopped, for a young man rounded the bushes and set a foot on the same log; then he and Kate looked straight into each other's eyes. Kate saw a clean- shaven, forceful young face, with strong lines and good colouring, clear gray eyes, sandy brown hair, even, hard, white teeth, and broad shoulders a little above her own. The man saw Kate, dressed in her best and looking her best. Slowly she extended her hand.

"I bet a picayune you are my new brother, Robert," she said.

The young man gripped her hand firmly, held it, and kept on looking in rather a stunned manner at Kate.

"Well, aren't you?" she asked, trying to withdraw the hand.

"I never, never would have believed it," he said.

"Believed what?" asked Kate, leaving the hand where it was.

"That there could be two in the same family," said he.

"But I'm as different from Nancy Ellen as night from day," said Kate, "besides, woe is me, I didn't wear a pink dress and pick you from the berry patch in a blue bowl."

Then the man released her hand and laughed. "You wouldn't have had the slightest trouble, if you had been there," he said.

"Except that I should have inverted my bowl," said Kate, calmly. "I am looking for a millionaire, riding a milk-white steed, and he must be much taller than you and have black hair and eyes. Good- bye, brother! I will see you this evening."

Then Kate went down the path to deliver the telescope, render her thanks, make her promise of speedy payment, and for the first time tell her good news about her school. She found that she was very happy as she went and quite convinced that her first flight would prove entirely successful.

A Question of Contracts

"Hello, Folks!" cried Kate, waving her hand to the occupants of the veranda as she went up the walk. "Glad to find you at home."

"That is where you will always find me unless I am forced away on business," said her brother as they shook hands.

Agatha was pleased with this, and stiff as steel, she bent the length of her body toward Kate and gave her a tight-lipped little peck on the cheek.

"I came over, as soon as I could," said Kate as she took the chair her brother offered, "to thank you for the big thing you did for me, Agatha, when you lent me that money. If I had known where I was going, or the help it would be to me, I should have gone if I'd had to walk and work for my board. Why, I feel so sure of myself! I've learned so much that I'm like the girl fresh from boarding school: 'The only wonder is that one small head can contain it all.' Thank you over and over and I've got a good school, so I can pay you back the very first month, I think. If there are things I must have, I can pay part the first month and the remainder the second. I am eager for pay-day. I can't even picture the bliss of having that much money in my fingers, all my own, to do with as I please. Won't it be grand?"

In the same breath said Agatha: "Procure yourself some clothes!" Said Adam: "Start a bank account!"

Said Kate: "Right you are! I shall do both."

"Even our little Susan has a bank account," said Adam, Jr., proudly.

"Which is no reflection whatever on me," laughed Kate. "Susan did not have the same father and mother I had. I'd like to see a girl of my branch of the Bates family start a bank account at ten."

"No, I guess she wouldn't," admitted Adam, dryly.

"But have you heard that Nancy Ellen has started?" cried Kate. "Only think! A lawn-mower! The house and barn to be painted! All the dinge possible to remove scoured away, inside! She must have worn her fingers almost to the bone! And really, Agatha, have you seen the man? He's as big as Adam, and just fine looking. I'm simply consumed with envy."

"Miss Medira, Dora, Ann, cast her net, and catched a man!" recited Susan from the top step, at which they all laughed.

"No, I have not had the pleasure of casting my optics upon the individual of Nancy Ellen's choice," said Agatha primly, "but Miss Amelia Lang tells me he is a very distinguished person, of quite superior education in a medical way. I shall call him if I ever have the misfortune to fall ill again. I hope you will tell Nancy Ellen that we shall be very pleased to have her bring him to see us some evening, and if she will let me know a short time ahead I shall take great pleasure in compounding a cake and freezing custard."

"Of course I shall tell her, and she will feel a trifle more stuck up than she does now, if that is possible," laughed Kate in deep amusement.

She surely was feeling fine. Everything had come out so splendidly. That was what came of having a little spirit and standing up for your rights. Also she was bubbling inside while Agatha talked. Kate wondered how Adam survived it every day. She glanced at him to see if she could detect any marks of shattered nerves, then laughed outright.

Adam was the finest physical specimen of a man she knew. He was good looking also, and spoke as well as the average, better in fact, for from the day of their marriage, Agatha sat on his lap each night and said these words: "My beloved, to-day I noted an error in your speech. It would put a former teacher to much embarrassment to have this occur in public. In the future will you not try to remember that you should say, 'have gone,' instead of 'have went?'" As she talked Agatha rumpled Adam's hair, pulled off his string tie, upon which she insisted, even when he was plowing; laid her hard little face against his, and held him tight with her frail arms, so that Adam being part human as well as part Bates, held her closely also and said these words: "You bet your sweet life I will!" And what is more he did. He followed a furrow the next day, softly muttering over to himself: "Langs have gone to town. I have gone to work. The birds have gone to building nests." So Adam seldom said: "have went," or made any other error in speech that Agatha had once corrected.

As Kate watched him leaning back in his chair, vital, a study in well-being, the supremest kind of satisfaction on his face, she noted the flash that lighted his eye when Agatha offered to "freeze a custard." How like Agatha! Any other woman Kate knew would have said, "make ice cream." Agatha explained to them that when they beat up eggs, added milk, sugar, and corn-starch it was custard. When they used pure cream, sweetened and frozen, it was iced cream. Personally, she preferred the custard, but she did not propose to call it custard cream. It was not correct. Why persist in misstatements and inaccuracies when one knew better? So Agatha said iced cream when she meant it, and frozen custard, when custard it was, but every other woman in the neighbourhood, had she acted as she felt, would have slapped Agatha's face when she said it: this both Adam and Kate well knew, so it made Kate laugh despite the fact that she would not have offended Agatha purposely.

"I think – I think," said Agatha, "that Nancy Ellen has much upon which to congratulate herself. More education would not injure her, but she has enough that if she will allow her ambition to rule her and study in private and spend her spare time communing with the best writers, she can make an exceedingly fair intellectual showing, while she surely is a handsome woman. With a good home and such a fine young professional man as she has had the good fortune to attract, she should immediately put herself at the head of society in Hartley and become its leader to a much higher moral and intellectual plane than it now occupies."

"Bet she has a good time," said young Adam. "He's awful nice."

"Son," said Agatha, "'awful,' means full of awe. A cyclone, a cloudburst, a great conflagration are awful things. By no stretch of the imagination could they be called nice."

"But, Ma, if a cyclone blew away your worst enemy wouldn't it be nice?"

Adam, Jr., and Kate laughed. Not the trace of a smile crossed Agatha's pale face.

"The words do not belong in contiguity," she said. "They are diametrically opposite in meaning. Please do not allow my ears to be offended by hearing you place them in propinquity again."

"I'll try not to, Ma," said young Adam; then Agatha smiled on him approvingly. "When did you meet Mr. Gray, Katherine?" she asked.

"On the foot-log crossing the creek beside Lang's line fence. Near the spot Nancy Ellen first met him I imagine."

"How did you recognize him?"

"Nancy Ellen had just been showing me his picture and telling me about him. Great Day, but she's in love with him!"

"And so he is with her, if Lang's conclusions from his behaviour can be depended upon. They inform me that he can be induced to converse on no other subject. The whole arrangement appeals to me as distinctly admirable."

"And you should see the lilac bush and the cabbage roses," said Kate. "And the strangest thing is Father. He is peaceable as a lamb. She is not to teach, but to spend the winter sewing on her clothes and bedding, and Father told her he would give her the necessary money. She said so. And I suspect he will. He always favoured her because she was so pretty, and she can come closer to wheedling him than any of the rest of us excepting you, Agatha."

"It is an innovation, surely!"

"Mother is nearly as bad. Father furnishing money for clothes and painting the barn is no more remarkable than Mother letting her turn the house inside out. If it had been I, Father would have told me to teach my school this winter, buy my own clothes and linen with the money I had earned, and do my sewing next summer. But I am not jealous. It is because she is handsome, and the man fine-looking and with such good prospects."

"There you have it!" said Adam emphatically. "If it were you, marrying Jim Lang, to live on Lang's west forty, you *would* pay your own way. But if it were you marrying a fine-looking young doctor, who will soon be a power in Hartley, no doubt, it would tickle Father's vanity until he would do the same for you."

"I doubt it!" said Kate. "I can't see the vanity in Father."

"You can't?" said Adam, Jr., bitterly. "Maybe not! You have not been with him in the Treasurer's office when he calls for 'the tax on those little parcels of land of mine.' He looks every inch of six feet six then, and swells like a toad. To hear him you would think sixteen hundred and fifty acres of the cream of this county could be tied in a bandanna and carried on a walking stick, he is so casual about it. And those men fly around like buttons on a barn door to wait on him and it's 'Mister Bates this' and 'Mister Bates that,' until it turns my stomach.

Vanity! He rolls in it! He eats it! He risks losing our land for us that some of us have slaved over for twenty years, to feed that especial vein of his vanity. Where should we be if he let anything happen to those deeds?"

"How refreshing!" cried Kate. "I love to hear you grouching! I hear nothing else from the women of the Bates family, but I didn't even know the men had a grouch. Are Peter, and John, and Hiram, and the other boys sore, too?"

"I should say they are! But they are too diplomatic to say so. They are afraid to cheep. I just open my head and say right out loud in meeting that since I've turned in the taxes and insurance for all these years and improved my land more than fifty per cent., I'd like to own it, and pay my taxes myself, like a man."

"I'd like to have some land under any conditions," said Kate, "but probably I never shall. And I bet you never get a flipper on that deed until Father has crossed over Jordan, which with his health and strength won't be for twenty-five years yet at least. He's performing a miracle that will make the other girls rave, when he gives Nancy Ellen money to buy her outfit; but they won't dare let him hear a whisper of it. They'll take it all out on Mother, and she'll be afraid to tell him."

"Afraid? Mother afraid of him? Not on your life. She is hand in glove with him. She thinks as he does, and helps him in everything he undertakes."

"That's so, too. Come to think of it, she isn't a particle afraid of him. She agrees with him perfectly. It would be interesting to hear them having a private conversation. They never talk a word before us. But they always agree, and they heartily agree on Nancy Ellen's man, that is plainly to be seen."

"It will make a very difficult winter for you, Katherine," said Agatha. "When Nancy Ellen becomes interested in dresses and table linen and bedding she will want to sew all the time, and leave the cooking and dishes for you as well as your schoolwork."

Kate turned toward Agatha in surprise. "But I won't be there! I told you I had taken a school."

"You taken a school!" shouted Adam. "Why, didn't they tell you that Father has signed up for the home school for you?"

"Good Heavens!" said Kate. "What will be to pay now?"

"Did you contract for another school?" cried Adam.

"I surely did," said Kate slowly. "I signed an agreement to teach the village school in Walden. It's a brick building with a janitor to sweep and watch fires, only a few blocks to walk, and it pays twenty dollars a month more than the home school where you can wade snow three miles, build your own fires, and freeze all day in a little frame building at that. I teach the school I have taken."

"And throw our school out of a teacher? Father could be sued, and probably will be," said Adam. "And throw the housework Nancy Ellen expected you to do on her," said Agatha, at the same time.

"I see," said Kate. "Well, if he is sued, he will have to settle. He wouldn't help me a penny to go to school, I am of age, the debt is my own, and I don't owe it to him. He's had all my work has been worth all my life, and I've surely paid my way. I shall teach the school I have signed for."

"You will get into a pretty kettle of fish!" said Adam.

"Agatha, will you sell me your telescope for what you paid for it, and get yourself a new one the next time you go to Hartley? It is only a few days until time to go to my school, it opens sooner than in the country, and closes later. The term is four months longer, so I earn that much more. I haven't gotten a telescope yet. You can add it to my first payment."

"You may take it," said Agatha, "but hadn't you better reconsider, Katherine? Things are progressing so nicely, and this will upset everything for Nancy Ellen."

"That taking the home school will upset everything for me, doesn't seem to count. It is late, late to find teachers, and I can be held responsible if I break the contract I have made. Father can stand the racket better than I can. When he wouldn't consent to my going, he had no business to make plans for me. I had to make my own plans and go in spite of him; he might have known I'd do all in my power to get a school. Besides, I don't want the home school, or the home work piled on me. My hands look like a human being's for the first time in my life; then I need all my time outside of school to study and map out lessons. I am going to try for a room in the Hartley schools next year, or the next after that, surely. They sha'n't change my plans and boss me, I am going to be free to work, and study, and help myself, like other teachers."

"A grand row this will be," commented young Adam. "And as usual Kate will be right, while all of them will be trying to use her to their advantage. Ma has done her share. Now it is your turn, Pa. Ain't you going to go over and help her?"

"What could I do?" demanded his father. "The mischief is done now."

"Well, if you can't do anything to help, you can let me have the buggy to drive her to Walden, if they turn her out."

"'Forcibly invite her to proceed to her destination,' you mean, son," said Agatha.

"Yes, Ma, that is exactly what I mean," said young Adam. "Do I get the buggy?"

"Yes, you may take my private conveyance. But do nothing to publish the fact. There is no need to incur antagonism if it can be avoided."

"Kate, I'll be driving past the privet bush about nine in the morning. If you need me, hang a white rag on it, and I'll stop at the corner of the orchard."

"I shall probably be standing in the road waiting for you," said Kate.

"Oh, I hope not," said Agatha.

"Looks remarkably like it to me," said Kate.

Then she picked up the telescope, said good-bye to each of them, and in acute misery started back to her home. This time she followed the footpath beside the highway. She was so busy with her indignant thought that she forgot to protect her skirts from the dust of wayside weeds, while in her excitement she walked so fast her face was red and perspiring when she approached the church.

"Oh, dear, I don't know about it," said Kate to the small, silent building. "I am trying to follow your advice, but it seems to me that life is very difficult, any way you go at it. If it isn't one thing, it is another. An hour ago I was the happiest I have ever been in my life; only look at me now! Any one who wants 'the wings of morning' may have them for all of me. It seems definitely settled that I walk, carry a load, and fight for the chance to do even that."

A big tear rolled down either side of Kate's nose and her face twisted in self-pity for an instant. But when she came in sight of home her shoulders squared, the blue-gray of her eyes deepened to steel, and her lips set in a line that was an exact counterpart of her father's when he had made up his mind and was ready to drive his family, with their consent or without it. As she passed the vegetable garden – there was no time or room for flowers in a Bates garden – Kate, looking ahead, could see Nancy Ellen and Robert Gray beneath the cherry trees. She hoped Nancy Ellen would see that she was tired and dusty, and should have time to brush and make herself more presentable to meet a stranger, and so Nancy Ellen did; for which reason she immediately arose and came to the gate, followed by her suitor whom she at once introduced. Kate was in no mood for words; one glance at her proved to Robert Gray that she was tired and dusty, that there were tear marks dried on her face. They hastily shook hands, but neither mentioned the previous meeting. Excusing herself Kate went into the house saying she would soon return.

Nancy Ellen glanced at Robert, and saw the look of concern on his face.

"I believe she has been crying," she said. "And if she has, it's something new, for I never saw a tear on her face before in my life."

"Truly?" he questioned in amazement.

"Why, of course! The Bates family are not weepers."

"So I have heard," said the man, rather dryly.

Nancy Ellen resented his tone.

"Would you like us better if we were?"

"I couldn't like you better than I do, but because of what I have heard and seen, it naturally makes me wonder what could have happened that has made her cry."

"We are rather outspoken, and not at all secretive," said Nancy Ellen, carelessly, "you will soon know."

Kate followed the walk around the house and entered at the side door, finding her father and mother in the dining room reading the weekly papers. Her mother glanced up as she entered.

"What did you bring Agatha's telescope back with you for?" she instantly demanded.

For a second Kate hesitated. It had to come, she might as well get it over. Possibly it would be easier with them alone than if Nancy Ellen were present.

"It is mine," she said. "It represents my first purchase on my own hook and line."

"You are not very choicy to begin on second-hand stuff. Nancy Ellen would have had a new one."

"No doubt!" said Kate. "But this will do for me."

Her father lowered his paper and asked harshly: "What did you buy that thing for?"

Kate gripped the handle and braced herself.

"To pack my clothes in when I go to my school next week," she said simply.

"What?" he shouted. "What?" cried her mother.

"I don't know why you seem surprised," said Kate. "Surely you knew I went to Normal to prepare myself to teach. Did you think I couldn't find a school?"

"Now look here, young woman," shouted Adam Bates, "you are done taking the bit in your teeth. Nancy Ellen is not going to teach this winter. I have taken the home school for you; you will teach it. That is settled. I have signed the contract. It must be fulfilled."

"Then Nancy Ellen will have to fulfill it," said Kate. "I also have signed a contract that must be fulfilled. I am of age, and you had no authority from me to sign a contract for me."

For an instant Kate thought there was danger that the purple rush of blood to her father's head might kill him. He opened his mouth, but no distinct words came. Her face paled with fright, but she was of his blood, so she faced him quietly. Her mother was quicker of wit, and sharper of tongue.

"Where did you get a school? Why didn't you wait until you got home?" she demanded.

"I am going to teach the village school in Walden," said Kate. "It is a brick building, has a janitor, I can board reasonably, near my work, and I get twenty dollars more a month than our school pays, while the term is four months longer."

"Well, it is a pity about that; but it makes no difference," said her mother. "Our home school has got to be taught as Pa contracted, and Nancy Ellen has got to have her chance."

"What about my chance?" asked Kate evenly. "Not one of the girls, even Exceptional Ability, ever had as good a school or as high wages to start on. If I do well there this winter, I am sure I can get in the Hartley graded schools next fall."

"Don't you dare nickname your sister," cried Mrs. Bates, shrilly. "You stop your impudence and mind your father."

"Ma, you leave this to me," said Adam Bates, thickly. Then he glared at Kate as he arose, stretching himself to full height. "You've signed a contract for a school?" he demanded.

"I have," said Kate.

"Why didn't you wait until you got home and talked it over with us?" he questioned.

"I went to you to talk over the subject to going," said Kate. "You would not even allow me to speak. How was I to know that you would have the slightest interest in what school I took, or where."

"When did you sign this contract?" he continued.

"Yesterday afternoon, in Hartley," said Kate.

"Aha! Then I did miss a letter from my pocket. When did you get to be a thief?" he demanded.

"Oh, Father!" cried Kate. "It was my letter. I could see my name on the envelope. I *asked* you for it, before I took it."

"From behind my back, like the sneak-thief you are. You are not fit to teach in a school where half the scholars are the children of your brothers and sisters, and you are not fit to live with honest people. Pack your things and be off!"

"Now? This afternoon?" asked Kate.

"This minute!" he cried.

"All right. You will be surprised at how quickly I can go," said Kate.

She set down the telescope and gathered a straw sunshade and an apron from the hooks at the end of the room, opened the dish cupboard, and took out a mug decorated with the pinkest of wild roses and the reddest and fattest of robins, bearing the inscription in gold, "For a Good Girl" on a banner in its beak. Kate smiled at it grimly as she took the telescope and ran upstairs. It was the work of only a few minutes to gather her books and clothing and pack the big telescope, then she went down the front stairs and left the house by the front door carrying in her hand everything she possessed on earth. As she went down the walk Nancy Ellen sprang up and ran to her while Robert Gray followed.

"You'll have to talk to me on the road," said Kate. "I am forbidden the house which also means the grounds, I suppose."

She walked across the road, set the telescope on the grass under a big elm tree, and sat down beside it.

"I find I am rather tired," she said. "Will you share the sofa with me?"

Nancy Ellen lifted her pink skirt and sat beside Kate. Robert Gray stood looking down at them.

"What in the world is the matter?" asked Nancy Ellen.

"You know, of course, that Father signed a contract for me to teach the home school this winter," explained Kate. "Well, I am of age, and he had no authority from me, so his contract isn't legal. None of you would lift a finger to help me get away to Normal, how was I to know that you would take any interest in finding me a school while I was gone? I thought it was all up to me, so I applied for the school in Walden, got it, and signed the contract to teach it. It is a better school, at higher wages. I thought you would teach here – I can't break my contract. Father is furious and has ordered me out of the house. So there you are, or rather here I am."

"Well, it isn't much of a joke," said Nancy Ellen, thinking intently.

What she might have said had they been alone, Kate always wondered. What she did say while her betrothed looked at her with indignant eyes was possibly another matter. It proved to be merely: "Oh, Kate, I am so sorry!"

"So am I," said Kate. "If I had known what your plans were, of course I should gladly have helped you out. If only you had written me and told me."

"I wanted to surprise you," said Nancy Ellen.

"You have," said Kate. "Enough to last a lifetime. I don't see how you figured. You knew how late it was. You knew it would be nip and tuck if I got a school at all."

"Of course we did! We thought you couldn't possibly get one, this late, so we fixed up the scheme to let you have my school, and let me sew on my linen this winter. We thought you would be as pleased as we were."

"I am too sorry for words," said Kate. "If I had known your plan, I would have followed it, even though I gave up a better school at a higher salary. But I didn't know. I thought I had to paddle my own canoe, so I made my own plans. Now I must live up to them, because my contract is legal, while Father's is not. I would have taught the school for you, in the circumstances, but since I can't, so far as I am concerned, the arrangement I have made is much better. The thing that really hurts the worst, aside from disappointing you, is that Father says I was not honest in what I did."

"But what *did* you do?" cried Nancy Ellen.

So Kate told them exactly what she had done.

"Of course you had a right to your own letter, when you could see the address on it, and it was where you could pick it up," said Robert Gray.

Kate lifted dull eyes to his face.

"Thank you for so much grace, at any rate," she said.

"I don't blame you a bit," said Nancy Ellen. "In the same place I'd have taken it myself."

"You wouldn't have had to," said Kate. "I'm too abrupt – too much like the gentleman himself. You would have asked him in a way that would have secured you the letter with no trouble."

Nancy Ellen highly appreciated these words of praise before her lover. She arose immediately.

"Maybe I could do something with him now," she said. "I'll go and see."

"You shall do nothing of the kind," said Kate. "I am as much Bates as he is. I won't be taunted afterward that he turned me out and that I sent you to him to plead for me."

"I'll tell him you didn't want me to come, that I came of my own accord," offered Nancy Ellen.

"And he won't believe you," said Kate.

"Would you consent for me to go?" asked Robert Gray.

"Certainly not! I can look out for myself."

"What shall you do?" asked Nancy Ellen anxiously.

"That is getting slightly ahead of me," said Kate. "If I had been diplomatic I could have evaded this until morning. Adam, 3d, is to be over then, prepared to take me anywhere I want to go. What I have to face now is a way to spend the night without letting the neighbours know that I am turned out. How can I manage that?"

Nancy Ellen and Robert each began making suggestions, but Kate preferred to solve her own problems.

"I think," she said, "that I shall hide the telescope under the privet bush, there isn't going to be rain to-night; and then I will go down to Hiram's and stay all night and watch for Adam when he passes in the morning. Hiram always grumbles because we don't come oftener."

"Then we will go with you," said Nancy Ellen. "It will be a pleasant evening walk, and we can keep you company and pacify my twin brother at the same time."

So they all walked to the adjoining farm on the south and when Nancy Ellen and Robert were ready to start back, Kate said she was tired and she believed she would stay until morning, which was agreeable to Hiram and his wife, a girlhood friend of Kate's. As Nancy Ellen and Robert walked back toward home: "How is this going to come out?" he asked, anxiously.

"It will come out all right," said Nancy Ellen, serenely. "Kate hasn't a particle of tact. She is Father himself, all over again. It will come out this way: he will tell me that Kate has gone back on him and I shall have to teach the school, and I will say that is the *only* solution and the *best* thing to do. Then I shall talk all evening about how provoking it is, and how I hate to change my plans, and say I am afraid I shall lose you if I have to put off our wedding to teach the school, and things like that," Nancy Ellen turned a flushed sparkling face to Robert, smiling quizzically, "and to-morrow I shall go early to see Serena Woodruff, who is a fine scholar and a good teacher, but missed her school in the spring by being so sick she was afraid to contract for it. She is all right now, and she will be delighted to have the school, and when I know she will take it then I shall just happen to think of her in a day or two and I'll suggest her, after I've wailed a lot more; and Father will go to see her of his own accord, and it will all be settled as easy as falling off a chunk, only I shall not get on so fast with my sewing, because of having to help Mother; but I shall do my best, and everything will be all right."

The spot was secluded. Robert Gray stopped to tell Nancy Ellen what a wonderful girl she was. He said he was rather afraid of such diplomacy. He foresaw clearly that he was going to be a managed man. Nancy Ellen told him of course he was, all men were, the thing was not to let them know it. Then they laughed and listened to a wood robin singing out his little heart in an evening song that was almost as melodious as his spring performances had been.

The Prodigal Daughter

Early in the morning Kate set her young nephew on the gate-post to watch for his cousin, and he was to have a penny for calling at his approach. When his lusty shout came, Kate said good-bye to her sister-in-law, paid the penny, kissed the baby, and was standing in the road when Adam stopped. He looked at her inquiringly.

"Well, it happened," she said. "He turned me out instanter, with no remarks about when I might return, if ever, while Mother cordially seconded the motion. It's a good thing, Adam, that you offered to take care of me, because I see clearly that you are going to have it to do."

"Of course I will," said Adam promptly. "And of course I can. Do you want to go to Hartley for anything? Because if you don't, we can cut across from the next road and get to Walden in about fifteen miles, while it's seventeen by Hartley; but if you want to go we can, for I needn't hurry. I've got a box of lunch and a feed for my horse in the back of the buggy. Mother said I was to stay with you until I saw you settled in your room, if you had to go; and if you do, she is angry with Grandpa, and she is going to give him a portion of her mentality the very first time she comes in contact with him. She said so."

"Yes, I can almost hear her," said Kate, struggling to choke down a rising laugh. "She will never know how I appreciate what she has done for me, but I think talking to Father will not do any good. Home hasn't been so overly pleasant. It's been a small, dark, cramped house, dingy and hot, when it might have been big, airy, and comfortable, well furnished and pretty as Father's means would allow, and as all the neighbours always criticize him for not having it; it's meant hard work and plenty of it ever since I was set to scouring the tinware with rushes at the mature age of four, but it's been home, all the home I have had, and it hurts more than I can tell you to be ordered out of it as I was, but if I do well and make a big success, maybe he will let me come back for Christmas, or next summer's vacation."

"If he won't, Ma said you could come to our house," said Adam.

"That's kind of her, but I couldn't do it," said Kate.

"She *said* you could," persisted the boy.

"But if I did it, and Father got as mad as he was last night and tore up your father's deed, then where would I be?" asked Kate.

"You'd be a sixteenth of two hundred acres better off than you are now," said Adam.

"Possibly," laughed Kate, "but I wouldn't want to become a land shark that way. Look down the road."

"Who is it?" asked Adam.

"Nancy Ellen, with my telescope," answered Kate. "I am to go, all right."

"All right, then we will go," said the boy, angrily. "But it is a blame shame and there is no sense to it, as good a girl as you have been, and the way you have worked. Mother said at breakfast there was neither sense nor justice in the way Grandpa always has acted and she said she would wager all she was worth that he would live to regret it. She said it wasn't natural, and when people undertook to controvert – ain't that a peach? Bet there isn't a woman in ten miles using that word except Ma – nature they always hurt themselves worse than they hurt their victims. And I bet he does, too, and I, for one, don't care. I hope he does get a good jolt, just to pay him up for being so mean."

"Don't, Adam, don't!" cautioned Kate.

"I mean it!" cried the boy.

"I know you do. That's the awful thing about it," said Kate. "I am afraid every girl he has feels the same way, and from what your father said yesterday, even the sons he favours don't feel any too good toward him."

"You just bet they don't! They are every one as sore as boiled owls. Pa said so, and he knows, for they all talk it over every time they meet. He said they didn't feel like men, they felt like a lot of 'spanked school-boys.'"

"They needn't worry," said Kate. "Every deed is made out. Father reads them over whenever it rains. They'll all get their land when he dies. It is only his way."

"Yes, and *this* is only his way, too, and it's a dern poor way," said Adam. "Pa isn't going to do this way at all. Mother said he could go and live on his land, and she'd stay home with Susan and me, if he tried it. And when I am a man I am going to do just like Pa and Ma because they are the rightest people I know, only I am not going to save *quite* so close as Pa, and if I died for it, I never could converse or dance like Ma."

"I should hope not!" said Kate, and then added hastily, "it's all right for a lady, but it would seem rather sissy for a man, I believe."

"Yes, I guess it would, but it is language let me tell you, when Ma cuts loose," said Adam.

"Hello, Nancy Ellen," said Kate as Adam stopped the buggy. "Put my telescope in the back with the horse feed. Since you have it, I don't need ask whether I am the Prodigal Daughter or not. I see clearly I am."

Nancy Ellen was worried, until she was pale.

"Kate," she said, "I never have seen Father so angry in all my life. I thought last night that in a day or two I could switch the school over to Serena Woodruff, and go on with my plans, but Father said at breakfast if the Bates name was to stand for anything approaching honour, a Bates would teach that school this winter or he'd know the reason why. And you know how easy it is to change him. Oh, Kate, won't you see if that Walden trustee can't possibly find another teacher, and let you off? I know Robert will be disappointed, for he's rented his office and bought a house and he said last night to get ready as soon after Christmas as I could. Oh, Kate, won't you see if you can't possibly get that man to hire another teacher?"

"Why, Nancy Ellen–" said Kate.

Nancy Ellen, with a twitching face, looked at Kate.

"If Robert has to wait months, there in Hartley, handsome as he is, and he has to be nice to everybody to get practice, and you know how those Hartley girls are–"

"Yes, Nancy Ellen, I know," said Kate. "I'll see what I can do. Is it understood that if I give up the school and come back and take ours, Father will let me come home?"

"Yes, oh, yes!" cried Nancy Ellen.

"Well, nothing goes on guess-work. I'll hear him say it, myself," said Kate.

She climbed from the buggy. Nancy Ellen caught her arm.

"Don't go in there! Don't you go there," she cried. "He'll throw the first thing he can pick up at you. Mother says he hasn't been asleep all night."

"Pooh!" said Kate. "How childish! I want to hear him say that, and he'll scarcely kill me."

She walked swiftly to the side door.

"Father," she said, "Nancy Ellen is afraid she will lose Robert Gray if she has to put off her marriage for months–"

Kate stepped back quickly as a chair crashed against the door facing. She again came into view and continued – "so she asked me if I would get out of my school and come back if I could" – Kate dodged another chair; when she appeared again – "To save the furniture, of which we have none too much, I'll just step inside," she said. When her father started toward her, she started around the dining table, talking as fast as she could, he lunging after her like a furious bull. "She asked me to come back and teach the school – to keep her from putting off her wedding – because she is afraid to – If I can break my contract there – may I come back and help her out here?"

The pace was going more swiftly each round, it was punctuated at that instant by a heavy meat platter aimed at Kate's head. She saw it picked up and swayed so it missed.

"I guess that is answer enough for me," she panted, racing on. "A lovely father you are – no wonder your daughters are dishonest through fear of you – no wonder your wife has no mind of her own – no wonder your sons hate you and wish you would die – so they could have their deeds and be like men – instead of 'spanked school-boys' as they feel now – no wonder the whole posse of us hate you."

Directly opposite the door Kate caught the table and drew it with her to bar the opening. As it crashed against the casing half the dishes flew to the floor in a heap. When Adam Bates pulled it from his path he stepped in a dish of fried potatoes and fell heavily. Kate reached the road, climbed in the buggy, and said the Nancy Ellen: "You'd better hide! Cut a bundle of stuff and send it to me by Adam and I'll sew my fingers to the bone for you every night. Now drive like sin, Adam!"

As Adam Bates came lurching down the walk in fury the buggy dashed past and Kate had not even time to turn her head to see what happened.

"Take the first turn," she said to Adam. "I've done an awful thing."

"What did you do?" cried the boy.

"Asked him as nicely as I could; but he threw a chair at me. Something funny happened to me, and I wasn't afraid of him at all. I dodged it, and finished what I was saying, and another chair came, so the two Bates went at it."

"Oh, Kate, what did you do?" cried Adam.

"Went inside and ran around the dining table while I told him what all his sons and daughters think of him. 'Spanked school-boys' and all–"

"Did you tell him my father said that?" he demanded.

"No. I had more sense left than that," said Kate. "I only said all his boys *felt* like that. Then I pulled the table after me to block the door, and smashed half the dishes and he slipped in the fried potatoes and went down with a crash–"

"Bloody Murder!" cried young Adam, aghast.

"Me, too!" said Kate. "I'll never step in that house again while he lives. I've spilled the beans, now."

"That you have," said Adam, slacking his horse to glance back. "He is standing in the middle of the road shaking his fist after you."

"Can you see Nancy Ellen?" asked Kate.

"No. She must have climbed the garden fence and hidden behind the privet bush."

"Well, she better make it a good long hide, until he has had plenty of time to cool off. He'd have killed me if he had caught me, after he fell – and wasted all those potatoes already cooked–"

Kate laughed a dry hysterical laugh, but the boy sat white-faced and awed.

"Never mind," said Kate, seeing how frightened he was. "When he has had plenty of time he'll cool off; but he'll never get over it. I hope he doesn't beat Mother, because I was born."

"Oh, drat such a man!" said young Adam. "I hope something worse that this happens to him. If ever I see Father begin to be the least bit like him as he grows older I shall–"

"Well, what shall you do?" asked Kate, as he paused.

"Tell Ma!" cried young Adam, emphatically.

Kate leaned her face in her hands and laughed. When she could speak she said: "Do you know, Adam, I think that would be the very best thing you could do."

"Why, of course!" said Adam.

They drove swiftly and reached Walden before ten o'clock. There they inquired their way to the home of the Trustee, but Kate said nothing about giving up the school. She merely made a few inquiries, asked for the key of the schoolhouse, and about boarding places. She was directed to four among which she might choose.

"Where would you advise me to go?" she asked the Trustee.

"Well, now, folks differ," said he. "All those folks is neighbours of mine and some might like one, and some might like another, best. I COULD say this: I think Means would be the cheapest, Knowls the dearest, but the last teacher was a good one, an' she seemed well satisfied with the Widder Holt."

"I see," said Kate, smiling.

Then she and young Adam investigated the schoolhouse and found it far better than any either of them had ever been inside. It promised every comfort and convenience, compared with schools to which they had been accustomed, so they returned the keys, inquired about the cleaning of the building, and started out to find a boarding place. First they went to the cheapest, but it could be seen at a glance that it was too cheap, so they eliminated that. Then they went to the most expensive, but it was obvious from the house and grounds that board there would be more than Kate would want to pay.

"I'd like to save my digestion, and have a place in which to study, where I won't freeze," said Kate, "but I want to board as cheaply as I can. This morning changes my plans materially. I shall want to go to school next summer part of the time, but the part I do not, I shall have to pay my way, so I mustn't spend money as I thought I would. Not one of you will dare be caught doing a thing for me. To make you safe I'll stay away, but it will cost me money that I'd hoped to have for clothes like other girls."

"It's too bad," said Adam, "but I'll stick to you, and so will Ma."

"Of course you will, you dear boy," said Kate. "Now let's try our third place; it is not far from here."

Soon they found the house, but Kate stopped short on sight of it.

"Adam, there has been little in life to make me particular," she said, "but I draw the line at that house. I would go crazy in a house painted bright red with brown and blue decoration. It should be prohibited by law. Let us hunt up the Widder Holt and see how her taste in colour runs."

"The joke is on you," said Adam, when they had found the house.

It was near the school, on a wide shady street across which big maples locked branches. There was a large lot filled with old fruit trees and long grass, with a garden at the back. The house was old and low, having a small porch in front, but if it ever had seen paint, it did not show it at that time. It was a warm linty gray, the shingles of the old roof almost moss-covered.

"The joke IS on me," said Kate. "I shall have no quarrel with the paint here, and will you look at that?"

Adam looked where Kate pointed across the street, and nodded.

"That ought to be put in a gold frame," he said.

"I think so, too," said Kate. "I shouldn't be a bit surprised if I stay where I can see it."

They were talking of a deep gully facing the house and running to a levee where the street crossed. A stream ran down it, dipped under a culvert, turned sharply, and ran away to a distant river, spanning which they could see the bridge. Tall old forest trees lined the banks, shrubs and bushes grew in a thicket. There were swaying, clambering vines and a babel of bird notes over the seed and berry bearing bushes.

"Let's go inside, and if we agree, then we will get some water and feed the horse and eat our lunch over there," said Kate.

"Just the thing!" said young Adam. "Come and we will proceed to the residence of Mrs. Holt and investigate her possibilities. How do you like that?"

"That is fine," said Kate gravely.

"It is," said Adam, promptly, "because it is Ma. And whatever is Ma, is right."

"Good for you!" cried Kate. "I am going to break a Bates record and kiss you good-bye, when you go. I probably shan't have another in years. Come on."

They walked up the grassy wooden walk, stepped on the tiny, vine- covered porch, and lifted and dropped a rusty old iron knocker. Almost at once the door opened, to reveal a woman of respectable appearance, a trifle past middle age. She made Kate think of dried sage because she had a dried-out look and her complexion, hair, and eyes were all that colour. She was neat and clean while the hall into which she invited them was clean and had a wholesome odour. Kate explained her errand. Mrs. Holt breathed a sigh of relief.

"Well, thank goodness I was before-handed," she said. "The teacher stayed here last year and she was satisfied, so I ast the Trustee to mention me to the new teacher. Nobody was expecting you until the last of the week, but I says to myself, 'always take time by the fetlock, Samantha, always be ready'; so last week I put in scouring my spare room to beat the nation, and it's all ready so's you can walk right in."

"Thank you," said Kate, rather resenting the assumption that she was to have no option in the matter. "I have four places on my list where they want the teacher, so I thought I would look at each of them and then decide."

"My, ain't we choicey!" said Mrs. Holt in sneering tones. Then she changed instantly, and in suave commendation went on: "That's exactly right. That's the very thing fer you to do. After you have seen what Walden has to offer, then a pretty young thing like you can make up your mind where you will have the most quiet fer your work, the best room, and be best fed. One of the greatest advantages here fer a teacher is that she can be quiet, an' not have her room rummaged. Every place else that takes boarders there's a lot of children; here there is only me and my son, and he is grown, and will be off to his medical work next week fer the year, so all your working time here, you'd be alone with me. This is the room."

"That surely would be a great advantage, because I have much studying to do," said Kate as they entered the room.

With one glance, she liked it. It was a large room with low ceiling, quaintly papered in very old creamy paper, scattered with delicately cut green leaves, but so carefully had the room been kept, that it was still clean. There were four large windows to let in light and air, freshly washed white curtains hanging over the deep green shades. The floor was carpeted with a freshly washed rag carpet stretched over straw, the bed was invitingly clean and looked comfortable, there was a wash stand with bowl and pitcher, soap and towels, a small table with a lamp, a straight- backed chair and a rocking chair. Mrs. Holt opened a large closet having hooks for dresses at one end and shelves at the other. On the top of these there were a comfort and a pair of heavy blankets.

"Your winter covers," said Mrs. Holt, indicating these, "and there is a good stove I take out in summer to make more room, and set up as soon as it gets cold, and that is a wood box."

She pointed out a shoe box covered with paper similar to that on the walls.

Kate examined the room carefully, the bed, the closet, and tried the chairs. Behind the girl, Mrs. Holt, with compressed lips, forgetting Adam's presence, watched in evident disapproval.

"I want to see the stove," said Kate.

"It is out in the woodhouse. It hasn't been cleaned up for the winter yet."

"Then it won't be far away. Let's look at it."

Almost wholly lacking experience, Kate was proceeding by instinct in exactly the same way her father would have taken through experience. Mrs. Holt hesitated, then turned: "Oh, very well," she said, leading the way down the hall, through the dining room, which was older in furnishing and much more worn, but still clean and wholesome, as were the small kitchen and back porch. From it there was only a step to the woodhouse, where on a little platform across one end sat two small stoves for burning wood, one so small as to be tiny. Kate walked to the larger, lifted the top, looked inside, tried the dampers and drafts and turning said: "That is very small. It will require more wood than a larger one."

Mrs. Holt indicated dry wood corded to the roof.

"We git all our wood from the thicket across the way. That little strip an' this lot is all we have left of father's farm. We kept this to live on, and sold the rest for town lots, all except that gully, which we couldn't give away. But I must say I like the trees and birds better than mebby I'd like people who might live there; we always git our wood from it, and the shade an' running water make it the coolest place in town."

"Yes, I suppose they do," said Kate.

She took one long look at everything as they returned to the hall.

"The Trustee told me your terms are four dollars and fifty cents a week, furnishing food and wood," she said, "and that you allowed the last teacher to do her own washing on Saturday, for nothing. Is that right?"

The thin lips drew more tightly. Mrs. Holt looked at Kate from head to foot in close scrutiny.

"I couldn't make enough to pay the extra work at that," she said. "I ought to have a dollar more, to really come out even. I'll have to say five-fifty this fall."

"If that is the case, good-bye," said Kate. "Thank you very much for showing me. Five-fifty is what I paid at Normal, it is more than I can afford in a village like this."

She turned away, followed by Adam. They crossed the street, watered the horse at the stream, placed his food conveniently for him, and taking their lunch box, seated themselves on a grassy place on the bank and began eating.

"Wasn't that a pretty nice room?" asked Adam. "Didn't you kind of hate to give it up?"

"I haven't the slightest intention of giving it up," answered Kate. "That woman is a skin-flint and I don't propose to let her beat me. No doubt she was glad to get four-fifty last fall. She's only trying to see if she can wring me for a dollar more. If I have to board all next summer, I shall have to watch every penny, or I'll not come out even, let alone saving anything. I'll wager you a nickel that before we leave, she comes over here and offers me the room at the same price she got last winter."

"I hope you are right," said Adam. "How do you like her?"

"Got a grouch, nasty temper, mean disposition; clean house, good room, good cook – maybe; lives just on the edge of comfort by daily skimping," summarized Kate.

"If she comes, are you going to try it?" asked Adam.

"Yes, I think I shall. It is nearest my purse and requirements and if the former teacher stayed there, it will seem all right for me; but she isn't going to put that little stove in my room. It wouldn't heat the closet. How did you like her?"

"Not much!" said Adam, promptly. "If glaring at your back could have killed you, you would have fallen dead when you examined the closet, and bedding, and stove. She honeyed up when she had to, but she was mad as hops. I nearly bursted right out when she talked about 'taking time by the fetlock.' I wanted to tell her she looked like she had, and almost got the life kicked out of her doing it, but I thought I'd better not."

Kate laughed. "Yes, I noticed," she said, "but I dared not look at you. I was afraid you'd laugh. Isn't this a fine lunch?"

"Bet your life it is," said Adam. "Ma never puts up any other kind."

"I wish someone admired me as much as you do your mother, Adam," said Kate.

"Well, you be as nice as Ma, and somebody is sure to," said he.

"But I never could," said Kate.

"Oh, yes, you could," said Adam, "if you would only set yourself to do it and try with all your might to be like her. Look, quick! That must be her 'Medical Course' man!"

Kate glanced across the way and saw a man she thought to be about thirty years of age. He did not resemble his mother in any particular, if he was the son of Mrs. Holt. He was above the average man in height, having broad, rather stooping shoulders, dark hair and eyes. He stopped at the gate and stood a few seconds looking at them, so they could not very well study him closely, then he went up the walk with loose, easy stride and entered the house.

"Yes, that is her son," said Kate. "That is exactly the way a man enters a house that belongs to him."

"That isn't the way I am going to enter my house," said Adam. "Now what shall we do?"

"Rest half an hour while they talk it over, and then get ready to go very deliberately. If she doesn't come across, literally and figuratively, we hunt another boarding place."

"I half believe she will come," said Adam. "She is watching us; I can see her pull back the blind of her room to peep."

"Keep looking ahead. Don't let her think you see her. Let's go up the creek and investigate this ravine. Isn't it a lovely place?"

"Yes. I'm glad you got it," said Adam, "that is, if she come across. I will think of you as having it to look at in summer; and this winter – my, what rabbit hunting there will be, and how pretty it will look!"

So they went wandering up the ravine, sometimes on one bank, sometimes crossing stepping-stones or logs to the other, looking, talking, until a full hour had passed when they returned to the buggy. Adam began changing the halter for the bridle while Kate shook out the lap robe.

"Nickel, please," whispered Kate.

Adam glanced across the street to see Mrs. Holt coming. She approached them and with no preliminaries said: "I have been telling my son about you an' he hates so bad to go away and leave me alone for the winter, that he says to take you at the same as the last teacher, even if I do lose money on it."

"Oh, you wouldn't do that, Mrs. Holt," said Kate, carelessly. "Of course it is for you to decide. I like the room, and if the board was right for the other teacher it will be for me. If you want me to stay, I'll bring my things over and take the room at once. If not, I'll look farther."

"Come right over," said Mrs. Holt, cordially. "I am anxious to git on the job of mothering such a sweet young lady. What will you have for your supper?"

"Whatever you are having," said Kate. "I am not accustomed to ordering my meals. Adam, come and help me unpack."

In half an hour Kate had her dresses on the hooks, her underclothing on the shelves, her books on the table, her pencils and pen in the robin cup, and was saying goodbye to Adam, and telling him what to tell his father, mother, and Nancy Ellen – if he could get a stolen interview with her on the way home. He also promised to write Kate what happened about the home school and everything in which she would be interested. Then she went back to her room, sat in the comfortable rocking chair, and with nothing in the world she was obliged to do immediately, she stared at the opposite wall and day by day reviewed the summer. She sat so long and stared at the wall so intently that gradually it dissolved and shaped into the deep green ravine across the way, which sank into soothing darkness and the slowly lightened until a peep of gold came over the tree tops; and then, a red sun crept up having a big wonderful widespread wing on each side of it. Kate's head fell with a jerk which awakened her, so she arose, removed her dress, washed and brushed her hair, put on a fresh dress and taking a book, she crossed the street and sat on the bank of the stream again, which she watched instead of reading, as she had intended.

Kate's Private Pupil

At first Kate merely sat in a pleasant place and allowed her nerves to settle, after the short nap she had enjoyed in the rocking chair. It was such a novel experience for her to sit idle, that despite the attractions of growing things, running water, and singing birds, she soon veered to thoughts of what she would be doing if she were at home, and that brought her to the fact that she was forbidden her father's house; so if she might not go there, she was homeless. As she had known her father for nearly nineteen years, for she had a birth anniversary coming in a few days, she felt positive that he never would voluntarily see her again, while with his constitution, he would live for years. She might as well face the fact that she was homeless; and prepare to pay her way all the year round. She wondered why she felt so forlorn and what made the dull ache in her throat.

She remembered telling Nancy Ellen before going away to Normal that she wished her father would drive her from home. Now that was accomplished. She was away from home, in a place where there was not one familiar face, object, or plan of life, but she did not wish for it at all. She devoutly wished that she were back at home even if she were preparing supper, in order that Nancy Ellen might hem towels. She wondered what they were saying: her mind was crystal clear as to what they were doing. She wondered if Nancy Ellen would send Adam, 3d, with a parcel of cut-out sewing for her to work on. She resolved to sew quickly and with stitches of machine-like evenness, if it came. She wondered if Nancy Ellen would be compelled to put off her wedding and teach the home school in order that it might be taught by a Bates, as her father had demanded. She wondered if Nancy Ellen was forced to this uncongenial task, whether it would sour the wonderful sweetness developed by her courtship, and make her so provoked that she would not write or have anything to do with her. They were nearly the same age; they had shared rooms, and, until recently, beds, and whatever life brought them; now Kate lifted her head and ran her hand against her throat to ease the ache gathering there more intensely every minute. With eyes that did not see, she sat staring at the sheer walls of the ravine as it ran toward the east, where the water came tumbling and leaping down over stones and shale bed. When at last she arose she had learned one lesson, not in the History she carried. No matter what its disadvantages are, having a home of any kind is vastly preferable to having none. And the casualness of people so driven by the demands of living and money making that they do not take time even to be slightly courteous and kind, no matter how objectionable it may be, still that, even that, is better than their active displeasure. So she sat brooding and going over and over the summer, arguing her side of the case, honestly trying to see theirs, until she was mentally exhausted and still had accomplished nothing further than arriving at the conclusion that if Nancy Ellen was forced to postpone her wedding she would turn against her and influence Robert Gray in the same feeling.

Then Kate thought of Him. She capitalized him in her thought, for after nineteen years of Bates men Robert Gray would seem a deified creature to their women. She reviewed the scene at the crossing log, while her face flushed with pleasure. If she had remained at home and had gone after the blackberries, as it was sure as fate that she would have done, then she would have met him first, and he would have courted her instead of Nancy Ellen. Suddenly Kate shook herself savagely and sat straight. "Why, you big fool!" she said. "Nancy Ellen went to the berry patch in a pink dress, wearing a sunbonnet to match, and carrying a blue bowl. Think of the picture she made! But if I had gone, I'd have been in a ragged old dirt-coloured gingham, Father's boots, and his old straw hat jammed down to my ears; I'd have been hot and in a surly temper, rebelling because I had the berries to pick. He would have taken one look at me, jumped the fence, and run to Lang's for dear life. Better cut that idea right out!"

So Kate "cut that idea out" at once, but the operation was painful, because when one turns mental surgeon and operates on the ugly spots in one's disposition, there is no anaesthetic, nor is the work done with skilful hands, so the wounds are numerous and leave ugly scars; but Kate was ruthless. She resolved never to think of that brook scene again. In life, as she had lived it, she would not have profited by having been first at the berry patch. Yet she had a right to think of Robert Gray's face, grave in concern for her, his offers to help, the influence he would have in her favour with Nancy Ellen. Of course if he was forced to postpone his wedding he would not be pleased; but it was impossible that the fears which were tormenting Nancy Ellen would materialize into action on his part. No sane man loved a woman as beautiful as her sister and cast her aside because of a few months' enforced waiting, the cause of which he so very well knew; but it would make both of them unhappy and change their beautiful plans, after he even had found and purchased the house. Still Nancy Ellen said that her father was making it a point of honour that a Bates should teach the school, because he had signed the contract for Kate to take the place Nancy Ellen had intended to fill, and then changed her plans. He had sworn that a Bates should teach the school. Well, Hiram had taken the county examination, as all pupils of the past ten years had when they finished the country schools. It was a test required to prove whether they had done their work well. Hiram held a certificate for a year, given him by the County Superintendent, when he passed the examinations. He had never used it. He could teach; he was Nancy Ellen's twin. School did not begin until the first of November. He could hire help with his corn if he could not finish alone. He could arise earlier than usual and do his feeding and milking; he could clean the stables, haul wood on Saturday and Sunday, if he must, for the Bates family looked on Sunday more as a day of rest for the horses and physical man than as one of religious observances. They always worked if there was anything to be gained by it. Six months being the term, he would be free by the first of May; surely the money would be an attraction, while Nancy Ellen could coach him on any new methods she had learned at Normal. Kate sprang to her feet, ran across the street, and entering the hall, hurried to her room. She found Mrs. Holt there in the act of closing her closet door. Kate looked at her with astonished eyes.

"I was just telling my son," Mrs. Holt said rather breathlessly, "that I would take a peep and see if I had forgot to put your extra covers on the shelf."

Kate threw her book on the bed and walked to the table. She had experienced her share of battle for the day. "No children to rummage," passed through her brain. It was the final week of hot, dry August weather, while a point had been made of calling her attention to the extra cover when the room had been shown her. She might have said these things, but why say them? The shamed face of the woman convicted her of "rummaging," as she had termed it. Without a word Kate sat down beside the table, drew her writing material before her, and began addressing an envelope to her brother Hiram. Mrs. Holt left the room, disliking Kate more than if she had said what the woman knew she thought.

Kate wrote briefly, convincingly, covering every objection and every advantage she could conceive, and then she added the strongest plea she could make. What Hiram would do, she had no idea. As with all Bates men, land was his God, but it required money to improve it. He would feel timid about making a first attempt to teach after he was married and a father of a child, but Nancy Ellen's marriage would furnish plausible excuse; all of the family had done their school work as perfectly as all work they undertook; he could teach if he wanted to; would he want to? If he did, at least, she would be sure of the continued friendship of her sister and Robert Gray. Suddenly Kate understood what that meant to her as she had not realized before. She was making long strides toward understanding herself, which is the most important feature of any life.

She sent a line of pleading to her sister-in-law, a word of love to the baby, and finishing her letter, started to post it, as she remembered the office was only a few steps down the street. In the hall it occurred to her that she was the "Teacher" now, and so should be an example. Possibly the women of Walden did not run bareheaded down the street on errands. She laid the letter on a small shelf of an old hatrack, and stepped back to her room to put on her hat. Her return was so immediate that Mrs. Holt had the letter in her fingers when Kate came back, and was reading the address so intently, that with extended hand, the girl said in cold tones: "My letter, please!" before the woman realized she was there. Their eyes met in a level look. Mrs. Holt's mouth opened in ready excuse, but this time Kate's temper overcame her better judgment.

"Can you read it clearly, without your glasses?" she asked politely. "I wouldn't for the world have you make a mistake as to whom my letter is addressed. It goes to my brother Hiram Bates, youngest son of Adam Bates, Bates Corners, Hartley, Indiana."

"I was going to give it to my son, so that he could take it to the office," said Mrs. Holt.

"And I am going to take it myself, as I know your son is down town and I want it to go over on the evening hack, so it will be sure to go out early in the morning."

Surprise overcame Mrs. Holt's discomfiture.

"Land sakes!" she cried. "Bates is such a common name it didn't mean a thing to me. Be you a daughter of Adam Bates, the Land King, of Bates Corners?"

"I be," said Kate tersely.

"Well, I never! All them hundreds of acres of land an' money in the bank an' mortgages on half his neighbours. Whut the nation! An' no more of better clo's an' you got! An' teachin' school! I never heard of the like in all my days!"

"If you have Bates history down so fine, you should know that every girl of the entire Bates family has taught from the time she finished school until she married. Also we never buy more clothing than we need, or of the kind not suitable for our work. This may explain why we own some land and have a few cents in the Bank. My letter, please."

Kate turned and went down the street, a dull red tingeing her face. "I could hate that woman cordially without half trying," she said.

The house was filled with the odour of cooking food when she returned and soon she was called to supper. As she went to the chair indicated for her, a step was heard in the hall. Kate remained standing and when a young man entered the room Mrs. Holt at once introduced her son, George. He did not take the trouble to step around the table and shake hands, but muttered a gruff "howdy do?" and seating himself, at once picked up the nearest dish and began filling his plate.

His mother would have had matters otherwise. "Why, George," she chided. "What's your hurry? Why don't you brush up and wait on Miss Bates first?"

"Oh, if she is going to be one of the family," he said, "she will have to learn to get on without much polly-foxing. Grub is to eat. We can all reach at a table of this size."

Kate looked at George Holt with a searching glance. Surely he was almost thirty, of average height, appeared strong, and as if he might have a forceful brain; but he was loosely jointed and there was a trace of domineering selfishness on his face that was repulsive to her. "I could hate that MAN cordially, without half trying," she thought to herself, smiling faintly at the thought.

The sharp eyes of Mrs. Holt detected the smile. She probably would have noticed it, if Kate had merely thought of smiling.

"Why do you smile, my dear?" she asked in melting tone.

"Oh, I was feeling so at home," answered Kate, suavely. "Father and the boys hold exactly those opinions and practise them in precisely the same way; only if I were to think about it at all, I should think that a man within a year of finishing a medical course would begin exercising politeness with every woman he meets. I believe a doctor depends on women to be most of his patients, and women don't like a rude doctor."

"Rot!" said George Holt.

"Miss Bates is exactly right," said his mother. "Ain't I been tellin' you the whole endurin' time that you'd never get a call unless you practised manners as well as medicine? Ain't I, now?"

"Yes, you have," he said, angrily. "But if you think all of a sudden that manners are so essential, why didn't you hammer some into me when you had the whip hand and could do what you pleased? You didn't find any fault with my manners, then."

"How of all the world was I to know that you'd grow up and go in for doctorin'? I s'pos'd then you'd take the farm an' run it like your pa did, stead of forcin' me to sell it off by inches to live, an' then you wastin' half the money."

"Go it, Mother," said George Holt, rudely. "Tell all you know, and then piece out with anything you can think of that you don't."

Mrs. Holt's face flushed crimson. She looked at Kate and said vindictively: "If you want any comfort in life, never marry and bring a son inter the world. You kin humour him, and cook for him, an work your hands to the bone fur him, and sell your land, and spend all you can raise educatin' him for half a dozen things, an' him never stickin to none or payin' back a cent, but sass in your old age–"

"Go it, Mother, you're doing fine!" said George. "If you keep on Miss Bates will want to change her boarding place before morning."

"It will not be wholly your mother's fault, if I do," said Kate. "I would suggest that if we can't speak civilly, we eat our supper in silence. This is very good food; I could enjoy it, if I had a chance."

She helped herself to another soda biscuit and a second piece of fried chicken and calmly began eating them.

"That's a good idy!" said Mrs. Holt.

"Then why don't you practice it?" said her son.

Thereupon began a childish battle for the last word. Kate calmly arose, picked up her plate, walked from the room, down the hall, and entering her own room, closed the door quietly.

"You fool! You great big dunderheaded fool!" cried Mrs. Holt. "Now you have done it, for the thousandth time. She will start out in less than no time to find some place else to stay, an' who could blame her? Don't you know who she is? Ain't you sense in your head? If there was ever a girl you ort to go after, and go quick an' hard, there she is!"

"What? That big beef! What for?" asked George.

"You idjit! You idjit! Don't you sense that she's a daughter of Adam Bates? Him they call the Land King. Ain't you sense ner reason? Drive her from the house, will you? An' me relyin' on sendin' you half her board money to help you out? You fool!"

"Why under the Heavens didn't you tell me? How could I know? No danger but the bowl is upset, and it's all your fault. She should be worth ten thousand, maybe twenty!"

"I never knew till jist before supper. I got it frum a letter she wrote to her brother. I'd no chanct to tell you. Course I meant to, first chanct I had; but you go to work an upset everything before I get a chanct. You never did amount to anything, an' you never will."

"Oh, well, now stop that. I didn't know. I thought she was just common truck. I'll fix it up with her right after supper. Now shut up."

"You can't do it! It's gone too far. She'll leave the house inside fifteen minutes," said Mrs. Holt.

"Well, I'll just show you," he boasted.

George Holt pushed back his plate, wiped his mouth, brushed his teeth at the washing place on the back porch, and sauntered around the house to seat himself on the front porch steps. Kate saw him there and remained in her room. When he had waited an hour he arose and tapped on her door. Kate opened it.

"Miss Bates," he said. "I have been doing penance an hour. I am very sorry I was such a boor. I was in earnest when I said I didn't get the gad when I needed it. I had a big disappointment to-day, and I came in sore and cross. I am ashamed of myself, but you will never see me that way again. I know I will make a failure of my profession if I don't be more polite than Mother ever taught me to be. Won't you let me be your scholar, too? Please do come over to the ravine where it is cool and give me my first lesson. I need you dreadfully."

Kate was desperately in need of human companionship in that instant, herself, someone who could speak, and sin, and suffer, and repent. As she looked straight in the face of the man before her she saw, not him being rude and quarrelling pettily with his mother, but herself racing around the dining table pursued by her father raving like an insane man. Who was she to judge or to refuse help when it was asked? She went with him; and Mrs. Holt, listening and peering from the side of the window blind of her room across the hall, watched them cross the road and sit beside each other on the bank of the ravine in what seemed polite and amicable conversation. So she heaved a deep sigh of relief and went to wash the dishes and plan breakfast. "Better feed her up pretty well 'til she gits the habit of staying here and mebby the rest who take boarders will be full," she said to herself. "Time enough to go at skimpin' when she's settled, and busy, an' I get the whip hand."

But in planning to get the "whip hand" Mrs. Holt reckoned without Kate. She had been under the whip hand all her life. Her dash to freedom had not been accomplished without both mental and physical hurt. She was doing nothing but going over her past life minutely, and as she realized more fully with each review how barren and unlovely it had been, all the strength and fresh young pride in her arose in imperative demand for something better in the future. She listened with interest to what George Holt said to her. All her life she had been driven by a man of inflexible will, his very soul inoculated with greed for possessions which would give him power; his body endowed with unfailing strength to meet the demands he made on it, and his heart wholly lacking in sentiment; but she did not propose to start her new life by speaking of her family to strangers. George

Holt's experiences had been those of a son spoiled by a weak woman, one day petted, the next bribed, the next nagged, again left to his own devices for days, with strong inherited tendencies to be fought, tendencies to what he did not say. Looking at his heavy jaw and swarthy face, Kate supplied "temper" and "not much inclination to work." He had asked her to teach him, she would begin by setting him an example in the dignity of self-control; then she would make him work. How she would make that big, strong man work! As she sat there on the bank of the ravine, with a background of delicately leafed bushes and the light of the setting sun on her face and her hair, George Holt studied her closely, mentally and physically, and would have given all he possessed if he had not been so hasty. He saw that she had a good brain and courage to follow her convictions, while on closer study he decided that she was moulded on the finest physical lines of any woman he ever had seen, also his study of medicine taught him to recognize glowing health, and to set a right estimate on it. Truly he was sorry, to the bottom of his soul, but he did not believe in being too humble. He said as much in apology as he felt forced, and then set himself the task of calling out and parading the level best he could think up concerning himself, or life in general. He had tried farming, teaching, merchandise, and law before he had decided his vocation was medicine.

On account of Robert Gray, Kate was much interested in this, but when she asked what college he was attending, he said he was going to a school in Chicago that was preparing to revolutionize the world of medicine. Then he started on a hobby that he had ridden for months, paying for the privilege, so Kate learned with surprise and no small dismay that in a few months a man could take a course in medicine that would enable him "to cure any ill to which the human flesh is heir," as he expressed it, without knowing anything of surgery, or drugs, or using either. Kate was amazed and said so at once. She disconcertingly inquired what he would do with patients who had sustained fractured skulls, developed cancers, or been exposed to smallpox. But the man before her proposed to deal with none of those disagreeable things, or their like. He was going to make fame and fortune in the world by treating mental and muscular troubles. He was going to be a Zonoletic Doctor. He turned teacher and spelled it for her, because she never had heard the word. Kate looked at George Holt long and with intense interest, while her mind was busy with new thoughts. On her pillow that night she decided that if she were a man, driven by a desire to heal the suffering of the world, she would be the man who took the long exhaustive course of training that enabled him to deal with accidents, contagions, and germ developments.

He looked at her with keen appreciation of her physical freshness and mental strength, and manoeuvred patiently toward the point where he would dare ask blankly how many there were in her family, and on exactly how many acres her father paid tax. He decided it would not do for at least a week yet; possibly he could raise the subject casually with someone down town who would know, so that he need never ask her at all. Whatever the answer might be, it was definitely settled in his own mind that Kate was the best chance he had ever had, or probably ever would have. He mapped out his campaign. This week, before he must go, he would be her pupil and her slave. The holiday week he would be her lover. In the spring he would propose, and in the fall he would marry her, and live on the income from her land ever afterward. It was a glowing prospect; so glowing that he seriously considered stopping school at once so that her could be at the courting part of his campaign three times a day and every evening. He was afraid to leave for fear people of the village would tell the truth about him. He again studied Kate carefully and decided that during the week that was coming, by deft and energetic work he could so win her approval that he could make her think that she knew him better than outsiders did. So the siege began.

Kate had decided to try making him work, to see if he would, or was accustomed to it. He was sufficiently accustomed to it that he could do whatever she suggested with facility that indicated practice, and there was no question of his willingness. He urged her to make suggestions as to what else he could do, after he had made all the needed repairs about the house and premises. Kate was enjoying herself immensely, before the week was over. She had another row of wood corded to the shed roof, in case the winter should be severe. She had the stove she thought would warm her room polished and set up while he was there to do it. She had the back porch mended and the loose board in the front walk replaced. She borrowed buckets and cloths and impressed George Holt for the cleaning of the school building which she superintended. Before the week was over she had every child of school age who came to the building to see what was going on, scouring out desks, blacking stoves, raking the yard, even cleaning the street before the building.

Across the street from his home George sawed the dead wood from the trees and then, with three days to spare, Kate turned her attention to the ravine. She thought that probably she could teach better there in the spring than in the school building. She and George talked it over. He raised all the objections he could think of that the townspeople would, while entirely agreeing with her himself, but it was of no use. She over-ruled the proxy objections he so kindly offered her, so he was obliged to drag his tired body up the trees on both banks for several hundred yards and drop the dead wood. Kate marshalled a corps of boys who would be her older pupils and they dragged out the dry branches, saved all that were suitable for firewood, and made bonfires from the remainder. They raked the tin cans and town refuse of years from the water and banks and induced the village delivery man to haul the stuff to the river bridge and dump it in the deepest place in the stream. They cleaned the creek bank to the water's edge and built rustic seats down the sides. They even rolled boulders to the bed and set them where the water would show their markings and beat itself to foam against them. Mrs. Holt looked on in breathless amazement and privately expressed to her son her opinion of him in terse and vigorous language. He answered laconically: "Has a fish got much to say about what happens to it after you get it out of the water?"

"No!" snapped Mrs. Holt, "and neither have you, if you kill yourself to get it."

"Do I look killed?" inquired her son.

"No. You look the most like a real man I ever saw you," she conceded.

"And Kate Bates won't need glasses for forty years yet," he said as he went back to his work in the ravine.

Kate was in the middle of the creek helping plant a big stone. He stood a second watching her as she told the boys surrounding her how best to help her, then he turned away, a dull red burning his cheek. "I'll have her if I die for it," he muttered, "but I hope to Heaven she doesn't think I am going to work like this for her every day of my life."

As the villagers sauntered past and watched the work of the new teacher, many of them thought of things at home they could do that would improve their premises greatly, and a few went home and began work of like nature. That made their neighbours' places look so unkempt that they were forced to trim, and rake, and mend in turn, so by the time the school began, the whole village was busy in a crusade that extended to streets and alleys, while the new teacher was the most popular person who had ever been there. Without having heard of such a thing, Kate had started Civic Improvement.

George Holt leaned against a tree trunk and looked down at her as he rested.

"Do you suppose there is such a thing as ever making anything out of this?" he asked.

"A perfectly lovely public park for the village, yes; money, selling it for anything, no! It's too narrow a strip, cut too deeply with the water, the banks too steep. Commercially, I can't see that it is worth ten cents."

"Cheering! It is the only thing on earth that truly and wholly belongs to me. The road divided the land. Father willed everything on the south side to Mother, so she would have the house, and the land on this side was mine. I sold off all I could to Jasper Linn to add to his farm, but he would only buy to within about twenty rods of the ravine. The land was too rocky and poor. So about half a mile of this comprises my earthly possessions."

"Do you keep up the taxes?" she asked.

"No. I've never paid them," he said carelessly.

"Then don't be too sure it is yours," she said. "Someone may have paid them and taken the land. You had better look it up."

"What for?" he demanded.

"It is beautiful. It is the shadiest, coolest place in town. Having it here doubles the value of your mother's house across the street. In some way, some day, it might turn out to be worth something."

"I can't see how," he said.

"Some of the trees may become valuable when lumber gets scarcer, as it will when the land grows older. Maybe a stone quarry could be opened up, if the stone runs back as far as you say. A lot of things might make it valuable. If I were you I would go to Hartley, quietly, to-morrow, and examine the records, and if there are back taxes I'd pay them."

"I'll look it up, anyway," he agreed. "You surely have made another place of it. It will be wonderful by spring."

"I can think of many uses for it," said Kate. "Here comes your mother to see how we are getting along."

Instead, she came to hand Kate a letter she had brought from the post office while doing her marketing. Kate took the letter, saw at a glance that it was from Nancy Ellen, and excusing herself, she went to one of the seats they had made, and turning her face so that it could not be seen, she read:

DEAR KATE: You can prepare yourself for the surprise of your life. Two Bates men have done something for one of their women. I hope you will survive the shock; it almost finished me and Mother is still speechless. I won't try to prepare you. I could not. Here it is. Father raged for three days and we got out of his way like scared rabbits. I saw I had to teach, so I said I would, but I had not told Robert, because I couldn't bear to. Then up came Hiram and offered to take the school for me. Father said no, I couldn't get out of it that way. Hiram said I had not seen him or sent him any word, and I could prove by mother I hadn't been away from the house, so Father believed him. He said he wanted the money to add two acres to his land from the Simms place; that would let his stock down to water on the far side of his land where it would be a great convenience and give him a better arrangement of fields so he could make more money. You know Father. He shut up like a clam and only said: "Do what you please. If a Bates teaches the school it makes my word good." So Hiram is going to teach for me. He is brushing up a little nights and I am helping him on "theory," and I am wild with joy, and so is Robert. I shall have plenty of time to do all my sewing and we shall be married at, or after, Christmas. Robert says to tell you to come to see him if you ever come to Hartley. He is there in his office now and it is lonesome, but I am busy and the time will soon pass. I might as well tell you that Father said right after you left that you should never enter his house again, and Mother and I should not speak your name before him. I do hope he gets over it before the wedding. Write me how you like your school, and where you board. Maybe Robert and I can slip off and drive over to see you some day. But that would make Father so mad if he found out that he would not give me the money he promised; so we had better not, but you come to see us as soon as we get in our home. Love from both, NANCY ELLEN.

Kate read the joyful letter slowly. It contained all she hoped for. She had not postponed Nancy Ellen's wedding. That was all she asked. She had known she would not be forgiven so soon, there was slight hope she ever would. Her only chance, thought Kate, lay in marrying a farmer having about a thousand acres of land. If she could do that, her father would let her come home again sometime. She read the letter slowly over, then tearing it in long strips she cross tore them and sifted the handful of small bits on the water, where they started a dashing journey toward the river. Mrs. Holt, narrowly watching her, turned with snaky gleaming eyes to her son and whispered: "A-ha! Miss Smart Alec has a secret!"

Helping Nancy Ellen and Robert to Establish a Home

The remainder of the time before leaving, George Holt spent in the very strongest mental and physical effort to show Kate how much of a man he was. He succeeded in what he hoped he might do. He so influenced her in his favour that during the coming year whenever any one showed signs of criticising him, Kate stopped them by commendation, based upon what she supposed to be knowledge of him.

With the schoolhouse and grounds cleaned as they never had been before, the parents and pupils naturally expected new methods. During the week spent in becoming acquainted with the teacher, the parents heartily endorsed her, while the pupils liked her cordially. It could be seen at a glance that she could pick up the brawniest of them, and drop him from the window, if she chose. The days at the stream had taught them her physical strength, while at the same time they had glimpses of her mental processes. The boys learned many things: that they must not lie or take anything which did not belong to them; that they must be considerate and manly, if they were to be her friends; yet not one word had been said on any of these subjects. As she spoke to them, they answered her, and soon spoke in the same way to each other. She was very careful about each statement she made, often adducing convenient proof, so they saw that she was always right, and never exaggerated. The first hour of this made the boys think, the second they imitated, the third they instantly obeyed. She started in to interest and educate these children; she sent them home to investigate more subjects the first day than they had ever carried home in any previous month. Boys suddenly began asking their fathers about business; girls questioned their mothers about marketing and housekeeping.

The week of Christmas vacation was going to be the hardest; everyone expected the teacher to go home for the Holidays. Many of them knew that her sister was marrying the new doctor of Hartley. When Kate was wondering how she could possibly conceal the rupture with her family, Robert Gray drove into Walden and found her at the schoolhouse. She was so delighted to see him that she made no attempt to conceal her joy. He had driven her way for exercise and to pay her a call. When he realized from her greeting how she had felt the separation from her family, he had an idea that he at once propounded: "Kate, I have come to ask a favour of you," he said.

"Granted!" laughed Kate. "Whatever can it be?"

"Just this! I want you to pack a few clothes, drive to Hartley with me and do what you can to straighten out the house, so there won't be such confusion when Nancy Ellen gets there."

Kate stared at him in a happy daze. "Oh, you blessed Robert Gray! What a Heavenly idea!" she cried. "Of course it wouldn't be possible for me to fix

Nancy Ellen's house the way she would, but I could put everything where it belonged, I could arrange well enough, and I could have a supper ready, so that you could come straight home."

"Then you will do it?" he asked.

"Do it?" cried Kate. "Do it! Why, I would be willing to pay you for the chance to do it. How do you think I'm to explain my not going home for the Holidays, and to my sister's wedding, and retain my self-respect before my patrons?"

"I didn't think of it in that way," he said.

"I'm crazy," said Kate. "Take me quickly! How far along are you?"

"House cleaned, blinds up, stoves all in, coal and wood, cellar stocked, carpets down, and furniture all there, but not unwrapped or in place. Dishes delivered but not washed; cooking utensils there, but not cleaned."

"Enough said," laughed Kate. "You go marry Nancy Ellen. I shall have the house warm, arranged so you can live in it, and the first meal ready when you come. Does Nancy Ellen know you are here?"

"No. I have enough country practice that I need a horse; I'm trying this one. I think of you often so I thought I'd drive out. How are you making it, Kate?"

"Just fine, so far as the school goes. I don't particularly like the woman I board with. Her son is some better, yes, he is much better. And Robert, what is a Zonoletic Doctor?"

"A poor fool, too lazy to be a real doctor, with no conscience about taking people's money for nothing," he said.

"As bad as *that*?" asked Kate.

"Worse! Why?" he said.

"Oh, I only wondered," said Kate. "Now I am ready, here; but I must run to the house where I board a minute. It's only a step. You watch where I go, and drive down."

She entered the house quietly and going back to the kitchen she said: "The folks have come for me, Mrs. Holt. I don't know exactly when I shall be back, but in plenty of time to start school. If George goes before I return, tell him 'Merry Christmas,' for me."

"He'll be most disappointed to death," said Mrs. Holt.

"I don't see why he should," said Kate, calmly. "You never have had the teacher here at Christmas."

"We never had a teacher that I wanted before," said Mrs. Holt; while Kate turned to avoid seeing the woman's face as she perjured herself. "You're like one of the family, George is crazy about you. He wrote me to be sure to keep you. Couldn't you possibly stay over Sunday?"

"No, I couldn't," said Kate.

"Who came after you?" asked Mrs. Holt.

"Dr. Gray," answered Kate.

"That new doctor at Hartley? Why, be you an' him friends?"

Mrs. Holt had followed down the hall, eagerly waiting in the doorway. Kate glanced at her and felt sudden pity. The woman was warped. Everything in her life had gone wrong. Possibly she could not avoid being the disagreeable person she was. Kate smiled at her.

"Worse than that," she said. "We be relations in a few days. He's going to marry my sister Nancy Ellen next Tuesday."

Kate understood the indistinct gurgle she heard to be approving, so she added: "He came after me early so I could go to Hartley and help get their new house ready for them to live in after the ceremony."

"Did your father give them the house?" asked Mrs. Holt eagerly.

"No. Dr. Gray bought his home," said Kate.

"How nice! What did your father give them?"

Kate's patience was exhausted. "You'll have to wait until I come back," she said. "I haven't the gift of telling about things before they have happened."

Then she picked up her telescope and saying "good-bye," left the house.

As they drove toward Hartley: "I'm anxious to see your house," said Kate. "Did you find one in a good neighbourhood?"

"The very best, I think," said the doctor. "That is all one could offer Nancy Ellen."

"I'm so glad for her! And I'm glad for you, too! She'll make you a beautiful wife in every way. She's a good cook, she knows how to economize, and she's too pretty for words, if she *is* my sister."

"I heartily agree with you," said the doctor. "But I notice you put the cook first and the beauty last."

"You will, too, before you get through with it," answered Kate.

"Here we are!" said he, soon after they entered Hartley. "I'll drive around the block, so you can form an idea of the location." Kate admired every house in the block, the streets and trees, the one house Robert Gray had selected in every particular. They went inside and built fires, had lunch together at the hotel, and then Kate rolled up her sleeves and with a few yards of cheese-cloth for a duster, began unwrapping furniture and standing it in the room where it belonged. Robert moved the heavy pieces, then he left to call on a patient and spend the evening with Nancy Ellen.

So Kate spent several happy days setting Nancy Ellen's new home in order. From basement to garret she had it immaculate and shining. No Bates girl, not even Agatha, ever had gone into a home having so many comforts and conveniences.

Kate felt lonely the day she knew her home was overcrowded with all their big family; she sat very still thinking of them during the hour of the ceremony; she began preparing supper almost immediately, because Robert had promised her that he would not eat any more of the wedding feast than he could help, and he would bring Nancy Ellen as soon afterward as possible. Kate saw them drive to the gate and come up the walk together. As they entered the door Nancy Ellen was saying: "Why, how does the house come to be all lighted up? Seems to me I smell things to eat. Well, if the table isn't all set!"

There was a pause and then Nancy Ellen's clear voice called: "Kate! Kate! Where are you? Nobody else would be *this* nice to me. You dear girl, where are you?"

"I'll get to stay until I go back to school!" was Kate's mental comment as she ran to clasp Nancy Ellen in her arms, while they laughed and very nearly cried together, so that the doctor felt it incumbent upon him to hug both of them. Shortly afterward he said: "There is a fine show in town to-night, and I have three tickets. Let's all go."

"Let's eat before we go," said Nancy Ellen, "I haven't had time to eat a square meal for a week and things smell deliciously."

They finished their supper leisurely, stacked the dishes and went to the theatre, where they saw a fair performance of a good play, which was to both of the girls a great treat. When they returned home, Kate left Nancy Ellen and Robert to gloat over the carpets they had selected, as they appeared on their floors, to arrange the furniture and re-examine their wedding gifts; while she slipped into the kitchen and began washing the dishes and planning what she would have for breakfast. But soon they came to her and Nancy Ellen insisted on wiping the dishes, while Robert carried them to the cupboard. Afterward, they sat before their fireplace and talked over events since the sisters' separation.

Nancy Ellen told about getting ready for her wedding, life at home, the school, the news of the family; the Kate drew a perfect picture of the Walden school, her boarding place, Mrs. Holt, the ravine, the town and the people, with the exception of George Holt – him she never mentioned.

After Robert had gone to his office the following morning, Kate said to Nancy Ellen: "Now I wish you would be perfectly frank with me–"

"As if I could be anything else!" laughed the bride.

"All right, then," said Kate. "What I want is this: that these days shall always come back to you in memory as nearly perfect as possible. Now if my being here helps ever so little, I like to stay, and I'll be glad to cook and wash dishes, while you fix your house to suit you. But if you'd rather be alone, I'll go back to Walden and be satisfied and happy with the fine treat this has been. I can look everyone in the face now, talk about the wedding, and feel all right."

Nancy Ellen said slowly: "I shan't spare you until barely time to reach your school Monday morning. And I'm not keeping you to work for me, either! We'll do everything together, and then we'll plan how to make the house pretty, and go see Robert in his office, and go shopping. I'll never forgive you if you go."

"Why, Nancy Ellen –!" said Kate, then fled to the kitchen too happy to speak further.

None of them ever forgot that week. It was such a happy time that all of them dreaded its end; but when it came they parted cheerfully, and each went back to work, the better for the happy reunion. Kate did not return to Walden until Monday; then she found Mrs. Holt in an evil temper. Kate could not understand it. She had no means of knowing that for a week George had nagged his mother unceasingly because Kate was gone on his return, and would not be back until after time for him to go again. The only way for him to see her during the week he had planned to come out openly as her lover, was to try to find her at her home, or at her sister's. He did not feel that it would help him to go where he never had been asked. His only recourse was to miss a few days of school and do extra work to make it up; but he detested nothing in life as he detested work, so the world's happy week had been to them one of constant sparring and unhappiness, for which Mrs. Holt blamed Kate. Her son had returned expecting to court Kate Bates strenuously; his disappointment was not lightened by his mother's constant nagging. Monday forenoon she went to market, and came in gasping.

"Land sakes!" she cried as she panted down the hall. "I've got a good one on that impident huzzy now!"

"You better keep your mouth shut, and not gossip about her," he said. "Everyone likes her!"

"No, they don't, for I hate her worse 'n snakes! If it wa'n't for her money I'd fix her so's 'at she'd never marry you in kingdom come."

George Holt clenched his big fist.

"Just you try it!" he threatened. "Just you try that!"

"You'll live to see the day you'd thank me if I did. She ain't been home. Mind you, she ain't been *home*! She never seen her sister married at all! Tilly Nepple has a sister, living near the Bates, who worked in the kitchen. She's visitin' at Tilly's now. Miss High-and-Mighty never seen her sister married at all! An' it looked mighty queer, her comin' here a week ahead of time, in the fall. Looks like she'd done somepin she don't *dare* go home. No wonder she tears every scrap of mail she gets to ribbons an' burns it. I told you she had a secret! If ever you'd listen to me."

"Why, you're crazy!" he exclaimed. "I did listen to you. What you told me was that I should go after her with all my might. So I did it. Now you come with this. Shut it up! Don't let her get wind of it for the world!"

"And Tilly Nepple's sister says old Land King Bates never give his daughter a cent, an' he never gives none of his girls a cent. It's up to the men they marry to take keer of them. The old skin- flint! What you want to do is to go long to your schoolin', if you reely are going to make somepin of yourself at last, an' let that big strap of a girl be, do–"

"Now, stop!" shouted George Holt. "Scenting another scandal, are you? Don't you dare mar Kate Bates' standing, or her reputation in this town, or we'll have a time like we never had before. If old Bates doesn't give his girls anything when they marry, they'll get more when he dies. And so far as money is concerned, this has gone *past* money with me. I'm going to marry Kate Bates, as soon as ever I can, and I've got to the place where I'd marry her if she hadn't a cent. If I can't take care of her, she can take care of me. I am crazy about her, an' I'm going to have her; so you keep still, an' do all you can to help me, or you'll regret it."

"It's you that will regret it!" she said.

"Stop your nagging, I tell you, or I'll come at you in a way you won't like," he cried.

"You do that every day you're here," said Mrs. Holt, starting to the kitchen to begin dinner.

Kate appeared in half an hour, fresh and rosy, also prepared; for one of her little pupils had said: "Tilly Nepple's sister say you wasn't at your sister's wedding at all. Did you cry 'cause you couldn't go?"

Instantly Kate comprehended what must be town gossip, so she gave the child a happy solution of the question bothering her, and went to her boarding house forewarned. She greeted both Mrs. Holt and her son cordially, then sat down to dinner, in the best of spirits. The instant her chance came, Mrs. Holt said: "Now tell us all about the lovely wedding."

"But I wasn't managing the wedding," said Kate cheerfully. "I was on the infare job. Mother and Nancy Ellen put the wedding through. You know our house isn't very large, and close relatives fill it to bursting. I've seen the same kind of wedding about every eighteen months all my life. I had a *new* job this time, and one I liked better."

She turned to George: "Of course your mother told you that Dr. Gray came after me. He came to ask me as an especial favour to go to his new house in Hartley, and do what I could to arrange it, and to have a supper ready. I was glad. I'd seen six weddings that I can remember, all exactly alike – there's nothing to them; but brushing those new carpets, unwrapping nice furniture and placing it, washing pretty new dishes, untying the loveliest gifts and arranging them – *that* was something new in a Bates wedding. Oh, but I had a splendid time!"

George Holt looked at his mother in too great disgust to conceal his feelings.

"*Another* gilt-edged scandal gone sky high," he said. Then he turned to Kate. "One of the women who worked in your mother's kitchen is visiting here, and she started a great hullabaloo because you were not at the wedding. You probably haven't got a leg left to stand on. I suspect the old cats of Walden have chewed them both off, and all the while you were happy, and doing the thing any girl would much rather have done. Lord, I hate this eternal picking! How did you come back, Kate?"

"Dr. Gray brought me."

"I should think it would have made talk, your staying there with him," commented Mrs. Holt.

"Fortunately, the people of Hartley seem reasonably busy attending their own affairs," said Kate. "Doctor Gray had been boarding at the hotel all fall, so he just went on living there until after the wedding."

George glared at his mother, but she avoided his eyes, and laughing in a silly, half-confused manner she said: "How much money did your father give the bride?"

"I can't tell you, in even dollars and cents," said Kate. "Nancy Ellen didn't say."

Kate saw the movement of George's foot under the table, and knew that he was trying to make his mother stop asking questions; so she began talking to him about his work. As soon as the meal was finished he walked with her to school, visiting until the session began. He remained three days, and before he left he told Kate he loved her, and asked her to be his wife. She looked at him in surprise and said: "Why, I never thought of such a thing! How long have you been thinking about it?"

"Since the first instant I saw you!" he declared with fervour.

"Hum! Matter of months," said Kate. "Well, when I have had that much time, I will tell you what I think about it."

The History of a Leghorn Hat

Kate finished her school in the spring, then went for a visit with Nancy Ellen and Robert, before George Holt returned. She was thankful to leave Walden without having seen him, for she had decided, without giving the matter much thought, that he was not the man she wanted to marry. In her heart she regretted having previously contracted for the Walden school another winter because she felt certain that with the influence of Dr. Gray, she could now secure a position in Hartley that would enable her either to live with, or to be near, her sister. With this thought in mind, she tried to make the acquaintance of teachers in the school who lived in Hartley and she soon became rather intimate with one of them.

It was while visiting with this teacher that Kate spoke of attending Normal again in an effort to prepare herself still better for the work of the coming year. Her new friend advised against it. She said the course would be only the same thing over again, with so little change or advancement, that the trip was not worth the time and money it would cost. She proposed that Kate go to Lake Chautauqua and take the teachers' course, where all spare time could be put in attending lectures, and concerts, and studying the recently devised methods of education. Kate went from her to Nancy Ellen and Robert, determined at heart to go.

She was pleased when they strongly advised her to, and offered to help her get ready. Aside from having paid Agatha, and for her board, Kate had spent almost nothing on herself. She figured the probable expenses of the trip for a month, what it would cost her to live until school began again, if she were forced to go to Walden, and then spent all her remaining funds on the prettiest clothing she had ever owned. Each of the sisters knew how to buy carefully; then the added advantage of being able to cut and make their own clothes, made money go twice as far as where a dressmaker had to be employed. When everything they had planned was purchased, neatly made, and packed in a trunk, into which Nancy Ellen slipped some of her prettiest belongings, Kate made a trip to a milliner's shop to purchase her first real hat.

She had decided on a big, wide-brimmed Leghorn, far from cheap. While she was trying the effect of flowers and ribbon on it, the wily milliner slipped up and with the hat on Kate's golden crown, looped in front a bow of wide black velvet ribbon and drooped over the brim a long, exquisitely curling ostrich plume. Kate had one good view of herself, before she turned her back on the temptation.

"You look lovely in that," said the milliner. "Don't you like it?"

"I certainly do," said Kate. "I look the best in that hat, with the black velvet and the plume, I ever did, but there's no use to look twice, I can't afford it."

"Oh, but it is very reasonable! We haven't a finer hat in the store, nor a better plume," said the milliner.

She slowly waved it in all its glory before Kate's beauty-hungry eyes. Kate turned so she could not see it.

"Please excuse one question. Are you teaching in Walden this winter?" asked the milliner.

"Yes," said Kate. "I have signed the contract for that school."

"Then charge the hat and pay for it in September. I'd rather wait for my money than see you fail to spend the summer under that plume. It really is lovely against your gold hair."

"'Get thee behind me, Satan,'" quoted Kate. "No. I never had anything charged, and never expect to. Please have the black velvet put on and let me try it with the bows set and sewed."

"All right," said the milliner, "but I'm sorry."

She was so sorry that she carried the plume to the work room, and when she walked up behind Kate, who sat waiting before the mirror, and carefully set the hat on her head, at exactly the right angle, the long plume crept down one side and drooped across the girl's shoulder.

"I will reduce it a dollar more," she said, "and send the bill to you at Walden the last week of September."

Kate moved her head from side to side, lifted and dropped her chin. Then she turned to the milliner.

"You should be killed!" she said.

The woman reached for a hat box.

"No, I shouldn't!" she said. "Waiting that long, I'll not make much on the hat, but I'll make a good friend who will come again, and bring her friends. What is your name, please?"

Kate took one look at herself – smooth pink cheeks, gray eyes, gold hair, the sweeping wide brim, the trailing plume.

"Miss Katherine Eleanor Bates," she said. "Bates Corners, Hartley, Indiana. Please call my carriage?"

The milliner laughed heartily. "That's the spirit of '76," she commended. "I'd be willing to wager something worth while that this very hat brings you the carriage before fall, if you show yourself in it in the right place. It's a perfectly stunning hat. Shall I send it, or will you wear it?"

Kate looked in the mirror again. "You may put a fresh blue band on the sailor I was wearing, and send that to Dr. Gray's when it is finished," she said. "And put in a fancy bow, for my throat, of the same velvet as the hat, please. I'll surely pay you the last week of September. And if you can think up an equally becoming hat for winter–"

"You just bet I can, young lady," said the milliner to herself as Kate walked down the street.

From afar, Kate saw Nancy Ellen on the veranda, so she walked slowly to let the effect sink in, but it seemed to make no impression until she looked up at Nancy Ellen's very feet and said: "Well, how do you like it?"

"Good gracious!" cried Nancy Ellen. "I thought I was having a stylish caller. I didn't know you! Why, I never saw *you* walk that way before."

"You wouldn't expect me to plod along as if I were plowing, with a thing like this on my head, would you?"

"I wouldn't expect you to have a thing like that on your head; but since you have, I don't mind telling you that you are stunning in it," said Nancy Ellen.

"Better and better!" laughed Kate, sitting down on the step. "The milliner said it was a stunning *hat*."

"The goose!" said Nancy Ellen. "You become that hat, Kate, quite as much as the hat becomes you."

The following day, dressed in a linen suit of natural colour, with the black bow at her throat, the new hat in a bandbox, and the renewed sailor on her head, Kate waved her farewells to Nancy Ellen and Robert on the platform, then walked straight to the dressing room of the car, and changed the hats. Nancy Ellen had told her this was *not* the thing to do. She should travel in a plain untrimmed hat, and when the dust and heat of her journey were past, she should bathe, put on fresh clothing, and wear such a fancy hat only with her best frocks, in the afternoon. Kate need not have been told that. Right instincts and Bates economy would have taught her the same thing, but she had a perverse streak in her nature. She had *seen* herself in the hat.

The milliner, who knew enough of the world and human nature to know how to sell Kate the hat, when she never intended to buy it, and knew she should not in the way she did, had said that before fall it would bring her a carriage, which put into bald terms meant a rich husband. Now Kate liked her school and she gave it her full attention; she had done, and still intended to keep on doing, first-class work in the future; but her school, or anything pertaining to it, was not worth mentioning beside Nancy Ellen's *home*, and the deep understanding and strong feeling that showed so plainly between her and Robert Gray. Kate expected to marry by the time she was twenty or soon after; all Bates girls had, most of them had married very well indeed. She frankly envied Nancy Ellen, while it never occurred to her that any one would criticise her for saying so. Only one thing could happen to her that would surpass what had come to her sister. If only she could have a man like Robert Gray, and have him on a piece of land of their own. Kate was a girl, but no man of the Bates tribe ever was more deeply bitten by the lust for land. She was the true daughter of her father, in more than one way. If that very expensive hat was going to produce the man why not let it begin to work from the very start? If her man was somewhere, only waiting to see her, and the hat would help him to speedy recognition, why miss a change?

She thought over the year, and while she deplored the estrangement from home, she knew that if she had to go back to one year ago, giving up the present and what it had brought and promised to bring, for a reconciliation with her father, she would not voluntarily return to the old driving, nagging, overwork, and skimping, missing every real comfort of life to buy land, in which she never would have any part.

"You get your knocks 'taking the wings of morning,'" thought Kate to herself, "but after all it is the only thing to do. Nancy Ellen says Sally Whistler is pleasing Mother very well, why should I miss my chance and ruin my temper to stay at home and do the work done by a woman who can do nothing else?"

Kate moved her head slightly to feel if the big, beautiful hat that sat her braids so lightly was still there. "Go to work, you beauty," thought Kate. "Do something better for me than George Holt. I'll have him to fall back on if I can't do better; but I think I can. Yes, I'm very sure I can! If you do your part, you lovely plume, I *know* I can!"

Toward noon the train ran into a violent summer storm. The sky grew black, the lightning flashed, the wind raved, the rain fell in gusts. The storm was at its height when Kate quit watching it and arose, preoccupied with her first trip to a dining car, thinking about how little food she could order and yet avoid a hunger headache. The twisting whirlwind struck her face as she stepped from the day coach to go to the dining car. She threw back her head and sucked her lungs full of the pure, rain-chilled air. She was accustomed to being out in storms, she liked them. One second she paused to watch the gale sweeping the fields, the next a twitch at her hair caused her to throw up her hands and clutch wildly at nothing. She sprang to the step railing and leaned out in time to see her wonderful hat whirl against the corner of the car, hold there an instant with the pressure of the wind, then slide down, draw under, and drop across the rail, where passing wheels ground it to pulp.

Kate stood very still a second, then she reached up and tried to pat the disordered strands of hair into place. She turned and went back into the day coach, opened the bandbox, and put on the sailor. She resumed her old occupation of thinking things over. All the joy had vanished from the day and the trip. Looking forward, it had seemed all right to defy custom and Nancy Ellen's advice, and do as she pleased. Looking backward, she saw that she had made a fool of herself in the estimation of everyone in the car by not wearing the sailor, which was suitable for her journey, and would have made no such mark for a whirling wind.

She found travelling even easier than any one had told her. Each station was announced. When she alighted, there were conveyances to take her and her luggage to a hotel, patronized almost exclusively by teachers, near the schools and lecture halls. Large front suites and rooms were out of the question for Kate, but luckily a tiny corner room at the back of the building was empty and when Kate specified how long she would remain, she secured it at a less figure than she had expected to pay. She began by almost starving herself at supper in order to save enough money to replace her hat with whatever she could find that would serve passably, and be cheap enough. That far she proceeded stoically; but when night settled and she stood in her dressing jacket brushing her hair, something gave way. Kate dropped on her bed and cried into her pillow, as she never had cried before about anything. It was not *all* about the hat. While she was at it, she shed a few tears about every cruel thing that had happened to her since she could remember that she had borne tearlessly at the time. It was a deluge that left her breathless and exhausted. When she finally sat up, she found the room so close, she gently opened her door and peeped into the hall. There was a door opening on an outside veranda, running across the end of the building and the length of the front.

As she looked from her door and listened intently, she heard the sound of a woman's voice in choking, stifled sobs, in the room having a door directly across the narrow hall from hers.

"My Lord! *There's two of us!" said* Kate.

She leaned closer, listening again, but when she heard a short groan mingled with the sobs, she immediately tapped on the door. Instantly the sobs ceased and the room became still. Kate put her lips to the crack and said in her off-hand way: "It's only a school-marm, rooming next you. If you're ill, could I get anything for you?"

"Will you please come in?" asked a muffled voice.

Kate turned the knob, and stepping inside, closed the door after her. She could dimly see her way to the dresser, where she found matches and lighted the gas. On the bed lay in a tumbled heap a tiny, elderly, Dresden-china doll-woman. She was fully dressed, even to her wrap, bonnet, and gloves; one hand clutched her side, the other held a handkerchief to her lips. Kate stood an instant under the light, studying the situation. The dark eyes in the narrow face looked appealingly at her. The woman tried to speak, but gasped for breath. Kate saw that she had heart trouble.

"The remedy! Where is it?" she cried.

The woman pointed to a purse on the dresser. Kate opened it, took out a small bottle, and read the directions. In a second, she was holding a glass to the woman's lips; soon she was better. She looked at Kate eagerly.

"Oh, please don't leave me," she gasped.

"Of course not!" said Kate instantly. "I'll stay as long as you want me."

She bent over the bed and gently drew the gloves from the frail hands. She untied and slipped off the bonnet. She hunted keys in the purse, opened a travelling bag, and found what she required. Then slowly and carefully, she undressed the woman, helped her into a night robe, and stooping she lifted her into a chair until she opened the bed. After giving her time to rest, Kate pulled down the white wavy hair and brushed it for the night. As she worked, she said a word of encouragement now and again; when she had done all she could see to do, she asked if there was more. The woman suddenly clung to her hand and began to sob wildly. Kate knelt beside the bed, stroked the white hair, patted the shoulder she could reach, and talked very much as she would have to a little girl.

"Please don't cry," she begged. "It must be your heart; you'll surely make it worse."

"I'm trying," said the woman, "but I've been scared sick. I most certainly would have died if you hadn't come to me and found the medicine. Oh, that dreadful Susette! How could she?"

The clothing Kate had removed from the woman had been of finest cloth and silk. Her hands wore wonderful rings. A heavy purse was in her bag. Everything she had was the finest that money could buy, while she seemed as if a rough wind never had touched her. She appeared so frail that Kate feared to let her sleep without knowing where to locate her friends.

"She should be punished for leaving you alone among strangers," said Kate indignantly.

"If I only could learn to mind John," sighed the little woman. "He never liked Susette. But she was the very best maid I ever had. She was like a loving daughter, until all at once, on the train, among strangers, she flared out at me, and simply raved. Oh, it was dreadful!"

"And knowing you were subject to these attacks, she did the thing that would precipitate one, and then left you alone among strangers. How wicked! How cruel!" said Kate in tense indignation.

"John didn't want me to come. But I used to be a teacher, and I came here when this place was mostly woods, with my dear husband. Then after he died, through the long years of poverty and struggle, I would read of the place and the wonderful meetings, but I could never afford to come. Then when John began to work and made good so fast I was dizzy half the time with his successes, I didn't think about the place. But lately, since I've had everything else I could think of, something possessed me to come back here, and take a suite among the women and men who are teaching our young people so wonderfully; and to sail on the lake, and hear the lectures, and dream my youth over again. I think that was it most of all, to dream my youth over again, to try to relive the past."

"There now, you have told me all about it," said Kate, stroking the white forehead in an effort to produce drowsiness, "close your eyes and go to sleep."

"I haven't even *begun* to tell you," said the woman perversely. "If I talked all night I couldn't tell you about John. How big he is, and how brave he is, and how smart he is, and how he is the equal of any business man in Chicago, and soon, if he keeps on, he will be worth as much as some of them – more than any one of his age, who has had a lot of help instead of having his way to make alone, and a sick old mother to support besides. No, I couldn't tell you in a week half about John, and he didn't want me to come. If I would come, then he wanted me to wait a few days until he finished a deal so he could bring me, but the minute I thought of it I was determined to come; you know how you get."

"I know how badly you want to do a thing you have set your heart on," admitted Kate.

"I had gone places with Susette in perfect comfort. I think the trouble was that she tried from the first to attract John. About the time we started, he let her see plainly that all he wanted of her was to take care of me; she was pretty and smart, so it made her furious. She was pampered in everything, as no maid I ever had before. John is young yet, and I think he is very handsome, and he wouldn't pay any attention to her. You see when other boys were going to school and getting acquainted with girls by association, even when he was a little bit of a fellow in knee breeches, I had to let him sell papers, and then he got into a shop, and he invented a little thing, and then a bigger, and bigger yet, and then he went into stocks and things, and he doesn't know anything about girls, only about sick old women like me. He never saw what Susette was up to. You do believe that I wasn't ugly to her, don't you?"

"You *couldn't* be ugly if you tried," said Kate.

The woman suddenly began to sob again, this time slowly, as if her forces were almost spent. She looked to Kate for the sympathy she craved and for the first time really saw her closely.

"Why, you dear girl," she cried. "Your face is all tear stained. You've been crying, yourself."

"Roaring in a pillow," admitted Kate.

"But my dear, forgive me! I was so upset with that dreadful woman. Forgive me for not having seen that you, too, are in trouble. Won't you please tell me?"

"Of course," said Kate. "I lost my new hat."

"But, my dear! Crying over a hat? When it is so easy to get another? How foolish!" said the woman.

"Yes, but you didn't see the hat," said Kate. "And it will be far from easy to get another, with this one not paid for yet. I'm only one season removed from sunbonnets, so I never should have bought it at all."

The woman moved in bed, and taking one of Kate's long, crinkly braids, she drew the wealth of gold through her fingers repeatedly.

"Tell me about your hat," she said.

So to humour this fragile woman, and to keep from thinking of her own trouble, Kate told the story of her Leghorn hat and ostrich plume, and many things besides, for she was not her usual terse self with her new friend who had to be soothed to forgetfulness.

Kate ended: "I was all wrong to buy such a hat in the first place. I couldn't afford it; it was foolish vanity. I'm not really good-looking; I shouldn't have flattered myself that I was. Losing it before it was paid for was just good for me. Never again will I be so foolish."

"Why, my dear, don't say such things or think them," chided the little woman. "You had as good a right to a becoming hat as any girl. Now let me ask you one question, and then I'll try to sleep. You said you were a teacher. Did you come here to attend the Summer School for Teachers?"

"Yes," said Kate.

"Would it make any great difference to you if you missed a few days?" she asked.

"Not the least," said Kate.

"Well, then, you won't be offended, will you, if I ask you to remain with me and take care of me until John comes? I could send him a message to-night that I am alone, and bring him by this time to-morrow; but I know he has business that will cause him to lose money should he leave, and I was so wilful about coming, I dread to prove him right so conclusively the very first day. That door opens into a room reserved for Susette, if only you'd take it, and leave the door unclosed to-night, and if only you would stay with me until John comes I could well afford to pay you enough to lengthen your stay as long as you'd like; and it makes me so happy to be with such a fresh young creature. Will you stay with me, my dear?"

"I certainly will," said Kate heartily. "If you'll only tell me what I should do; I'm not accustomed to rich ladies, you know."

"I'm not myself," said the little woman, "but I do seem to take to being waited upon with the most remarkable facility!"

A Sunbonnet Girl

With the first faint light of morning, Kate slipped to the door to find her charge still sleeping soundly. It was eight o'clock when she heard a movement in the adjoining room and went again to the door. This time the woman was awake and smilingly waved to Kate as she called: "Good morning! Come right in. I was wondering if you were regretting your hasty bargain."

"Not a bit of it!" laughed Kate. "I am here waiting to be told what to do first. I forgot to tell you my name last night. It is Kate Bates. I'm from Bates Corners, Hartley, Indiana."

The woman held out her hand. "I'm so very glad to meet you, Miss Bates," she said. "My name is Mariette Jardine. My home is in Chicago."

They shook hands, smiling at each other, and then Kate said: "Now, Mrs. Jardine, what shall I do for you first?"

"I will be dressed, I think, and then you may bring up the manager until I have an understanding with him, and give him a message I want sent, and an order for our breakfast. I wonder if it wouldn't be nice to have it served on the corner of the veranda in front of our rooms, under the shade of that big tree."

"I think that would be famous," said Kate.

They ate together under the spreading branches of a giant maple tree, where they could see into the nest of an oriole that brooded in a long purse of gray lint and white cotton cord. They could almost reach out and touch it. The breakfast was good, nicely served by a neat maid, evidently doing something so out of the ordinary that she was rather stunned; but she was a young person of some self-possession, for when she removed the tray, Mrs. Jardine thanked her and gave her a coin that brought a smiling: "Thank you very much. If you want your dinner served here and will ask for Jennie Weeks, I'd like to wait on you again."

"Thank you," said Mrs. Jardine, "I shall remember that. I don't like changing waiters each meal. It gives them no chance to learn what I want or how I want it."

Then she and Kate slowly walked the length of the veranda several times, while she pointed out parts of the grounds they could see that remained as she had known them formerly, and what were improvements.

When Mrs. Jardine was tired, they returned to the room and she lay on the bed while they talked of many things; talked of things with which Kate was familiar, and some concerning which she unhesitatingly asked questions until she felt informed. Mrs. Jardine was so dainty, so delicate, yet so full of life, so well informed, so keen mentally, that as she talked she kept Kate chuckling most of the time. She talked of her home life, her travels, her friends, her son. She talked of politics, religion, and education; then she talked of her son again. She talked of social conditions, Civic Improvement, and Woman's Rights, then she came back to her son, until Kate saw that he was the real interest in the world to her. The mental picture she drew of him was peculiar. One minute Mrs. Jardine spoke of him as a man among men, pushing, fighting, forcing matters to work to his will, so Kate imagined him tall, broad, and brawny, indefatigable in his undertakings; the next, his mother was telling of such thoughtfulness, such kindness, such loving care that Kate's mental picture shifted to a neat, exacting little man, purely effeminate as men ever can be; but whatever she thought, some right instinct prevented her from making a comment or asking a question.

Once she sat looking far across the beautiful lake with such an expression on her face that Mrs. Jardine said to her: "What are you thinking of, my dear?"

Kate said smilingly: "Oh, I was thinking of what a wonderful school I shall teach this winter."

"Tell me what you mean," said Mrs. Jardine.

"Why, with even a month of this, I shall have riches stored for every day of the year," said Kate. "None of my pupils ever saw a lake, that I know of. I shall tell them of this with its shining water, its rocky, shady, sandy shore lines; of the rowboats and steam-boats, and the people from all over the country. Before I go back, I can tell them of wonderful lectures, concerts, educational demonstrations here. I shall get much from the experiences of other teachers. I shall delight my pupils with just you."

"In what way?" asked Mrs. Jardine.

"Oh, I shall tell them of a dainty little woman who know everything. From you I shall teach my girls to be simple, wholesome, tender, and kind; to take the gifts of God thankfully, reverently, yet with self-respect. From you I can tell them what really fine fabrics are, and about laces, and linens. When the subjects arise, as they always do in teaching, I shall describe each ring you wear, each comb and pin, even the handkerchiefs you carry, and the bags you travel with. To teach means to educate, and it is a big task; but it is almost painfully interesting. Each girl of my school shall go into life a gentler, daintier woman, more careful of her person and speech because of my having met you. Isn't that a fine thought?"

"Why, you darling!" cried Mrs. Jardine. "Life is always having lovely things in store for me. Yesterday I thought Susette's leaving me as she did was the most cruel thing that ever happened to me. To-day I get from it this lovely experience. If you are straight from sunbonnets, as you told me last night, where did you get these advanced ideas?"

"If sunbonnets could speak, many of them would tell of surprising heads they have covered," laughed Kate. "Life deals with women much the same as with men. If we go back to where we start, history can prove to you that there are ten sunbonnets to one Leghorn hat, in the high places of the world."

"Not to entertain me, but because I am interested, my dear, will you tell me about your particular sunbonnet?" asked Mrs. Jardine.

Kate sat staring across the blue lake with wide eyes, a queer smile twisting her lips. At last she said slowly: "Well, then, my sunbonnet is in my trunk. I'm not so far away from it but that it still travels with me. It's blue chambray, made from pieces left from my first pretty dress. It is ruffled, and has white stitching. I made it myself. The head that it fits is another matter. I didn't make that, or its environment, or what was taught it, until it was of age, and had worked out its legal time of service to pay for having been a head at all. But my head is now free, in my own possession, ready to go as fast and far on the path of life as it develops the brains to carry it. You'd smile if I should tell you what I'd ask of life, if I could have what I want."

"I scarcely think so. Please tell me."

"You'll be shocked," warned Kate.

"Just so it isn't enough to set my heart rocking again," said Mrs. Jardine.

"We'll stop before that," laughed Kate. "Then if you will have it, I want of life by the time I am twenty a man of my stature, dark eyes and hair, because I am so light. I want him to be honest, forceful, hard working, with a few drops of the milk of human kindness in his heart, and the same ambitions I have."

"And what *are* your ambitions?" asked Mrs. Jardine.

"To own, and to cultivate, and to bring to the highest state of efficiency at least two hundred acres of land, with convenient and attractive buildings and pedigreed stock, and to mother at least twelve perfect physical and mental boys and girls."

"Oh, my soul!" cried Mrs. Jardine, falling back in her chair, her mouth agape. "My dear, you don't *mean* that? You only said that to shock me."

"But why should I wish to shock you? I sincerely mean it," persisted Kate.

"You amazing creature! I never heard a girl talk like that before," said Mrs. Jardine.

"But you can't look straight ahead of you any direction you turn without seeing a girl working for dear life to attract the man she wants; if she can't secure him, some other man; and in lieu of him, any man at all, in preference to none. Life shows us woman on the age-old quest every day, everywhere we go; why be so secretive about it? Why not say honestly what we want, and take it if we can get it? At any rate, that is the most important thing inside my sunbonnet. I knew you'd be shocked."

"But I am not shocked at what you say, I agree with you. What I am shocked at is your ideals. I thought you'd want to educate yourself to such superiority over common woman that you could take the platform, and backed by your splendid physique, work for suffrage or lecture to educate the masses."

"I think more could be accomplished with selected specimens, by being steadily on the job, than by giving an hour to masses. I'm not much interested in masses. They are too abstract for me; I prefer one stern reality. And as for Woman's Rights, if anybody gives this woman the right to do anything more than she already has the right to do, there'll surely be a scandal."

Mrs. Jardine lay back in her chair laughing.

"You are the most refreshing person I have met in all my travels. Then to put it baldly, you want of life a man, a farm, and a family."

"You comprehend me beautifully," said Kate. "All my life I've worked like a towhead to help earn two hundred acres of land for someone else. I think there's nothing I want so much as two hundred acres of land for myself. I'd undertake to do almost anything with it, if I had it. I know I could, if I had the shoulder-to-shoulder, real man. You notice it will take considerable of a man to touch shoulders with me; I'm a head taller than most of them."

Mrs. Jardine looked at her speculatively. "Ummm!" she murmured. Kate laughed.

"For eighteen years I have been under marching orders," said Kate. "Over a year ago I was advised by a minister to 'take the wings of morning' so I took wing. I started on one grand flight and fell ker-smash in short order. Life since has been a series of battering my wings until I have almost decided to buy some especially heavy boots, and walk the remainder of the way. As a concrete example, I started out yesterday morning wearing a hat that several very reliable parties assured me would so assist me to flight that I might at least have a carriage. Where, oh, where are my hat and my carriage now? The carriage, non est! The hat – I am humbly hoping some little country girl, who has lived a life as barren as mine, will find the remains and retrieve the velvet bow for a hair-ribbon. As for the man that Leghorn hat was supposed to symbolize, he won't even look my way when I appear in my bobby little sailor. He's as badly crushed out of existence as my beautiful hat."

"You never should have been wearing such a hat to travel in, my dear," murmured Mrs. Jardine.

"Certainly not!" said Kate. "I knew it. My sister told me that. Common sense told me that! But what has that got to do with the fact that I WAS wearing the hat? I guess I have you there!"

"Far from it!" said Mrs. Jardine. "If you're going to start out in life, calmly ignoring the advice of those who love you, and the dictates of common sense, the result will be that soon the wheels of life will be grinding you, instead of a train making bag-rags of your hat."

"Hummm!" said Kate. "There IS food for reflection there. But wasn't it plain logic, that if the hat was to bring the man, it should be worn where at any minute he might see it?"

"But my dear, my dear! If such a man as a woman like you should have, had seen you wearing that hat in the morning, on a railway train, he would merely have thought you prideful and extravagant. You would have been far more attractive to any man I know in your blue sunbonnet."

"I surely have learned that lesson," said Kate. "Hereafter, sailors or sunbonnets for me in the morning. Now what may I do to add to your comfort?"

"Leave me for an hour until I take a nap, and then we'll have lunch and go to a lecture. I can go to-day, perfectly well, after an hour's rest."

So Kate went for a very interesting walk around the grounds. When she returned Mrs. Jardine was still sleeping so she wrote Nancy Ellen, telling all about her adventure, but not a word about losing her hat. Then she had a talk with Jennie Weeks whom she found lingering in the hall near her door. When at last that nap was over, a new woman seemed to have developed. Mrs. Jardine was so refreshed and interested the remainder of the day that it was easier than

before for Kate to see how shocked and ill she had been. As she helped dress her
for lunch, Kate said to Mrs. Jardine: "I met the manager as I was going to post
a letter to my sister, so I asked him always to send you the same waiter. He said
he would, and I'd like you to pay particular attention to her appearance, and the
way she does her work."

"Why?" asked Mrs. Jardine.

"I met her in the hall as I came back from posting my letter, so we 'visited' a
little, as the country folks say. She has taught one winter of country school, a
small school in an out county. She's here waiting table two hours three times a
day, to pay for her room and board. In the meantime, she attends all the sessions
and studies as much as she can; but she's very poor material for a teacher. I pity
her pupils. She's a little thing, bright enough in her way, but she has not much
initiative, not strong enough for the work, and she has not enough spunk. She'll
never lead the minds of school children anywhere that will greatly benefit them."

"And your deduction is—"

"That she would make you a kind, careful, obedient maid, who is capable
enough to be taught to wash your hair and manicure you with deftness, and who
would serve you for respect as well as hire. I think it would be a fine arrangement
for you and good for her."

"This surely is kind of you," said Mrs. Jardine. "I'll keep strict watch of
Jennie Weeks. If I could find a really capable maid here and not have to wire
John to bring one, I'd be so glad. It does so go against the grain to prove to a man
that he has a right to be more conceited than he is naturally."

As they ate lunch Kate said to Mrs. Jardine: "I noticed one thing this morning
that is going to be balm to my soul. I passed many teachers and summer resorters
going to the lecture halls and coming from them, and half of them were
bareheaded, so my state will not be remarkable, until I can get another hat."

"'God moves in a mysterious way, His wonders to perform,'" laughingly
quoted Mrs. Jardine. "You thought losing that precious hat was a calamity; but
if you hadn't lost it, you probably would have slept soundly while I died across
the hall. My life is worth the price of a whole millinery shop to me; I think you
value the friendship we are developing; I foresee I shall get a maid who will not
disgrace my in public; you will have a full summer here; now truly, isn't all this
worth many hats?"

"Of course! It's like a fairy tale," said Kate. "Still, you didn't see the hat!"

"But you described it in a truly graphic manner," said Mrs. Jardine.

"When I am the snowiest of great-grandmothers, I shall still be telling small
people about the outcome of my first attempt at vanity," laughed Kate.

The third morning dawned in great beauty, a "misty, moisty morning," Mrs.
Jardine called it. The sun tried to shine but could not quite pierce the intervening
clouds, so on every side could be seen exquisite pictures painted in delicate pastel
colours. Kate, fresh and rosy, wearing a blue chambray dress, was a picture well
worth seeing. Mrs. Jardine kept watching her so closely that Kate asked at last:
"Have you made up your mind, yet?"

"No, and I am afraid I never shall," answered Mrs. Jardine. "You are rather an astonishing creature. You're so big, so vital; you absorb knowledge like a sponge takes water–"

"And for the same purpose," laughed Kate. "That it may be used for the benefit of others. Tell me some more about me. I find me such an interesting subject."

"No doubt!" admitted Mrs. Jardine. "Not a doubt about that! We are all more interested in ourselves than in any one else in this world, until love comes; then we soon learn to a love man more than life, and when a child comes we learn another love, so clear, so high, so purifying, that we become of no moment at all, and live only for those we love."

"You speak for yourself, and a class of women like you," answered Kate gravely. "I'm very well acquainted with many women who have married and borne children, and who are possibly more selfish than before. The Great Experience never touched them at all."

There was a tap at the door. Kate opened it and delivered to Mrs. Jardine a box so big that it almost blocked the doorway.

Mrs. Jardine lifted from the box a big Leghorn hat of weave so white and fine it almost seemed like woven cloth instead of braid. There was a bow in front, but the bow was nested in and tied through a web of flowered gold lace. One velvet end was slightly long and concealed a wire which lifted one side of the brim a trifle, beneath which was fastened a smashing big, pale-pink velvet rose. There was an ostrich plume even longer than the other, broader, blacker, as wonderful a feather as ever dropped from the plumage of a lordly bird. Mrs. Jardine shook the hat in such a way as to set the feather lifting and waving after the confinement of the box. With slender, sure fingers she set the bow and lace as they should be, and touched the petals of the rose. She inspected the hat closely, shook it again, and held it toward Kate.

"A very small price to pay for the breath of life, which I was rapidly losing," she said. "Do me the favour to accept it as casually as I offer it. Did I understand your description anywhere near right? Is this your hat?"

"Thank you," said Kate. "It is just 'the speaking image' of my hat, but it's a glorified, sublimated, celestial image. What I described was merely a hat. This is what I think I have lately heard Nancy Ellen mention as a 'creation.' Wheuuuuuu!"

She went to the mirror, arranged her hair, set the hat on her head, and turned.

"Gracious Heaven!" said Mrs. Jardine. "My dear, I understand NOW why you wore that hat on your journey."

"I wore that hat," said Kate, "as an ascension stalk wears its crown of white lilies, as a bobolink wears its snowy courting crest, as a bride wears her veil; but please take this from me to- night, lest I sleep in it!"

That night Mrs. Jardine felt tired enough to propose resting in her room, with Jennie Weeks where she could be called; so for the first time Kate left her, and, donning her best white dress and the hat, attended a concert. At its close she walked back to the hotel with some of the other teachers stopping there, talked a few minutes in the hall, went to the office desk for mail, and slowly ascended the stairs, thinking intently. What she thought was: "If I am not mistaken, my hat did a small bit of execution to-night." She stepped to her room to lock the door and stopped a few minutes to arrange the clothing she had discarded when she dressed hurriedly before going to the concert, then, the letters in her hand, she opened Mrs. Jardine's door.

A few minutes before, there had been a tap on that same door.

"Come in," said Mrs. Jardine, expecting Kate or Jennie Weeks. She slowly lifted her eyes and faced a tall, slender man standing there.

"John Jardine, what in the world are you doing here?" she demanded after the manner of mothers, "and what in this world has happened to you?"

"Does it show on me like that?" he stammered.

"Was your train in a wreck? Are you in trouble?" she asked. "Something shows plainly enough, but I don't understand what it is."

"Are you all right, Mother?" He advanced a step, looking intently at her.

"Of course I'm all right! You can see that for yourself. The question is, what's the matter with you?"

"If you will have it, there is something the matter. Since I saw you last I have seen a woman I want to marry, that's all; unless I add that I want her so badly that I haven't much sense left. Now you have it!"

"No, I don't have it, and I won't have it! What designing creature has been trying to intrigue you now?" she demanded.

"Not any one. She didn't see me, even. I saw her. I've been following her for nearly two hours instead of coming straight to you, as I always have. So you see where I am. I expect you won't forgive me, but since I'm here, you must know that I could only come on the evening train."

He crossed the room, knelt beside the chair, and took it and its contents in his arms.

"Are you going to scold me?" he asked.

"I am," she said. "I am going to take you out and push you into the deepest part of the lake. I'm so disappointed. Why, John, for the first time in my life I've selected a girl for you, the very most suitable girl I ever saw, and I hoped and hoped for three days that when you came you'd like her. Of course I wasn't so rash as to say a word to her! But I've thought myself into a state where I'm going to be sick with disappointment."

"But wait, Mother, wait until I can manage to meet the girl I've seen. Wait until I have a chance to show her to you!" he begged.

"I suppose I shall be forced," she said. "I've always dreaded it, now here it comes. Oh, why couldn't it have been Kate? Why did she go to that silly concert? If only I'd kept her here, and we'd walked down to the station. I'd half a mind to!"

Then the door opened, and Kate stepped into the room. She stood still, looking at them. John Jardine stood up, looking at her. His mother sat staring at them in turn. Kate recovered first.

"Please excuse me," she said.

She laid the letters on a small table and turned to go. John caught his mother's hand closer, when he found himself holding it.

"If you know the young lady, Mother," he said, "why don't you introduce us?"

"Oh, I was so bewildered by your coming," she said. "Kate, dear, let me present my son."

Kate crossed the room, and looking straight into each other's eyes they shook hands and found chairs.

"How was your concert, my dear?" asked Mrs. Jardine.

"I don't think it was very good," said Kate. "Not at all up to my expectations. How did you like it, Mr. Jardine?"

"Was that a concert?" he asked.

"It was supposed to be," said Kate.

"Thank you for the information," he said. "I didn't see it, I didn't hear it, I don't know where I was."

"This is most astonishing," said Kate.

Mrs. Jardine looked at her son, her eyes two big imperative question marks. He nodded slightly.

"My soul!" she cried, then lay back in her chair half-laughing, half-crying, until Kate feared she might have another attack of heart trouble.

John Jardine's Courtship

The following morning they breakfasted together under the branches of the big maple tree in a beautiful world. Mrs. Jardine was so happy she could only taste a bite now and then, when urged to. Kate was trying to keep her head level, and be natural. John Jardine wanted to think of everything, and succeeded fairly well. It seemed to Kate that he could invent more ways to spend money, and spend it with freer hand, than any man she ever had heard of, but she had to confess that the men she had heard about were concerned with keeping their money, not scattering it.

"Did you hear unusual sounds when John came to bid me good-night?" asked Mrs. Jardine of Kate.

"Yes," laughed Kate, "I did. And I'm sure I made a fairly accurate guess as to the cause."

"What did you think?" asked Mrs. Jardine.

"I thought Mr. Jardine had missed Susette, and you'd had to tell him," said Kate.

"You're quite right. It's a good thing she went on and lost herself in New York. I'm not at all sure that he doesn't contemplate starting out to find her yet."

"Let Susette go!" said Kate. "We're interested in forgetting her. There's a little country school-teacher here, who wants to take her place, and it will be the very thing for your mother and for her, too. She's the one serving us; notice her in particular."

"If she's a teacher, how does she come to be serving us?" he asked.

"I'm a teacher; how do I come to be dining with you?" said Kate. "This is such a queer world, when you go adventuring in it. Jennie had a small school in an out county, a widowed mother and a big family to help support; so she figured that the only way she could come here to try to prepare herself for a better school was to work for her room and board. She serves the table two hours, three times a day, and studies between times. She tells me that almost every waiter in the dining hall is a teacher. Please watch her movements and manner and see if you think her suitable. Goodness knows she isn't intended for a teacher."

"I like her very much," said John Jardine. "I'll engage her as soon as we finish."

Kate smiled, but when she saw the ease and dexterity with which he ended Jennie Weeks' work as a waiter and installed her as his mother's maid, making the least detail all right with his mother, with Jennie, with the manager, she realized that there had been nothing for her to smile about. Jennie was delighted, and began her new undertaking earnestly, with sincere desire to please. Kate helped her all she could, while Mrs. Jardine developed a fund of patience commensurate with the need of it. She would have endured more inconvenience than resulted from Jennie's inexperienced hands because of the realization that her son and the girl she had so quickly learned to admire were on the lake, rambling the woods, or hearing lectures together.

When she asked him how long he could remain, he said as long as she did. When she explained that she was enjoying herself thoroughly and had no idea how long she would want to stay, he said that was all right; he had only had one vacation in his life; it was time he was having another. When she marvelled at this he said: "Now, look here, Mother, let's get this business straight, right at the start. I told you when I came I'd seen the woman I wanted. If you want me to go back to business, the way to do it is to help me win her."

"But I don't want you 'to go back to business'; I want you to have a long vacation, and learn all you can from the educational advantages here."

"It's too late for me to learn more than I get every day by knocking around and meeting people. I've tried books two or three times, and I've given them up; I can't do it. I've waited too long, I've no way to get down to it, I can't remember to save my soul."

"But you can remember anything on earth about a business deal," she urged.

"Of course I can. I was born with a business head. It was remember, or starve, and see you starve. If I'd had the books at the time they would have helped; now it's too late, and I'll never try it again, that's settled. Much as I want to marry Miss Bates, she'll have to take me or leave me as I am. I can't make myself over for her or for you. I would if I could, but that's one of the things I can't do, and I admit it. If I'm not good enough for her as I am, she'll have the chance to tell me so the very first minute I think it's proper to ask her."

"John, you are good enough for the best woman on earth. There never was a better lad, it isn't that, and you know it. I am so anxious that I can scarcely wait; but you must wait. You must give her time and go slowly, and you must be careful, oh, so very careful! She's a teacher and a student; she came here to study."

"I'll fix that. I can rush things so that there'll be no time to study."

"You'll make a mistake if you try it. You'd far better let her go her own way and only appear when she has time for you," she advised.

"That's a fine idea!" he cried. "A lot of ice I'd cut, sitting back waiting for a signal to run after a girl, like a poodle. The way to do is the same as with any business deal. See what you want, overcome anything in your way, and get it. I'd go crazy hanging around like that. You've always told me I couldn't do the things in business I said I would; and I've always proved to you that I could, by doing them. Now watch me do this."

"You know I'll do anything to help you, John. You know how proud I am of you, how I love you! I realize now that I've talked volumes to Kate about you. I've told her everything from the time you were a little boy and I slaved for you, until now, when you slave for me."

"Including how many terms I'd gone to school?"

"Yes, I even told her that," she said.

"Well, what did she seem to think about it?" he asked.

"I don't know what she thought, she didn't say anything. There was nothing to say. It was a bare-handed fight with the wolf in those days. I'm sure I made her understand that," she said.

"Well, I'll undertake to make her understand this," he said. "Are you sure that Jennie Weeks is taking good care of you?"

"Jennie is well enough and is growing better each day, now be off to your courting, but if you love me, remember, and be careful," she said.

"Remember – one particular thing – you mean?" he asked.

She nodded, her lips closed.

"You bet I will!" he said. "All there is of me goes into this. Isn't she a wonder, Mother?"

Mrs. Jardine looked closely at the big man who was all the world to her, so like her in mentality, so like his father with his dark hair and eyes and big, well-rounded frame; looked at him with the eyes of love, then as he left her to seek the girl she had learned to love, she shut her eyes and frankly and earnestly asked the Lord to help her son to marry Kate Bates.

One morning as Kate helped Mrs. Jardine into her coat and gloves, preparing for one of their delightful morning drives, she said to her: "Mrs. Jardine, may I ask you a *real* question?"

"Of course you may," said Mrs. Jardine, "and I shall give you a 'real' answer if it lies in my power."

"You'll be shocked," warned Kate.

"Shock away," laughed Mrs. Jardine. "By now I flatter myself that I am so accustomed to you that you will have to try yourself to shock me."

"It's only this," said Kate: "If you were a perfect stranger, standing back and looking on, not acquainted with any of the parties, merely seeing things as they happen each day, would it be your honest opinion – would you say that I am being *courted*?"

Mrs. Jardine laughed until she was weak. When she could talk, she said: "Yes, my dear, under the conditions, and in the circumstances you mention, I would cheerfully go on oath and testify that you are being courted more openly, more vigorously, and as tenderly as I ever have seen woman courted in all my life. I always thought that John's father was a master hand at courting, but John has him beaten in many ways. Yes, my dear, you certainly are being courted assiduously."

"Now, then, on that basis," said Kate, "just one more question and we'll proceed with our drive. From the same standpoint: would you say from your observation and experience that the mother of the man had any insurmountable objection to the proceedings?"

Mrs. Jardine laughed again. Finally she said: "No, my dear. It's my firm conviction that the mother of the man in the case would be so delighted if you should love and marry her son that she would probably have a final attack of heart trouble and pass away from sheer joy."

"Thank you," said Kate. "I wasn't perfectly sure, having had no experience whatever, and I didn't want to make a mistake."

That drive was wonderful, over beautiful country roads, through dells, and across streams and hills. They stopped where they pleased, gathering flowers and early apples, visiting with people they met, lunching wherever they happened to be.

"If it weren't for wishing to hear John A. Logan to-night," said Kate, "I'd move that we drive on all day. I certainly am having the grandest time."

She sat with her sailor hat filled with Early Harvest apples, a big bunch of Canadian anemones in her belt, a little stream at her feet, July drowsy fullness all around her, congenial companions; taking the "wings of morning" paid, after all.

"Why do you want to hear him so much?" asked John.

Kate looked up at him in wonder.

"Don't you want to see and hear him?" she asked.

He hesitated, a thoughtful expression on his face. Finally he said: "I can't say that I do. Will you tell me why I should?"

"You should because he was one of the men who did much to preserve our Union, he may tell us interesting things about the war. Where were you when it was the proper time for you to be studying the speech of Logan's ancestor in McGuffey's Fourth?"

"That must have been the year I figured out the improved coupling pin in the C. N. W. shops, wouldn't you think, Mother?"

"Somewhere near, my dear," she said.

So they drove back as happily as they had set out, made themselves fresh, and while awaiting the lecture hour, Kate again wrote to Robert and Nancy Ellen, telling plainly and simply all that had occurred. She even wrote "John Jardine's mother is of the opinion that he is courting me. I am so lacking in experience myself that I scarcely dare venture an opinion, but it has at times appealed to me that if he isn't really, he certainly must be going through the motions."

Nancy Ellen wrote:

I have read over what you say about John Jardine several times. Then I had Robert write Bradstreet's and look him up. He is rated so high that if he hasn't a million right now, he soon will have. You be careful, and do your level best. Are your clothes good enough? Shall I send more of my things? You know I'll do anything to help you. Oh, yes, that George Holt from your boarding place was here the other day hunting you. He seemed determined to know where you were and when you would be back, and asked for your address. I didn't think you had any time for him and I couldn't endure him or his foolish talk about a new medical theory; so I said you'd no time for writing and were going about so much I had no idea if you'd get a letter if he sent one, and I didn't give him what he wanted. He'll probably try general delivery, but you can drop it in the lake. I want you to be sure to change your boarding place this winter, if you teach; but

I haven't an idea you will. Hadn't you better bring matters to a close if you can, and let the Director know? Love from us both, NANCY ELLEN.

Kate sat very still, holding this letter in her hand, when John Jardine came up and sat beside her. She looked at him closely. He was quite as good looking as his mother thought him, in a brawny masculine way; but Kate was not seeking the last word in mental or physical refinement. She was rather brawny herself, and perfectly aware of the fact. She wanted intensely to learn all she could, she disliked the idea that any woman should have more stored in her head than she, but she had no time to study minute social graces and customs. She wanted to be kind, to be polite, but she told Mrs. Jardine flatly the "she didn't give a flip about being overly nice," which was the exact truth. That required subtleties beyond Kate's depth, for she was at times alarmingly casual. So she held her letter and thought about John Jardine. As she thought, she decided that she did not know whether she was in love with him or not; she thought she was. She liked being with him, she liked all he did for her, she would miss him if he went away, she would be proud to be his wife, but she did wish that he were interested in land, instead of inventions and stocks and bonds. Stocks and bonds were almost as evanescent as rainbows to Kate. Land was something she could understand and handle. Maybe she could interest him in land; if she could, that would be ideal. What a place his wealth would buy and fit up. She wondered as she studied John Jardine, what was in his head; if he truly intended to ask her to be his wife, and since reading Nancy Ellen's letter, when? She should let the Trustee know if she were not going to teach the school again; but someway, she rather wanted to teach the school. When she started anything she did not know how to stop until she finished. She had so much she wanted to teach her pupils the coming winter.

Suddenly John asked: "Kate, if you could have anything you wanted, what would you have?"

"Two hundred acres of land," she said.

"How easy!" laughed John, rising to find a seat for his mother who was approaching them. "What do you think of that, Mother? A girl who wants two hundred acres of land more than anything else in the world."

"What is better?" asked Mrs. Jardine.

"I never heard you say anything about land before."

"Certainly not," said his mother, "and I'm not saying anything about it now, for myself; but I can see why it means so much to Kate, why it's her natural element."

"Well, I can't," he said. "I meet many men in business who started on land, and most of them were mighty glad to get away from it. What's the attraction?"

Kate waved her hand toward the distance.

"Oh, merely sky, and land, and water, and trees, and birds, and flowers, and fruit, and crops, and a few other things scarcely worth mentioning," she said, lightly. "I'm not in the mood to talk bushels, seed, and fertilization just now; but I understand them, they are in my blood. I think possibly the reason I want two hundred acres of land for myself is because I've been hard on the job of getting them for other people ever since I began to work, at about the age of four."

"But if you want land personally, why didn't you work to get it for yourself?" asked John Jardine.

"Because I happened to be the omega of my father's system," answered Kate.

Mrs. Jardine looked at her interestedly. She had never mentioned her home or parents before. The older woman did not intend to ask a word, but if Kate was going to talk, she did not want to miss one. Kate evidently was going to talk, for she continued: "You see my father is land mad, and son crazy. He thinks a *boy* of all the importance in the world; a *girl* of none whatever. He has the biggest family of any one we know. From birth each girl is worked like a man, or a slave, from four in the morning until nine at night. Each boy is worked exactly the same way; the difference lies in the fact that the girls get plain food and plainer clothes out of it; the boys each get two hundred acres of land, buildings and stock, that the girls have been worked to the limit to help pay for; they get nothing personally, worth mentioning. I think I have two hundred acres of land on the brain, and I think this is the explanation of it. It's a pre-natal influence at our house; while we nurse, eat, sleep, and above all, *work* it, afterward."

She paused and looked toward John Jardine calmly: "I think," she said, "that there's not a task ever performed on a farm that I haven't had my share in. I have plowed, hoed, seeded, driven reapers and bound wheat, pitched hay and hauled manure, chopped wood and sheared sheep, and boiled sap; if you can mention anything else, go ahead, I bet a dollar I've done it."

"Well, what do you think of that?" he muttered, looking at her wonderingly.

"If you ask me, and want the answer in plain words, I think it's a shame!" said Kate. "If it were *one hundred* acres of land, and the girls had as much, and were as willing to work it as the boys are, well and good. But to drive us like cattle, and turn all we earn into land for the boys, is another matter. I rebelled last summer, borrowed the money and went to Normal and taught last winter. I'm going to teach again this winter; but last summer and this are the first of my life that I haven't been in the harvest fields, at this time. Women in the harvest fields of Land King Bates are common as men, and wagons, and horses, but not nearly so much considered. The women always walk on Sunday, to save the horses, and often on week days."

"Mother has it hammered into me that it isn't polite to ask questions," said John, "but I'd like to ask one."

"Go ahead," said Kate. "Ask fifty! What do I care?"

"How many boys are there in your family?"

"There are seven," said Kate, "and if you want to use them as a basis for a land estimate add two hundred and fifty for the home place. Sixteen hundred and fifty is what Father pays tax on, besides the numerous mortgages and investments. He's the richest man in the county we live in; at least he pays the most taxes."

Mother and son looked at each other in silence. They had been thinking her so poor that she would be bewildered by what they had to offer. But if two hundred acres of land were her desire, there was a possibility that she was a women who was not asking either ease or luxury of life, and would refuse it if it were proffered.

"I hope you will take me home with you, and let me see all that land, and how it is handled," said John Jardine. "I don't own an acre. I never even have thought of it, but there is no reason why I, or any member of my family shouldn't have all the land they want. Mother, do you feel a wild desire for two hundred acres of land? Same kind of a desire that took you to come here?"

"No, I don't," said Mrs. Jardine. "All I know about land is that I know it when I see it, and I know if I think it's pretty; but I can see why Kate feels that she would like that amount for herself, after having helped earn all those farms for her brothers. If it's land she wants, I hope she speedily gets all she desires in whatever location she wants it; and then I hope she lets me come to visit her and watch her do as she likes with it."

"Surely," said Kate, "you are invited right now; as soon as I ever get the land, I'll give you another invitation. And of course you may go home with me, Mr. Jardine, and I'll show you each of what Father calls 'those little parcels of land of mine.' But the one he lives on we shall have to gaze at from afar, because I'm a Prodigal Daughter. When I would leave home in spite of him for the gay and riotous life of a school-marm, he ordered me to take all my possessions with me, which I did in one small telescope. I was not to enter his house again while he lived. I was glad to go, he was glad to have me, while I don't think either of us has changed our mind since. Teaching school isn't exactly gay, but I'll fill my tummy with quite a lot of symbolical husks before he'll kill the fatted calf for me. They'll be glad to see you at my brother Adam's, and my sister, Nancy Ellen, would greatly enjoy meeting you. Surely you may go home with me, if you'd like."

"I can think of only one thing I'd like better," he said. "We've been such good friends here and had such a good time, it would be the thing I'd like best to take you home with us, and show you where and how we live. Mother, did you ever invite Kate to visit us?"

"I have, often, and she has said that she would," replied Mrs. Jardine. "I think it would be nice for her to go from here with us; and then you can take her home whenever she fails to find us interesting. How would that suit you for a plan, my dear?"

"I think that would be a perfect ending to a perfect summer," said Kate. "I can't see an objection in any way. Thank you very much."

"Then we'll call that settled," said John Jardine.

A Business Proposition

Mid-August saw them on their way to Chicago. Kate had taken care of Mrs. Jardine a few days while Jennie Weeks went home to see her mother and arrange for her new work. She had no intention of going back to school teaching. She preferred to brush Mrs. Jardine's hair, button her shoes, write her letters, and read to her.

In a month, Jennie had grown so deft at her work and made herself so appreciated, that she was practically indispensable to the elderly woman, and therefore the greatest comfort to John. Immediately he saw that his mother was properly cared for, sympathetically and even lovingly, he made it his business to smooth Jennie's path in every way possible. In turn she studied him, and in many ways made herself useful to him. Often she looked at him with large and speculative eyes as he sat reading letters, or papers, or smoking.

The world was all right with Kate when they crossed the sand dunes as they neared the city. She was sorry about the situation in her home, but she smiled sardonically as she thought how soon her father would forget his anger when he heard about the city home and the kind of farm she could have, merely by consenting to take it. She was that sure of John Jardine; yet he had not asked her to marry him. He had seemed on the verge of it a dozen times, and then had paused as if better judgment told him it would be wise to wait a little longer. Now Kate had concluded that there was a definite thing he might be waiting for, since that talk about land.

She thought possibly she understood what it was. He was a business man; he knew nothing else; he said so frankly. He wanted to show her his home, his business, his city, his friends, and then he required – he had almost put it into words – that he be shown her home and her people. Kate not only acquiesced, she approved. She wanted to know as much of a man she married as Nancy Ellen had known, and Robert had taken her to his home and told his people she was his betrothed wife before he married her.

Kate's eyes were wide open and her brain busy, as they entered a finely appointed carriage and she heard John say: "Rather sultry. Home down the lake shore, George." She wished their driver had not been named "George," but after all it made no difference. There could not be a commoner name than John, and she knew of but one that she liked better. For the ensuing three days she lived in a Lake Shore home of wealth. She watched closely not to trip in the heavy rugs and carpets. She looked at wonderful paintings and long shelves of books. She never had touched such china, or tasted such food or seen so good service. She understood why John had opposed his mother's undertaking the trip without him, for everyone in the house seemed busy serving the little woman.

Jennie Weeks was frankly enchanted.

"My sakes!" she said to Kate. "If I'm not grateful to you for getting me into a place like this. I wouldn't give it up for all the school-teaching in the world. I'm going to snuggle right in here, and make myself so useful I won't have to leave until I die. I hope you won't turn me out when to come to take charge."

"Don't you think you're presuming?" said Kate.

Jennie drew back with a swift apology, but there was a flash in the little eyes and a spiteful look on the small face as she withdrew.

Then Kate was shown each of John's wonderful inventions. To her they seemed almost miracles, because they were so obvious, so simple, yet brought such astounding returns. She saw offices and heard the explanation of big business; but did not comprehend, farther than that when an invention was completed, the piling up of money began. Before the week's visit was over, Kate was trying to fit herself and her aims and objects of life into the surroundings, with no success whatever. She felt housed in, cribbed, confined, frustrated. When she realized that she was becoming plainly cross, she began keen self-analysis and soon admitted to herself that she did not belong there.

Kate watched with keen eyes. Repeatedly she tried to imagine herself in such surroundings for life, a life sentence, she expressed it, for soon she understood that it would be to her, a prison. The only way she could imagine herself enduring it at all was to think of the promised farm, and when she began to think of that on Jardine terms, she saw that it would mean to sit down and tell someone else what she wanted done. There would be no battle to fight. Her mind kept harking back to the day when she had said to John that she hoped there would be a lake on the land she owned, and he had answered casually: "If there isn't a lake, make one!" Kate thought that over repeatedly. "Make one!" Make a lake? It would have seemed no more magical to her if he had said, "Make a cloud," "Make a star," or "Make a rainbow." "What on earth would I do with myself, with my time, with my life?" pondered Kate.

She said "Good-bye" to Mrs. Jardine and Jennie Weeks, and started home with John, still pondering. When the train pulled into Hartley, Nancy Ellen and Robert were on the platform to meet them. From that time, Kate was on solid ground. She was reckoning in terms she could comprehend. All her former assurance and energy came back to her. She almost wished the visit were over, and that she were on the way to Walton to clean the school-house. She was eager to roll her sleeves and beat a tub of soapy clothes to foam, and boil them snowy white. She had a desire she could scarcely control to sweep, and dust, and cook. She had been out of the environment she thought she disliked and found when she returned to it after a wider change than she could have imagined, that she did not dislike it at all. It was her element, her work, what she knew. She could attempt it with sure foot, capable hand, and certain knowledge.

Sunday morning she said to Nancy Ellen as they washed the breakfast dishes, while the men smoked on the veranda: "Nancy Ellen, I don't believe I was ever cut out for a rich woman! If I have got a chance, I wish *you* had it, and I had *this*. This just suits my style to a T."

"Tell me about it," said Nancy Ellen.

Kate told all she could remember.

"You don't mean to say you didn't *like* it?" cried Nancy Ellen.

"I didn't say anything," said Kate, "but if I were saying exactly what I feel, you'd know I despise it all."

"Why, Kate Barnes!" cried the horrified Nancy Ellen, "Whatever do you mean?"

"I haven't thought enough to put it to you clearly," said Kate, "but someway the city repels me. Facilities for manufacturing something start a city. It begins with the men who do the work, and the men who profit from that work, living in the same coop. It expands, and goes on, and grows, on that basis. It's the laborer, living on his hire, and the manufacturer living on the laborer's productions, coming in daily contact. The contrast is too great, the space is too small. Somebody is going to get the life crowded out of him at every turn, and it isn't always the work hand in the factory. The money kings eat each other for breakfast every day. As for work, we always thought we worked. You should take a peep into the shops and factories I've seen this week. Work? Why, we don't know what work is, and we waste enough food every day to keep a workman's family, and we're dressed liked queens, in comparison with them right now."

"Do you mean to say if he asks you –?" It was a small explosion.

"I mean to say if he asks me, 'buy me that two hundred acres of land where I want it, build me the house and barns I want, and guarantee that I may live there as I please, and I'll marry you to-morrow.' If it's Chicago – Never! I haven't stolen, murdered, or betrayed, who should I be imprisoned?"

"Why, you hopeless anarchist!" said Nancy Ellen, "I am going to tell John Jardine on you."

"Do!" urged Kate. "Sound him on the land question. It's our only hope of a common foundation. Have you send Agatha word that we will be out this afternoon?"

"I have," said Nancy Ellen. "And I don't doubt that now, even now, she is in the kitchen – how would she put it?"

"'Compounding a cake,'" said Kate, "while Adam is in the cellar 'freezing a custard.' Adam, 3d, will be raking the yard afresh and Susan will be sweeping the walks steadily from now until they sight us coming down the road. What you bet Agatha asked John his intentions? I almost wish she would," she added. "He has some, but there is a string to them in some way, and I can't just make out where, or why it is."

"Not even a guess?" asked Nancy Ellen.

"Not even a guess, with any sense to it. I've thought it was coming repeatedly; but I've got a stubborn Bates streak, and I won't lift a finger to help him. He'll speak up, loud and plain, or there will be no 'connubial bliss' for us, as Agatha says. I think he has ideas about other things than freight train gear. According to his programme we must have so much time to become acquainted, I must see his home and people, he must see mine. If there's more after that, I'm not informed. Like as not there is. It may come after we get back to-night, I can't say."

"Have you told him –?" asked Nancy Ellen.

"Not the details, but the essentials. He knows that I can't go home. It came up one day in talking about land. I guess they had thought before, that my people were poor as church mice. I happened to mention how much land I had helped earn for my brothers, and they seemed so interested I finished the job. Well, after they had heard about the Land King, it made a noticeable difference in their treatment of me. Not that they weren't always fine, but it made, I scarcely know how to put it, it was so intangible – but it was a difference, an added respect. You bet money is a power! I can see why Father hangs on to those deeds, when I get out in the world. They are his compensation for his years of hard work, the material evidence that he has succeeded in what he undertook. He'd show them to John Jardine with the same feeling John showed me improved car couplers, brakes, and air cushions. They stand for successes that win the deference of men. Out in the little bit of world I've seen, I notice that men fight, bleed, and die for even a tiny fraction of deference. Aren't they funny? What would I care –?"

"Well, *I'd* care a lot!" said Nancy Ellen.

Kate surveyed her slowly. "Yes, I guess you would."

They finished the dishes and went to church, because Robert was accustomed to going. They made a remarkable group. Then they went to the hotel for dinner, so that the girls would not have to prepare it, and then in a double carriage Robert had secured for the occasion, they drove to Bates Corners and as Kate said, "Viewed the landscape o'er." Those eight pieces of land, none under two hundred acres, some slightly over, all in the very highest state of cultivation, with modern houses, barns, outbuildings, and fine stock grazing in the pastures, made an impressive picture. It was probably the first time that any of the Bates girls had seen it all at once, and looked on it merely as a spectacle. They stopped at Adam's last, and while Robert was busy with the team and John had alighted to help him, Nancy Ellen, revealing tight lips and unnaturally red cheeks, leaned back to Kate.

"This is about as mean a trick, and as big a shame as I've ever seen," she said, hotly. "You know I was brought up with this, and I never looked at it with the eyes of a stranger before. If ever I get my fingers on those deeds, I'll make short work of them!"

"And a good job, too!" assented Kate, instantly. "Look out! There comes Adam."

"I'd just as soon tell him so as not!" whispered Nancy Ellen.

"Which would result in the deeds being recorded to-morrow and spoiling our trip to-day, and what good would it do you?" said Kate.

"None, of course! Nothing ever does a Bates girl any good, unless she gets out and does it for herself," retorted Nancy Ellen spitefully.

"There, there," said Robert as he came to help Nancy Ellen protect her skirts in alighting. "I was afraid this trip would breed discontent."

"What's the trouble?" asked John, as he performed the same service for Kate.

"Oh, the girls are grouching a little because they helped earn all this, and are to be left out of it," explained Robert in a low voice.

"Let's get each one of them a farm that will lay any of these completely in the shade," suggested John.

"All right for you, if you can do it," said Robert, laughing, "but I've gone my limit for the present. Besides, if you gave each of them two hundred acres of the Kingdom of Heaven, it wouldn't stop them from feeling that they had been defrauded of their birthright here."

"How would you feel if you was served the same way?" asked John, and even as she shook hands with Adam, and introduced John Jardine, Kate found herself wishing that he had said "were."

As the girls had predicted, the place was immaculate, the yard shady and cool from the shelter of many big trees, the house comfortable, convenient, the best of everything in sight. Agatha and Susan were in new white dresses, while Adam Jr. and 3d wore tan and white striped seersucker coats, and white duck trousers. It was not difficult to feel a glow of pride in the place and people. Adam made them cordially welcome.

"You undoubtedly are blessed with good fortune," said Agatha. "Won't you please enlighten us concerning your travels, Katherine?"

So Kate told them everything she could think of that she thought would interest and amuse them, even outlining for Agatha speeches she had heard made by Dr. Vincent, Chaplain McCabe, Jehu DeWitt Miller, a number of famous politicians, teachers, and ministers. Then all of them talked about everything. Adam took John and Robert to look over the farm, whereupon Kate handed over her hat for Agatha to finger and try on.

"And how long will it be, my dear," said Agatha to Kate, "before you enter connubial bliss?"

"My goodness! I'm glad you asked me that while the men are at the barn," said Kate. "Mr. Jardine hasn't said a word about it himself, so please be careful what you say before him."

Agatha looked at Kate in wonder.

"You amaze me," she said. "Why, he regards you as if he would devour you. He hasn't proposed for your hand, you say? Surely you're not giving him proper encouragement!"

"She isn't giving him any, further than allowing him to be around," said Nancy Ellen.

"Do enlighten me!" cried the surprised Agatha. "How astonishing! Why, Kate, my dear, there is a just and proper amount of encouragement that *must* be given any self-respecting youth, before he makes his declarations. You surely know that."

"No, I do not know it!" said Kate. "I thought it was a man's place to speak up loud and plain and say what he had to propose."

"Oh, dear!" wailed Agatha, wringing her thin hands, her face a mirror of distress. "Oh, dear, I very much fear you will lose him. Why, Katherine, after a man has been to see you a certain number of times, and evidenced enough interest in you, my dear, there are a thousand strictly womanly ways in which you can lend his enterprise a little, only a faint amount of encouragement, just enough to allow him to recognize that he is not – not – er – repulsive to you."

"But how many times must he come, and how much interest must he evince?" asked Kate.

"I can scarcely name an exact number," said Agatha. "That is personal. You must decide for yourself what is the psychological moment at which he is to be taken. Have you even signified to him that you – that you – that you could be induced, even to *contemplate* marriage?"

"Oh, yes," said Kate, heartily. "I told his mother that it was the height of my ambition to marry by the time I'm twenty. I told her I wanted a man as tall as I am, two hundred acres of land, and at least twelve babies."

Agatha collapsed suddenly. She turned her shocked face toward Nancy Ellen.

"Great Day of Rest!" she cried. "No wonder the man doesn't propose!"

When the men returned from their stroll, Agatha and Susan served them with delicious frozen custard and Angel's food cake. Then they resumed their drive, passing Hiram's place last. At the corner Robert hesitated and turned to ask: "Shall we go ahead, Kate?"

"Certainly," said Kate. "I want Mr. Jardine to see where I was born and spent my time of legal servitude. I suppose we daren't stop. I doubt if Mother would want to see me, and I haven't the slightest doubt that Father would *not*; but he has no jurisdiction over the road. It's the shortest way – and besides, I want to see the lilac bush and the cabbage roses."

As they approached the place Nancy Ellen turned.

"Father's standing at the gate. What shall we do?"

"There's nothing you can do, but drive straight ahead and you and Robert speak to him," said Kate. "Go fast, Robert."

He touched the team and at fair speed they whirled past the white house, at the gate of which, stiffly erect, stood a brawny man of six feet six, his face ruddy and healthy in appearance. He was dressed as he prepared himself to take a trip to pay his taxes, or to go to Court. He stood squarely erect, with stern, forbidding face, looking directly at them. Robert spoke to him, and Nancy Ellen leaned forward and waved, calling "Father," that she might be sure he knew her, but he gave not the slightest sign of recognition. They carried away a distinct picture of him, at his best physically and in appearance; at his worst mentally.

"There you have it!" said Kate, bitterly. "I'd be safe in wagering a thousand dollars, if I had it, that Agatha or the children told, at Hiram's or to Mother's girl, that we were coming. They knew we would pass about this time. Mother was at the side door watching, and Father was in his Sunday best, waiting to show us what would happen if we stopped, and that he never changes his mind. It didn't happen by accident that he was standing there dressed that way. What do you think, Nancy Elen?"

"That he was watching for us!" said Nancy Ellen.

"But why do you suppose that he did it?" asked Kate.

"He thought that if he were *not* standing guard there, we might stop in the road and at least call Mother out. He wanted to be seen, and seen at his best; but as always, in command, showing his authority."

"Don't mind," said John Jardine. "It's easy to understand the situation."

"Thank you," said Kate. "I hope you'll tell your mother that. I can't bear her to think that the trouble is wholly my fault."

"No danger of that," he said. "Mother thinks there's nobody in all the world like you, and so do I."

Nancy Ellen kicked Robert's shin, to let him know that she heard. Kate was very depressed for a time, but she soon recovered and they spent a final happy evening together. When John had parted from Robert and Nancy Ellen, with the arrangement that he was to come again the following Saturday evening and spend Sunday with them, he asked Kate to walk a short distance with him. He seemed to be debating some proposition in his mind, that he did not know how to approach. Finally he stopped abruptly and said: "Kate, Mother told me that she told you how I grew up. We have been together most of every day for six weeks. I have no idea how a man used to women goes at what I want, so I can only do what I think is right, and best, and above all honest, and fair. I'd be the happiest I've ever been, to do anything on earth I've got the money to do, for you. There's a question I'm going to ask you the next time I come. You can think over all you know of me, and of Mother, and of what we have, and are, and be ready to tell me how you feel about everything next Sunday. There's one question I want to ask you before I go. In case we can plan for a life together next Sunday, what about my mother?"

"Whatever pleases her best, of course," said Kate. "Any arrangement that you feel will make her happy, will be all right with me; in the event we agree on other things."

He laughed, shortly.

"This sounds cold-blooded and business-like," he said. "But Mother's been all the world to me, until I met you. I must be sure about her, and one other thing. I'll write you about that this week. If that is all right with you, you can get ready for a deluge. I've held in as long as I can. Kate, will you kiss me good-bye?"

"That's against the rules," said Kate. "That's getting the cart before the horse."

"I know it," he said. "But haven't I been an example for six weeks? Only one. Please?"

They were back at Dr. Gray's gate, standing in the deep shelter of a big maple. Kate said: "I'll make a bargain with you. I'll kiss you to-night, and if we come to an agreement next Sunday night, you shall kiss me. Is that all right?"

The reply was so indistinct Kate was not sure of it; but she took his face between her hands and gave him exactly the same kind of kiss she would have given Adam, 3d. She hesitated an instant, then gave him a second. "You may take that to your mother," she said, and fled up the walk.

Two Letters

Nancy Ellen and Robert were sitting on the side porch, not seeming in the least sleepy, when Kate entered the house. As she stepped out to them, she found them laughing mysteriously.

"Take this chair, Kate," said Nancy Ellen. "Come on, Robert, let's go stand under the maple tree and let her see whether she can see us."

"If you're going to rehearse any momentous moment of your existence," said Kate, "I shouldn't think of even being on the porch. I shall keep discreetly in the house, even going at once to bed. Good-night! Pleasant dreams!"

"Now we've made her angry," said Robert.

"I think there *was* 'a little touch of asperity,' as Agatha would say, in that," said Nancy Ellen, "but Kate has a good heart. She'll get over it before morning."

"Would Agatha use such a common word as 'little'?" asked Robert.

"Indeed, no!" said Nancy Ellen. "She would say 'infinitesimal.' But all the same he kissed her."

"If she didn't step up and kiss him, never again shall I trust my eyes!" said the doctor.

"Hush!" cautioned Nancy Ellen. "She's provoked now; if she hears that, she'll never forgive us."

Kate did not need even a hint to start her talking in the morning. The day was fine, a snappy tinge of autumn in the air, her head and heart were full. Nancy Ellen would understand and sympathize; of course Kate told her all there was to tell.

"And even at that," said Nancy Ellen, "he hasn't just come out right square and said 'Kate, will you marry me?' as I understand it."

"Same here," laughed Kate. "He said he had to be sure about his mother, and there was 'one other thing' he'd write me about this week, and he'd come again next Sunday; then if things were all right with me – the deluge!"

"And what is 'the other thing?'" asked Nancy Ellen.

"There he has me guessing. We had six, long, lovely weeks of daily association at the lake, I've seen his home, and his inventions, and as much of his business as is visible to the eye of a woman who doesn't know a tinker about business. His mother has told me minutely of his life, every day since he was born, I think. She insists that he never paid the slightest attention to a girl before, and he says the same, so there can't be any hidden ugly feature to mar my joy. He is thoughtful, quick, kind, a self-made business man. He looks well enough, he acts like a gentleman, he seldom makes a mistake in speech–"

"He doesn't say enough to *make* any mistakes. I haven't yet heard him talk freely, give an opinion, or discuss a question," said Nancy Ellen.

"Neither have I," said Kate. "He's very silent, thinking out more inventions, maybe. The worst thing about him is a kind of hard- headed self-assurance. He got it fighting for his mother from boyhood. He knew she would freeze and starve if he didn't take care of her; he *had* to do it. He soon found he could. It took money to do what he had to do. He got the money. Then he began performing miracles with it. He lifted his mother out of poverty, he dressed her 'in purple and fine linen,' he housed her in the same kind of home other rich men of the Lake Shore Drive live in, and gave her the same kind of service. As most men do, when things begin to come their way, he lived for making money alone. He was so keen on the chase he wouldn't stop to educate and culture himself; he drove headlong on, and on, piling up more, far more than any one man should be allowed to have; so you can see that it isn't strange that he thinks there's nothing on earth that money can't do. You can see *that* sticking out all over him. At the hotel, on boats, on the trains, anywhere we went, he pushed straight for the most conspicuous place, the most desirable thing, the most expensive. I almost prayed sometimes that in some way he would strike *one single thing* that he couldn't make come his way with money; but he never did. No. I haven't an idea what he has in his mind yet, but he's going to write me about it this week, and if I agree to whatever it is, he is coming Sunday; then he has threatened me with a 'deluge,' whatever he means by that."

"He means providing another teacher for Walden, taking you to Chicago shopping for a wonderful trousseau, marrying you in his Lake Shore palace, no doubt."

"Well, if that's what he means by a 'deluge,'" said Kate, "he'll find the flood coming his way. He'll strike the first thing he can't do with money. I shall teach my school this winter as I agreed to. I shall marry him in the clothes I buy with what I earn. I shall marry him quietly, here, or at Adam's, or before a Justice of the Peace, if neither of you wants me. He can't pick me up, and carry me away, and dress me, and marry me, as if I were a pauper."

"You're *right* about it," said Nancy Ellen. "I don't know how we came to be so different. I should do at once any way he suggested to get such a fine-looking man and that much money. That it would be a humiliation to me all my after life, I wouldn't think about until the humiliation began, and then I'd have no way to protect myself. You're right! But I'd get out of teaching this winter if I could. I'd love to have you here."

"But I must teach to the earn money for my outfit. I'll have to go back to school in the same old sailor."

"Don't you care," laughed Nancy Ellen. "We know a secret!"

"That we do!" agreed Kate.

Wednesday Kate noticed Nancy Ellen watching for the boy Robert had promised to send with the mail as soon as it was distributed, because she was, herself. Twice Thursday, Kate hoped in vain that the suspense would be over. It had to end Friday, if John were coming Saturday night. She began to resent the length of time he was waiting. It was like him to wait until the last minute, and then depend on money to carry him through.

"He is giving me a long time to think things over," Kate said to Nancy Ellen when there was no letter in the afternoon mail Thursday.

"It may have been lost or delayed," said Nancy Ellen. "It will come to-morrow, surely."

Both of them saw the boy turn in at the gate Friday morning. Each saw that he carried more than one letter. Nancy Ellen was on her feet and nearer to the door; she stepped to it, and took the letters, giving them a hasty glance as she handed them to Kate.

"Two," she said tersely. "One, with the address written in the clear, bold hand of a gentleman, and one, the straggle of a country clod-hopper."

Kate smiled as she took the letters: "I'll wager my hat, which is my most precious possession," she said, "that the one with the beautifully written address comes from the 'clod-hopper,' and the 'straggle' from the 'gentleman.'"

She glanced at the stamping and addresses and smiled again: "So it proves," she said. "While I'm about it, I'll see what the 'clod-hopper' has to say, and then I shall be free to give my whole attention to the 'gentleman.'"

"Oh, Kate, how can you!" cried Nancy Ellen.

"Way I'm made, I 'spect," said Kate. "Anyway, that's the way this is going to be done."

She dropped the big square letter in her lap and ran her finger under the flap of the long, thin, beautifully addressed envelope, and drew forth several quite as perfectly written sheets. She read them slowly and deliberately, sometimes turning back a page and going over a part of it again. When she finished, she glanced at Nancy Ellen while slowly folding the sheets. "Just for half a cent I'd ask you to read this," she said.

"I certainly shan't pay anything for the privilege, but I'll read it, if you want me to," offered Nancy Ellen.

"All right, go ahead," said Kate. "It might possibly teach you that you can't always judge a man by appearance, or hastily; though just why George Holt looks more like a 'clod-hopper' than Adam, or Hiram, or Andrew, it passes me to tell."

She handed Nancy Ellen the letter and slowly ripped open the flap of the heavy white envelope. She drew forth the sheet and sat an instant with it in her fingers, watching the expression of Nancy Ellen's face, while she read the most restrained yet impassioned plea that a man of George Holt's nature and opportunities could devise to make to a woman after having spent several months in the construction of it. It was a masterly letter, perfectly composed, spelled, and written; for among his other fields of endeavour, George Holt had taught several terms of country school, and taught them with much success; so that he might have become a fine instructor, had it been in his blood to stick to anything long enough to make it succeed. After a page as she turned the second sheet Nancy Ellen glanced at Kate, and saw that she had not opened the creased page in her hands. She flamed with sudden irritation.

"You do beat the band!" she cried. "You've watched for two days and been provoked because that letter didn't come. Now you've got it, there you sit like a mummy and let your mind be so filled with this idiotic drivel that you're not ever reading John Jardine's letter that is to tell you what both of us are crazy to know."

"If you were in any mood to be fair and honest, you'd admit that you never read a finer letter than *that*," said Kate. "As for *this*, I never was so *afraid* in all my life. Look at that!"

She threw the envelope in Nancy Ellen's lap.

"That is the very first line of John Jardine's writing I have ever seen," she said. "Do you see anything about it to *encourage* me to go farther?"

"You Goose!" cried the exasperated Nancy Ellen. "I suppose he transacts so much business he scarcely ever puts pen to paper. What's the difference how he writes? Look at what he is and what he does! Go on and read his letter."

Kate arose and walked to the window, turning her back to Nancy Ellen, who sat staring at her, while she read John Jardine's letter. Once Nancy Ellen saw Kate throw up her head and twist her neck as if she were choking; then she heard a great gulping sob down in her throat; finally Kate turned and stared at her with dazed, incredulous eyes. Slowly she dropped the letter, deliberately set her foot on it, and leaving the room, climbed the stairs. Nancy Ellen threw George Holt's letter aside and snatched up John Jardine's. She read:

MY DEREST KATE: I am a day late with this becos as I told you I have no schooling and in writing a letter is where I prove it, so I never write them, but it was not fare to you for you not to know what kind of a letter I would write if I did write one, so here it is very bad no dout but the best I can possably do which has got nothing at all to do with my pashion for you and the aughful time I will have till I here from you. If you can stand for this telagraf me and I will come first train and we will forget this and I will never write another letter. With derest love from Mother, and from me all the love of my hart. Forever yours only, JOHN JARDINE.

The writing would have been a discredit to a ten-year-old schoolboy. Nancy Ellen threw the letter back on the floor; with a stiffly extended finger, she poked it into the position in which she thought she had found it, and slowly stepped back.

"Great God!" she said amazedly. "What does the man mean? Where does that dainty and wonderful little mother come in? She must be a regular parasite, to take such ease and comfort for herself out of him, and not see that he had time and chance to do better than *that* for himself. Kate will never endure it, never in the world! And by the luck of the very Devil, there comes that school-proof thing in the same mail, from that abominable George Holt, and Kate reads it *first*. It's too bad! I can't believe it! What did his mother mean?"

Suddenly Nancy Ellen began to cry bitterly; between sobs she could hear Kate as she walked from closet and bureau to her trunk which she was packing. The lid slammed heavily and a few minutes later Kate entered the room dressed for the street.

"Why are you weeping?" she asked casually.

Her eyes were flaming, her cheeks scarlet, and her lips twitching. Nancy Ellen sat up and looked at her. She pointed to the letter: "I read that," she said.

"Well, what do I care?" said Kate. "If he has no more respect for me than to write me such an insult as that, why should I have the respect for him to protect him in it? Publish it in the paper if you want to."

"Kate, what are you going to do?" demanded Nancy Ellen.

"Three things," said Kate, slowly putting on her long silk gloves. "First, I'm going to telegraph John Jardine that I never shall see him again, if I can possibly avoid it. Second, I'm going to send a drayman to get my trunk and take it to Walden. Third, I'm going to start out and walk miles, I don't know or care where; but in the end, I'm going to Walden to clean the schoolhouse and get ready for my winter term of school."

"Oh, Kate, you are such a fine teacher! Teach him! Don't be so hurried! Take more time to think. You will break his heart," pleaded Nancy Ellen.

Kate threw out both hands, palms down.

"P-a-s-h, a-u-g-h, h-a-r-t, d-o-u-t, d-e-r-e," she slowly spelled out the letters. "What about my heart and my pride? Think I can respect that, or ask my children to respect it? But thank you and Robert, and come after me as often as you can, as a mercy to me. If John persists in coming, to try to buy me, as he thinks he can buy anything he wants, you needn't let him come to Walden; for probably I won't be there until I have to, and I won't see him, or his mother, so he needn't try to bring her in. Say good-bye to Robert for me."

She walked from the house, head erect, shoulders squared, and so down the street from sight. In half an hour a truckman came for her trunk, so Nancy Ellen made everything Kate had missed into a bundle to send with it. When she came to the letters, she hesitated.

"I guess she didn't want them," she said. "I'll just keep them awhile and if she doesn't ask about them, the next time she comes, I'll burn them. Robert must go after her every Friday evening, and we'll keep her until Monday, and do all we can to cheer her; and this very day he must find out all there is to know about that George Holt. That *is* the finest letter I ever read; she does kind of stand up for him; and in the reaction, impulsive as she is and self-confident – of course she wouldn't, but you never can tell what kind of fool a girl will make of herself, in some cases."

Kate walked swiftly, finished two of the errands she set out to do, then her feet carried her three miles from Hartley on the Walden road, before she knew where she was, so she proceeded to the village.

Mrs. Holt was not at home, but the house was standing open. Kate found her room cleaned, shining, and filled with flowers. She paid the drayman, opened her trunk, and put away her dresses, laying out all the things which needed washing; then she bathed, put on heavy shoes, and old skirt and waist, and crossing the road sat in a secluded place in the ravine and looked stupidly at the water. She noticed that everything was as she had left it in the spring, with many fresher improvements, made, no doubt, to please her. She closed her eyes, leaned against a big tree, and slow, cold and hot shudders alternated in shaking her frame.

She did not open her eyes when she heard a step and her name called. She knew without taking the trouble to look that George had come home, found her luggage in her room, and was hunting for her. She heard him come closer and knew when he seated himself that he was watching her, but she did not care enough even to move. Finally she shifted her position to rest herself, opened her eyes, and looked at him without a word. He returned her gaze steadily, smiling gravely. She had never seen him looking so well. He had put in the summer grooming himself, he had kept up the house and garden, and spent all his spare time on the ravine, and farming on the shares with his mother's sister who lived three miles east of them. At last she roused herself and again looked at him.

"I had your letter this morning," she said.

"I was wondering about that," he replied.

"Yes, I got it just before I started," said Kate. "Are you surprised to see me?"

"No," he answered. "After last year, we figured you might come the last of this week or the first of next, so we got your room ready Monday."

"Thank you," said Kate. "It's very clean and nice."

"I hope soon to be able to offer you such a room and home as you should have," he said. "I haven't opened my office yet. It was late and hot when I got home in June and Mother was fussing about this winter – that she had no garden and didn't do her share at Aunt Ollie's, so I have farmed most of the summer, and lived on hope; but I'll start in and make things fly this fall, and by spring I'll be sailing around with a horse and carriage like the best of them. You bet I am going to make things hum, so I can offer you anything you want."

"You haven't opened an office yet?" she asked for the sake of saying something, and because a practical thing would naturally suggest itself to her.

"I haven't had a breath of time," he said in candid disclaimer.

"Why don't you ask me what's the matter?"

"Didn't figure that it was any of my business in the first place," he said, "and I have a pretty fair idea, in the second."

"But how could you have?" she asked in surprise.

"When your sister wouldn't give me your address, she hinted that you had all the masculine attention you cared for; then Tilly Nepple visited town again last week and she had been sick and called Dr. Gray. She asked him about you, and he told what I fine time you had at Chautauqua and Chicago, with the rich new friends you'd made. I was watching for you about this time, and I just happened to be at the station in Hartley last Saturday when you got off the train with your fine gentleman, so I stayed over with some friends of mine, and I saw you several times Sunday. I saw that I'd practically no chance with you at all; but I made up my mind I'd stick until I saw you marry him, so I wrote just as I would if I hadn't known there was another man in existence."

"That was a very fine letter," said Kate.

"It is a very fine, deep, sincere love that I am offering you," said George Holt. "Of course I could see prosperity sticking out all over that city chap, but it didn't bother me much, because I knew that you, of all women, would judge a man on his worth. A rising young professional man is not to be sneered at, at least until he makes his start and proves what he can do. I couldn't get an early start, because I've always had to work, just as you've seen me last summer and this, so I couldn't educate myself so fast, but I've gone as fast and far as I could."

Kate winced. This was getting on places that hurt and to matters she well understood, but she was the soul of candour. "You did very well to educate yourself as you have, with no help at all," she said.

"I've done my best in the past, I'm going to do marvels in the future, and whatever I do, it is all for you and yours for the taking," he said grandiosely.

"Thank you," said Kate. "But are you making that offer when you can't help seeing that I'm in deep trouble?"

"A thousand times over," he said. "All I want to know about your trouble is whether there is anything a man of my size and strength can do to help you."

"Not a thing," said Kate, "in the direction of slaying a gay deceiver, if that's what you mean. The extent of my familiarities with John Jardine consists in voluntarily kissing him twice last Sunday night for the first and last time, once for himself, and once for his mother, whom I have since ceased to respect."

George Holt was watching her with eyes lynx-sharp, but Kate never saw it. When she mentioned her farewell of Sunday night, a queer smile swept over his face and instantly disappeared.

"I should thing any girl might be permitted that much, in saying a final good-bye to a man who had shown her a fine time for weeks," he commented casually.

"But I didn't know I was saying good-bye," explained Kate. "I expected him back in a week, and that I would then arrange to marry him. That was the agreement we made then."

As she began to speak, George Holt's face flashed triumph at having led her on; at what she said it fell perceptibly, but he instantly controlled it and said casually: "In any event, it was your own business."

"It was," said Kate. "I had given no man the slightest encouragement, I was perfectly free. John Jardine was courting me openly in the presence of his mother and any one who happened to be around. I intended to marry him. I liked him as much as any man need be liked. I don't know whether it was the same feeling Nancy Ellen had for Robert Gray or not, but it was a whole lot of feeling of some kind. I was satisfied with it, and he would have been. I meant to be a good wife to him and a good daughter to his mother, and I could have done much good in the world and extracted untold pleasure from the money he would have put in my power to handle. All was going 'merry as a marriage bell,' and then this morning came my Waterloo, in the same post with your letter."

"Do you know what you are doing?" cried George Holt, roughly, losing self-control with hope. *"You are proving to me, and admitting to yourself, that you never loved that man at all.* You were flattered, and tempted with position and riches, but your heart was not his, or you would be mighty SURE of it, don't you forget that!"

"I am not interested in analyzing exactly what I felt for him," said Kate. "It made small difference then; it makes none at all now. I would have married him gladly, and I would have been to him all a good wife is to any man; then in a few seconds I turned squarely against him, and lost my respect for him. You couldn't marry me to him if he were the last and only man on earth; but it hurt terribly, let me tell you that!"

George Holt suddenly arose and went to Kate. He sat down close beside her and leaned toward her.

"There isn't the least danger of my trying to marry you to him," he said, "because I am going to marry you myself at the very first opportunity. Why not now? Why not have a simple ceremony somewhere at once, and go away until school begins, and forget him, having a good time by ourselves? Come on, Kate, let's do it! We can go stay with Aunt Ollie, and if he comes trying to force himself on you, he'll get what he deserves. He'll learn that there is something on earth he can't buy with his money."

"But I don't love you," said Kate.

"Neither did you love him," retorted George Holt. "I can prove it by what you say. Neither did you love him, but you were going to marry him, and use all his wonderful power of position and wealth, and trust to association to *bring* love. You can try that with me. As for wealth, who cares? We are young and strong, and we have a fine chance in the world. You go on and teach this year, and I'll get such a start that by next year you can be riding around in your carriage, proud as Pompey."

"Of course we could make it all right, as to a living," said Kate. "Big and strong as we are, but–"

Then the torrent broke. At the first hint that she would consider his proposal George Holt drew her to him and talked volumes of impassioned love to her. He gave her no chance to say anything; he said all there was to say himself; he urged that Jardine would come, and she should not be there. He begged, he pleaded, he reasoned. Night found Kate sitting on the back porch at Aunt Ollie's with a confused memory of having stood beside the little stream with her hand in George Holt's while she assented to the questions of a Justice of the Peace, in the presence of the School Director and Mrs. Holt. She knew that immediately thereafter they had walked away along a hot, dusty country road; she had tried to eat something that tasted like salted ashes. She could hear George's ringing laugh of exultation breaking out afresh every few minutes; in sudden irritation at the latest guffaw she clearly remembered one thing: in her dazed and bewildered state she had forgotten to tell him that she was a Prodigal Daughter.

The Bride

Only one memory in the ten days that followed before her school began ever stood out clearly and distinctly with Kate. That was the morning of the day after she married George Holt. She saw Nancy Ellen and Robert at the gate so she went out to speak with them. Nancy Ellen was driving, she held the lines and the whip in her hands. Kate in dull apathy wondered why they seemed so deeply agitated. Both of them stared at her as if she might be a maniac.

"Is this thing in the morning paper true?" cried Nancy Ellen in a high, shrill voice that made Kate start in wonder. She did not take the trouble to evade by asking "what thing?" she merely made assent with her head.

"You are married to that – that–" Nancy Ellen choked until she could not say what.

"It's *time* to stop, since I am married to him," said Kate, gravely.

"You rushed in and married him without giving Robert time to find out and tell you what everybody knows about him?" demanded Nancy Ellen.

"I married him for what I knew about him myself," said Kate. "We shall do very well."

"Do well!" cried Nancy. "Do well! You'll be hungry and in rags the rest of your life!"

"Don't, Nancy Ellen, don't!" plead Robert. "This is Kate's affair, wait until you hear what she has to say before you go further."

"I don't care what she has to say!" cried Nancy Ellen. "I'm saying my say right now. This is a disgrace to the whole Bates family. We may not be much, but there isn't a lazy, gambling, drunken loafer among us, and there won't be so far as I'm concerned."

She glared at Kate who gazed at her in wonder.

"You really married this lout?" she demanded.

"I told you I was married," said Kate, patiently, for she saw that Nancy Ellen was irresponsible with anger.

"You're going to live with him, you're going to stay in Walden to live?" she cried.

"That is my plan at present," said Kate.

"Well, see that *you stay there*," said Nancy Ellen. "You can't bring that – that creature to my house, and if you're going to be his wife, you needn't come yourself. That's all I've got to say to you, you shameless, crazy–"

"Nancy Ellen, you shall not!" cried Robert Gray, deftly slipping the lines from her fingers, and starting the horse full speed. Kate saw Nancy Ellen's head fall forward, and her hands lifted to cover her face. She heard the deep, tearing sob that shook her, and then they were gone. She did not know what to do, so she stood still in the hot sunshine, trying to think; but her brain refused to act at her will. When the heat became oppressive, she turned back to the shade of a tree, sat down, and leaned against it. There she got two things clear after a time. She had married George Holt, there was nothing to do but make the best of it. But Nancy Ellen had said that if she lived with him she should not come to her home. Very well. She had to live with him, since she had consented to marry him, so she was cut off from Robert and Nancy Ellen. She was now a prodigal, indeed. And those things Nancy Ellen had said – she was wild with anger. She had been misinformed. Those things could not be true.

"Shouldn't you be in here helping Aunt Ollie?" asked George's voice from the front step where he seated himself with his pipe.

"Yes, in a minute," said Kate, rising. "Did you see who came?"

"No. I was out doing the morning work. Who was it?" he asked.

"Nancy Ellen and Robert," she answered.

He laughed hilariously: "Brought them in a hurry, didn't we? Why didn't they come in?"

"They came to tell me," said Kate, slowly, "that if I had married you yesterday, as I did, that they felt so disgraced that I wasn't to come to their home again."

"'Disgraced?'" he cried, his colour rising. "Well, what's the matter with me?"

"Not the things they said, I fervently hope."

"Well, they have some assurance to come out here and talk about me, and you've got as much to listen, and then come and tell me about it," he cried.

"It was over in a minute," said Kate. "I'd no idea what they were going to say. They said it, and went. Oh, I can't spare Nancy Ellen, she's all I had!"

Kate sank down on the step and covered her face. George took one long look at her, arose, and walked out of hearing. He went into the garden and watched from behind a honeysuckle bush until he saw her finally lift her head and wipe her eyes; then he sauntered back, and sat down on the step beside her.

"That's right," he said. "Cry it out, and get it over. It was pretty mean of them to come out here and insult you, and tell any lie they could think up, and then drive away and leave you; but don't mind, they'll soon get over it. Nobody ever keeps up a fuss over a wedding long."

"Nancy Ellen never told a lie in her life," said Kate. "She has too much self-respect. What she said she *thought* was true. My only chance is that somebody has told her a lie. You know best if they did."

"Of course they did," he broke in, glibly. "Haven't you lived in the same house with me long enough to know me better than any one else does?"

"You can live in the same house with people and know less about them than any one else, for that matter," said Kate, "but that's neither here nor there. We're in this together, we got to get on the job and pull, and make a success out of it that will make all of them proud to be our friends. That's the only thing left for me. As I know the Bates, once they make up their minds, they never change. With Nancy Ellen and Father both down on me, I'm a prodigal for sure."

"What?" he cried, loudly. "What? Is your father in this, too? Did he send you word you couldn't come home, either? This is a hell of a mess! Speak up!"

Kate closed her lips, looked at him with deep scorn, and walked around the corner of the house. For a second he looked after her threateningly, then he sprang to his feet, and ran to her, catching her in his arms.

"Forgive me, dearest," he cried. "That took the wind out of my sails until I was a brute. You'd no business to *say* a thing like that. Of course we can't have the old Land King down on us. We've got to have our share of that land and money to buy us a fine home in Hartley, and fix me up the kind of an office I should have. We'll borrow a rig and drive over to-morrow and fix things solid with the old folks. You bet I'm a star-spangled old persuader, look what I did with you–"

"You stop!" cried Kate, breaking from his hold. "You will drive me crazy! You're talking as if you married me expecting land and money from it. I haven't been home in a year, and my father would deliberately kill me if I went within his reach."

"Well, score one for little old scratchin', pickin', Mammy!" he cried. "She *said* you had a secret!"

Kate stood very still, looking at him so intently that a sense of shame must have stirred in his breast.

"Look here, Kate," he said, roughly. "Mother did say you had a secret, and she hinted at Christmas that the reason you didn't go home was because your folks were at outs with you, and you can ask her if I didn't tell her to shut up and leave you alone, that I was in love with you, and I'd marry you and we'd get along all right, even if you were barred from home, and didn't get a penny. I just dare you to ask her."

"It's no matter," said Kate, wearily. "I'd rather take your word."

"All right, you take it, for that's the truth," he said. "But what was the rumpus? How did you come to have a racket with your old man?"

"Over my wanting to teach," said Kate. Then she explained in detail.

"Pother! Don't you fret about that!" said George. "I'm taking care of you now, and I'll see that you soon get home and to Grays', too; that's all buncombe. As for your share of your father's estate, you watch me get it! You are his child, and there is law!"

"There's law that allows him to deed his land to his sons before he dies, and that is exactly what he has done," said Kate.

"The Devil, you say!" shouted George Holt, stepping back to stare at her. "You tell that at the Insane Asylum or the Feeble Minded Home! I've seen the records! I know to the acre how much land stands in your father's name. Don't try to work that on me, my lady."

"I am not trying to work anything on you," said Kate, dully, wondering to herself why she listened, why she went on with it. "I'm merely telling you. In Father's big chest at the head of his bed at home lies a deed for two hundred acres of land for each of his seven sons, all signed and ready to deliver. He keeps the land in his name on record to bring him distinction and feed his vanity. He makes the boys pay the taxes, and ko-tow, and help with his work; he keeps them under control; but the land is theirs; none of the girls get a penny's worth of it!"

George Holt cleared his face with an effort.

"Well, we are no worse off than the rest of them, then," he said, trying to speak naturally and cheerfully. "But don't you ever believe it! Little old Georgie will sleep with this in his night cap awhile, and it's a problem he will solve if he works himself to death on it."

"But that is Father's affair," said Kate. "You had best turn your efforts, and lie awake nights thinking how to make enough money to buy some land for us, yourself."

"Certainly! Certainly! I see myself doing it!" laughed George Holt. "And now, knowing how you feel, and feeling none to good myself, we are going to take a few days off and go upstream, fishing. I'll take a pack of comforts to sleep on, and the tackle and some food, and we will forget the whole bunch and go have a good time. There's a place, not so far away, where I have camped beside a spring since I was a little shaver, and it's quiet and cool. Go get what you can't possibly exist without, nothing more."

"But we must dig the potatoes," protested Kate.

"Let them wait until we get back; it's a trifle early, anyway," he said. "Stop objecting and get ready! I'll tell Aunt Ollie. We're chums. Whatever I do is always all right with her. Come on! This is our wedding trip. Not much like the one you had planned, no doubt, but one of some kind."

So they slipped beneath the tangle of vines and bushes, and, following the stream of the ravine, they walked until mid- afternoon, when they reached a spot that was very lovely, a clear, clean spring, grassy bank, a sheltered cave-in floored with clean sand, warm and golden. From the depths of the cave George brought an old frying pan and coffee pot. He spread a comfort on the sand of the cave for a bed, produced coffee, steak, bread, butter, and fruit from his load, and told Kate to make herself comfortable while he got dinner. They each tried to make allowances for, and to be as decent as possible with, the other, with the result that before they knew it, they were having a good time; at least, they were keeping the irritating things they thought to themselves, and saying only the pleasant ones.

After a week, which George enjoyed to the fullest extent, while Kate made the best of everything, they put away the coffee pot and frying pan, folded the comforts, and went back to Aunt Ollie's for dinner; then to Walden in the afternoon. Because Mrs. Holt knew they would be there that day she had the house clean and the best supper she could prepare ready for them. She was in a quandary as to how to begin with Kate. She heartily hated her. She had been sure the girl had a secret, now she knew it; for if she did not attend the wedding of her sister, if she had not been at home all summer, if her father and mother never mentioned her name or made any answer to any one who did, there was a reason, and a good reason. Of course a man as rich as Adam Bates could do no wrong; whatever the trouble was, Kate was at fault, she had done some terrible thing.

"Hidin' in the bushes!" spat Mrs. Holt. "Hidin' in the bushes! Marry a man who didn't know he was goin' to be married an hour before, unbeknownst to her folks, an' wouldn't even come in the house, an' have a few of the neighbours in. Nice doin's for the school-ma'am! Nice prospect for George."

Mrs. Holt hissed like a copperhead, which was a harmless little creature compared with her, as she scraped, and slashed, and dismembered the chicken she was preparing to fry. She had not been able, even by running into each store in the village, and the post office, to find one person who would say a word against Kate. The girl had laid her foundations too well. The one thing people could and did say was: "How could she marry George Holt?" The worst of them could not very well say it to his mother. They said it frequently to each other and then supplied the true answers. "Look how he spruced up after she came!" "Look how he worked!" "Look how he ran after and waited on her!" "Look how nice he has been all summer!" Plenty was being said in Walden, but not one word of it was for the itching ears of Mrs. Holt. They had told her how splendid Kate was, how they loved her, how glad they were that she was to have the school again, how fortunate her son was, how proud she should be, until she was almost bursting with repressed venom.

She met them at the gate, after their week's camping. They were feeling in splendid health, the best spirits possible in the circumstances, but appearing dirty and disreputable. They were both laughing as they approached the gate.

"Purty lookin' bride you be!" Mrs. Holt spat at Kate.

"Yes, aren't I?" laughed Kate. "But you just give me a tub of hot soapsuds and an hour, and you won't know me. How are you? Things look as if you were expecting us."

"Hump!" said Mrs. Holt.

Kate laughed and went into the house. George stepped in front of his mother.

"Now you look here," he said. "I know every nasty thing your mind has conjured up that you'd *like* to say, and have other folks say, about Kate. And I know as well as if you were honest enough to tell me, that you haven't been able to root out one living soul who would say a single word against her. Swallow your secret! Swallow your suspicions! Swallow your venom, and forget all of them. Kate is as fine a woman as God ever made, and anybody who has common sense knows it. She can just *make* me, if she wants to, and she will; she's coming on fine, much faster and better than I hoped for. Now you drop this! Stop it! Do you hear?"

He passed her and hurried up the walk. In an hour, both George and Kate had bathed and dressed in their very best. Kate put on her prettiest white dress and George his graduation suit. Then together they walked to the post office for their mail, which George had ordered held, before they left. Carrying the bundle, they entered several stores on trifling errands, and then went home. They stopped and spoke to everyone. Kate kissed all her little pupils she met, and told them to come to see her, and to be ready to help clean the schoolhouse in the morning. Word flew over town swiftly. The Teacher was back, wearing the loveliest dress, and nicer than ever, and she had invited folks to come to see her.

Kate and George had scarcely finished their supper, when the first pair of shy little girls came for their kisses and to bring "Teacher" a bunch of flowers and a pretty pocket handkerchief from each. They came in flocks, each with flowers, most with a towel or some small remembrance; then the elders began to come, merchants with comforts, blankets, and towels, hardware men with frying pans, flat irons, and tinware. By ten o'clock almost everyone in Walden had carried Kate some small gift, wished her joy all the more earnestly, because they felt the chances of her ever having it were so small, and had gone their way, leaving her feeling better than she had thought possible.

She slipped into her room alone and read two letters, one a few typewritten lines from John Jardine, saying he had been at Hartley, also at Walden, and having found her married and gone, there was nothing for him to do but wish that the man she married had it in his heart to guard her life and happiness as he would have done. He would never cease to love her, and if at any time in her life there was anything he could do for her, would she please let him know. Kate dropped the letter on her dresser, with a purpose, and let it lie there. The other was from Robert. He said he was very sorry, but he could do nothing with Nancy Ellen at present. He hoped she would change later. If there was ever anything he could do, to let him know. Kate locked that letter in her trunk. She wondered as she did so why both of them seemed to think she would need them in the future. She felt perfectly able to take care of herself.

Monday morning George carried Kate's books to school for her, saw that she was started on her work in good shape, then went home, put on his old clothes, and began the fall work at Aunt Ollie's. Kate, wearing her prettiest blue dress, forgot even the dull ache in her heart, as she threw herself into the business of educating those young people. She worked as she never had before. She seemed to have developed fresh patience, new perception, keener penetration; she made the dullest of them see her points, and interested the most inattentive. She went home to dinner feeling better. She decided to keep on teaching a few years until George was well started in his practice; if he ever got started. He was very slow in action it seemed to her, compared with his enthusiasm when he talked.

Starting Married Life

For two weeks Kate threw herself into the business of teaching with all her power. She succeeded in so interesting herself and her pupils that she was convinced she had done a wise thing. Marriage did not interfere with her teaching; she felt capable and independent so long as she had her salary. George was working and working diligently, to prepare for winter, whenever she was present or could see results. With her first month's salary she would buy herself a warm coat, a wool suit, an extra skirt for school, and some waists. If there was enough left, she would have another real hat. Then for the remainder of the year she would spend only for the barest necessities and save to help toward a home something like Nancy Ellen's. Whenever she thought of Nancy Ellen and Robert there was a choking sensation in her throat, a dull ache where she had been taught her heart was located.

For two weeks everything went as well as Kate hoped: then Mrs. Holt began to show the results of having been partially bottled up, for the first time in her life. She was careful to keep to generalities which she could claim meant nothing, if anything she said was taken up by either George or Kate. George was too lazy to quarrel unless he was personally angered; Kate thought best to ignore anything that did not come in the nature of a direct attack. So long as Mrs. Holt could not understand how some folks could see their way to live off of other folks, or why a girl who had a chance to marry a fortune would make herself a burden to a poor man, Kate made the mistake of ignoring her. Thus emboldened she soon became personal. It seemed as if she spent her spare time and mental force thinking up suggestive, sarcastic things to say, where Kate could not help hearing them. She paid no attention unless the attack was too mean and premeditated; but to her surprise she found that every ugly, malicious word the old woman said lodged in her brain and arose to confront her at the most inopportune times – in the middle of a recitation or when she roused enough to turn over in her bed at night. The more vigorously she threw herself into her school work, the more she realized a queer lassitude, creeping over her. She kept squaring her shoulders, lifting her chin, and brushing imaginary cobwebs from before her face.

The final Friday evening of the month, she stopped at the post office and carried away with her the bill for her Leghorn hat, mailed with nicely conceived estimate as to when her first check would be due. Kate visited the Trustee, and smiled grimly as she slipped the amount in an envelope and gave it to the hack driver to carry to Hartley on his trip the following day. She had intended all fall to go with him and select a winter headpiece that would be no discredit to her summer choice, but a sort of numbness was in her bones; so she decided to wait until the coming week before going. She declined George's pressing invitation to go along to Aunt Ollie's and help load and bring home a part of his share of their summer's crops, on the ground that she had some work to prepare for the coming week.

Then Kate went to her room feeling faint and heavy. She lay there most of the day, becoming sorrier for herself, and heavier every passing hour. By morning she was violently ill; when she tried to leave her bed, dizzy and faint. All day she could not stand. Toward evening, she appealed to George either to do something for her himself, or to send for the village doctor. He asked her a few questions and then, laughing coarsely, told her that a doctor would do her no good, and that it was very probable that she would feel far worse before she felt better. Kate stared at him in dumb wonder.

"But my school!" she cried. "My school! I must be able to go to school in the morning. Could that spring water have been infected with typhus? I've never been sick like this before."

"I should hope not!" said George. And then he told her bluntly what caused her trouble. Kate had been white to begin with, now she slowly turned greenish as she gazed at him with incredulous eyes. Then she sprang to her feet.

"But I can't be ill!" she cried. "I can't! There is my school! I've got to teach! Oh, what shall I do?"

George had a very clear conception of what she could do, but he did not intend to suggest it to her. She could think of it, and propose it herself. She could not think of anything at that minute, because she fainted, and fell half on the bed, half in his arms as he sprang to her. He laid her down, and stood a second smiling triumphantly at her unheeding face.

"Easy snap for you this winter, Georgie, my boy!" he muttered. "I don't see people falling over each other to get to you for professional services, and it's hard work anyway. Zonoletics are away above the head of these country ignoramuses; blue mass and quinine are about their limit."

He took his time to bathe Kate's face. Presently she sat up, then fell on the pillow again.

"Better not try that!" warned George. "You'll hurt yourself, and you can't make it. You're out of the game; you might as well get used to it."

"I won't be out of the game!" cried Kate. "I can't be! What will become of my school? Oh, George, could you possibly teach for me, only for a few days, until I get my stomach settled?"

"Why, I'd like to help you," he said, "but you see how it is with me. I've got my fall work finished up, and I'm getting ready to open my office next week. I'm going to rent that nice front room over the post office."

"But, George, you must," said Kate. "You've taught several terms. You've a license. You can take it until this passes. If you have waited from June to October to open your office, you can wait a few more days. Suppose you *open* the office and patients don't come, or we haven't the school; what would we *live* on? What would I buy things with, and pay doctor bills?"

"Why didn't you think of that before you got married? What was your rush, anyway? I can't figure it to save my soul," he said.

"George, the school can't go," she cried. "If what you say is true, and I suspect it is, I must have money to see me through."

"Then set your wits to work and fix things up with your father," he said casually.

Kate arose tall and straight, standing unwaveringly as she looked at him in blazing contempt.

"So?" she said. "This is the kind of man you are? I'm not so helpless as you think me. I have a refuge. I know where to find it. You'll teach my school until I'm able to take it myself, if the Trustee and patrons will allow you, or I'll sever my relations with you as quickly as I formed them. You have no practice; I have grave doubts if you can get any; this is our only chance for the money we must have this winter. Go ask the Trustee to come here until I can make arrangements with him."

Then she wavered and rolled on the bed again. George stood looking at her between narrowed eyelids.

"Tactics I use with Mother don't go with you, old girl," he said to himself. "Thing of fire and tow, stubborn as an ox; won't be pushed a hair's breadth; old Bates over again – alike as two peas. But I'll break you, damn you, I'll break you; only, I *want* that school. Lots easier than kneading somebody's old stiff muscles, while the money is sure. Oh, I go after the Trustee, all right!"

He revived Kate, and telling her to keep quiet, and not excite herself, he explained that it was a terrible sacrifice to him to put off opening his office any longer; she must forgive him for losing self-control when he thought of it; but for her dear sake he would teach until she was better – possibly she would be all right in a few days, and then she could take her work again. Because she so devoutly hoped it, Kate made that arrangement with the Trustee. Monday, she lay half starved, yet gagging and ill, while George went to teach her school. As she contemplated that, she grew sicker than she had been before. When she suddenly marshalled all the facts she knew of him, she stoutly refused to think of what Nancy Ellen had said; when she reviewed his character and disposition, and thought of him taking charge of the minds of her pupils, Kate suddenly felt she must not allow that to happen, she must not! Then came another thought, even more personal and terrible, a thought so disconcerting she mercifully lost consciousness again.

She sent for the village doctor, and found no consolation from her talk with him. She was out of the school; that was settled. No harpy ever went to its meat with one half the zest Mrs. Holt found in the situation. With Kate so ill she could not stand on her feet half the time, so ill she could not reply, with no spirit left to appeal to George, what more could be asked? Mrs. Holt could add to every grievance she formerly had, that of a sick woman in the house for her to wait on. She could even make vile insinuations to Kate, prostrate and helpless, that she would not have dared otherwise. She could prepare food that with a touch of salt or sugar where it was not supposed to be, would have sickened a well person.

One day George came in from school and saw a bowl of broth sitting on a chair beside Kate's bed.

"Can't you drink it?" he asked. "Do, if you possibly can," he urged. "You'll get so weak you'll be helpless."

"I just can't," said Kate. "Things have such a sickening, sweetish taste, or they are bitter, or sour; not a thing is as it used to be. I simply can't!"

A curious look crept over George's face. He picked up the bowl and tasted the contents. Instantly his face went black; he started toward the kitchen. Kate heard part of what happened, but she never lifted her head. After a while he came back with more broth and a plate of delicate toast.

"Try this," he said. "I made it myself."

Kate ate ravenously.

"That's good!" she cried.

"I'll tell you what I'm going to do," he said. "I'm going to take you out to Aunt Ollie's for a week after school to-night. Want to go?"

"Yes! Oh, yes!" cried Kate.

"All right," he said. "I know where I can borrow a rig for an hour. Get ready if you are well enough, if you are not, I'll help you after school."

That week with Aunt Ollie remained a bright spot in Kate's memory. The October days were beginning to be crisp and cool. Food was different. She could sleep, she could eat many things Aunt Ollie knew to prepare especially; soon she could walk and be outdoors. She was so much better she wrote George a note, asking him to walk out and bring her sewing basket, and some goods she listed, and in the afternoons the two women cut and sewed quaint, enticing little garments. George found Kate so much better when he came that he proposed she remain another week. Then for the first time he talked to her about her theory of government and teaching, until she realized that the School Director had told him he was dissatisfied with him – so George was trying to learn her ways. Appalled at what might happen if he lost the school, Kate made notes, talked at length, begged him to do his best, and to come at once if anything went wrong. He did come, and brought the school books so she went over the lessons with him, and made marginal notes of things suggested to her mind by the text, for him to discuss and elucidate. The next time he came, he was in such good spirits she knew his work had been praised, so after that they went over the lessons together each evening. Thinking of what would help him also helped fill her day.

He took her home, greatly improved, in much better spirits, to her room, cleaned and ready for winter, with all of her things possible to use in place, so that it was much changed, prettier, and more convenient. As they drove in she said of him: "George, what about it? Did your mother purposely fix my food so I could not eat it?"

"Oh, I wouldn't say that," he said. "You know neither of you is violently attached to the other. She'll be more careful after this, I'm sure she will."

"Why, have you been sick?" asked Kate as soon as she saw Mrs. Holt.

She seemed so nervous and appeared so badly Kate was sorry for her; but she could not help noticing how she kept watch on her son. She seemed to keep the width of the room and a piece of furniture between them, while her cooking was so different that it was not in the least necessary for George to fix things for Kate himself, as he had suggested. Everything was so improved, Kate felt better. She began to sew, to read, to sit for long periods in profound thought, then to take walks that brought back her strength and colour. So through the winter and toward the approach of spring they lived in greater comfort. With Kate's help, George was doing so well with the school that he was frequently complimented by the parents. That he was trying to do good work and win the approval of both pupils and parents was evident to Kate. Once he said to her that he wondered if it would be a good thing for him to put in an application for the school the coming winter. Kate stared at him in surprise: "But your profession," she objected. "You should be in your office and having enough practice to support us by then."

"Yes, I should!" he said. "But this is a new thing, and you know how these clodhoppers are."

"If I came as near living in the country, and worked at farming as much as you do, that's the last thing I would call any human being," said Kate. "I certainly do know how they are, and what I know convinces me that you need not look to them for any patients."

"You seem to think I won't have any from any source," he said hotly.

"I confess myself dubious," said Kate. "You certainly are, or you wouldn't be talking of teaching."

"Well, I'll just show you!" he cried.

"I'm waiting," said Kate. "But as we must live in the meantime, and it will be so long before I can earn anything again, and so much expense, possibly it would be a good idea to have the school to fall back on, if you shouldn't have the patients you hope for this summer. I think you have done well with the school. Do your level best until the term closes, and you may have a chance."

Laughing scornfully, he repeated his old boast: "I'll just show you!"

"Go ahead," said Kate. "And while you are at it, be generous. Show me plenty. But in the meantime, save every penny you can, so you'll be ready to pay the doctor's bills and furnish your office."

"I love you advice; it's so Batesy," he said. "I have money saved for both contingencies you mention, but I'll tell you what I think, and about this I'm the one who knows. I've told you repeatedly winter is my best time. I've lost the winter trying to help you out; and I've little chance until winter comes again. It takes cold weather to make folks feel what ails their muscles, and my treatment is mostly muscular. To save so we can get a real start, wouldn't it be a good idea for you to put part of your things in my room, take what you must have, and fix Mother's bedroom for you, let her move her bed into her living room, and spare me all you can of your things to fix up your room for my office this summer. That would save rent, it's only a few steps from downtown, and when I wasn't busy with patients, I could be handy to the garden, and to help you."

"If your mother is willing, I'll do my share," said Kate, "although the room's cramped, and where I'll put the small party when he comes I don't know, but I'll manage someway. The big objection to it is that it will make it look to people as if it were a makeshift, instead of starting a real business."

"Real," was the wrong word. It was the red rag that started George raging, until to save her self-respect, Kate left the room. Later in the day he announced that his mother was willing, she would clean the living room and move in that day. How Kate hated the tiny room with its one exterior wall, only one small window, its scratched woodwork, and soiled paper, she could not say. She felt physically ill when she thought of it, and when she thought of the heat of the coming summer, she wondered what she would do; but all she could do was to acquiesce. She made a trip downtown and bought a quart of white paint and a few rolls of dainty, fresh paper. She made herself ill with turpentine odours in giving the woodwork three coats, and fell from a table almost killing herself while papering the ceiling. There was no room for her trunk; the closet would not hold half her clothes; her only easy chair was crowded out; she was sheared of personal comfort at a clip, just at a time when every comfort should have been hers. George ordered an operating table, on which to massage his patients, a few other necessities, and in high spirits, went about fixing up his office and finishing his school. He spent hours in the woodshed with the remainder of Kate's white paint, making a sign to hang in front of the house.

He was so pathetically anxious for a patient, after he had put his table in place, hung up his sign, and paid for an announcement in the county paper and the little Walden sheet, that Kate was sorry for him.

On a hot July morning Mrs. Holt was sweeping the front porch when a forlorn specimen of humanity came shuffling up the front walk and asked to see Dr. Holt. Mrs. Holt took him into the office and ran to the garden to tell George his first patient had come. His face had been flushed from pulling weeds, but it paled perceptibly as he started to the back porch to wash his hands.

"Do you know who it is, Mother?" he asked.

"It's that old Peter Mines," she said, "an' he looks fit to drop."

"Peter Mines!" said George. "He's had about fifty things the matter with him for about fifty years."

"Then you're a made man if you can even make him think he feels enough better so's he'll go round talking about it," said Mrs. Holt, shrewdly.

George stood with his hands dripping water an instant, thinking deeply.

"Well said for once, old lady," he agreed. "You are just exactly right."

He hurried to his room, and put on his coat.

"A patient that will be a big boom for me," he boasted to Kate as he went down the hall.

Mrs. Holt stood listening at the hall door. Kate walked around the dining room, trying to occupy herself. Presently cringing groans began to come from the room, mingling with George's deep voice explaining, and trying to encourage the man. Then came a wild shriek and then silence. Kate hurried out to the back walk and began pacing up and down in the sunshine. She did not know it, but she was praying.

A minute later George's pallid face appeared at the back door: "You come in here quick and help me," he demanded.

"What's the matter?" asked Kate.

"He's fainted. His heart, I think. He's got everything that ever ailed a man!" he said.

"Oh, George, you shouldn't have touched him," said Kate.

"Can't you see it will make me, if I can help him! Even Mother could see that," he cried.

"But if his heart is bad, the risk of massaging him is awful," said Kate as she hurried after George.

Kate looked at the man on the table, ran her hand over the heart region, and lifted terrified eyes to George.

"Do you think –?" he stammered.

"Sure of it!" she said, "but we can try. Bring your camphor bottle, and some water," she cried to Mrs. Holt.

For a few minutes, they worked frantically. Then Kate stepped back. "I'm scared, and I don't care who knows it," she said. "I'm going after Dr. James."

"No, you are not!" cried George. "You just hold yourself. I'll have him out in a minute. Begin at his feet and rub the blood up to his heart."

"They are swollen to a puff, he's got no circulation," said Kate. "Oh, George, how could you ever hope to do anything for a man in this shape, with MUSCULAR treatment?"

"You keep still and rub, for God's sake," he cried, frantically. "Can't you see that I am ruined if he dies on this table?"

"No, I can't," said Kate. "Everybody would know that he was practically dying when he came here. Nobody will blame you, only, you never should have touched him! George, I AM going after Dr. James."

"Well, go then," he said wildly.

Kate started. Mrs. Holt blocked the doorway.

"You just stop, Missy!" she cried. "You're away too smart, trying to get folks in here, and ruin my George's chances. You just stay where you are till I think what to do, to put the best face on this!"

"He may not be really gone! The doctor might save him!" cried Kate.

Mrs. Holt looked long at the man.

"He's deader 'an a doornail," she said. "You stay where you are!"

Kate picked her up by the shoulders, set her to one side, ran from the room and down the street as fast as possible. She found the doctor in his office with two patients. She had no time to think or temporize.

"Get your case and come to our house quick, doctor," she cried. "An old man they call Peter Mines came to see George, and his heart has failed. Please hurry!"

"Heart, eh?" said the doctor. "Well, wait a minute. No use to go about a bad heart without digitalis."

He got up and put on his hat, told the men he would be back soon, and went to the nearest drug store. Kate followed. The men who had been in the office came also.

"Doctor, hurry!" she panted. "I'm so frightened."

"You go to some of the neighbours, and stay away from there," he said.

"Hurry!" begged Kate. "Oh, do hurry!"

She was beside him as they sped down the street, and at his shoulder as they entered the room. With one glance she lurched against the casing and then she plunged down the hall, entered her room, closed the door behind her, and threw herself on the bed. She had only a glance, but in that glance she had seen Peter Mines sitting fully clothed, his hat on his head, his stick in his hands, in her easy chair; the operating table folded and standing against the wall; Mrs. Holt holding the camphor bottle to Peter's nose, while George had one hand over Peter's heart, the other steadying his head.

The doctor swung the table in place, and with George's help laid Peter on it, then began tearing open his clothes. As they worked the two men followed into the house to see if they could do anything and excited neighbours began to gather. George and his mother explained how Peter had exhausted himself walking two miles from the country that hot morning, how he had entered the office, tottering with fatigue, and had fallen in the chair in a fainting condition. Everything was plausible until a neighbour woman, eager to be the centre of attention for a second, cried: "Yes, we all see him come more'n an hour ago; and when he begin to let out the yells we says to each other, '*there*! George has got his first patient, sure!' An' we all kind of waited to see if he'd come out better."

The doctor looked at her sharply: "More than an hour ago?" he said. "You heard cries?"

"Yes, more'n a good hour ago. Yes, we all heard him yell, jist once, good and loud!" she said.

The doctor turned to George. Before he could speak his mother intervened.

"That was our Kate done the yellin'," she said. "She was scart crazy from the start. He jest come in, and set in the chair and he's been there ever since."

"You didn't give him any treatment, Holt?" asked the doctor.

Again Mrs. Holt answered: "Never touched him! Hadn't even got time to get his table open. Wa'n't nothing he could 'a' done for him anyway. Peter was good as gone when he got here. His fool folks never ought 'a' let him out this hot day, sick as he was."

The doctor looked at George, at his mother, long at Peter. "He surely was too sick to walk that far in this heat," he said. "But to make sure, I'll look him over. George, you help me. Clear the room of all but these two men."

He began minutely examining Peter's heart region. Then he rolled him over and started to compress his lungs. Long white streaks marked the puffy red of the swollen, dropsical flesh. The doctor examined the length of the body, and looked straight into George Holt's eyes.

"No use," he said. "Bill, go to the 'phone in my office, and tell Coroner Smith to get here from Hartley as soon as he can. All that's left to do here is to obey the law, and have a funeral. Better some of the rest of you go tell his folks. I've done all I can do. It's up to the Coroner now. The rest of you go home, and keep still till he comes."

When he and George were left alone he said tersely: "Of course you and your mother are lying. You had this man stripped, he did cry out, and he did die from the pain of the treatment you tried to give him, in his condition. By the way, where's your wife? This is a bad thing for her right now. Come, let's find her and see what state she is in."

Together they left the room and entered Kate's door. As soon as the doctor was busy with her, George slipped back into the closed room, rolled Peter on his back and covered him, in the hope that the blood would settle until it would efface the marks of his work before the Coroner arrived. By that time the doctor was too busy to care much what happened to Peter Mines; he was a poor old soul better off as he was. Across Kate's unconscious body he said to George Holt: "I'm going to let the Coroner make what he pleases out of this, solely for your wife's sake. But two things: take down that shingle. Take it down now, and never put it up again if you want me to keep still. I'll give you what you paid for that table. It's a good one. Get him out as soon as you can. Set him in another room. I've got to have Mrs. Holt where I can work. And send Sarah Nepple here to help me. Move fast! This is going to be a close call. And the other thing: I've heard you put in an application for our school this winter. Withdraw it! Now move!"

So they set Peter in the living room, cleaned Kate's room quickly, and moved in her bed. By the time the Coroner arrived, the doctor was too busy to care what happened. On oath he said a few words that he hoped would make life easier for Kate, and at the same time pass muster for truth; told the Coroner what witnesses to call; and gave an opinion as to Peter's condition. He also added that he was sure Peter's family would be very glad he was to suffer no more, and then he went back to Kate who was suffering entirely too much for safety. Then began a long vigil that ended at midnight with Kate barely alive and Sarah Nepple, the Walden mid-wife, trying to divide a scanty wardrobe between a pair of lusty twins.

A New Idea

Kate slowly came back to consciousness. She was conscious of her body, sore from head to foot, with plenty of pain in definite spots. Her first clear thought was that she was such a big woman; it seemed to her that she filled the room, when she was one bruised ache from head to heels. Then she became conscious of a moving bundle on the bed beside her, and laid her hand on it to reassure herself. The size and shape of the bundle were not reassuring.

"Oh, Lord!" groaned Kate. "Haven't You any mercy at all? It was Your advice I followed when I took wing and started out in life."

A big sob arose in her throat, while at the same time she began to laugh weakly. Dr. James heard her from the hall and entered hastily. At the sight of him, Kate's eyes filled with terrified remembrance. Her glance swept the room, and rested on her rocking chair. "Take that out of here!" she cried. "Take it out, split it into kindling wood, and burn it."

"All right," said Dr. James calmly. "I'll guarantee that you never see it again. Is there anything else you want?"

"You – you didn't –?"

The doctor shook his head. "Very sorry," he said, "but there wasn't a thing could be done."

"Where is he?" she asked in a whisper.

"His people took him home immediately after the Coroner's inquest, which found that he died from heart failure, brought on by his long walk in the heat."

Kate stared at him with a face pitiful to behold.

"You let him think *that?*" she whispered again.

"I did," said the old doctor. "I thought, and still think, that for the sake of you and yours," he waved toward the bundle, "it was the only course to pursue."

"Thank you," said Kate. "You're very kind. But don't you think that I and mine are going to take a lot of shielding? The next man may not be so kindly disposed. Besides, is it right? Is it honest?"

"It is for you," said the doctor. "You had nothing to do with it. If you had, things would not have gone as they did. As for me, I feel perfectly comfortable about it in my conscience, which is my best guide. All I had to do was to let them tell their story. I perjured myself only to the extent of testifying that you knew nothing about it. The Coroner could well believe that. George and his mother could easily manage the remainder."

Kate waved toward the bundle: "Am I supposed to welcome and love them?"

"A poet might expect you to," said the doctor. "In the circumstances, I do not. I shall feel that you have done your whole duty if you will try to nurse them when the time comes. You must have a long rest, and they must grow some before you'll discover what they mean to you. There's always as much chance that they'll resemble your people as that they will not. The boy will have dark hair and eyes I think, but he looks exactly like you. The girl is more Holt."

"Where is George?" she asked.

"He was completely upset," said the doctor. "I suggested that he go somewhere to rest up a few days, so he took his tackle and went fishing, and to the farm."

"Shouldn't he have stayed and faced it?" asked Kate.

"There was nothing for him to face, except himself, Kate," said the doctor.

Kate shook her head. She looked ghastly ill.

"Doctor," she said, "couldn't you have let me die?"

"And left your son and your little daughter to them?" he asked. "No, Kate, I couldn't have let you die; because you've your work in the world under your hand right now."

He said that because when he said "left your son and your little daughter to them," Kate had reached over and laid her hand possessively, defensively, on the little, squirming bundle, which was all Dr. James asked of her. Presently she looked the doctor straight in the face. "Exactly what do you know?" she asked.

"Everything," said the doctor. "And you?"

"Everything," said Kate.

There was a long silence. Then Kate spoke slowly: "That George didn't know that he shouldn't have touched that man, proves him completely incompetent," she said. "That he did, and didn't have the courage to face the results, proves him lacking in principle. He's not fit for either work to which he aspires."

"You are talking too much," said the doctor. "Nurse Nepple is in charge here, and Aunt Ollie. George's mother went to the farm to cook for him. You're in the hands of two fine women, who will make you comfortable. You have escaped lasting disgrace with your skirts clear, now rest and be thankful."

"I can't rest until I know one thing," said Kate. "You're not going to allow George to kill any one else?"

"No," said the doctor. "I regretted telling him very much; but I had to tell him *that* could not happen."

"And about the school?" she asked. "I half thought he might get it."

"He *won't!*" said the doctor. "I'm in a position to know that. Now try to take some rest."

Kate waved toward the babies: "Will you please take them away until they need me?" she asked.

"Of course," said the doctor. "But don't you want to see them, Kate? There isn't a mark or blemish on either of them. The boy weighs seven pounds and the girl six; they seem as perfect as children can be."

"You needn't worry about that," said Kate. "Twins are a Bates habit. My mother had three pairs, always a boy and a girl, always big and sound as any children; mine will be all right, too."

The doctor started to turn back the blanket. Kate turned her head away: "Don't you think I have had about enough at present?" she asked. "I'd stake my life that as a little further piece of my punishment, the girl looks exactly like Mrs. Holt."

"By Jove," said the doctor, "I couldn't just think who it was."

He carried the babies from the room, lowered the blinds, and Kate tried to sleep, and did sleep, because she was so exhausted she could not keep awake.

Later in the evening Aunt Ollie slipped in, and said George was in the woodhouse, almost crying himself to death, and begging to see her.

"You tell him I'm too sick to be seen for at least a week," said Kate.

"But, my dear, he's so broken up; he feels so badly," begged Aunt Ollie.

"So do I," said Kate. "I feel entirely too badly to be worried over seeing him. I must take the babies now."

"I do wish you would!" persisted Aunt Ollie.

"Well, I won't," said Kate. "I don't care if I never see him again. He knows *why* he is crying; ask him."

"I'll wager they ain't a word of truth in that tale they're telling," she said.

Kate looked straight at her: "Well, for their sakes and my sake, and the babies' sake, don't *talk* about it."

"You poor thing!" said Aunt Ollie, "I'll do anything in the world to help you. If ever you need me, just call on me. I'll go start him back in a hurry."

He came every night, but Kate steadily refused, until she felt able to sit up in a chair, to see him, or his mother when she came to see the babies. She had recovered rapidly, was over the painful part of nursing the babies, and had a long talk with Aunt Ollie, before she consented to see George. At times she thought she never could see him again; at others, she realized her helplessness. She had her babies to nurse for a year; there was nothing she could think of she knew to do, that she could do, and take proper care of two children. She was tied "hand and foot," as Aunt Ollie said. And yet it was Aunt Ollie who solved her problem for her. Sitting beside the bed one day she said to Kate: "My dear, do you know that I'm having a mighty good time? I guess I was lonesomer than I thought out there all alone so much, and the work was nigh to breaking me during the long, cold winter. I got a big notion to propose somepin' to you that might be a comfort to all of us."

"Propose away," said Kate. "I'm at my wit's end."

"Well, what would you think of you and George taking the land, working it on the shares, and letting me have this room, an' live in Walden, awhile?"

Kate sat straight up in bed: "Oh, Aunt Ollie! Would you?" she cried. "Would you? That would be a mercy to me; it would give George every chance to go straight, if there is a straight impulse in him."

"Yes, I will," said Aunt Ollie, "and you needn't feel that I am getting the little end of the bargain, either. The only unpleasant thing about it will be my sister, and I'll undertake to manage her. I read a lot, an' I can always come to see you when mortal sperrits will bear her no more. She'll be no such trial to me, as she is to you."

"You're an angel," said Kate. "You've given me hope where I had not a glimmer. If I have George out there alone, away from his mother, I can bring out all the good there is in him, and we can get some results out of life, or I can assure myself that it is impossible, so that I can quit with a clear conscience. I do thank you."

"All right, then, I'll go out and begin packing my things, and see about moving this afternoon. I'll leave my stoves, and beds, and tables, and chairs for you; you can use your wedding things, and be downright comfortable. I'll like living in town a spell real well."

So once more Kate saw hope a beckoning star in the distance, and ruffled the wings of the spirit preparatory to another flight: only a short, humble flight this time, close earth; but still as full of promise as life seemed to hold in any direction for her. She greeted George casually, and as if nothing had happened, when she was ready to see him.

"You're at the place where words are not of the slightest use to me," she said. "I'm giving you one, and a final chance to *act*. This seems all that is open to us. Go to work like a man, and we will see what we can make of our last chance."

Kate was so glad when she sat in the carriage that was to take her from the house and the woman she abominated that she could scarcely behave properly. She clasped Adam tightly in her arms, and felt truly his mother. She reached over and tucked the blanket closer over Polly, but she did not carry her, because she resembled her grandmother, while Adam was a Bates.

George drove carefully. He was on behaviour too good to last, but fortunately both women with him knew him well enough not to expect that it would. When they came in sight of the house, Kate could see that the grass beside the road had been cut, the trees trimmed, and Oh, joy, the house freshly painted a soft, creamy white she liked, with a green roof. Aunt Ollie explained that she furnished the paint and George did the work. He had swung oblong clothes baskets from the ceiling of a big, cheery, old-fashioned bedroom for a cradle for each baby, and established himself in a small back room adjoining the kitchen. Kate said nothing about the arrangement, because she supposed it had been made to give her more room, and that George might sleep in peace, while she wrestled with two tiny babies.

There was no doubt about the wrestling. The babies seemed of nervous temperament, sleeping in short naps and lightly. Kate was on her feet from the time she reached her new home, working when she should not have worked; so that the result developed cross babies, each attacked with the colic, which raged every night from six o'clock until twelve and after, both frequently shrieking at the same time. George did his share by going to town for a bottle of soothing syrup, which Kate promptly threw in the creek. Once he took Adam and began walking the floor with him, extending his activities as far as the kitchen. In a few minutes he had the little fellow sound asleep and he did not waken until morning; then he seemed to droop and feel listless. When he took the baby the second time and made the same trip to the kitchen, Kate laid Polly on her bed and silently followed. She saw George lay the baby on the table, draw a flask from his pocket, pour a spoon partly full, filling it the remainder of the way from the teakettle. As he was putting the spoon to the baby's lips, Kate stepped beside him and taking it, she tasted the contents. Then she threw the spoon into the dishpan standing near and picked up the baby.

"I knew it!" she said. "Only I didn't know what. He acted like a drugged baby all last night and to-day. Since when did you begin carrying that stuff around with you, and feeding it to tiny babies?"

"It's a good thing. Dr. James recommended it. He said it was harmful to let them strain themselves crying, and very hard on you. You could save yourself a lot," he urged.

"I need saving all right," said Kate, "but I haven't a picture of myself saving myself by drugging a pair of tiny babies."

He slipped the bottle back in his pocket. Kate stood looking at him so long and so intently, he flushed and set the flask on a shelf in the pantry. "It may come in handy some day when some of us have a cold," he said.

Kate did her best, but she was so weakened by nursing both of the babies, by loss of sleep, and overwork in the house, that she was no help whatever to George in getting in the fall crops and preparing for spring. She had lost none of her ambition, but there was a limit to her capacity.

In the spring the babies were big and lusty, eating her up, and crying with hunger, until she was forced to resort to artificial feeding in part, which did not agree with either of them. As a saving of time and trouble she decided to nurse one and feed the other. It was without thought on her part, almost by chance, yet the chance was that she nursed Adam and fed Polly. Then the babies began teething, so that she was rushed to find time to prepare three regular meals a day, and as for the garden and poultry she had planned, George did what he pleased about them, which was little, if anything.

He would raise so much to keep from being hungry, he would grow so many roots, and so much cabbage for winter, he would tend enough corn for a team and to fatten pork; right there he stopped and went fishing, while the flask was in evidence on the pantry shelf only two days. Kate talked crop rotation, new seed, fertilization, until she was weary; George heartily agreed with her, but put nothing of it all into practice.

"As soon as the babies are old enough to be taken out," she said, "things will be better. I just can't do justice to them and my work, too. Three pairs! My poor mother! And she's alive yet! I marvel at it."

So they lived, and had enough to eat, and were clothed, but not one step did they advance toward Kate's ideals of progression, economy, accumulation. George always had a little money, more than she could see how he got from the farming. There were a few calves and pigs to sell occasionally; she thought possibly he saved his share from them.

For four years, Kate struggled valiantly to keep pace with what her mother always had done, and had required of her at home; but she learned long before she quit struggling that farming with George was hopeless. So at last she became so discouraged she began to drift into his way of doing merely what would sustain them, and then reading, fishing, or sleeping the remainder of the time. She began teaching her children while very small, and daily they had their lessons after dinner, while their father slept.

Kate thought often of what was happening to her; she hated it, she fought it; but with George Holt for a partner she could not escape it. She lay awake nights, planning ways to make a start toward prosperity; she propounded her ideas at breakfast. To save time in getting him early to work she began feeding the horses as soon as she was up, so that George could go to work immediately after breakfast; but she soon found she might as well save her strength. He would not start to harness until he had smoked, mostly three quarters of an hour. That his neighbours laughed at him and got ahead of him bothered him not at all. All they said and all Kate said, went, as he expressed it, "in at one ear, out at the other."

One day in going around the house Kate was suddenly confronted by a thing she might have seen for three years, but had not noticed. Leading from the path of bare, hard-beaten earth that ran around the house through the grass, was a small forking path not so wide and well defined, yet a path, leading to George's window. She stood staring at it a long time with a thoughtful expression on her face.

That night she did not go to bed when she went to her room. Instead she slipped out into the night and sitting under a sheltering bush she watched that window. It was only a short time until George crawled from it, went stealthily to the barn, and a few minutes later she saw him riding barebacked on one of the horses he had bridled, down the footpath beside the stream toward town. She got up and crossing the barnyard shut the gate after him, and closed the barn door. She went back to the house and closed his window and lighting a lamp set it on his dresser in front of his small clock. His door was open in the morning when she passed it on her way to the kitchen, so she got breakfast instead of feeding the horses. He came in slowly, furtively watching her. She worked as usual, saying no unpleasant word. At length he could endure it no longer.

"Kate," he said, "I broke a bolt in the plow yesterday, and I never thought of it until just as I was getting into bed, so to save time I rode in to Walden and got another last night. Ain't I a great old economist, though?"

"You are a great something," she said. "'Economist' would scarcely be my name for it. Really, George, can't you do better than that?"

"Better than what?" he demanded.

"Better than telling such palpable lies," she said. "Better than crawling out windows instead of using your doors like a man; better than being the most shiftless farmer of your neighbourhood in the daytime, because you have spend most of your nights, God and probably all Walden know how. The flask and ready money I never could understand give me an inkling."

"Anything else?" he asked, sneeringly.

"Nothing at present," said Kate placidly. "I probably could find plenty, if I spent even one night in Walden when you thought I was asleep."

"Go if you like," he said. "If you think I'm going to stay here, working like a dog all day, year in and year out, to support a daughter of the richest man in the county and her kids, you fool yourself. If you want more than you got, call on your rich folks for it. If you want to go to town, either night or day, go for all I care. Do what you damn please; that's what I am going to do in the future and I'm glad you know it. I'm tired climbing through windows and slinking like a dog. I'll come and go like other men after this."

"I don't know what other men you are referring to," said Kate. "You have a monopoly of your kind in this neighbourhood; there is none other like you. You crawl and slink as 'to the manner born.'"

"Don't you go too far," he menaced with an ugly leer.

"Keep that for your mother," laughed Kate. "You need never try a threat with me. I am stronger than you are, and you may depend upon it I shall see that my strength never fails me again. I know now that you are all Nancy Ellen said you were."

"Well, if you married me knowing it, what are you going to do about it?" he sneered.

"I didn't know it then. I thought I knew you. I thought she had been misinformed," said Kate, in self-defence.

"Well," he said insultingly, "if you hadn't been in such a big hurry, you could soon have found out all you wanted to know. I took advantage of it, but I never did understand your rush."

"You never will," said Kate.

Then she arose and went to see if the children had wakened. All day she was thinking so deeply she would stumble over the chairs in her preoccupation. George noticed it, and it frightened him. After supper he came and sat on the porch beside her.

"Kate," he said, "as usual you are 'making mountains out of mole hills.' It doesn't damn a fellow forever to ride or walk, I almost always walk, into town in the evening, to see the papers and have a little visit with the boys. Work all day in a field is mighty lonesome; a man has got the have a little change. I don't deny a glass of beer once in awhile, or a game of cards with the boys occasionally; but if you have lived with me over five years here, and never suspected it before, it can't be so desperately bad, can it? Come now, be fair!"

"It's no difference whether I am fair or unfair," Kate said, wearily. "It explains why you simply will not brace up, and be a real man, and do a man's work in the world, and achieve a man's success."

"Who can get anywhere, splitting everything in halves?" he demanded.

"The most successful men in this neighbourhood got their start exactly that way," she said.

"Ah, well, farming ain't my job, anyway," he said. "I always did hate it. I always will. If I could have a little capital to start with, I know a trick that would suit you, and make us independent in no time."

Kate said no word, and seeing she was not going to, he continued: "I've thought about this till I've got it all down fine, and it's a great scheme; you'll admit that, even angry as you are. It is this: get enough together to build a saw mill on my strip of ravine. A little damming would make a free water power worth a fortune. I could hire a good man to run the saw and do the work, and I could take a horse and ride, or drive around among the farmers I know, and buy up timber cheaper than most men could get it. I could just skin the eyes out of them."

"Did it ever occur to you that you could do better by being honest?" asked Kate, wearily.

"Aw, well, Smarty! you know I didn't mean that literally!" he scoffed. "You know I only meant I could talk, and jolly, and buy at bed-rock prices; I know where to get the timber, and the two best mill men in the country; we are near the railroad; it's the dandiest scheme that ever struck Walden. What do you think about it?"

"I think if Adam had it he'd be rich from it in ten years," she said, quietly.

"Then you *do* think it's a bully idea," he cried. "You *would* try it if we had a chance?"

"I might," said Kate.

"You know," he cried, jumping up in excitement, "I've never mentioned this to a soul, but I've got it all thought out. Would you go to see your brother Adam, and see if you could get him to take an interest for young Adam? He could manage the money himself."

"I wouldn't go to a relative of mine for a cent, even if the children were starving," said Kate. "Get, and keep, *that* clear in your head."

"But you think there is something in it?" he persisted.

"I know there is," said Kate with finality. "In the hands of the right man, and with the capital to start."

"Kate, you can be the meanest," he said.

"I didn't intend to be, in this particular instance," she said. "But honestly, George, what have I ever seen of you in the way of financial success in the past that would give me hope for the future?"

"I know it," he said, "but I've never struck exactly the right thing. This is what I could make a success of, and I would make a good big one, you bet! Kate, I'll not go to town another night. I'll stop all that." He drew the flask from his pocket and smashed it against the closest tree. "And I'll stop all there ever was of that, even to a glass of beer on a hot day; if you say so, if you'll stand by me this once more, if I fail this time, I'll never ask you again; honest, I won't."

"If I had money, I'd try it, keeping the building in my own name and keeping the books myself; but I've none, and no way to get any, as you know," she said. "I can see what could be done, but I'm helpless."

"*I'm not!*" said George. "I've got it all worked out. You see I was doing something useful with my head, if I wasn't always plowing as fast as you thought I should. If you'll back me, if you'll keep books, if you'll handle the money until she is paid back, I know Aunt Ollie will sell enough of this land to build the mill and buy the machinery. She could keep the house, and orchard, and barn, and a big enough piece, say forty acres, to live on and keep all of us in grub. She and Mother could move out here – she said the other day she was tired of town and getting homesick – and we could go to town to put the children in school, and be on the job. I won't ever ask you and Mother to live together again. Kate, will you go in with me? Will you talk to Aunt Ollie? Will you let me show you, and explain, and prove to you?"

"I won't be a party to anything that would even remotely threaten to lose Aunt Ollie's money for her," she said.

"She's got nobody on earth but me. It's all mine in the end. Why not let me have this wonderful chance with it? Kate, will you?" he begged.

"I'll think about it," she conceded. "If I can study out a sure, honourable way. I'll promise to think. Now go out there, and hunt the last scrap of that glass; the children may cut their feet in the morning."

Then Kate went in to bed. If she had looked from her window, she might have seen George scratching matches and picking pieces of glass from the grass. When he came to the bottom of the bottle with upstanding, jagged edges, containing a few drops, he glanced at her room, saw that she was undressing in the dark, and lifting it, he poured the liquid on his tongue to the last drop that would fall.

The Work of the Sun

Before Kate awakened the following morning George was out feeding the horses, cattle, and chickens, doing the milking, and working like the proverbial beaver. By the time breakfast was ready, he had convinced himself that he was a very exemplary man, while he expected Kate to be convinced also. He stood ready and willing to forgive her for every mean deceit and secret sin he ever had committed, or had it in his heart to commit in the future. All the world was rosy with him, he was flying with the wings of hope straight toward a wonderful achievement that would bring pleasure and riches, first to George Holt, then to his wife and children, then to the old aunt he really cared more for than any one else.

Incidentally, his mother might have some share, while he would bring such prosperity and activity to the village that all Walden would forget every bad thing it had ever thought or known of him, and delight to pay him honour. Kate might have guessed all this when she saw the pails full of milk on the table, and heard George whistling "Hail the Conquering Hero Comes," as he turned the cows into the pasture; but she had not slept well. Most of the night she had lain staring at the ceiling, her brain busy with calculations, computations, most of all with personal values.

She dared not be a party to anything that would lose Aunt Ollie her land; that was settled; but if she went into the venture herself, if she kept the deeds in Aunt Ollie's name, the bank account in hers, drew all the checks, kept the books, would it be safe? Could George buy timber as he thought; could she, herself, if he failed? The children were old enough to be in school now, she could have much of the day, she could soon train Polly and Adam to do even more than sweep and run errands; the scheme could be materialized in the Bates way, without a doubt; but could it be done in a Bates way, hampered and impeded by George Holt? Was the plan feasible, after all? She entered into the rosy cloud enveloping the kitchen without ever catching the faintest gleam of its hue. George came to her the instant he saw her and tried to put his arm around her. Kate drew back and looked at him intently.

"Aw, come on now, Kate," he said. "Leave out the heroics and be human. I'll do exactly as you say about everything if you will help me wheedle Aunt Ollie into letting me have the money."

Kate stepped back and put out her hands defensively: "A rare bargain," she said, "and one eminently worthy of you. You'll do what I say, if I'll do what you say, without the slightest reference as to whether it impoverishes a woman who has always helped and befriended you. You make me sick!"

"What's biting you now?" he demanded, sullenly.

Kate stood tall and straight before and above him

"If you have a good plan, if you can prove that it will work, what is the necessity for 'wheedling' anybody? Why not state what you propose in plain, unequivocal terms, and let the dear, old soul, who has done so much for us already, decide what she will do?"

"That's what I meant! That's all I meant!" he cried.

"In that case, 'wheedle' is a queer word to use."

"I believe you'd throw up the whole thing; I believe you'd let the chance to be a rich woman slip through your fingers, if it all depended on your saying only one word you thought wasn't quite straight," he cried, half in assertion, half in question.

"I honour you in that belief," said Kate. "I most certainly would."

"Then you turn the whole thing down? You won't have anything to do with it?" he cried, plunging into stoop-shouldered, mouth- sagging despair.

"Oh, I didn't *say* that!" said Kate. "Give me time! Let me think! I've got to know that there isn't a snare in it, from the title of the land to the grade of the creek bed. Have you investigated that? Is your ravine long enough and wide enough to dam it high enough at our outlet to get your power, and yet not back water on the road, and the farmers above you? Won't it freeze in winter? and can you get strong enough power from water to run a large saw? I doubt it!"

"Oh, gee! I never thought about that!" he cried.

"And if it would work, did you figure the cost of a dam into your estimate of the building and machinery?"

He snapped his fingers in impatience.

"By heck!" he cried, "I forgot *that*, too! But that wouldn't cost much. Look what we did in that ravine just for fun. Why, we could build that dam ourselves!"

"Yes, strong enough for conditions in September, but what about the January freshet?" she said.

"Croak! Croak! You blame old raven," cried George.

"And have you thought," continued Kate, "that there is no room on the bank toward town to set your mill, and it wouldn't be allowed there, if there were?"

"You bet I have!" he said defiantly. "I'm no such slouch as you think me. I've even stepped off the location!"

"Then," said Kate, "will you build a bridge across the ravine to reach it, or will you buy a strip from Linn and build a road?"

George collapsed with a groan.

"That's the trouble with you," said Kate. "You always build your castle with not even sand for a foundation. The most nebulous of rosy clouds serve you as perfectly as granite blocks. Before you go glimmering again, double your estimate to cover a dam and a bridge, and a lot of incidentals that no one ever seems able to include in a building contract. And whatever you do, keep a still head until we get these things figured, and have some sane idea of what the venture would cost."

"How long will it take?" he said sullenly.

"I haven't an idea. I'd have to go the Hartley and examine the records and be sure that there was no flaw in the deeds to the land; but the first thing is to get a surveyor and know for sure if you have a water-power that will work and not infringe on your neighbours. A thing like this can't be done in a few minutes' persuasive conversation. It will take weeks."

It really seemed as if it would take months. Kate went to Walden that afternoon, set the children playing in the ravine while she sketched it, made the best estimate she could of its fall, and approved the curve on the opposite bank which George thought could be cleared for a building site and lumber yard. Then she added a location for a dam and a bridge site, and went home to figure and think. The further she went in these processes the more hopeless the project seemed. She soon learned that there must be an engine with a boiler to run the saw. The dam could be used only to make a pond to furnish the water needed; but at that it would be cheaper than to dig a cistern or well. She would not even suggest to Aunt Ollie to sell any of the home forty. The sale of the remainder at the most hopeful price she dared estimate would not bring half the money needed, and it would come in long-time payments. Lumber, bricks, machinery, could not be had on time of any length, while wages were cash every Saturday night.

"It simply can't be done," said Kate, and stopped thinking about it, so far as George knew.

He was at once plunged into morose moping; he became sullen and indifferent about the work, ugly with Kate and the children, until she was driven almost frantic, and projects nearly as vague as some of George's began to float through her head.

One Saturday morning Kate had risen early and finished cleaning up her house, baking, and scrubbing porches. She had taken a bath to freshen and cool herself and was standing before her dresser, tucking the last pins in her hair, when she heard a heavy step on the porch and a loud knock on the screen door. She stood at an angle where she could peep; she looked as she reached for her dress. What she saw carried her to the door forgetful of the dress. Adam, Jr., stood there, white and shaken, steadying himself against the casing.

"Adam!" cried Kate. "Is Mother –?"

He shook his head.

"Father –?" she panted.

He nodded, seeming unable to speak. Kate's eyes darkened and widened. She gave Adam another glance and opened the door. "Come in," she said. "When did it happen? How did he get hurt?"

In that moment she recalled that she had left her father in perfect health, she had been gone more than seven years. In that time he could not fail to illness; how he had been hurt was her first thought. As she asked the question, she stepped into her room and snatched up her second best summer dress, waiting for Adam to speak as she slipped into it. But speaking seemed to be a very difficult thing for Adam. He was slow in starting and words dragged and came singly: "Yesterday – tired – big dinner – awful hot – sunstroke–"

"He's gone?" she cried.

Adam nodded in that queer way again.

"Why did you come? Does Mother want me?" the questions leaped from Kate's lips; her eyes implored him. Adam was too stricken to heed his sister's unspoken plea.

"Course," he said. "All there – your place – I want you. Only one in the family – not stark mad!"

Kate straightened tensely and looked at him again. "All right," she said. "I can throw a few things in my telescope, write the children a note to take to their father in the field, and we can stop in Walden and send Aunt Ollie out to cook for them; I can go as well as not, for as long as Mother wants me."

"Hurry!" said Adam.

In her room Kate stood still a second, her eyes narrow, her underlip sucked in, her heart almost stopped. Then she said aloud: "Father's sons have wished he would die too long for his death to strike even the most tolerant of them like that. Something dreadful has happened. I wonder to my soul – !"

She waited until they were past Hartley and then she asked suddenly: "Adam, what is the matter?"

Then Adam spoke: "I am one of a pack of seven poor fools, and every other girl in the family has gone raving mad, so I thought I'd come after you, and see if you had sense, or reason, or justice, left in you."

"What do you want of me?" she asked dazedly.

"I want you to be fair, to be honest, to do as you'd be done by. You came to me when you were in trouble," he reminded her.

Kate could not prevent the short laugh that sprang to her lips, nor what she said: "And you would not lift a finger; young Adam *made* his *mother* help me. Why don't you go to George for what you want?"

Adam lost all self-control and swore sulphurously.

"I thought you'd be different," he said, "but I see you are going to be just like the rest of the –!"

"Stop that!" said Kate. "You're talking about my sisters – and yours. Stop this wild talk, and tell me exactly what is the matter."

"I'm telling nothing," said Adam. "You can find out what is the matter and go it with the rest of them, when you get there. Mother said this morning she wished you were there, because you'd be the only *sane* one in the family, so I thought I'd bring you; but I wish now I hadn't done it, for it stands to reason that you will join the pack, and run as fast as the rest of the wolves."

"*From* a prairie fire, or *to* a carcass?" asked Kate.

"I told you, you could find out when you got there. I'm not going to have them saying I influenced you, or bribed you," he said.

"Do you really think that they think you could, Adam?" asked Kate, wonderingly.

"I have said all I'm going to say," said Adam, and then he began driving his horse inhumanely fast, for the heat was deep, slow, and burning.

"Adam, is there any such hurry?" asked Kate. "You know you are abusing your horse dreadfully."

Adam immediately jerked the horse with all his might, and slashed the length of its body with two long stripes that rapidly raised in high welts, so Kate saw that he was past reasoning with and said no other word. She tried to think who would be at home, how they would treat her, the Prodigal, who had not been there in seven years; and suddenly it occurred to Kate that, if she had known all she now knew in her youth, and had the same decision to make again as when she knew nothing, she would have taken wing, just as she had. She had made failures, she had hurt herself, mind and body, but her honour, her self-respect were intact. Suddenly she sat straight. She was glad that she had taken a bath, worn a reasonably decent dress, and had a better one in the back of the buggy. She would cut the Gordian knot with a vengeance. She would not wait to see how they treated her, she would treat them! As for Adam's state, there was only one surmise she could make, and that seemed so incredible, she decided to wait until her mother told her all about whatever the trouble was.

As they came in sight of the house, queer feelings took possession of Kate. She struggled to think kindly of her father; she tried to feel pangs of grief over his passing. She was too forthright and had too good memory to succeed. Home had been so unbearable that she had taken desperate measures to escape it, but as the white house with its tree and shrub filled yard could be seen more plainly, Kate suddenly was filled with the strongest possessive feeling she ever had known. It was home. It was her home. Her place was there, even as Adam had said. She felt a sudden revulsion against herself that she had stayed away seven years; she should have taken her chances and at least gone to see her mother. She leaned from the buggy and watched for the first glimpse of the tall, gaunt, dark woman, who had brought their big brood into the world and stood squarely with her husband, against every one of them, in each thing he proposed.

Now he was gone. No doubt he had carried out his intentions. No doubt she was standing by him as always. Kate gathered her skirts, but Adam passed the house, driving furiously as ever, and he only slackened speed when he was forced to at the turn from the road to the lane. He stopped the buggy in the barnyard, got out, and began unharnessing the horse. Kate sat still and watched him until he led it away, then she stepped down and started across the barnyard, down the lane leading to the dooryard. As she closed the yard gate and rounded a widely spreading snowball bush, her heart was pounding wildly. What was coming? How would the other boys act, if Adam, the best balanced man of them all, was behaving as he was? How would her mother greet her? With the thought, Kate realized that she was so homesick for her mother that she would do or give anything in the world to see her. Then there was a dragging step, a short, sharp breath, and wheeling, Kate stood facing her mother. She had come from the potato patch back of the orchard, carrying a pail of potatoes in each hand. Her face was haggard, her eyes bloodshot, her hair falling in dark tags, her cheeks red with exertion. They stood facing each other. At the first glimpse Kate cried,

"Oh, Mother," and sprang toward her. Then she stopped, while her heart again failed her, for from the astonishment on her mother's face, Kate saw instantly that she was surprised, and had neither sent for nor expected her. She was nauseatingly disappointed. Adam had said she was wanted, had been sent for. Kate's face was twitching, her lips quivering, but she did not hesitate more than an instant.

"I see you were not expecting me," she said. "I'm sorry. Adam came after me. I wouldn't have come if he hadn't said you sent for me."

Kate paused a minute hopefully. Her mother looked at her steadily.

"I'm sorry," Kate repeated. "I don't know why he said that."

By that time the pain in her heart was so fierce she caught her breath sharply, and pressed her hand hard against her side. Her mother stooped, set down the buckets, and taking off her sunbonnet, wiped the sweat from her lined face with the curtain.

"Well, I do," she said tersely.

"Why?" demanded Kate.

"To see if he could use you to serve his own interests, of course," answered her mother. "He lied good and hard when he said I sent for you; I didn't. I probably wouldn't a-had the sense to do it. But since you are here, I don't mind telling you that I never was so glad to see any one in all my born days."

Mrs. Bates drew herself full height, set her lips, stiffened her jaw, and again used the bonnet skirt on her face and neck. Kate picked up the potatoes, to hide the big tears that gushed from her eyes, and leading the way toward the house she said: "Come over here in the shade. Why should you be out digging potatoes?"

"Oh, they's enough here, and willing enough," said Mrs. Bates. "Slipped off to get away from them. It was the quietest and the peacefullest out there, Kate. I'd most liked to stay all day, but it's getting on to dinner time, and I'm short of potatoes."

"Never mind the potatoes," said Kate. "Let the folks serve themselves if they are hungry."

She went to the side of the smoke house, picked up a bench turned up there, and carrying it to the shady side of a widely spreading privet bush, she placed it where it would be best screened from both house and barn. Then setting the potatoes in the shade, she went to her mother, put her arm around her, and drew her to the seat. She took her handkerchief and wiped her face, smoothed back her straggled hair, and pulling out a pin, fastened the coil better.

"Now rest a bit," she said, "and then tell me why you are glad to see me, and exactly what you'd like me to do here. Mind, I've been away seven years, and Adam told me not a word, except that Father was gone."

"Humph! All missed the mark again," commented Mrs. Bates dryly. "They all said he'd gone to fill you up, and get you on his side."

"Mother, what is the trouble?" asked Kate. "Take your time and tell me what has happened, and what *you* want, not what Adam wants."

Mrs. Bates relaxed her body a trifle, but gripped her hands tightly together in her lap.

"Well, it was quick work," she said. "It all came yesterday afternoon just like being hit by lightning. Pa hadn't failed a particle that any one could see. Ate a big dinner of ham an' boiled dumplings, an' him an' Hiram was in the west field. It was scorchin' hot an' first Hiram saw, Pa was down. Sam Langley was passin' an' helped get him in, an' took our horse an' ran for Robert. He was in the country but Sam brought another doctor real quick, an' he seemed to fetch Pa out of it in good shape, so we thought he'd be all right, mebby by morning, though the doctor said he'd have to hole up a day or two. He went away, promisin' to send Robert back, and Hiram went home to feed. I set by Pa fanning him an' putting cloths on his head. All at once he began to chill.

"We thought it was only the way a-body was with sunstroke, and past pilin' on blankets, we didn't pay much attention. He *said* he was all right, so I went to milk. Before I left I gave him a drink, an' he asked me to feel in his pants pocket an' get the key an' hand him the deed box, till he'd see if everything was right. Said he guessed he'd had a close call. You know how he was. I got him the box and went to do the evening work. I hurried fast as I could. Coming back, clear acrost the yard I smelt burning wool, an' I dropped the milk an' ran. I dunno no more about just what happened 'an you do. The house was full of smoke. Pa was on the floor, most to the sitting-room door, his head and hair and hands awfully burned, his shirt burned off, laying face down, and clear gone. The minute I seen the way he laid, I knew he was gone. The bed was pourin' smoke and one little blaze about six inches high was shootin' up to the top. I got that out, and then I saw most of the fire was smothered between the blankets where he'd thrown them back to get out of the bed. I dunno why he fooled with the lamp. It always stood on the little table in his reach, but it was light enough to read fine print. All I can figure is that the light was going out of his *eyes*, an' he thought *it was gettin' dark*, so he tried to light the lamp to see the deeds. He was fingerin' them when I left, but he didn't say he couldn't see them. The lamp was just on the bare edge of the table, the wick way up an' blackened, the chimney smashed on the floor, the bed afire."

"Those deeds are burned?" gasped Kate. "All of them? Are they all gone?"

"Every last one," said Mrs. Bates.

"Well, if *one* is gone, thank God they all are," said Kate.

Her mother turned swiftly and caught her arm.

"Say that again!" she cried eagerly.

"Maybe I'm *wrong* about it, but it's what I think," said Kate. "If the boys are crazy over all of them being gone, they'd do murder if part had theirs, and the others had not."

Mrs. Bates doubled over on Kate's shoulder suddenly and struggled with an inward spasm.

"You poor thing," said Kate. "This is dreadful. All of us know how you loved him, how you worked together. Can you think of anything I can do? Is there any special thing the matter?"

"I'm afraid!" whispered Mrs. Bates. "Oh, Katie, I'm so afraid. You know how *set* he was, you know how he worked himself and all of us – he had to know what he was doing, when he fought the fire till the shirt burned off him" – her voice dropped to a harsh whisper – "what do you s'pose he's doing now?"

Any form of religious belief was a subject that never had been touched upon or talked of in the Bates family. Money was their God, work their religion; Kate looked at her mother curiously.

"You mean you believe in after life?" she asked.

"Why, I suppose there must be *something*," she said.

"I think so myself," said Kate. "I always have. I think there is a God, and that Father is facing Him now, and finding out for the first time in his experience that he is very small potatoes, and what he planned and slaved for amounted to nothing, in the scheme of the universe. I can't imagine Father being subdued by anything on earth, but it appeals to me that he will cut a pathetic figure before the throne of an Almighty God."

A slow grin twisted Mrs. Bates' lips.

"Well, wherever he went," she said, "I guess he found out pretty quick that he was some place at last where he couldn't be boss."

"I'm very sure he has," said Kate, "and I am equally sure the discipline will be good for him. But his sons! His precious sons! What are they doing?"

"Taking it according to their bent," said Mrs. Bates. "Adam is insane, Hiram is crying."

"Have you had a lawyer?" asked Kate.

"What for? We all know the law on this subject better than we know our a, b, c's."

"Did your deed for this place go, too?" asked Kate.

"Yes," said Mrs. Bates, "but mine was recorded, none of the others were. I get a third, and the rest will be cut up and divided, share and share alike, among *all of you*, equally. I think it's going to kill Adam and ruin Andrew."

"It won't do either. But this is awful. I can see how the boys feel, and really, Mother, this is no more fair to them than things always have been for the girls. By the way, what are they doing?"

"Same as the boys, acting out their natures. Mary is openly rejoicing. So is Nancy Ellen. Hannah and Bertha at least can see the boys' side. The others say one thing before the boys and another among themselves. In the end the girls will have their shares and nobody can blame them. I don't myself, but I think Pa will rise from his grave when those farms are torn up."

"Don't worry," said Kate. "He will have learned by now that graves are merely incidental, and that he has no option on real estate where he is. Leave him to his harp, and tell me what you want done."

"I want you to see that it was all accidental. I want you to take care of me. I want you should think out the *fair* thing for all of us to *do*. I want you to keep sane and cool-headed and shame the others into behaving themselves. And I want you to smash down hard on their everlasting, 'why didn't you do this?' and 'why didn't you do that?' I reckon I've been told five hundred times a-ready that I shouldn't a-give him the deeds. Josie say it, an' then she sings it. *Not give them to him*! How could I help giving them to him? He'd a-got up and got them himself if I hadn't–"

"You have cut out something of a job for me," said Kate, "but I'll do my best. Anyway, I can take care of you. Come on into the house now, and let me clean you up, and then I'll talk the rest of them into reason, if you stand back of me, and let them see I'm acting for you."

"You go ahead," said Mrs. Bates. "I'll back whatever you say. But keep them off of me! Keep them off of me!"

After Kate had bathed her mother, helped her into fresh clothes, and brushed her hair, she coaxed her to lie down, and by diplomatic talk and stroking her head, finally soothed her to sleep. Then she went down and announced the fact, asked them all to be quiet, and began making her way from group to group in an effort to restore mental balance and sanity. After Kate had invited all of them to go home and stay until time for the funeral Sunday morning, and all of them had emphatically declined, and eagerly had gone on straining the situation to the breaking point, Kate gave up and began setting the table. When any of them tried to talk or argue with her she said conclusively: "I shall not say one word about this until Monday. Then we will talk things over, and find where we stand, and what Mother wants. This would be much easier for all of us, if you'd all go home and calm down, and plan out what you think would be the fair and just thing to do."

Before evening Kate was back exactly where she left off, for when Mrs. Bates came downstairs, her nerves quieted by her long sleep, she asked Kate what would be best about each question that arose, while Kate answered as nearly for all of them as her judgment and common sense dictated; but she gave the answer in her own way, and she paved the way by making a short, sharp speech when the first person said in her hearing that "Mother never should have given him the deeds." Not one of them said that again, while at Kate's suggestion, mentally and on scraps of paper, every single one of them figured that one third of sixteen hundred and fifty was five hundred and fifty; subtracted from sixteen hundred and fifty this left one thousand one hundred, which, divided by sixteen, gave sixty-eight and three fourths. This result gave Josie the hysterics, strong and capable though she was; made Hiram violently ill, so that he resorted to garden palings for a support; while Agatha used her influence suddenly, and took Adam, Jr., home.

As she came to Kate to say that they were going, Agatha was white as possible, her thin lips compressed, a red spot burning on either cheek.

"Adam and I shall take our departure now, Katherine," she said, standing very stiffly, her head held higher than Kate ever had thought it could be lifted. Kate put her arm around her sister-in-law and gave her a hearty hug: "Tell Adam I'll do what I think is fair and just; and use all the influence I have to get the others to do the same," she said.

"Fruitless!" said Agatha. "Fruitless! Reason and justice have departed from this abode. I shall hasten my pace, and take Adam where my influence is paramount. The state of affairs here is deplorable, perfectly deplorable! I shall not be missed, and I shall leave my male offspring to take the place of his poor, defrauded father."

Adam, 3d, was now a tall, handsome young man of twenty-two, quite as fond of Kate as ever. He wiped the dishes, and when the evening work was finished, they talked with Mrs. Bates until they knew her every wish. The children had planned for a funeral from the church, because it was large enough to seat the family and friends in comfort; but when they mentioned this to Mrs. Bates, she delivered an ultimatum on the instant: "You'll do no such thing!" she cried. "Pa never went to that church living; I'll not sanction his being carried there feet first, when he's helpless. And we'll not scandalize the neighbours by fighting over money on Sunday, either. You'll all come Monday morning, if you want anything to say about this. If you don't, I'll put through the business in short order. I'm sick to my soul of the whole thing. I'll wash my hands of it as quick as possible."

So the families all went to their homes; Kate helped her mother to bed; and then she and Adam, 3d, tried to plan what would be best for the morrow; afterward they sat down and figured until almost dawn.

"There's no faintest possibility of pleasing everyone," said Kate. "The level best we can do is to devise some scheme whereby everyone will come as nearly being satisfied as possible."

"Can Aunt Josie and Aunt Mary keep from fighting across the grave?" asked Adam.

"Only Heaven knows," said Kate.

The Banner Hand

Sunday morning Kate arose early and had the house clean and everything ready when the first carriage load drove into the barnyard. As she helped her mother to dress, Mrs. Bates again evidenced a rebellious spirit. Nancy Ellen had slipped upstairs and sewed fine white ruching in the neck and sleeves of her mother's best dress, her only dress, in fact, aside from the calicoes she worked in. Kate combed her mother's hair and drew it in loose waves across her temples. As she produced the dress, Mrs. Bates drew back.

"What did you stick them gew-gaws onto my dress for?" she demanded.

"I didn't," said Kate.

"Oh, it was Nancy Ellen! Well, I don't see why she wanted to make a laughing stock of me," said Mrs. Bates.

"She didn't!" said Kate. "Everyone is wearing ruching now; she wanted her mother to have what the best of them have."

"Humph!" said Mrs. Bates. "Well, I reckon I can stand it until noon, but it's going to be a hot dose."

"Haven't you a thin black dress, Mother?" asked Kate.

"No," said Mrs. Bates, "I haven't; but you can make a pretty safe bet that I will have one before I start anywhere again in such weather as this."

"That's the proper spirit," said Kate. "There comes Andrew. Let me put your bonnet on."

She set the fine black bonnet Nancy Ellen had bought on Mrs. Bates' head at the proper angle and tied the long, wide silk ribbon beneath her chin. Mrs. Bates sat in martyr-like resignation. Kate was pleased with her mother's appearance.

"Look in the mirror," she said. "See what a handsome lady you are."

"I ain't seen in a looking-glass since I don't know when," said Mrs. Bates. "Why should I begin now? Chances are 'at you have rigged me up until I'll set the neighbours laughing, or else to saying that I didn't wait until the breath was out of Pa's body to begin primping."

"Nonsense, Mother," said Kate. "Nobody will say or think anything. Everyone will recognize Nancy Ellen's fine Spencerian hand in that bonnet and ruching. Now for your veil!"

Mrs. Bates arose from her chair, and stepped back.

"There, there, Katie!" she said. "You've gone far enough. I'll be sweat to a lather in this dress; I'll wear the head-riggin', because I've go to, or set the neighbours talkin' how mean Pa was not to let me have a bonnet; and between the two I'd rather they'd take it out on me than on him." She steadied herself by the chair back and looked Kate in the eyes. "Pa was always the banner hand to boss everything," she said. "He was so big and strong, and so all-fired sure he was right, I never contraried him in the start, so before I knowed it, I was waiting for him to say what to do, and then agreeing with him, even when I knowed he was *wrong.* So goin' we got along *fine,* but it give me an awful smothered feeling at times."

Kate stood looking at her mother intently, her brain racing, for she was thinking to herself: "Good Lord! She means that to preserve the appearance of self-respect she systematically agreed with him, whether she thought he was right or wrong; because she was not able to hold her own against him. Nearly fifty years of life like that!"

Kate tossed the heavy black crepe veil back on the bed. "Mother," she said, "here alone, and between us, if I promise never to tell a living soul, will you tell me the truth about that deed business?" Mrs. Bates seemed so agitated Kate added: "I mean how it started. If you thought it was right and a fair thing to do."

"Yes, I'll tell you that," said Mrs. Bates. "It was not fair, and I saw it; I saw it good and plenty. There was no use to fight him; that would only a-drove him to record them, but I was sick of it, an' I told him so."

Kate was pinning her hat.

"I have planned for you to walk with Adam," she said.

"Well, you can just change *that* plan, so far as I am concerned," said Mrs. Bates with finality. "I ain't a-goin' with Adam. Somebody had told him about the deeds before he got here. He came in ravin', and he talked to me something terrible. He was the first to say I shouldn't a-give Pa the box. *Not give it to him!* An' he went farther than that, till I just rose up an' called him down proper; but I ain't feelin' good at him, an' I ain't goin' with him. I am goin' with you. I want somebody with me that understands me, and feels a little for me, an' I want the neighbours to see that the minute I'm boss, such a fine girl as you has her rightful place in her home. I'll go with you, or I'll sit down on this chair, and sit here."

"But you didn't send for me," said Kate.

"No, I hadn't quite got round to it yet; but I was coming. I'd told all of them that you were the only one in the lot who had any sense; and I'd said I *wished* you were here, and as I see it, I'd a-sent for you yesterday afternoon about three o'clock. I was coming to it fast. I didn't feel just like standing up for myself; but I'd took about all fault-finding it was in me to bear. Just about three o'clock I'd a-sent for you, Katie, sure as God made little apples."

"All right then," said Kate, "but if you don't tell them, they'll always say I took the lead."

"Well, they got to say something," said Mrs. Bates. "Most of 'em would die if they had to keep their mouths shut awhile; but I'll tell them fast enough."

Then she led the way downstairs. There were enough members of the immediate family to pack the front rooms of the house, the neighbours filled the dining room and dooryard. The church choir sang a hymn in front of the house, the minister stood on the front steps and read a chapter, and told where Mr. Bates had been born, married, the size of his family and possessions, said he was a good father, an honest neighbour, and very sensibly left his future with his God. Then the choir sang again and all started to their conveyances. As the breaking up began outside, Mrs. Bates arose and stepped to the foot of the casket. She steadied herself by it and said: "Some time back, I promised Pa that if he went before I did, at this time in his funeral ceremony I would set his black tin box on the foot of his coffin and unlock before all of you, and in the order in which they lay, beginning with Adam, Jr., hand each of you boys the deed Pa had made you for the land you live on. You all know *what* happened. None of you know just *how*. It wouldn't bring the deeds *back* if you did. They're gone. But I want you boys to follow your father to his grave with nothing in your hearts against *him*. He was all for the men. I don't ever want to hear any of you criticize him about this, or me, either. He did his best to make you upstanding men in your community, his one failing being that he liked being an upstanding man himself so well that he carried it too far; but his intentions was the best. As for me, I'd no idea how sick he was, and nobody else did. I minded him just like all the rest of you always did; the *boys* especially. From the church I want all of you to go home until to-morrow morning, and then I want my sons and daughters by *Birth* only, to come here, and we'll talk things over, quietly, *quietly*, mind you; and decide what to do. Katie, will you come with me?"

It was not quite a tearless funeral. Some of the daughters-in-law wept from nervous excitement; and some of the little children cried with fear, but there were no tears from the wife of Adam Bates, or his sons and daughters. And when he was left to the mercies of time, all of them followed Mrs. Bates' orders, except Nancy Ellen and Robert, who stopped to help Kate with the dinner. Kate slipped into her second dress and went to work. Mrs. Bates untied her bonnet strings and unfastened her dress neck as they started home. She unbuttoned her waist going up the back walk and pulled it off at the door.

"Well, if I ever put that thing on in July again," she said, "you can use my head for a knock-maul. Nancy Ellen, can't you stop at a store as you come out in the morning and get the goods, and you girls run me up a dress that is nice enough to go out in, and not so hot it starts me burning before my time?"

"Of course I can," said Nancy Ellen. "About what do you want to pay, Mother?"

"Whatever it takes to get a decent and a cool dress; cool, mind you," said Mrs. Bates, "an' any colour but black."

"Why, Mother!" cried Nancy Ellen "it must be black!"

"No," said Mrs. Bates. "Pa kept me in black all my life on the supposition it showed the dirt the least. There's nothing in that. It shows dirt worse 'an white. I got my fill of black. You can get a nice cool gray, if you want me to wear it."

"Well, I never!" said Nancy Ellen. "What will the neighbours say?"

"What do I care?" asked Mrs. Bates. "They've talked about me all my life, I'd be kinda lonesome if they's to quit."

Dinner over, Kate proposed that her mother should lie down while they washed the dishes.

"I would like a little rest," said Mrs. Bates. "I guess I'll go upstairs."

"You'll do nothing of the kind," said Kate. "It's dreadfully hot up there. Go in the spare room, where it is cool; we'll keep quiet. I am going to stay Tuesday until I move you in there, anyway. It's smaller, but it's big enough for one, and you'll feel much better there."

"Oh, Katie, I'm so glad you thought of that," cried Mrs. Bates. "I been thinking and thinking about it, and it just seems as if I can't ever steel myself to go into that room to sleep again. I'll never enter that door that I don't see–"

"You'll never enter it again as your room," said Kate. "I'll fix you up before I go; and Sally Whistler told me last evening she would come and make her home with you if you wanted her. You like Sally, don't you?"

"Yes, I like her fine," said Mrs. Bates.

Quietly as possible the girls washed the dishes, pulled down the blinds, closed the front door, and slipped down in the orchard with Robert to talk things over. Nancy Ellen was stiffly reserved with Kate, but she *would* speak when she was spoken to, which was so much better than silence that Kate was happy over it. Robert was himself. Kate thought she had never liked him so well. He seemed to grow even kinder and more considerate as the years passed. Nancy Ellen was prettier than Kate ever had seen her, but there was a line of discontent around her mouth, and she spoke pettishly on slight provocation, or none at all. Now she was openly, brazenly, brutally, frank in her rejoicing. She thought it was the best "*joke*" that ever happened to the boys; and she said so repeatedly. Kate found her lips closing more tightly and a slight feeling of revulsion growing in her heart. Surely in Nancy Ellen's lovely home, cared for and shielded in every way, she had no such need of money as Kate had herself. She was delighted when Nancy Ellen said she was sleepy, and was going to the living-room lounge for a nap. Then Kate produced her sheet of figures. She and Robert talked the situation over and carefully figured on how an adjustment, fair to all, could be made, until they were called to supper.

After supper Nancy Ellen and Robert went home, while Kate and her mother sat on the back porch and talked until Kate had a clear understanding and a definite plan in her mind, which was that much improvement over wearing herself out in bitter revilings, or selfish rejoicing over her brothers' misfortune. Her mother listened to all she had to say, asked a question occasionally, objected to some things, and suggested others. They arose when they had covered every contingency they could think of and went upstairs to bed, even though the downstairs was cooler.

As she undressed, Mrs. Bates said slowly: "Now in the morning, I'll speak my piece first; and I'll say it pretty plain. I got the whip-hand here for once in my life. They can't rave and fight here, and insult me again, as they did Friday night and Saturday till you got here an' shut 'em up. I won't stand it, that's flat! I'll tell 'em so, and that you speak for me, because you can figure faster and express yourself plainer; but insist that there be no fussing, an' I'll back you. I don't know just what life has been doing to you, Katie, but Lord! it has made a fine woman of you."

Kate set her lips in an even line and said nothing, but her heart was the gladdest it had been in years.

Her mother continued: "Seems like Nancy Ellen had all the chance. Most folks thought she was a lot the purtiest to start with, though I can't say that I ever saw so much difference. She's had leisure an' pettin', and her husband has made a mint o' money; she's gone all over the country with him, and the more chance she has, the narrower she grows, and the more discontenteder. One thing, she is awful disappointed about havin' no children. I pity her about that."

"Is it because she's a twin?" asked Kate.

"I'm afraid so," said Mrs. Bates. "You can't tell much about those things, they just seem to happen. Robert and Nancy Ellen feel awful bad about it. Still, she might do for others what she would for her own. The Lord knows there are enough mighty nice children in the world who need mothering. I want to see your children, Katie. Are they nice little folks, straight and good looking?"

"The boy is," said Kate. "The girl is good, with the exception of being the most stubborn child I've ever seen. She looks so much like a woman it almost sickens me to think of that I have to drive myself to do her justice."

"What a pity!" said Mrs. Bates, slowly.

"Oh, they are healthy, happy youngsters," said Kate. "They get as much as we ever did, and don't expect any more. I have yet to see a demonstrative Bates."

"Humph!" said Mrs. Bates. "Well, you ought to been here Friday night, and I thought Adam came precious near it Saturday."

"Demonstrating power, or anger, yes," said Kate. "I meant affection. And isn't it the queerest thing how people are made? Of all the boys, Adam is the one who has had the most softening influences, and who has made the most money, and yet he's acting the worst of all. It really seems as if failure and hardship make more of a human being of folks than success."

"You're right," said Mrs. Bates. "Look at Nancy Ellen and Adam. Sometimes I think Adam has been pretty much galled with Agatha and her money all these years; and it just drives him crazy to think of having still less than she has. Have you got your figures all set down, to back you up, Katie?"

"Yes," said Kate. "I've gone all over it with Robert, and he thinks it's the best and only thing that can be done. Now go to sleep."

Each knew that the other was awake most of the night, but very few words passed between them. They were up early, dressed, and waiting when the first carriage stopped at the gate. Kate told her mother to stay where she would not be worried until she was needed, and went down herself to meet her brothers and sisters in the big living room. When the last one arrived, she called her mother. Mrs. Bates came down looking hollow-eyed, haggard, and grim, as none of her children ever before had seen her. She walked directly to the little table at the end of the room, and while still standing she said: "Now I've got a few words to say, and then I'll turn this over to a younger head an' one better at figures than mine. I've said my say as to Pa, yesterday. Now I'll say THIS, for myself. I got my start, minding Pa, and agreeing with him, young; but you needn't any of you throw it in my teeth now, that I did. There is only *one* woman among you, and no *man* who ever disobeyed him. Katie stood up to him once, and got seven years from home to punish her and me. He wasn't *right* then, and I knew it, as I'd often known it before, and pretty often since; but no woman God ever made could have lived with Adam Bates as his wife and contraried him. I didn't mind him any quicker or any oftener than the rest of you; keep that pretty clear in your heads, and don't one of you dare open your mouth again to tell me, as you did Saturday, what I *should* a-done, and what I *shouldn't*. I've had the law of this explained to me; you all know it for that matter. By the law, I get this place and one third of all the other land and money. I don't know just what money there is at the bank or in notes and mortgages, but a sixteenth of it after my third is taken out ain't going to make or break any of you. I've told Katie what I'm willing to do on my part and she will explain it, and then tell you about a plan she has fixed up. As for me, you can take it or leave it. If you take it, well and good; if you don't, the law will be set in motion to-day, and it will take its course to the end. It all depends on *you*.

"Now two things more. At the start, what Pa wanted to do seemed to me right, and I agreed with him and worked with him. But when my girls began to grow up and I saw how they felt, and how they struggled and worked, and how the women you boys married went ahead of my own girls, and had finer homes, an' carriages, and easier times, I got pretty sick of it, and I told Pa so more'n once. He just raved whenever I did, an' he always carried his keys in his pocket. I never touched his chest key in my life, till I handed him his deed box Friday afternoon. But I agree with my girls. It's fair and right, since things have come out as they have, that they should have their shares. I would, too.

"The other thing is just this: I'm tired to death of the whole business. I want peace and rest and I want it quick. Friday and Saturday I was so scared and so knocked out I s'pose I'd 'a' took it if one of the sucking babies had riz up and commenced to tell me what I should a-done, and what I shouldn't. I'm *through* with that. You will all keep civil tongues in your heads this morning, or I'll get up and go upstairs, an' lock myself in a room till you're gone, an' if I go, it will mean that the law takes its course; and if it does, there will be three hundred acres less land to divide. You've had Pa on your hands all your lives, now you will go civil, and you will go easy, or you will get a taste of Ma. I take no more talk from anybody. Katie, go ahead with your figures."

Kate spread her sheet on the table and glanced around the room:

"The Milton County records show sixteen hundred and fifty acres standing in Father's name," she said. "Of these, Mother is heir to five hundred and fifty acres, leaving one thousand one hundred acres to be divided among sixteen of us, which give sixty-eight and three-fourths acres to each. This land is the finest that proper fertilization and careful handling can make. Even the poorest is the cream of the country as compared with the surrounding farms. As a basis of estimate I have taken one hundred dollars an acre as a fair selling figure. Some is worth more, some less, but that is a good average. This would make the share of each of us in cash that could easily be realized, six thousand eight hundred and seventy-five dollars. Whatever else is in mortgages, notes, and money can be collected as it is due, deposited in some bank, and when it is all in, divided equally among us, after deducting Mother's third. Now this is the law, and those are the figures, but I shall venture to say that none of us feel *right* about it, or ever will."

An emphatic murmur of approval ran among the boys, Mary and Nancy Ellen stoutly declared that they did.

"Oh, no, you don't!" said Kate. "If God made any woman of you so that she feels right and clean in her conscience about this deal, he made her *wrong,* and that is a thing that has not yet been proven of God. As I see it, here is the boys' side: from childhood they were told, bribed, and urged to miss holidays, work all week, and often on Sunday, to push and slave on the promise of this land at twenty-one. They all got the land and money to stock it and build homes. They were told it was theirs, required to pay the taxes on it, and also to labour at any time and without wages for Father. Not one of the boys but has done several hundred dollars' worth of work on Father's farm for nothing, to keep him satisfied and to insure getting his deed. All these years, each man has paid his taxes, put thousands in improvements, in rebuilding homes and barns, fertilizing, and developing his land. Each one of these farms is worth nearly twice what it was the day it was received. That the boys should lose all this is no cause for rejoicing on the part of any true woman; as a fact, no true woman would allow such a thing to happen–"

"Speak for yourself!" cried several of the girls at once.

"Now right here is where we come to a perfect understanding," said Kate. "I did say that for myself, but in the main what I say, I say for *mother.* Now you will not one of you interrupt me again, or this meeting closes, and each of you stands to lose more than two thousand dollars, which is worth being civil for, for quite a while. No more of that! I say any woman should be ashamed to take advantage of her brother through an accident; and rob him of years of work and money he was perfectly justified in thinking was his. I, for one, refuse to do it, and I want and need money probably more than any of you. To tear up these farms, to take more than half from the boys, is too much. On the other hand, for the girls to help earn the land, to go with no inheritance at all, is even more unfair. Now in order to arrive at a compromise that will leave each boy his farm, and give each girl the nearest possible to a fair amount, figuring in what the boys have spent in taxes and work for Father, and what each girl has *lost* by not having her money to handle all these years, it is necessary to split the difference between the time Adam, the eldest, has had his inheritance, and Hiram, the youngest, came into possession, which by taking from and adding to, gives a fair average of fifteen years. Now Mother proposes if we will enter into an agreement this morning with no words and no wrangling, to settle on this basis: she will relinquish her third of all other land, and keep only this home farm. She even will allow the fifty lying across the road to be sold and the money put into a general fund for the share of the girls. She will turn into this fund all money from notes and mortgages, and the sale of all stock, implements, etc., here, except what she wants to keep for her use, and the sum of three thousand dollars in cash, to provide against old age. This releases quite a sum of money, and three hundred and fifty acres of land, which she gives to the boys to start this fund as her recompense for their work and loss through a scheme in which she had a share in the start. She does this only on the understanding that the boys form a pool, and in some way take from what they have saved, sell timber or cattle, or borrow enough money to add to this sufficient to pay to each girl six thousand dollars in cash, in three months. Now get out your pencils and figure. Start with the original number of acres at fifty dollars an acre which is what it cost Father on an average. Balance against each other what the boys have lost in tax and work, and the girls have lost in not having their money to handle, and cross it off. Then figure, not on a basis of what the boys have made this land worth, but on what it cost Father's estate to buy, build on, and stock each farm. Strike the fifteen-year average on prices and profits. Figure that the girls get all their money practically immediately, to pay for the time they have been out of it; while each boy assumes an equal share of the indebtedness required to finish out the six thousand, after Mother has turned in what she is willing to, if this is settled *here and now.*"

"Then I understand," said Mary, "that if we take under the law, each of us is entitled to sixty-eight and three quarter acres; and if we take under Mother's proposition we are entitled to eighty- seven and a half acres."

"No, no, E. A.," said Kate, the old nickname for "Exceptional Ability" slipping out before she thought. "No, no! Not so! You take sixty-eight and three quarters under the law. Mother's proposition is made *only* to the boys, and only on condition that they settle here and now; because she feels responsible to them for her share in rearing them and starting them out as she did. By accepting her proposition you lose eight hundred and seventy- five dollars, approximately. The boys lose on the same basis, figuring at fifty dollars and acre, six thousand five hundred and sixty-two dollars and fifty cents, plus their work and taxes, and minus what Mother will turn in, which will be about, let me see – It will take a pool of fifty-four thousand dollars to pay each of us six thousand. If Mother raises thirty-five thousand, plus sale money and notes, it will leave about nineteen thousand for the boys, which will divide up at nearly two thousand five hundred for them to lose, as against less than a thousand for us. That should be enough to square matters with any right-minded woman, even in our positions. It will give us that much cash in hand, it will leave the boys, some of the younger ones, in debt for years, if they hold their land. What more do you want?"

"I want the last cent that is coming to me," said Mary.

"I thought you would," said Kate. "Yet you have the best home, and the most money, of any of the girls living on farms. I settle under this proposition, because it is fair and just, and what Mother wants done. If she feels that this is defrauding the girls any, she can arrange to leave what she has to us at her death, which would more than square matters in our favour–"

"You hold on there, Katie," said Mrs. Bates. "You're going too fast! I'll get what's coming to me, and hang on to it awhile, before I decide which way the cat jumps. I reckon you'll all admit that in mothering the sixteen of you, doing my share indoors and out, and living with PA for all these years, I've earned it. I'll not tie myself up in any way. I'll do just what I please with mine. Figure in all I've told you to; for the rest – let be!"

"I beg your pardon," said Kate. "You're right, of course. I'll sign this, and I shall expect every sister I have to do the same, quickly and cheerfully, as the best way out of a bad business that has hurt all of us for years, and then I shall expect the boys to follow like men. It's the fairest, decentest thing we can do, let's get it over."

Kate picked up the pen, handed it to her mother, signed afterward herself, and then carried it to each of her sisters, leaving Nancy Ellen and Mary until last. All of them signed up to Nancy Ellen. She hesitated, and she whispered to Kate: "Did Robert –?" Kate nodded. Nancy Ellen thought deeply a minute and then said slowly: "I guess it is the quickest and best we can do." So she signed. Mary hesitated longer, but finally added her name. Kate passed on to the boys, beginning with Adam. Slowly he wrote his name, and as he handed back the paper he said: "Thank you, Kate, I believe it's the sanest thing we can do. I can make it easier than the younger boys."

"Then *help* them," said Kate tersely, passing on.

Each boy signed in turn, all of them pleased with the chance. It was so much better than they had hoped, that it was a great relief, which most of them admitted; so they followed Adam's example in thanking Kate, for all of them knew that in her brain had originated the scheme, which seemed to make the best of their troubles.

Then they sat closer and talked things over calmly and dispassionately. It was agreed that Adam and his mother should drive to Hartley the following afternoon and arrange for him to take out papers of administration for her, and start the adjustment of affairs. They all went home thinking more of each other, and Kate especially, than ever before. Mrs. Bates got dinner while Kate and Nancy Ellen went to work on the cool gray dress, so that it would be ready for the next afternoon. While her mother was away Kate cleaned the spare bedroom and moved her mother's possessions into it. She made it as convenient and comfortable and as pretty as she could, but the house was bare to austerity, so that her attempt at prettifying was rather a failure. Then she opened the closed room and cleaned it, after studying it most carefully as it stood. The longer she worked, the stronger became a conviction that was slowly working its way into her brain. When she could do no more she packed her telescope, installed Sally Whistler in her father's room, and rode to Hartley with a neighbour. From there she took the Wednesday hack for Walden.

Kate Takes the Bit in her Teeth

The hackman was obliging, for after delivering the mail and some parcels, he took Kate to her home. While she waited for him, she walked the ravine bank planning about the mill which was now so sure that she might almost begin work. Surely she might as soon as she finished figuring, for she had visited the Court House in Hartley and found that George's deeds were legal, and in proper shape. Her mind was filled with plans which this time must succeed.

As she approached the house she could see the children playing in the yard. It was the first time she ever had been away from them; she wondered if they had missed her. She was amazed to find that they were very decidedly disappointed to see her; but a few pertinent questions developed the reason. Their grandmother had come with her sister; she had spent her time teaching them that their mother was cold, and hard, and abused them, by not treating them as other children were treated. So far as Kate could see they had broken every rule she had ever laid down for them: eaten until their stomachs were out of order, and played in their better clothing, until it never would be nice again, while Polly shouted at her approach: "Give *me* the oranges and candy. I want to divide them."

"Silly," said Kate. "This is too soon. I've no money yet, it will be a long time before I get any; but you shall each have an orange, some candy, and new clothing when I do. Now run see what big fish you can catch."

Satisfied, the children obeyed and ran to the creek. Aunt Ollie, worried and angered, told Adam to tell his father that Mother was home and for him to come and take her and grandmother to Walden at once. She had not been able to keep Mrs. Holt from one steady round of mischief; but she argued that her sister could do less, with her on guard, than alone, so she had stayed and done her best; but she knew how Kate would be annoyed, so she believed the best course was to leave as quickly as possible. Kate walked into the house, spoke to both women, and went to her room to change her clothing. Before she had finished, she heard George's voice in the house demanding: "Where's our millionaire lady? I want a look at her."

Kate was very tired, slowly relaxing from intense nerve strain, she was holding herself in check about the children. She took a tighter grip, and vowed she would not give Mrs. Holt the satisfaction of seeing her disturbed and provoked, if she killed herself in the effort at self-control. She stepped toward the door.

"Here," she called in a clear voice, the tone of which brought George swiftly.

"What was he worth, anyway?" he shouted.

"Oh, millions and millions," said Kate, sweetly, "at least I *think* so. It was scarcely a time to discuss finances, in the face of that horrible accident."

George laughed. "Oh, you're a good one!" he cried. "Think you can keep a thing like that still? The cats, and the dogs, and the chickens of the whole county know about the deeds the old Land King had made for his sons; and how he got left on it. Served him right, too! We could here Andrew swear, and see Adam beat his horse, clear over here! That's right! Go ahead! Put on airs! Tell us something we don't *know*, will you? Maybe you think I wasn't hanging pretty close around that neighbourhood, myself!"

"Spying?" cried Kate.

"Looking for timber," he sneered. "And never in all my life have I seen anything to beat it. Sixteen hundred and fifty acres of the best land in the world. Your share of land and money together will be every cent of twelve thousand. Oh, I guess I know what you've got up your sleeve, my lady. Come on, shell out! Let's all go celebrate. What did you bring the children?"

Kate was rapidly losing patience in spite of her resolves.

"Myself," she said. "From their appearance and actions, goodness knows they needed me. I have been to my father's funeral, George; not to a circus."

"Humph!" said George. "And home for the first time in seven years. You needn't tell me it wasn't the biggest picnic you ever had! And say, about those deeds burning up – wasn't that too grand?"

"Even if my father burned with them?" she asked. "George, you make me completely disgusted."

"Big hypocrite!" he scoffed. "You know you're tickled silly. Why, you will get ten times as much as you would if those deeds hadn't burned. I know what that estate amounts to. I know what that land is worth. I'll see that you get your share to the last penny that can be wrung out of it. You bet I will! Things are coming our way at last. Now we can build the mill, and do everything we planned. I don't know as we will build a mill. With your fifteen thousand we could start a store in Hartley, and do bigger things."

"The thing for you to do right now is to hitch up and take Aunt Ollie and your mother home," said Kate. "I'll talk to you after supper and tell you all there is to know. I'm dusty and tired now."

"Well, you needn't try to fix up any shenanigan for me," he said. "I know to within five hundred dollars of what your share of that estate is worth, and I'll see that you get it."

"No one has even remotely suggested that I shouldn't have my share of that estate," said Kate.

While he was gone, Kate thought intently as she went about her work. She saw exactly what her position was, and what she had to do. Their talk would be disagreeable, but the matter had to gone into and gotten over. She let George talk as he would while she finished supper and they ate. When he went for his evening work, she helped the children scale their fish for breakfast and as they worked she talked to them, sanely, sensibly, explaining what she could, avoiding what she could not. She put them to bed, her heart almost sickened at what they had been taught and told. Kate was in no very propitious mood for her interview with George. As she sat on the front porch waiting for him, she was wishing with all her heart that she was back home with the children, to remain forever. That, of course, was out of the question, but she wished it. She had been so glad to be with her mother again, to be of service, to hear a word of approval now and then. She must be worthy of her mother's opinion, she thought, just as George stepped on the porch, sat on the top step, leaned against a pillar, and said: "Now go on, tell me all about it."

Kate thought intently a second. Instead of beginning with leaving Friday morning: "I was at the Court House in Hartley this morning," she said.

"You needn't have done that," he scoffed. "I spent most of the day there Monday. You bet folks shelled out the books when I told them who I was, and what I was after. I must say you folks have some little reason to be high and mighty. You sure have got the dough. No wonder the old man hung on to his deeds himself. He wasn't so *far* from a King, all right, all right."

"You mean you left your work Monday, and went to the Court House in Hartley and told who you were, and spent the day nosing into my father's affairs, before his *sons* had done anything, or you had any idea *what* was to be done?" she demanded.

"Oh, you needn't get so high and mighty," he said. "I propose to know just where I am, about this. I propose to have just what is coming to me – to you, to the last penny, and no Bates man will manage the affair, either."

Suddenly Kate leaned forward.

"I foresee that you've fixed yourself up for a big disappointment," she said. "My mother and her eldest son will settle my father's estate; and when it is settled I shall have exactly what the other girls have. Then if I still think it is wise, I shall at once go to work building the mill. Everything must be shaved to the last cent, must be done with the closest economy, I *must* come out of this with enough left to provide us a comfortable home."

"Do that from the first profits of the mill," he suggested.

"I'm no good at 'counting chickens before they're hatched,'" said Kate. "Besides, the first profits from the mill, as you very well know, if you would ever stop to think, must go to pay for logs to work on, and there must always be a good balance for that purpose. No. I reserve enough from my money to fix the home I want; but I shall wait to do it until the mill is working, so I can give all my attention to it, while you are out looking up timber."

"Of course I can do all of it perfectly well," he said. "And it's a *man's* business. You'll make me look like fifty cents if you get out among men and go to doing a thing no woman in this part of the country ever did. Why, it will look like you didn't *trust* me!"

"I can't help how it will look," said Kate. "This is my last and only dollar; if I lose it, I am out for life; I shall take no risk. I've no confidence in your business ability, and you know it. It need not hurt your pride a particle to say that we are partners; that I'm going to build the mill, while you're going to bring in the timber. It's the only way I shall touch the proposition. I will give you two hundred dollars for the deed and abstract of the ravine. I'll give your mother eight hundred for the lot and house, which is two hundred more than it is worth.

I'll lay away enough to rebuild and refurnish it, and with the remainder I'll build the dam, bridge, and mill, just as quickly as it can be done. As soon as I get my money, we'll buy timber for the mill and get it sawed and dried this winter. We can be all done and running by next June."

"Kate, how are you going to get all that land sold, and the money in hand to divide up that quickly? I don't think it ever can be done. Land is always sold on time, you know," he said.

Kate drew a deep breath. "*This* land isn't going to be sold," she said. "Most of the boys have owned their farms long enough to have enabled them to buy other land, and put money in the bank. They're going to form a pool, and put in enough money to pay the girls the share they have agreed to take; even if they have to borrow it, as some of the younger ones will; but the older ones will help them; so the girls are to have their money in cash, in three months. I was mighty glad of the arrangement for my part, because we can begin at once on our plans for the mill."

"And how much do the girls get?" he asked darkly.

"Can't say just yet," said Kate. "The notes and mortgages have to be gone over, and the thing figured out; it will take some time. Mother and Adam began yesterday; we shall know in a few weeks."

"Sounds to me like a cold-blooded Bates steal," he cried. "Who figured out what WAS a fair share for the girls; who planned that arrangement? Why didn't you insist on the thing going through court; the land belong sold, and equal divisions of all the proceeds?"

"Now if you'll agree not to say a word until I finish, I'll show you the figures," said Kate. "I'll tell you what the plan is, and why it was made, and I'll tell you further that it is already recorded, and in action. There are no minor heirs. We could make an agreement and record it. There was no will. Mother will administer. It's all settled. Wait until I get the figures."

Then slowly and clearly she went over the situation, explaining everything in detail. When she finished he sat staring at her with a snarling face.

"You signed that?" he demanded. "You signed that! *You threw away at least half you might have had*! You let those lazy scoundrels of brothers of yours hoodwink you, and pull the wool over your eyes like that? Are you mad? Are you stark, staring mad?"

"No, I'm quite sane," said Kate. "It is you who are mad. You know my figures, don't you? Those were the only ones used yesterday. The whole scheme was mine, with help from Mother to the extent of her giving up everything except the home farm."

"You crazy fool!" he cried, springing up.

"Now stop," said Kate. "Stop right there! I've done what I think is right, and fair, and just, and I'm happy with the results. Act decently, I'll stay and build the mill. Say one, only one more of the nasty, insulting things in your head, and I'll go in there and wake up the children and we will leave now and on foot."

Confronted with Kate and her ultimatum, George arose and walked down to the road; he began pacing back and forth in the moonlight, struggling to regain command of himself. He had no money. He had no prospect of any until Aunt Ollie died and left him her farm. He was, as he expressed it, "up against it" there. Now he was "up against it" with Kate. What she decided upon and proposed to do was all he could do. She might shave prices, and cut, and skimp, and haggle to buy material, and put up her building at the least possible expense. She might sit over books and figure herself blind. He would be driving over the country, visiting with the farmers, booming himself for a fat county office maybe, eating big dinners, and being a jolly good fellow generally. Naturally as breathing, there came to him a scheme whereby he could buy at the very lowest figure he could extract; then he would raise the price to Kate enough to make him a comfortable income besides his share of the business. He had not walked the road long until his anger was all gone.

He began planning the kind of horse he would have to drive, the buggy he would want, and a box in it to carry a hatchet, a square, measures, an auger, other tools he would need, and by Jove! it would be a dandy idea to carry a bottle of the real thing. Many a farmer, for a good cigar and a few swallows of the right thing, would warm up and sign such a contract as could be got in no other manner; while he would need it on cold days himself. George stopped in the moonlight to slap his leg and laugh over the happy thought. "By George, Georgie, my boy," he said, "most days will be cold, won't they?"

He had no word to say to Kate of his change of feeling in the matter. He did not want to miss the chance of twitting her at every opportunity he could invent with having thrown away half her inheritance; but he was glad the whole thing was settled so quickly and easily. He was now busy planning how he would spend the money Kate agreed to pay him for the ravine; but that was another rosy cloud she soon changed in colour, for she told him if he was going to be a partner he could put in what money he had, as his time was no more valuable than she could make hers teaching school again – in other words, he could buy his horse and buggy with the price she paid for the location, so he was forced to agree. He was forced to do a great many things in the following months that he hated; but he had to do them or be left out of the proposition altogether.

Mrs. Bates and Adam administered the Bates estate promptly and efficiently. The girls had their money on time, the boys adjusted themselves as their circumstances admitted. Mrs. Bates had to make so many trips to town, before the last paper was signed, and the last transfer was made, that she felt she could not go any farther, so she did not. Nancy Ellen had reached the point where she would stop and talk a few minutes to Kate, if she met her on the streets of Hartley, as she frequently did now; but she would not ask her to come home with her, because she would not bring herself in contact with George Holt. The day Kate went to Hartley to receive and deposit her check, and start her bank account, her mother asked her if she had any plan as to what she would do with her money. Kate told her in detail. Mrs. Bates listened with grim face: "You better leave it in the bank," she said, "and use the interest to help you live, or put it in good farm mortgages, where you can easily get ten per cent."

Kate explained again and told how she was doing all the buying, how she would pay all bills, and keep the books. It was no use. Mrs. Bates sternly insisted that she should do no such thing. In some way she would be defrauded. In some way she would lose the money. What she was proposing was a man's work. Kate had most of her contracts signed and much material ordered, she could not stop. Sadly she saw her mother turn from her, declaring as she went that Kate would lose every cent she had, and when she did she need not come hanging around her. She had been warned. If she lost, she could take the consequences. For an instant Kate felt that she could not endure it then she sprang after her mother.

"Oh, but I won't lose!" she cried. "I'm keeping my money in my own hands. I'm spending it myself. Please, Mother, come and see the location, and let me show you everything."

"Too late now," said Mrs. Bates grimly, "the thing is done. The time to have told me was before you made any contracts. You're always taking the bit in your teeth and going ahead. Well, go! But remember, 'as you make your bed, so you can lie.'"

"All right," said Kate, trying to force a laugh. "Don't you worry. Next time you get into a tight place and want to borrow a few hundreds, come to me."

Mrs. Bates laughed derisively. Kate turned away with a faint sickness in her heart and when half an hour later she met Nancy Ellen, fresh from an interview with her mother, she felt no better – far worse, in fact – for Nancy Ellen certainly could say what was in her mind with free and forceful directness. With deft tongue and nimble brain, she embroidered all Mrs. Bates had said, and prophesied more evil luck in three minutes than her mother could have thought of in a year. Kate left them with no promise of seeing either of them again, except by accident, her heart and brain filled with misgivings. "Must I always have 'a fly in my ointment'?" she wailed to herself. "I thought this morning this would be the happiest day of my life. I felt as if I were flying. Ye Gods, but wings were never meant for me. Every time I take them, down I come kerflop, mostly in a 'gulf of dark despair,' as the hymn book says. Anyway, I'll keep my promise and give the youngsters a treat."

So she bought each of them an orange, some candy, and goods for a new Sunday outfit and comfortable school clothing. Then she took the hack for Walden, feeling in a degree as she had the day she married George Holt. As she passed the ravine and again studied the location her spirits arose. It WAS a good scheme. It would work. She would work it. She would sell from the yards to Walden and the surrounding country. She would see the dealers in Hartley and talk the business over, so she would know she was not being cheated in freight rates when she came to shipping. She stopped at Mrs. Holt's, laid a deed before her for her signature, and offered her a check for eight hundred for the Holt house and lot, which Mrs. Holt eagerly accepted. They arranged to move immediately, as the children were missing school. She had a deed with her for the ravine, which George signed in Walden, and both documents were acknowledged; but she would not give him the money until he had the horse and buggy he was to use, at the gate, in the spring.

He wanted to start out buying at once, but that was going too far in the future for Kate. While the stream was low, and the banks firm, Kate built her dam, so that it would be ready for spring, put in the abutments, and built the bridge. It was not a large dam, and not a big bridge, but both were solid, well constructed, and would serve every purpose. Then Kate set men hauling stone for the corner foundations. She hoped to work up such a trade and buy so much and so wisely in the summer that she could run all winter, so she was building a real mill in the Bates way, which way included letting the foundations freeze and settle over winter. That really was an interesting and a comfortable winter.

Kate and George both watched the children's studies at night, worked their plans finer in the daytime, and lived as cheaply and carefully as they could. Everything was going well. George was doing his best to promote the mill plan, to keep Kate satisfied at home, to steal out after she slept, and keep himself satisfied in appetite, and some ready money in his pockets, won at games of chance, at which he was an expert, and at cards, which he handled like a master.

"As a Man Soweth"

At the earliest possible moment in the spring, the building of the mill began. It was scarcely well under way when the work was stopped by a week of heavy rains. The water filled the ravine to dangerous height and the roaring of the dam could be heard all over town. George talked of it incessantly. He said it was the sweetest music his ears had ever heard. Kate had to confess that she like the sound herself, but she was fearful over saying much on the subject because she was so very anxious about the stability of the dam. There was a day or two of fine weather; then the rains began again. Kate said she had all the music she desired; she proposed to be safe; so she went and opened the sluiceway to reduce the pressure on the dam. The result was almost immediate. The water gushed through, lowering the current and lessening the fall. George grumbled all day, threatening half a dozen times to shut the sluice; but Kate and the carpenter were against him, so he waited until he came slipping home after midnight, his brain in a muddle from drink, smoke, and cards. As he neared the dam, he decided that the reason he felt so badly was because he had missed hearing it all day, but he would have it to go to sleep by. So he crossed the bridge and shut the sluice gate. Even as he was doing it the thunder pealed; lightning flashed, and high Heaven gave him warning that he was doing a dangerous thing; but all his life he had done what he pleased; there was no probability that he would change then. He needed the roar of the dam to quiet his nerves.

The same roar that put him to sleep, awakened Kate. She lay wondering at it and fearing. She raised her window to listen. The rain was falling in torrents, while the roar was awful, so much worse than it had been when she fell asleep, that she had a suspicion of what might have caused it. She went to George's room and shook him awake.

"Listen to the dam!" she cried. "It will go, as sure as fate. George, did you, Oh, did you, close the sluice-gate when you came home?"

He was half asleep, and too defiant from drink to take his usual course.

"Sure!" he said. "Sweesish mushich ever hearsh. Push me shleep."

He fell back on the pillow and went on sleeping. Kate tried again to waken him, but he struck at her savagely. She ran to her room, hurried into a few clothes, and getting the lantern, started toward the bridge. At the gate she stepped into water. As far as she could see above the dam the street was covered. She waded to the bridge, which was under at each end but still bare in the middle, where it was slightly higher. Kate crossed it and started down the yard toward the dam. The earth was softer there, and she mired in places almost to her knees. At the dam, the water was tearing around each end in a mad race, carrying earth and everything before it. The mill side was lower than the street. The current was so broad and deep she could not see where the sluice was. She hesitated a second to try to locate it from the mill behind her; and in that instant there was a crack and a roar, a mighty rush that swept her from her feet and washed away the lantern. Nothing saved her but the trees on the bank. She struck one, clung to it, pulled herself higher, and in the blackness gripped the tree, while she heard the dam going gradually after the first break.

There was no use to scream, no one could have heard her. The storm raved on; Kate clung to her tree, with each flash of lightning trying to see the dam. At last she saw that it was not all gone. She was not much concerned about herself. She knew the tree would hold. Eagerly she strained her eyes toward the dam. She could feel the water dropping lower, while the roar subsided to a wild rush, and with flashes of lightning she could see what she thought was at least half of the dam holding firm. By that time Kate began to chill. She wrapped her arms around the tree, and pressing her cheek against the rough bark, she cried as hard as she could and did not care. God would not hear; the neighbours could not. She shook and cried until she was worn out. By that time the water was only a muddy flow around her ankles; if she had a light she could wade back to the bridge and reach home. But if she missed the bridge and went into the ravine, the current would be too strong for her. She held with one arm and tried to wipe her face with the other hand. "What a fool to cry!" she said. "As if there were any more water needed here!"

Then she saw a light in the house, and the figures of the children, carrying it from room to room, so she knew that one of them had awakened for a drink, or with the storm, and they had missed her. Then she could see them at the front door, Adam's sturdy feet planted widely apart, bracing him, as he held up the lamp which flickered in the wind. Then she could hear his voice shouting: "Mother!" Instantly Kate answered. Then she was sorry she had, for both of them began to scream wildly. There was a second of that, then even the children realized its futility.

"She is out there in the water, *we got to get her*," said Adam. "We got to do it!"

He started with the light held high. The wind blew it out. They had to go back to relight it. Kate knew they would burn their fingers, and she prayed they would not set the house on fire. When the light showed again, at the top of her lungs she screamed: "Adam, set the broom on fire and carry it to the end of the bridge; the water isn't deep enough to hurt you." She tried twice, then she saw him give Polly the lamp, and run down the hall. He came back in an instant with the broom. Polly held the lamp high, Adam went down the walk to the gate and started up the sidewalk. "He's using his head," said Kate to the tree. "He's going to wait until he reaches the bridge to start his light, so it will last longer. *That* is *bates*, anyway. Thank God!"

Adam scratched several matches before he got the broom well ignited, then he held it high, and by its light found the end of the bridge. Kate called to him to stop and plunging and splashing through mud and water, she reached the bridge before the broom burned out. There she clung to the railing she had insisted upon, and felt her way across to the boy. His thin cotton night shirt was plastered to his sturdy little body. As she touched him Kate lifted him in her arms, and almost hugged the life from him.

"You big man!" she said. "You could help Mother! Good for you!"

"Is the dam gone?" he asked.

"Part of it," said Kate, sliding her feet before her, as she waded toward Polly in the doorway.

"Did Father shut the sluice-gate, to hear the roar?"

Kate hesitated. The shivering body in her arms felt so small to her.

"I 'spect he did," said Adam. "All day he was fussing after you stopped the roar." Then he added casually: "The old fool ought-a known better. I 'spect he was drunk again!"

"Oh, Adam!" cried Kate, setting him on the porch. "Oh, Adam! What makes you say that?"

"Oh, all of them at school say that," scoffed Adam. "Everybody knows it but you, don't they, Polly?"

"Sure!" said Polly. "Most every night; but don't you mind, Mother, Adam and I will take care of you."

Kate fell on her knees and gathered both of them in a crushing hug for an instant; then she helped them into to dry nightgowns and to bed. As she covered them she stooped and kissed each of them before she went to warm and put on dry clothes, and dry her hair. It was almost dawn when she walked to George Holt's door and looked in at him lying stretched in deep sleep.

"You may thank your God for your children," she said. "If it hadn't been for them, I know what I would have done to you."

Then she went to her room and lay down to rest until dawn. She was up at the usual time and had breakfast ready for the children. As they were starting to school George came into the room.

"Mother," said Polly, "there is a lot of folks over around the dam. What shall we tell them?"

Kate's heart stopped. She had heard that question before.

"Tell them the truth," said Adam scornfully, before Kate could answer. "Tell them that Mother opened the sluiceway to save the dam and Father shut it to hear it roar, and it busted!"

"Shall I, Mother?" asked Polly.

A slow whiteness spread over George's face; he stared down the hall to look.

"Tell them exactly what you please," said Kate, "only you watch yourself like a hawk. If you tell one word not the way it was, or in any way different from what happened, I'll punish you severely."

"May I tell them I held the lamp while Adam got you out of the water?" asked Polly. "That would be true, you know."

George turned to listen, his face still whiter.

"Yes, that would be true," said Kate, "but if you tell them that, the first thing they will ask will be 'where was your father?' What will you say then?"

"Why, we'll say that he was so drunk we couldn't wake him up," said Polly conclusively. "We pulled him, an' we shook him, an' we yelled at him. Didn't we, Adam?"

"I was not drunk!" shouted George.

"Oh, yes, you were," said Adam. "You smelled all sour, like it does at the saloon door!"

George made a rush at Adam. The boy spread his feet and put up his hands, but never flinched or moved. Kate looking on felt something in her heart that never had been there before. She caught George's arm, as he reached the child.

"You go on to school, little folks," she said. "And for Mother's sake try not to talk at all. If people question you, tell them to ask Mother. I'd be so proud of you, if you would do that."

"I *will*, if you'll hold me and kiss me again like you did last night when you got out of the water," said Polly.

"It is a bargain," said Kate. "How about you, Adam?"

"I will for *that*, too," said Adam, "but I'd like awful well to tell how fast the water went, and how it poured and roared, while I held the light, and you got across. Gee, if was awful, Mother! So black, and so crashy, and so deep. I'd *like* to tell!"

"But you *won't* if I ask you not to?" queried Kate.

"I will not," said Adam.

Kate went down on her knees again, she held out her arms and both youngsters rushed to her. After they were gone, she and George Holt looked at each other an instant, then Kate turned to her work. He followed: "Kate—" he began.

"No use!" said Kate. "If you go out and look at the highest water mark, you can easily imagine what I had to face last night when I had to cross the bridge to open the sluice-gate, or the bridge would have gone, too. If the children had not wakened with the storm, and hunted me, I'd have had to stay over there until morning, if I could have clung to the tree that long. First they rescued me; and then they rescued *you*, if you only but knew it. By using part of the money I had saved for the house, I can rebuild the dam; but I am done with you. We're partners no longer. Not with business, money, or in any other way, will I ever trust you again. Sit down there and eat your breakfast, and then leave my sight."

Instead George put on his old clothing, crossed the bridge, and worked all day with all his might trying to gather building material out of the water, save debris from the dam, to clear the village street. At noon he came over and got a drink, and a piece of bread. At night he worked until he could see no longer, and then ate some food from the cupboard and went to bed. He was up and at work before daybreak in the morning, and for two weeks he kept this up, until he had done much to repair the work of the storm. The dam he almost rebuilt himself, as soon as the water lowered to normal again. Kate knew what he was trying to do, and knew also that in a month he had the village pitying him, and blaming her because he was working himself to death, and she was allowing it.

She doggedly went on with her work; the contracts were made; she was forced to. As the work neared completion, her faith in the enterprise grew. She studied by the hour everything she could find pertaining to the business. When the machinery began to arrive, George frequently spoke about having timber ready to begin work on, but he never really believed the thing which did happen, would happen, until the first load of logs slowly crossed the bridge and began unloading in the yards. A few questions elicited from the driver the reply that he had sold the timber to young Adam Bates of Bates Corners, who was out buying right and left and paying cash on condition the seller did his own delivering. George saw the scheme, and that it was good. Also the logs were good, while the price was less than he hoped to pay for such timber. His soul was filled with bitterness. The mill was his scheme. He had planned it all. Those thieving Bates had stolen his plan, and his location, and his home, and practically separated him from his wife and children. It was his mill, and all he was getting from it was to work with all his might, and not a decent word from morning until night. That day instead of working as before, he sat in the shade most of the time, and that night instead of going to bed he went down town.

When the mill was almost finished Kate employed two men who lived in Walden, but had been working in the Hartley mills for years. They were honest men of much experience. Kate made the better of them foreman, and consulted with him in every step of completing the mill, and setting up the machinery. She watched everything with sharp eyes, often making suggestions that were useful about the placing of different parts as a woman would arrange them. Some of these the men laughed at, some they were more than glad to accept. When the engine was set up, the big saw in place, George went to Kate.

"See here!" he said roughly. "I know I was wrong about the sluice-gate. I was a fool to shut it with the water that high, but I've learned my lesson; I'll never touch it again; I've worked like a dog for weeks to pay for it; now where do I come in? What's my job, how much is my share of the money, and when do I get it?"

"The trouble with you, George, is that you have to learn a new lesson about every thing you attempt. You can't carry a lesson about one thing in your mind, and apply it to the next thing that comes up. I know you have worked, and I know why. It is fair that you should have something, but I can't say what, just now. Having to rebuild the dam, and with a number of incidentals that have come up, in spite of the best figuring I could do, I have been forced to use my money saved for rebuilding the house; and even with that, I am coming out a hundred or two short. I'm strapped; and until money begins to come in I have none myself. The first must go toward paying the men's wages, the next for timber. If Jim Milton can find work for you, go to work at the mill, and when we get started I'll pay you what is fair and just, you may depend on that. If he hasn't work for you, you'll have to find a job at something else."

"Do you mean that?" he asked wonderingly.

"I mean it," said Kate.

"After stealing my plan, and getting my land for nothing, you'd throw me out entirely?" he demanded.

"You entreated me to put all I had into your plan, you told me repeatedly the ravine was worth nothing, you were not even keeping up the taxes on it until I came and urged you to, the dam is used merely for water, the engine furnishes the real power, and if you are thrown out, you have thrown yourself out. You have had every chance."

"You are going to keep your nephew on the buying job?" he asked

"I am," said Kate. "You can have no job that will give you a chance to involve me financially."

"Then give me Milton's place. It's so easy a baby could do it, and the wages you have promised him are scandalous," said George.

Kate laughed. "Oh, George," she said, "you can't mean that! Of all your hare-brained ideas, that you could operate that saw, is the wildest. Oh course you could start the engine, and set the saw running – I could myself; but to regulate its speed, to control it with judgment, you could no more do it than Polly. As for wages, Milton is working for less than he got in Hartley, because he can be at home, and save his hack fare, as you know."

George went over to Jim Milton, and after doing all he could see to do and ordering Milton to do several things he thought might be done, he said casually: "Of course I am *boss* around this shack, but this is new to me. You fellows will have to tell me what to do until I get my bearings. As soon as we get to running, I'll be yard-master, and manage the selling and shipping. I'm good at figures, and that would be the best place for me."

"You'll have to settle with Mrs. Holt about that," said Jim Milton.

"Of course," said George. "Isn't she a wonder? With my help, we'll soon wipe the Hartley mills off the map, and be selling till Grand Rapids will get her eye peeled. With you to run the machinery, me to manage the sales, and her to keep the books, we got a combination to beat the world."

"In the meantime," said Jim Milton dryly, "you might take that scoop shovel and clean the shavings and blocks off this floor. Leave me some before the engine to start the first fire, and shovel the rest into that bin there where it's handy. It isn't safe to start with so much loose, dry stuff lying around."

George went to work with the scoop shovel, but he watched every movement Jim Milton made about the engine and machinery. Often he dropped the shovel and stood studying things out for himself, and asking questions. Not being sure of his position, Jim Milton answered him patiently, and showed him all he wanted to know; but he constantly cautioned him not to touch anything, or try to start the machinery himself, as he might lose control of the gauge and break the saw, or let the power run away with him. George scoffed at the idea of danger and laughed at the simplicity of the engine and machinery. There was little for him to do. He hated to be seen cleaning up the debris; men who stopped in passing kept telling what a fine fellow young Bates was, what good timber he was sending in. Several of them told George frankly they thought that was to be his job. He was so ashamed of that, he began instant improvisation.

"That was the way we first planned things," he said boastfully, "but when it came to working out our plans, we found I would be needed here till I learned the business, and then I'm going on the road. I am going to be the salesman. To travel, dress well, eat well, flirt with the pretty girls, and take big lumber orders will just about suit little old Georgie."

"Wonder you remembered to put the orders in at all," said Jim Milton dryly.

George glared at him. "Well, just remember whom you take orders from," he said, pompously.

"I take them from Mrs. Holt, and nobody else," said Milton, with equal assurance. "And I've yet to hear her say the first word about this wonderful travelling proposition. She thinks she will do well to fill home orders and ship to a couple of factories she already has contracts with. Sure you didn't dream that travelling proposition, George?"

At that instant George wished he could slay Jim Milton. All day he brooded and grew sullen and ugly. By noon he quit working and went down town. By suppertime he went home to prove to his wife that he was all right. She happened to be coming across from the mill, where she had helped Milton lay the first fire under the boiler ready to touch off, and had seen the first log on the set carriage. It had been agreed that she was to come over at opening time in the morning and start the machinery. She was a proud and eager woman when she crossed the bridge and started down the street toward the gate. From the opposite direction came George, so unsteady that he was running into tree boxes, then lifting his hat and apologizing to them for his awkwardness. Kate saw at a glance that he might fall any instant. Her only thought was to help him from the street, to where children would not see him.

She went to him and taking his arm started down the walk with him. He took off his hat to her also, and walked with wavering dignity, setting his steps as if his legs were not long enough to reach the walk, so that each step ended with a decided thump. Kate could see the neighbours watching at their windows, and her own children playing on the roof of the woodshed. When the children saw their parents, they both stopped playing to stare at them. Then suddenly, shrill and high, arose Adam's childish voice:

"Father came home the other night,   Tried to blow out the 'lectric light, Blew and blew with all his might,   And the blow almost killed Mother."

Polly joined him, and they sang and shrilled, and shrieked it; they jumped up and down and laughed and repeated it again and again. Kate guided George to his room and gave him a shove that landed him on his bed. Then to hush the children she called them to supper. They stopped suddenly, as soon as they entered the kitchen door, and sat, sorry and ashamed while she went around, her face white, her lips closed, preparing their food. George was asleep. The children ate alone, as she could take no food. Later she cleaned the kitchen, put the children to bed, and sat on the front porch looking at the mill, wondering, hoping, planning, praying unconsciously. When she went to bed at ten o'clock George was still asleep.

He awakened shortly after, burning with heat and thirst. He arose and slipped to the back porch for a drink. Water was such an aggravation, he crossed the yard, went out the back gate, and down the alley. When he came back up the street, he was pompously, maliciously, dangerously drunk. Either less or more would have been better. When he came in sight of the mill, standing new and shining in the moonlight, he was a lord of creation, ready to work creation to his will. He would go over and see if things were all right. But he did not cross the bridge, he went down the side street, and entered the yard at the back. The doors were closed and locked, but there was as yet no latch on the sliding windows above the work bench. He could push them open from the ground. He leaned a board against the side of the mill, set his foot on it, and pulled himself up, so that he could climb on the bench.

That much achieved, he looked around him. After a time his eyes grew accustomed to the darkness, so that he could see his way plainly. Muddled half-thoughts began to filter through his brain. He remembered he was abused. He was out of it. He remembered that he was not the buyer for the mill. He remembered how the men had laughed when he had said that he was to be the salesman. He remembered that Milton had said that he was not to touch the machinery. He at once slid from the bench and went to the boiler. He opened the door of the fire-box and saw the kindling laid ready to light, to get up steam. He looked at the big log on the set carriage. They had planned to start with a splurge in the morning. Kate was to open the throttle that started the machinery. He decided to show them that they were not so smart. He would give them a good surprise by sawing the log. That would be a joke on them to brag about the remainder of his life. He took matches from his pocket and started the fire. It seemed to his fevered imagination that it burned far too slowly. He shoved in more kindling, shavings, ends left from siding. This smothered his fire, so he made trip after trip to the tinder box, piling in armloads of dry, inflammable stuff.

Then suddenly the flames leaped up. He slammed shut the door and started toward the saw. He could not make it work. He jammed and pulled everything he could reach. Soon he realized the heat was becoming intense, and turned to the boiler to see that the fire- box was red hot almost all over, white hot in places.

"My God!" he muttered. "Too hot! Got to cool that down."

Then he saw the tank and the dangling hose, and remembered that he had not filled the boiler. Taking down the hose, he opened the watercock, stuck in the nozzle, and turned on the water full force. Windows were broken across the street. Parts of the fire- box, boiler, and fire flew everywhere. The walls blew out, the roof lifted and came down, the fire raged among the new, dry timbers of the mill.

When her windows blew in, Kate was thrown from her bed to the floor. She lay stunned a second, then dragged herself up to look across the street. There was nothing where the low white expanse of roof had spread an hour before, while a red glare was creeping everywhere over the ground. She ran to George's room and found it empty. She ran to the kitchen, calling him, and found the back door standing open. She rushed back to her room and began trying to put on her dress over her nightrobe. She could not control her shaking fingers, while at each step she cut her feet on broken glass. She reached the front door as the children came screaming with fright. In turning to warn them about the glass, she stumbled on the top step, pitched forward headlong, then lay still. The neighbours carried her back to her bed, called the doctor, and then saved all the logs in the yard they could. The following day, when the fire had burned itself out, the undertaker hunted assiduously, but nothing could be found to justify a funeral.

"For a Good Girl"

For a week, Kate lay so dazed she did not care whether she lived or died; then she slowly crept back to life, realizing that whether she cared or not, she must live. She was too young, too strong, to quit because she was soul sick; she had to go on. She had life to face for herself and her children. She wondered dully about her people, but as none of the neighbours who had taken care of her said anything concerning them, she realized that they had not been there. At first she was almost glad. They were forthright people. They would have had something to say; they would have said it tersely and to the point.

Adam, 3d, had wound up her affairs speedily by selling the logs he had bought for her to the Hartley mills, paying what she owed, and depositing the remainder in the Hartley Bank to her credit; but that remainder was less than one hundred dollars. That winter was a long, dreadful nightmare to Kate. Had it not been for Aunt Ollie, they would have been hungry some of the time; they were cold most of it. For weeks Kate thought of sending for her mother, or going to her; then as not even a line came from any of her family, she realized that they resented her losing that much Bates money so bitterly that they wished to have nothing to do with her. Often she sat for hours staring straight before her, trying to straighten out the tangle she had made of her life. As if she had not suffered enough in the reality of living, she now lived over in day and night dreams, hour by hour, her time with George Holt, and gained nothing thereby.

All winter Kate brooded, barely managing to keep alive, and the children in school. As spring opened, she shook herself, arose, and went to work. It was not planned, systematic, effective, Bates work. Piecemeal she did anything she saw needed the doing. The children helped to make garden and clean the yard. Then all of them went out to Aunt Ollie's and made a contract to plant and raise potatoes and vegetables on shares. They passed a neglected garden on the way, and learning that the woman of the house was ill, Kate stopped and offered to tend it for enough cords of windfall wood to pay her a fair price, this to be delivered in mid-summer.

With food and fire assured, Kate ripped up some of George's clothing, washed, pressed, turned, and made Adam warm clothes for school. She even achieved a dress for Polly by making a front and back from a pair of her father's trouser legs, and setting in side pieces, a yoke and sleeves from one of her old skirts. George's underclothing she cut down for both of the children; then drew another check for taxes and second-hand books. While she was in Hartley in the fall paying taxes, she stopped at a dry goods store for thread, and heard a customer asking for knitted mittens, which were not in stock. After he had gone, she arranged with the merchant for a supply of yarn which she carried home and began to knit into mittens such as had been called for. She used every minute of leisure during the day, she worked hours into the night, and soon small sums began coming her way. When she had a supply of teamster's heavy mittens, she began on fancy coloured ones for babies and children, sometimes crocheting, sometimes using needles. Soon she started both children on the rougher work with her. They were glad to help for they had a lively remembrance of one winter of cold and hunger, with no Christmas. That there were many things she might have done that would have made more money with less exertion Kate never seemed to realize. She did the obvious thing. Her brain power seemed to be on a level with that of Adam and Polly.

When the children began to carry home Christmas talk, Kate opened her mouth to say the things that had been said to her as a child; then tightly closed it. She began getting up earlier, sitting up later, knitting feverishly. Luckily the merchant could sell all she could furnish. As the time drew nearer, she gathered from the talk of the children what was the deepest desire of their hearts. One day a heavy wind driving ice-coated trees in the back yard broke quite a large limb from a cherry tree. Kate dragged it into the woodhouse to make firewood. She leaned it against the wall to wait until the ice melted, and as it stood there in its silvery coat, she thought how like a small tree the branch was shaped, and how pretty it looked. After the children had gone to school the next day she shaped it with the hatchet and saw, and fastened it in a small box. This she carried to her bedroom and locked the door. She had not much idea what she was going to do, but she kept thinking. Soon she found enough time to wrap every branch carefully with the red tissue paper her red knitting wool came in, and to cover the box smoothly. Then she thought of the country Christmas trees she had seen decorated with popcorn and cranberries. She popped the corn at night and the following day made a trip up the ravine, where she gathered all the bittersweet berries, swamp holly, and wild rose seed heads she could find. She strung the corn on fine cotton cord putting a rose seed pod between each grain, then used the bittersweet berries to terminate the blunt ends of the branches, and climb up the trunk. By the time she had finished this she was really interested. She achieved a gold star for the top from a box lid and a piece of gilt paper Polly had carried home from school. With yarn ends and mosquito netting, she whipped up a few little mittens, stockings, and bags. She cracked nuts from their fall store and melting a little sugar stirred in the kernels until they were covered with a sweet, white glaze. Then she made some hard candy, and some fancy cookies with a few sticks of striped candy cut in circles and dotted on the top. She polished red, yellow, and green apples and set them under the tree.

When she made her final trip to Hartley before Christmas the spirit of the day was in the air. She breathed so much of it that she paid a dollar and a half for a stout sled and ten cents for a dozen little red candles, five each for two oranges, and fifteen each for two pretty little books, then after long hesitation added a doll for Polly. She felt that she should not have done this, and said so, to herself; but knew if she had it to do over, she would do the same thing again. She shook her shoulders and took the first step toward regaining her old self-confidence.

"Pshaw! Big and strong as I am, and Adam getting such a great boy, we can make it," she said. Then she hurried to the hack and was driven home barely in time to rush her bundles into her room before school was out. She could scarcely wait until the children were in bed to open the parcels. The doll had to be dressed, but Kate was interested in Christmas by that time, and so contemplated the spider-waisted image with real affection. She never had owned a doll herself. She let the knitting go that night, and cut up an old waist to make white under-clothing with touches of lace, and a pretty dress. Then Kate went to her room, tied the doll in a safe place on the tree, put on the books, and set the candles with pins. As she worked she kept biting her lips, but when it was all finished she thought it was lovely, and so it was. As she set the sled in front of the tree she said: "There, little folks, I wonder what you will think of that! It's the best I can do. I've a nice chicken to roast; now if only, if only Mother or Nancy Ellen would come, or write a line, or merely send one word by Tilly Nepple."

Suddenly Kate lay down on the bed, buried her face in the pillow while her shoulders jerked and shook in dry sobs for a long time. At last she arose, went to the kitchen, bathed her face, and banked the fires. "I suppose it is the Bates way," she said, "but it's a cold, hard proposition. I know what's the matter with all of them. They are afraid to come near me, or show the slightest friendliness, for fear I'll ask them to help support us. They needn't worry, we can take care of ourselves."

She set her tree on the living room table, arranged everything to the best advantage, laid a fire in the stove, and went to sleep Christmas eve, feeling more like herself than she had since the explosion. Christmas morning she had the house warm and the tree ready to light while the children dressed. She slipped away their every-day clothing and laid out their best instead. She could hear them talking as they dressed, and knew the change of clothing had filled them with hope. She hastily lighted the tree, and was setting the table as they entered the dining room.

"Merry Christmas, little people," she cried in a voice they had not heard in a long time. They both rushed to her and Kate's heart stood still as they each hugged her tight, kissed her, and offered a tiny packet. From the size and feeling of these, she realized that they were giving her the candy they had received the day before at school. Surprises were coming thick and fast with Kate. That one shook her to her foundations. They loved candy. They had so little! They had nothing else to give. She held them an instant so tightly they were surprised at her, then she told them to lay the packages on the living room table until after breakfast. Polly opened the door, and screamed. Adam ran, and then both of them stood silently before the brave little tree, flaming red, touched with white, its gold star shining. They looked at it, and then at each other, while Kate, watching at an angle across the dining room, distinctly heard Polly say in an awed tone: "Adam, hadn't we better pray?"

Kate lifted herself full height, and drew a deep breath. "Well, I guess I manage a little Christmas after this," she said, "and maybe a Fourth of July, and a birthday, and a few other things. I needn't be such a coward. I believe I can make it."

From that hour she began trying to think of something she could do that would bring returns more nearly commensurate with the time and strength she was spending. She felt tied to Walden because she owned the house, and could rely on working on shares with Aunt Ollie for winter food; but there was nothing she could do there and take care of the children that would bring more than the most meagre living. Still they were living, each year more comfortably; the children were growing bigger and stronger; soon they could help at something, if only she could think what. The time flew, each day a repetition of yesterday's dogged, soul- tiring grind, until some days Kate was close to despair. Each day the house grew shabbier; things wore out and could not be replaced; poverty showed itself more plainly. So three more years of life in Walden passed, setting their indelible mark on Kate. Time and again she almost broke the spell that bound her, but she never quite reached the place where her thought cleared, her heart regained its courage, her soul dared take wing, and try another flight. When she thought of it, "I don't so much mind the falling," said Kate to herself; "but I do seem to select the hardest spots to light on."

Kate sat on the back steps, the sun shone, her nearest neighbour was spading an onion bed. She knew that presently she would get out the rake and spade and begin another year's work; but at that minute she felt too hopeless to move. Adam came and sat on the step beside her. She looked at him and was surprised at his size and apparent strength. Someway he gave her hope. He was a good boy, he had never done a mean, sneaking thing that she knew of. He was natural, normal, mischievous; but he had not an underhand inclination that she could discover. He would make a fine- looking, big man, quite as fine as any of the Bates men; even Adam, 3d, was no handsomer than the fourth Adam would be. Hope arose in her with the cool air of spring on her cheek and its wine in her nostrils. Then out of the clear sky she said it: "Adam, how long are we going to stay in the beggar class?"

Adam jumped, and turned surprised eyes toward her. Kate was forced to justify herself.

"Of course we give Aunt Ollie half we raise," she said, "but anybody would do that. We work hard, and we live little if any better than Jasons, who have the County Trustee in three times a winter. I'm big and strong, you're almost a man, why don't we *do* something? Why don't we have some decent clothes, some money for out work and" – Kate spoke at random – "a horse and carriage?"

"A horse and carriage?" repeated Adam, staring at her.

"Why not?" said Kate, casually.

"But how?" cried the amazed boy.

"Why, earn the money, and buy it!" said Kate, impatiently. "I'm about fed up on earning cabbage, and potatoes, and skirmishing for wood. I'd prefer to have a dollar in my pocket, and *buy* what we need. Can't you use your brain and help me figure out a way to earn some *money*?"

"I meant to pretty soon now, but I thought I had to go to school a few years yet," he said.

"Of course you do," said Kate. "I must earn the money, but can't you help me think how?"

"Sure," said Adam, sitting straight and seeming thoughtful, "but give me a little time. What would you – could you, do?"

"I taught before I was married," said Kate; "but methods of teaching change so I'd have to have a Normal term to qualify for even this school. I could put you and Polly with Aunt Ollie this summer; but I wouldn't, not if we must freeze and starve together–"

"Because of Grandma?" asked the boy. Kate nodded.

"I borrowed money to go once, and I could again; but I have been away from teaching so long, and I don't know what to do with you children. The thing I would *like* would be to find a piece of land somewhere, with a house, any kind of one on it, and take it to rent. Land is about all I really know. Working for money would be of some interest. I am so dead tired working for potatoes. Sometimes I see them flying around in the air at night."

"Do you know of any place you would like?" asked Adam.

"No, I don't," said Kate, "but I am going to begin asking and I'm going to keep my eyes open. I heard yesterday that Dr. James intends to build a new house. This house is nothing, but the lot is in the prettiest place in town. Let's sell it to him, and take the money, and buy us some new furniture and a cow, and a team, and wagon, and a buggy, and go on a piece of land, and live like other people. Seems to me I'll die if I have to work for potatoes any longer. I'm heart sick of them. Don't say a word to anybody, but Oh, Adam, *think*! Think *hard*! Can't you just help me *think*?"

"You are sure you want land?" asked the boy.

"It is all I know," said Kate. "How do you feel about it?"

"I want horses, and cows, and pigs – lots of pigs – and sheep, and lots of white hens," said Adam, promptly.

"Get the spade and spade the onion bed until I think," said Kate. "And that reminds me, we didn't divide the sets last fall. Somebody will have to go after them."

"I'll go," said Adam, "but it's awful early. It'll snow again. Let me go after school Friday and stay over night. I'd like to go and stay over night with Aunt Ollie. Grandma can't say anything to me that I'll listen to. You keep Polly, and let me go alone. Sure I can."

"All right," said Kate. "Spade the bed, and let it warm a day. It will be good for it. But don't tell Polly you're going, or she'll want to go along."

Until Friday night, Kate and Adam went around in such a daze of deep thought that they stumbled, and ran against each other; then came back to their affairs suddenly, looking at each other and smiling understandingly. After one of these encounters Kate said to the boy: "You may not arrive at anything, Adam, but I certainly can't complain that you are not thinking."

Adam grinned: "I'm not so sure that I haven't got it," he said.

"Tell me quick and let me think, too" said Kate.

"But I can't tell you yet," said Adam. "I have to find out something first."

Friday evening he wanted to put off his trip until Saturday morning, so Kate agreed. She was surprised when he bathed and put on his clean shirt and trousers, but said not a word. She had made some study of child psychology, she thought making the trip alone was of so much importance to Adam that he was dressing for the occasion. She foresaw extra washing, yet she said nothing to stop the lad. She waved good-bye to him, thinking how sturdy and good looking he was, as he ran out of the front door. Kate was beginning to be worried when Adam had not returned toward dusk Sunday evening, and Polly was cross and fretful. Finally they saw him coming down the ravine bank, carrying his small bundle of sets. Kate felt a glow of relief; Polly ran to meet him. Kate watched as they met and saw Adam take Polly's hand.

"If only they looked as much alike as some twins do, I'd be thankful," said Kate.

Adam delivered the sets, said Aunt Ollie and Grandma were all right, that it was an awful long walk, and he was tired. Kate noticed that his feet were dust covered, but his clothes were so clean she said to him: "You didn't fish much."

"I didn't fish any," said Adam, "not like I always fish," he added.

"Had any time to *think*?" asked Kate.

"You just bet I did," said the boy. "I didn't waste a minute."

"Neither did I," said Kate. "I know exactly what the prettiest lot in town can be sold for."

"Good!" cried Adam. "Fine!"

Monday Kate wanted to get up early and stick the sets, but Adam insisted that Aunt Ollie said the sign would not be right until Wednesday. If they were stuck on Monday or Tuesday, they would all grow to top.

"My goodness! I knew that," said Kate. "I am thinking so hard I'm losing what little sense I had; but anyway, mere thinking is doing me a world of good. I am beginning to feel a kind of rising joy inside, and I can't imagine anything else that makes it."

Adam went to school, laughing. Kate did the washing and ironing, and worked in the garden getting beds ready. Tuesday she was at the same occupation, when about ten o'clock she dropped her spade and straightened, a flash of perfect amazement crossing her face. She stood immovable save for swaying forward in an attitude of tense listening.

"Hoo! hoo!"

Kate ran across the yard and as she turned the corner of the house she saw a one-horse spring wagon standing before the gate, while a stiff, gaunt figure sat bolt upright on the seat, holding the lines. Kate was at the wheel looking up with a face of delighted amazement.

"Why, Mother!" she cried. "Why, Mother!"

"Go fetch a chair and help me down," said Mrs. Bates, "this seat is getting tarnation hard."

Kate ran after a chair, and helped her mother to alight. Mrs. Bates promptly took the chair, on the sidewalk.

"Just drop the thills," she said. "Lead him back and slip on the halter. It's there with his feed."

Kate followed instructions, her heart beating wildly. Several times she ventured a quick glance at her mother. How she had aged! How lined and thin she was! But Oh, how blessed good it was to see her! Mrs. Bates arose and they walked into the house, where she looked keenly around, while her sharp eyes seemed to appraise everything as she sat down and removed her bonnet.

"Go fetch me a drink," she said, "and take the horse one and then I'll tell you why I came."

"I don't care why you came," said Kate, "but Oh, Mother, thank God you are here!"

"Now, now, don't get het up!" cautioned Mrs. Bates. "Water, I said."

Kate hurried to obey orders; then she sank on a chair and looked at her mother. Mrs. Bates wiped her face and settled in the chair comfortably.

"They's no use to waste words," she said. "Katie, you're the only one in the family that has any sense, and sometimes you ain't got enough so's you could notice it without a magnifyin' glass; but even so, you're ahead of the rest of them. Katie, I'm sick an' tired of the Neppleses and the Whistlers and being bossed by the whole endurin' Bates tribe; sick and tired of it, so I just came after you."

"Came after me?" repeated Kate stupidly.

"Yes, parrot, 'came after you,'" said Mrs. Bates. "I told you, you'd no great amount of sense. I'm speakin' plain, ain't I? I don't see much here to hold you. I want you should throw a few traps, whatever you are beholden to, in the wagon - that's why I brought it - and come on home and take care of me the rest of my time. It won't be so long; I won't interfere much, nor be much bother. I've kep' the place in order, but I'm about fashed. I won't admit it to the rest of them; but I don't seem to mind telling you, Katie, that I am almost winded. Will you come?"

"Of course I will," said Kate, a tide of effulgent joy surging up in her heart until it almost choked her. "Of course I will, Mother, but my children, won't they worry you?"

"Never having had a child about, I s'pect likely they may," said Mrs. Bates, dryly. "Why, you little fool! I think likely it's the children I am pinin' for most, though I couldn't a-stood it much longer without *you*. Will you get ready and come with me to- day?"

"Yes," said Kate, "if I can make it. There's very little here I care for; I can have the second-hand man give me what he will for the rest; and I can get a good price for the lot to-day, if I say so. Dr. James wants it to build on. I'll go and do the very best I can, and when you don't want me any longer, Adam will be bigger and we can look out for ourselves. Yes, I'll get ready at once if you want me to."

"Not much of a haggler, are you, Katie?" said Mrs. Bates. "Why don't you ask what rooms you're to have, and what I'll pay you, and how much work you'll have to do, and if you take charge of the farm, and how we share up?"

Kate laughed: "Mother," she said, "I have been going to school here, with the Master of Life for a teacher; and I've learned so many things that really count, that I know now *none* of the things you mention are essential. You may keep the answers to all those questions; I don't care a cent about any of them. If you want me, and want the children, all those things will settle themselves as we come to them. I didn't use to understand you; but we got well enough acquainted at Father's funeral, and I do, now. Whatever you do will be fair, just, and right. I'll obey you, as I shall expect Adam and Polly to."

"Well, for lands sakes, Katie," said Mrs. Bates. "Life must a- been weltin' it to you good and proper. I never expected to see you as meek as Moses. That Holt man wasn't big enough to beat you, was he?"

"The ways in which he 'beat' me no Bates would understand. I had eight years of them, and I don't understand them yet; but I am so cooked with them, that I shall be wild with joy if you truly mean for me to pack up and come home with you for awhile."

"Oh, Lordy, Katie!" said Mrs. Bates. "This whipped out, take-anything-anyway style ain't becomin' to a big, fine, upstanding woman like you. Hold up your head, child! Hold up your head, and say what you want, an' how you want it!"

"Honestly, Mother, I don't want a thing on earth but to go home with you and do as you say for the next ten years," said Kate.

"Stiffen up!" cried Mrs. Bates. "Stiffen up!" "Don't be no broken reed, Katie! I don't want you dependin' on ME; I came to see if you would let ME lean on *you* the rest of the way. I wa'n't figuring that there was anything on this earth that could get you down; so's I was calculatin' you'd be the very one to hold me up. Since you seem to be feeling unaccountably weak in the knees, let's see if we can brace them a little. Livin' with Pa so long must kind of given me a tendency toward nussin' a deed. I've got one here I had executed two years ago, and I was a coming with it along about now, when 'a little bird tole me' to come to-day, so here I am. Take that, Katie."

Mrs. Bates pulled a long sealed envelope from the front of her dress and tossed it in Kate's lap.

"Mother, what is this?" asked Kate in a hushed voice.

"Well, if you'd rather use your ears than your eyes, it's all the same to me," said Mrs. Bates. "The boys always had a mortal itchin' to get their fingers on the papers in the case. I can't say I don't like the difference; and I've give you every chance, too, an you *wouldn't* demand, you *wouldn't* specify. Well, I'll just specify myself. I'm dead tired of the neighbours taking care of me, and all of the children stoppin' every time they pass, each one orderin' or insinuatin' according to their lights, as to what I should do. I've always had a purty clear idea of what I wanted to do myself. Over forty years, I sided with Pa, to keep the peace; *now* I reckon I'm free to do as I like. That's my side. You can tell me yours, now."

Kate shook her head: "I have nothing to say."

"Jest as well," said Mrs. Bates. "Re-hashing don't do any good. Come back, and come to-day; but stiffen up. That paper you are holding is a warrantee deed to the home two hundred to you and your children after you. You take possession to-day. There's money in the bank to paper, an' paint, and make any little changes you'd like, such as cutting doors or windows different places, floorin' the kitchen new, or the like. Take it an' welcome. I got more 'an enough to last me all my days; all I ask of you is my room, my food, and your company. Take the farm, and do what you pretty please with it."

"But, Mother!" cried Kate. "The rest of them! They'd tear me limb for limb. I don't *dare* take this."

"Oh, don't you?" asked Mrs. Bates. "Well, I still stand for quite a bit at Bates Corners, and I say you *will* take that farm, and run it as you like. It is mine, I give it to you. We all know it wasn't your fault you lost your money, though it was a dose it took some of us a good long time to swallow. You are the only one out of your share; you settled things fine for the rest of them; and they all know it, and feel it. You'll never know what you did for me the way you put me through Pa's funeral; now if you'll just shut up, and stick that deed somewhere it won't burn, and come home an' plant me as successfully as you did Pa, you'll have earned all you'll get, an' something coming. Now set us out a bite to eat, and let's be off."

Kate slowly arose and handed back the deed.

"I'll be flying around so lively I might lose that," she said, "you put it where you had it, till we get to Hartley, and then I'll get a place in the bank vault for it. I can't quite take this in, just yet, but you know I'll do my best for you, Mother!"

"Tain't likely I'd be here else," said Mrs. Bates, "and tea, Katie. A cup of good strong hot tea would fix me up about proper, right now."

Kate went to the kitchen and began setting everything she had to eat on the table. As she worked Polly came flying in the door crying: "Mother, who has come?" so Kate stepped toward the living room to show the child to her grandmother and as she advanced she saw a queer thing. Adam was sitting on his grandmother's lap. Her arms were tight around him, her face buried in his crisp hair, and he was patting her shoulder and telling her he would take care of her, while her voice said distinctly: "Of course you will, birdie!" Then the lad and the old woman laid their heads together and laughed almost hysterically.

"*Well, if that isn't quick work!*" said Kate to herself. Then she presented Polly, who followed Adam's lead in hugging the stranger first and looking at her afterward. God bless all little children. Then Adam ran to tell the second-hand man to come at one o'clock and Dr. James that he might have the keys at three. They ate hurriedly. Kate set out what she wished to save; the children carried things to the wagon; she packed while they ran after their books, and at three o'clock all of them climbed into the spring wagon, and started to Bates Corners.

Kate was the last one in. As she climbed on the seat beside her mother and took the lines, she handed Mrs. Bates a small china mug to hold for her. It was decorated with a very fat robin and on a banner floating from its beak was inscribed: "For a Good Girl."

Life's Boomerang

As they drove into Hartley, Mrs. Bates drew forth the deed.

"You are right about the bank being a safe place for this," she said. "I've had it round the house for two years, and it's a fair nervous thing to do. I wish I'd a-had sense to put it there and come after you the day I made it. But there's no use crying over spilt milk, nor fussin' with the grease spot it makes; salt it down safely now, and when you get it done, beings as this setting is fairly comfortable, take time to run into Harding's and pick up some Sunday-school clothes for the children that will tally up with the rest of their relations'; an' get yourself a cheap frock or two that will spruce you up a bit till you have time to decide what you really want."

Kate passed the lines to her mother, and climbed from the wagon. She returned with her confidence partly restored and a new look on her face. Her mother handed her two dimes.

"I can wait five minutes longer," she said. "Now get two nice oranges and a dime's worth of candy."

Kate took the money and obeyed orders. She handed the packages to her mother as she climbed into the wagon and again took the lines, heading the horse toward the old, familiar road. Her mother twisted around on the seat and gave each of the children an orange and a stick of candy.

"There!" she said. "Go on and spoil yourselves past redemption."

Kate laughed. "But, Mother," she said, "you never did that for us."

"Which ain't saying I never *wanted* to," said Mrs. Bates, sourly. "You're a child only once in this world; it's a little too rough to strip childhood of everything. I ain't so certain Bates ways are right, that for the rest of my time I'm goin' to fly in the face of all creation to prove it. If God lets me live a few years more, I want the faces around me a little less discontenteder than those I've been used to. If God Almighty spares me long enough, I lay out to make sure that Adam and Polly will squeeze out a tear or two for Granny when she is laid away."

"I think you are right, Mother," said Kate. "It didn't cost anything, but we had a real pretty Christmas tree this year, and I believe we can do better next time. I want the children to love you, but don't *buy* them."

"Well, I'd hardly call an orange and a stick of candy traffickin' in affection," said Mrs. Bates. "They'll survive it without underminin' their principles, I'll be bound, or yours either. Katie, let's make a beginning to-day. *Let's work what is right, and healthy, a fair part of the day, and then each day, and sunday especially, let's play and rest, just as hard as we work. It's been all work and no play till we've been mighty 'dull boys' at our house; I'm free to say that I hanker for a change before I die.*"

"Don't speak so often of dying," said Kate. "You're all right. You've been too much alone. You'll feel like yourself as soon as you get rested."

"I guess I been thinking about it too much," said Mrs. Bates. "I ain't been so well as I might, an' not being used to it, it worries me some. I got to buck up. The one thing I *can't* do is to die; but I'm most tired enough to do it right now. I'll be glad when we get home."

Kate drove carefully, but as fast as she dared with her load. As they neared Bates Corners, the way became more familiar each mile. Kate forgot the children, forgot her mother, forgot ten years of disappointment and failure, and began a struggle to realize what was happening to her now. The lines slipped down, the horse walked slowly, the first thing she knew, big hot tears splashed on her hand. She gathered up the lines, drew a deep breath, and glanced at her mother, meeting her eye fairly. Kate tried to smile, but her lips were quivering.

"Glad, Katie?" asked Mrs. Bates.

Kate nodded.

"Me, too!" said Mrs. Bates.

They passed the orchard.

"There's the house, there, Polly!" cried Adam.

"Why, Adam, how did you know the place?" asked Kate, turning.

Adam hesitated a second. "Ain't you told us times a-plenty about the house and the lilac, and the snowball bush–" "Yes, and the cabbage roses," added Polly.

"So I have," said Kate. "Mostly last winter when we were knitting. Yes, this will be home for all the rest of our lives. Isn't it grand? How will we ever thank Grandmother? How will we ever be good enough to pay her?"

Both children thought this a hint, so with one accord they arose and fell on Mrs. Bates' back, and began to pay at once in coin of childhood.

"There, there," said Kate, drawing them away as she stopped the horse at the gate. "There, there, you will choke Grandmother."

Mrs. Bates pushed Kate's arm down.

"Mind your own business, will you?" she said. "I ain't so feeble that I can't speak for myself awhile yet."

In a daze Kate climbed down, and ran to bring a chair to help her mother. The children were boisterously half eating Mrs. Bates up; she had both of them in her arms, with every outward evidence of enjoying the performance immensely. That was a very busy evening, for the wagon was to be unpacked; all of them were hungry, while the stock was to be fed, and the milking done. Mrs. Bates and Polly attempted supper; Kate and Adam went to the barn; but they worked very hurriedly, for Kate could see how feeble her mother had grown.

When at last the children were bathed and in bed, Kate and her mother sat on the little front porch to smell spring a few minutes before going to rest. Kate reached over and took her mother's hand.

"There's no word I know in any language big enough to thank you for this, Mother," she said. "The best I can do is make each day as nearly a perfect expression of what I feel as possible."

Mrs. Bates drew away her hand and used it to wipe her eyes; but she said with her usual terse perversity: "My, Kate! You're most as wordy as Agatha. I'm no glibtonguer, but I bet you ten dollars it will hustle you some to be any gladder than I am."

Kate laughed and gave up the thanks question.

"To-morrow we must get some onions in," she said. "Have you made any plans about the farm work for this year yet?"

"No," said Mrs. Bates. "I was going to leave that till I decided whether I'd come after you this spring or wait until next. Since I decided to come now, I'll just leave your farm to you. Handle it as you please."

"Mother, what will the other children say?" implored Kate.

"Humph! You are about as well acquainted with them as I am. Take a shot at it yourself. If it will avoid a fuss, we might just say you had to come to stay with me, and run the farm for me, and let them get used to your being here, and bossing things by degrees; like the man that cut his dog's tail off an inch at a time, so it wouldn't hurt so bad."

"But by inches, or 'at one fell swoop,' it's going to hurt," said Kate.

"Sometimes it seems to me," said Mrs. Bates, "that the more we get *hurt* in this world the decenter it makes us. All the boys were hurt enough when Pa went, but every man of them has been a *bigger, better* man since. Instead of competing as they always did, Adam and Andrew and the older, beforehandeder ones, took hold and helped the younger as you told them to, and it's done the whole family a world of good. One thing is funny. To hear Mary talk now, you'd think she engineered that plan herself. The boys are all thankful, and so are the girls. I leave it to you. Tell them or let them guess it by degrees, it's all one to me."

"Tell me about Nancy Ellen and Robert," said Kate.

"Robert stands head in Hartley. He gets bigger and broader every year. He is better looking than a man has any business to be; and I hear the Hartley ladies give him plenty of encouragement in being stuck on himself, but I think he is true to Nancy Ellen, and his heart is all in his work. No children. That's a burning shame! Both of them feel it. In a way, and strictly between you and me, Nancy Ellen is a disappointment to me, an' I doubt if she ain't been a mite of a one to him. He had a right to expect a good deal of Nancy Ellen. She had such a good brain, and good body, and purty face. I may miss my guess, but it always strikes me that she falls *short* of what he expected of her. He's coined money, but she hasn't spent it in the ways he would. Likely I shouldn't say it, but he strikes me as being just a leetle mite too good for her."

"Oh, Mother!" said Kate.

"Now you lookey here," said Mrs. Bates. "Suppose you was a man of Robert's brains, and education, and professional ability, and you made heaps of money, and no children came, and you had to see all you earned, and stood for, and did in a community spent on the *selfishness* of one woman. How big would you feel? What end is that for the ambition and life work of a real man? How would you like it?"

"I never thought of such a thing," said Kate.

"Well, mark my word, you *will* think of it when you see their home, and her clothes, and see them together," said Mrs. Bates.

"She still loves pretty clothing so well?" asked Kate.

"She is the best-dressed woman in the county, and the best looking," said Mrs. Bates, "and that's all there is to her. I'm free to say with her chances, I'm ashamed of what she has, and hasn't made of herself. I'd rather stand in your shoes, than hers, this minute, Katie."

"Does she know I'm here?" asked Kate.

"Yes. I stopped and told her on my way out, this morning," said Mrs. Bates. "I asked them to come out for Sunday dinner, and they are coming."

"Did you deliver the invitation by force?" asked Kate.

"Now, none of your meddling," said Mrs. Bates. "I got what I went after, and that was all I wanted. I've told her an' told her to come to see you during the last three years, an' I know she *wanted* to come; but she just had that stubborn Bates streak in her that wouldn't let her change, once her mind was made up. It did give us a purty severe jolt, Kate, havin' all that good Bates money burn up."

"I scarcely think it jolted any of you more than it did me," said Kate dryly.

"No, I reckon it didn't," said Mrs. Bates. "But they's no use hauling ourselves over the coals to go into that. It's past. You went out to face life bravely enough and it threw you a boomerang that cut a circle and brought you back where you started from. Our arrangements for the future are all made. Now it's up to us to live so that we get the most out of life for us an' the children. Those are mighty nice children of yours, Kate. I take to that boy something amazin', and the girl is the nicest little old lady I've seen in many a day. I think we will like knittin' and sewin' together, to the top of our bent."

"My, but I'm glad you like them, Mother," said Kate. "They are all I've got to show for ten years of my life."

"Not by a long shot, Katie," said Mrs. Bates. "Life has made a real woman of you. I kept watchin' you to-day comin' over; an' I was prouder 'an Jehu of you. It's a debatable question whether you have thrown away your time and your money. I say you've got something to show for it that I wish to God the rest of my children had. I want you should brace your back, and stiffen your neck, and make things hum here. Get a carpenter first. Fix the house the way it will be most convenient and comfortable. Then paint and paper, and get what new things you like, in reason – of course, in reason – and then I want you should get all of us clothes so's there ain't a noticeable difference between us and the others when we come together here or elsewhere. Put in a telephone; they're mighty handy, and if you can scrape up a place – I washed in Nancy Ellen's tub a few weeks ago. I never was wet all over at once before in my life, and I'm just itching to try it again. I say, let's have it, if it knocks a fair-sized hole in a five-hundred-dollar bill. An' if we had the telephone right now, we could call up folks an' order what we want without ever budgin' out of our tracks. Go up ahead, Katie, I'll back you in anything you can think of. It won't hurt my feelings a mite if you can think of one or two things the rest of them haven't got yet. Can't you think of something that will lay the rest of them clear in the shade? I just wish you could. Now, I'm going to bed."

Kate went with her mother, opened her bed, pulled out the pins, and brushed her hair, drew the thin cover over her, and blew out the light. Then she went past the bed on her way to the door, and stooping, she kissed her mother for the first time since she could remember.

Then she lighted a lamp, hunted a big sheet of wrapping paper, and sitting down beside the living room table, she drew a rough sketch of the house. For hours she pored over it, and when at last she went to bed, on the reverse of the sheet she had a drawing that was quite a different affair; yet it was the same house with very few and easily made changes that a good contractor could accomplish in a short time. In the morning, she showed these ideas to her mother who approved all of them, but still showed disappointment visibly.

"That's nothing but all the rest of them have," she said. "I thought you could think up some frills that would be new, and different."

"Well," said Kate, "would you want to go to the expense of setting up a furnace in the cellar? It would make the whole house toasty warm; it would keep the bathroom from freezing in cold weather; and make a better way to heat the water."

"Now you're shouting!" cried Mrs. Bates. "That's it! But keep still. Don't you tell a soul about it, but go on and do it, Katie. Wade right in! What else can you think of?"

"A brain specialist for you," said Kate. "I think myself this is enough for a start; but if you insist on more, there's a gas line passing us out there on the road; we could hitch on for a very reasonable sum, and do away with lamps and cooking with wood."

"Goody for you! That's it!" cried Mrs. Bates. "That's the very thing! Now brush up your hair your prettiest, and put on your new blue dress, and take the buggy, and you and Adam go see how much of this can be started to-day. Me and Polly will keep house."

In a month all of these changes had been made, and were in running order; the painting was finished, new furniture in place, a fair start made on the garden, while a strong, young, hired man was not far behind Hiram with his plowing. Kate was so tired she almost staggered; but she was so happy she arose each morning refreshed, and accomplished work enough for three average women before the day was over. She suggested to her mother that she use her money from the sale of the Walden home to pay for what furniture she had bought, and then none of the others could feel that they were entitled to any share in it, at any time. Mrs. Bates thought that a good idea, so much ill will was saved among the children.

They all stopped in passing; some of them had sharp words to say, which Kate instantly answered in such a way that this was seldom tried twice. In two months the place was fresh, clean, convenient, and in good taste. All of them had sufficient suitable clothing, while the farm work had not been neglected enough to hurt the value of the crops.

In the division of labour, Adam and the hired man took the barn and field work, Mrs. Bates and Polly the house, while Kate threw all her splendid strength wherever it was most needed. If a horse was sick, she went to the barn and doctored it. If the hay was going to get wet, she pitched hay. If the men had not time for the garden she attended it, and hoed the potatoes. For a change, everything went right. Mrs. Bates was happier than she ever had been before, taking the greatest interest in the children. They had lived for three years in such a manner that they would never forget it. They were old enough to appreciate what changes had come to them, and to be very keen about their new home and life. Kate threw herself into the dream of her heart with all the zest of her being. Always she had loved and wanted land. Now she had it. She knew how to handle it. She could make it pay as well as any Bates man, for she had man strength, and all her life she had heard men discuss, and helped men apply man methods.

There was a strong strain of her father's spirit of driving in Kate's blood; but her mother was so tired of it that whenever Kate had gone just so far the older woman had merely to caution: "Now, now, Katie!" to make Kate realized what she was doing and take a slower pace. All of them were well, happy, and working hard; but they also played at proper times, and in convenient places. Kate and her mother went with the children when they fished in the meadow brook, or hunted wild flowers in the woods for Polly's bed in the shade of the pear tree beside the garden. There were flowers in the garden now, as well as vegetables. There was no work done on Sunday. The children always went to Sunday-school and the full term of the District School at Bates Corners. They were respected, they were prosperous, they were finding a joy in life they never before had known, while life had taught them how to appreciate its good things as they achieved them.

The first Christmas Mrs. Bates and Kate made a Christmas tree from a small savine in the dooryard that stood where Kate wanted to set a flowering shrub she had found in the woods. Guided by the former year, and with a few dollars they decided to spend, these women made a real Christmas tree, with gifts and ornaments, over which Mrs. Bates was much more excited than the children. Indeed, such is the perversity of children that Kate's eyes widened and her mouth sagged when she heard Adam say in a half-whisper to Polly: "This is mighty pretty, but gee, Polly, there'll never be another tree as pretty as ours last year!"

While Polly answered: "I was just thinking about it, Adam. Wasn't it the grandest thing?"

The next Christmas Mrs. Bates advanced to a tree that reached the ceiling, with many candles, real ornaments, and an orange, a stocking of candy and nuts, and a doll for each girl, and a knife for each boy of her grandchildren, all of whom she invited for dinner. Adam, 3d, sat at the head of the table, Mrs. Bates at the foot. The tiniest tots that could be trusted without their parents ranged on the Dictionary and the Bible, of which the Bates family possessed a fat edition for birth records; no one had ever used it for any other purpose, until it served to lift Hiram's baby, Milly, on a level with her roast turkey and cranberry jelly. For a year before her party Mrs. Bates planned for it. The tree was beautiful, the gifts amazing, the dinner, as Kate cooked and served it, a revelation, with its big centre basket of red, yellow, and green apples, oranges, bananas, grapes, and flowers. None of them ever had seen a table like that. Then when dinner was over, Kate sat before the fire and in her clear voice, with fine inflections, she read from the Big Book the story of the guiding star and the little child in the manger. Then she told stories, and they played games until four o'clock; and then Adam rolled all of the children into the big wagon bed mounted on the sled runners, and took them home. Then he came back and finished the day. Mrs. Bates could scarcely be persuaded to go to bed. When at last Kate went to put out her mother's light, and see that her feet were warm and her covers tucked, she found her crying.

"Why, Mother!" exclaimed Kate in frank dismay. "Wasn't everything all right?"

"I'm just so endurin' mad," sobbed Mrs. Bates, "that I could a- most scream and throw things. Here I am, closer the end of my string than anybody knows. Likely I'll not see another Christmas. I've lived the most of my life, and never knowed there was a time like that on earth to be had. There wasn't expense to it we couldn't easy have stood, always. Now, at the end of my tether, I go and do this for my grandchildren. 'Tween their little shining faces and me, there kept coming all day the little, sad, disappointed faces of you and Nancy Ellen, and Mary, and Hannah, and Adam, and Andrew, and Hiram and all the others. Ever since he went I've thought the one thing *I couldn't do was to die and face Adam Bates*, but to-day I ain't felt so scared of him. Seems to me HE has got about as much to account for as I have."

Kate stood breathlessly still, looking at her mother. Mrs. Bates wiped her eyes. "I ain't so mortal certain," she said, "that I don't open up on him and take the first word. I think likely I been defrauded out of more that really counts in this world, than he has. Ain't that little roly-poly of Hannah's too sweet? Seems like I'll hardly quit feeling her little sticky hands and her little hot mouth on my face when I die; and as she went out she whispered in my ear: 'Do it again, Grandma, Oh, please do it again!' an it's more'n likely I'll not get the chance, no matter how willing I am. Kate, I am going to leave you what of my money is left – I haven't spent so much – and while you live here, I wish each year you would have this same kind of a party and pay for it out of that money, and call it 'Grandmother's Party.' Will you?"

"I surely will," said Kate. "And hadn't I better have *all* of them, and put some little thing from you on the tree for them? You know how Hiram always was wild for cuff buttons, and Mary could talk by the hour about a handkerchief with lace on it, and Andrew never yet has got that copy of 'Aesop's Fables,' he always wanted. Shall I?"

"Yes," said Mrs. Bates. "Oh, yes, and when you do it, Katie, if they don't chain me pretty close in on the other side, I think likely I'll be sticking around as near as I can get to you."

Kate slipped a hot brick rolled in flannel to the cold old feet, and turning out the light she sat beside the bed and stroked the tired head until easy breathing told her that her mother was sound asleep. Then she went back to the fireplace and sitting in the red glow she told Adam, 3d, *part* of what her mother had said. Long after he was gone, she sat gazing into the slowly graying coals, her mind busy with what she had *not* told.

That spring was difficult for Kate. Day after day she saw her mother growing older, feebler, and frailer. And as the body failed, up flamed the wings of the spirit, carrying her on and on, each day keeping her alive, when Kate did not see how it could be done. With all the force she could gather, each day Mrs. Bates struggled to keep going, denied that she felt badly, drove herself to try to help about the house and garden. Kate warned the remainder of the family what they might expect at any hour; but when they began coming in oftener, bringing little gifts and being unusually kind, Mrs. Bates endured a few of the visits in silence, then she turned to Kate and said after her latest callers: "I wonder what in the name of all possessed ails the folks? Are they just itching to start my funeral? Can't they stay away until you send them word that the breath's out of my body?"

"Mother, you shock me," said Kate. "They come because they *love* you. They try to tell you so with the little things they bring. Most people would think they were neglected, if their children did *not* come to see them when they were not so well."

"Not so well!" cried Mrs. Bates. "Folly! I am as well as I ever was. They needn't come snooping around, trying to make me think I'm not. If they'd a-done it all their lives, well and good; it's no time for them to begin being cotton-mouthed now."

"Mother," said Kate gently, "haven't *you* changed, yourself, about things like Christmas, for example? Maybe your children are changing, too. Maybe they feel that they have missed something they'd like to have from you, and give back to you, before it's too late. Just maybe," said Kate.

Mrs. Bates sat bolt upright still, but her flashing eyes softened.

"I hadn't just thought of that," she said. "I think it's more than likely. Well, if it's *that* way, I s'pose I've got to button up my lip and stand it; but it's about more than I can go, when I know that the first time I lose my grip I'll land smash up against Adam Bates and my settlement with him."

"Mother," said Kate still more gently, "I thought we had it settled at the time Father went that each of you would be accountable to *god*, not to each other. I am a wanderer in darkness myself, when it come to talking about God, but this I know, He is *somewhere* and He is *redeeming* love. If Father has been in the light of His love all these years, he must have changed more, far more than you have. He'll understand now how wrong he was to force ways on you he knew you didn't think right; he'll have more to account to you for than you ever will to him; and remember this only, neither of you is accountable, save to your God."

Mrs. Bates arose and walked to the door, drawn to full height, her head very erect. The world was at bloom-time. The evening air was heavily sweet with lilacs, and the widely branching, old apple trees of the dooryard with loaded with flowers. She stepped outside. Kate followed. Her mother went down the steps and down the walk to the gate. Kate kept beside her, in reach, yet not touching her. At the gate she gripped the pickets to steady herself as she stared long and unflinchingly at the red setting sun dropping behind a white wall of bloom. Then she slowly turned, life's greatest tragedy lining her face, her breath coming in short gasps. She spread her hands at each side, as if to balance herself, her passing soul in her eyes, and looked at Kate.

"Katherine Eleanor," she said slowly and distinctly, "I'm going now. I can't fight it off any longer. I confess myself. I burned those deeds. Every one of them. Pa got himself afire, but he'd thrown *them* out of it. It was my chance. I took it. Are you going to tell them?"

Kate was standing as tall and straight as her mother, her hands extended the same, but not touching her.

"No," she said. "You were an instrument in the hands of God to right a great wrong. No! I shall never tell a soul while I live. In a minute God himself will tell you that you did what He willed you should."

"Well, we will see about that right now," said Mrs. Bates, lifting her face to the sky. "Into thy hands, O Lord, into thy hands!"

Then she closed her eyes and ceased to breathe. Kate took her into her arms and carried her to her bed.

Somewhat of Polly

If the spirit of Mrs. Bates hovered among the bloom-whitened apple trees as her mortal remains were carried past the lilacs and cabbage rose bushes, through a rain of drifting petals, she must have been convinced that time had wrought one great change in the hearts of her children. They had all learned to weep; while if the tears they shed were a criterion of their feelings for her, surely her soul must have been satisfied. They laid her away with simple ceremony and then all of them went to their homes, except Nancy Ellen and Robert, who stopped in passing to learn if there was anything they could do for Kate. She was grieving too deeply for many words; none of them would ever understand the deep bond of sympathy and companionship that had grown to exist between her and her mother. She stopped at the front porch and sat down, feeling unable to enter the house with Nancy Ellen, who was deeply concerned over the lack of taste displayed in Agatha's new spring hat. When Kate could endure it no longer she interrupted: "Why didn't all of them come?"

"What for?" asked Nancy Ellen.

"They had a right to know what Mother had done," said Kate in a low voice.

"But what was the use?" asked Nancy Ellen. "Adam had been managing the administrator business for Mother and paying her taxes with his, of course when she made a deed to you, and had it recorded, they told him. All of us knew it for two years before she went after you. And the new furniture was bought with your money, so it's yours; what was there to have a meeting about?"

"Mother didn't understand that you children knew," said Kate.

"Sometimes I thought there were a lot of things Mother didn't understand," said Nancy Ellen, "and sometimes I thought she understood so much more than any of the rest of us, that all of us would have had a big surprise if we could have seen her brain."

"Yes, I believe we would," said Kate. "Do you mind telling me how the boys and girls feel about this?"

Nancy Ellen laughed shortly. "Well, the boys feel that you negotiated such a fine settlement of Father's affairs for them, that they owe this to you. The girls were pretty sore at first, and some of them are nursing their wrath yet; but there wasn't a thing on earth they could do. All of them were perfectly willing that you should have something – after the fire – of course, most of them thought Mother went too far."

"I think so myself," said Kate. "But she never came near me, or wrote me, or sent me even one word, until the day she came after me. I had nothing to do with it–"

"All of us know that, Kate," said Nancy Ellen. "You needn't worry. We're all used to it, and we're all at the place where we have nothing to say."

To escape grieving for her mother, Kate worked that summer as never before. Adam was growing big enough and strong enough to be a real help. He was interested in all they did, always after the reason, and trying to think of a better way. Kate secured the best agricultural paper for him and they read it nights together. They kept an account book, and set down all they spent, and balanced against it all they earned, putting the difference, which was often more than they hoped for, in the bank.

So the years ran. As the children grew older, Polly discovered that the nicest boy in school lived across the road half a mile north of them; while Adam, after a real struggle in his loyal twin soul, aided by the fact that Henry Peters usually had divided his apples with Polly before Adam reached her, discovered that Milly York, across the road, half a mile south, liked his apples best, and was as nice a girl as Polly ever dared to be. In a dazed way, Kate learned these things from their after-school and Sunday talk, saw that they nearly reached her shoulder, and realized that they were sixteen. So quickly the time goes, when people are busy, happy, and working together. At least Kate and Adam were happy, for they were always working together. By tacit agreement, they left Polly the easy housework, and went themselves to the fields to wrestle with the rugged work of a farm. They thought they were shielding Polly, teaching her a woman's real work, and being kind to her.

Polly thought they were together because they liked to be; doing the farm work because it suited them better; while she had known from babyhood that for some reason her mother did not care for her as she did for Adam. She thought at first that it was because Adam was a boy. Later, when she noticed her mother watching her every time she started to speak, and interrupting with the never-failing caution: "Now be careful! *Think* before you speak! Are you *sure?*" she wondered why this should happen to her always, to Adam never. She asked Adam about it, but Adam did not know. It never occurred to Polly to ask her mother, while Kate was so uneasy it never occurred to her that the child would notice or what she would think. The first time Polly deviated slightly from the truth, she and Kate had a very terrible time. Kate felt fully justified; the child astonished and abused.

Polly arrived at the solution of her problem slowly. As she grew older, she saw that her mother, who always was charitable to everyone else, was repelled by her grandmother, while she loved Aunt Ollie. Older still, Polly realized that *she* was a reproduction of her grandmother. She had only to look at her to see this; her mother did not like her grandmother, maybe Mother did not like her as well as Adam, because she resembled her grandmother. By the time she was sixteen, Polly had arrived at a solution that satisfied her as to why her mother liked Adam better, and always left her alone in the house to endless cooking, dishwashing, sweeping, dusting, washing, and ironing, while she hoed potatoes, pitched hay, or sheared sheep. Polly thought the nicer way would have been to do the housework together and then go to the fields together; but she was a good soul, so she worked alone and brooded in silence, and watched up the road for a glimpse of Henry Peters, who liked to hear her talk, and to whom it mattered not a mite that her hair was lustreless, her eyes steel coloured, and her nose like that of a woman he never had seen. In her way, Polly admired her mother, loved her, and worked until she was almost dropping for Kate's scant, infrequent words of praise.

So Polly had to be content in the kitchen. One day, having finished her work two hours before dinnertime, she sauntered to the front gate. How strange that Henry Peters should be at the end of the field joining their land. When he waved, she waved back. When he climbed the fence she opened the gate. They met halfway, under the bloomful shade of a red haw. Henry wondered who two men he had seen leaving the Holt gate were, and what they wanted, but he was too polite to ask. He merely hoped they did not annoy her. Oh, no, they were only some men to see Mother about some business, but it was most kind of him to let her know he was looking out for her. She got so lonely; Mother never would let her go to the field with her. Of course not! The field was no place for such a pretty girl; there was enough work in the house for her. His sister should not work in the field, if he had a sister, and Polly should not work there, if she belonged to him; No-sir-ee! Polly looked at Henry with shining, young girl eyes, and when he said she was pretty, her blue-gray eyes softened, her cheeks pinked up, the sun put light in her hair nature had failed to, and lo and behold, the marvel was wrought – plain little Polly became a thing of beauty. She knew it instantly, because she saw herself in Henry Peters' eyes. And Henry was so amazed when this wonderful transformation took place in little Polly, right there under the red haw tree, that his own eyes grew big and tender, his cheeks flooded with red blood, his heart shook him, and he drew to full height, and became possessed of an overwhelming desire to dance before Polly, and sing to her. He grew so splendid, Polly caught her breath, and then she smiled on him a very wondering smile, over the great discovery; and Henry grew so bewildered he forgot either to dance or sing as a preliminary. He merely, just merely, reached out and gathered Polly in his arms, and held her against him, and stared down at her wonderful beauty opening right out under his eyes.

"Little Beautiful!" said Henry Peters in a hushed, choking voice, "Little Beautiful!"

Polly looked up at him. She was every bit as beautiful as he thought her, while he was so beautiful to Polly that she gasped for breath. How did he happen to look as he did, right under the red haw, in broad daylight? He had been hers, of course, ever since, shy and fearful, she had first entered Bates Corners school, and found courage in his broad, encouraging smile. Now she smiled on him, the smile of possession that was in her heart. Henry instantly knew she always had belonged to him, so he grasped her closer, and bent his head.

When Henry went back to the plow, and Polly ran down the road, with the joy of the world surging in her heart and brain, she knew that she was going to have to account to her tired, busy mother for being half an hour late with dinner; and he knew he was going to have to explain to an equally tired father why he was four furrows short of where he should be.

He came to book first, and told the truth. He had seen some men go to the Holts'. Polly was his little chum; and she was always alone all summer, so he just walked that way to be sure she was safe. His father looked at him quizzically.

"So *that's* the way the wind blows!" he said. "Well, I don't know where you could find a nicer little girl or a better worker. I'd always hoped you'd take to Milly York; but Polly is better; she can work three of Milly down. Awful plain, though!"

This sacrilege came while Henry's lips were tingling with their first kiss, and his heart was drunken with the red wine of innocent young love.

"Why, Dad, you're crazy!" he cried. "There isn't another girl in the whole world as pretty and sweet as Polly. Milly York? She can't hold a candle to Polly! Besides, she's been Adam's as long as Polly has been mine!"

"God bless my soul!" cried Mr. Peters. "How these youngsters to run away with us. And are you the most beautiful young man at Bates Corners, Henry?"

"I'm beautiful enough that Polly will put her arms around my neck and kiss me, anyway," blurted Henry. "So you and Ma can get ready for a wedding as soon as Polly says the word. I'm ready, right now."

"So am I," said Mr. Peters, "and from the way Ma complains about the work I and you boys make her, I don't think she will object to a little help. Polly is a good, steady worker."

Polly ran, but she simply could not light the fire, set the table, and get things cooked on time, while everything she touched seemed to spill or slip. She could not think what, or how, to do the usual for the very good reason that Henry Peters was a Prince, and a Knight, and a Lover, and a Sweetheart, and her Man; she had just agreed to all this with her soul, less than an hour ago under the red haw. No wonder she was late, no wonder she spilled and smeared; and red of face she blundered and bungled, for the first time in her life. Then in came Kate. She must lose no time, the corn must be finished before it rained. She must hurry – for the first time dinner was late, while Polly was messing like a perfect little fool.

Kate stepped in and began to right things with practised hand. Disaster came when she saw Polly, at the well, take an instant from bringing in the water, to wave in the direction of the Peters farm. As she entered the door, Kate swept her with a glance.

"Have to upset the bowl, as usual?" she said, scathingly. "Just as I think you're going to make something of yourself, and be of some use, you begin mooning in the direction of that big, gangling Hank Peters. Don't you ever let me see you do it again. You are too young to start that kind of foolishness. I bet a cow he was hanging around here, and made you late with dinner."

"He was not! He didn't either!" cried Polly, then stopped in dismay, her cheeks burning. She gulped and went on bravely: "That is, he wasn't here, and he didn't make *me* late, any more than I kept *him* from his work. He always watches when there are tramps and peddlers on the road, because he knows I'm alone. I knew he would be watching two men who stopped to see you, so I just went as far as the haw tree to tell him I was all right, and we got to talking—"

If only Kate had been looking at Polly then! But she was putting the apple butter and cream on the table. As she did so, she thought possibly it was a good idea to have Henry Peters seeing that tramps did not frighten Polly, so she missed dawn on the face of her child, and instead of what might have been, she said: "Well, I must say *that* is neighbourly of him; but don't you dare let him get any foolish notions in his head. I think Aunt Nancy Ellen will let you stay at her house after this, and go to the Hartley High School in winter, so you can come out of that much better prepared to teach than I ever was. I had a surprise planned for you to-night, but now I don't know whether you deserve it or not. I'll have to think."

Kate did not think at all. After the manner of parents, she *said* that, but her head was full of something she thought vastly more important just then; of course Polly should have her share in it. Left alone to wash the dishes and cook supper while her mother went to town, it was Polly, who did the thinking. She thought entirely too much, thought bitterly, thought disappointedly, and finally thought resentfully, and then alas, Polly thought deceitfully. Her mother had said: "Never let me see you." Very well, she would be extremely careful that she was *not* seen; but before she slept she rather thought she would find a way to let Henry know how she was being abused, and about that plan to send her away all the long winter to school. She rather thought Henry would have something to say about how his "Little Beautiful" was being treated. Here Polly looked long and searchingly in the mirror to see if by any chance Henry was mistaken, and she discovered he was. She stared in amazement at the pink-cheeked, shining eyed girl she saw mirrored. She pulled her hair looser around the temples, and drew her lips over her teeth. Surely Henry was mistaken. "Little Beautiful" was too moderate. She would see that he said "perfectly lovely," the next time, and he did.

Kate's Heavenly Time

One evening Kate and Polly went to the front porch to rest until bedtime and found a shining big new trunk sitting there, with Kate's initials on the end, her name on the check tag, and a key in the lock. They unbuckled the straps, turned the key, and lifted the lid. That trunk contained underclothing, hose, shoes, two hats, a travelling dress with half a dozen extra waists, and an afternoon and an evening dress, all selected with especial reference to Kate's colouring, and made one size larger than Nancy Ellen wore, which fitted Kate perfectly. There were gloves, a parasol, and a note which read:

DEAR KATE: Here are some clothes. I am going to go North a week after harvest. You can be spared then as well as not. Come on! Let's run away and have one good time all by ourselves. It is my treat from start to finish. The children can manage the farm perfectly well. Any one of her cousins will stay with Polly, if she will be lonely. Cut loose and come on, Kate. I am going. Of course Robert couldn't be pried away from his precious patients; we will have to go alone; but we do not care. We like it. Shall we start about the tenth, on the night train, which will be cooler? NANCY ELLEN.

"We shall!" said Kate emphatically, when she finished the note. "I haven't cut loose and had a good time since I was married; not for eighteen years. If the children are not big enough to take care of themselves, they never will be. I can go as well as not."

She handed the note to Polly, while she shook out dresses and gloated over the contents of the trunk.

"Of course you shall go!" shouted Polly as she finished the note, but even as she said it she glanced obliquely up the road and waved a hand behind her mother's back.

"Sure you shall go!" cried Adam, when he finished the note, and sat beside the trunk seeing all the pretty things over again. "You just bet you shall go. Polly and I can keep house, fine! We don't need any cousins hanging around. I'll help Polly with her work, and then we'll lock the house and she can come out with me. Sure you go! We'll do all right." Then he glanced obliquely down the road, where a slim little figure in white moved under the cherry trees of the York front yard, aimlessly knocking croquet balls here and there.

It was two weeks until time to go, but Kate began taking care of herself at once, solely because she did not want Nancy Ellen to be ashamed of her. She rolled her sleeves down to meet her gloves and used a sunbonnet instead of a sunshade. She washed and brushed her hair with care she had not used in years. By the time the tenth of July came, she was in very presentable condition, while the contents of the trunk did the remainder. As she was getting ready to go, she said to Polly: "Now do your best while I'm away, and I am sure I can arrange with Nancy Ellen about school this winter. When I get back, the very first thing I shall do will be to go to Hartley and buy some stuff to begin on your clothes. You shall have as nice dresses as the other girls, too. Nancy Ellen will know exactly what to get you."

But she never caught a glimpse of Polly's flushed, dissatisfied face or the tightening of her lips that would have suggested to her, had she seen them, that Miss Polly felt perfectly capable of selecting the clothing she was to wear herself. Adam took his mother's trunk to the station in the afternoon. In the evening she held Polly on her knee, while they drove to Dr. Gray's. Kate thought the children would want to wait and see them take the train, but Adam said that would make them very late getting home, they had better leave that to Uncle Robert and go back soon; so very soon they were duly kissed and unduly cautioned; then started back down a side street that would not even take them through the heart of the town. Kate looked after them approvingly: "Pretty good youngsters," she said. "I told them to go and get some ice cream; but you see they are saving the money and heading straight home." She turned to Robert. "Can anything happen to them?" she asked, in evident anxiety.

"Rest in peace, Kate," laughed the doctor. "You surely know that those youngsters are going to be eighteen in a few weeks. You've reared them carefully. Nothing can, or will, happen to them, that would not happen right under your nose if you were at home. They will go from now on according to their inclinations."

Kate looked at him sharply: "What do you mean by that?" she demanded.

He laughed: "Nothing serious," he said. "Polly is half Bates, so she will marry in a year or two, while Adam is all Bates, so he will remain steady as the Rock of Ages, and strictly on the job. Go have your good time, and if I possibly can, I'll come after you."

"You'll do nothing of the kind," said Nancy Ellen, with finality. "You wouldn't leave your patients, and you couldn't leave dear Mrs. Southey."

"If you feel that way about it, why do you leave me?" he asked.

"To show the little fool I'm not afraid of her, for one thing," said Nancy Ellen with her head high. She was very beautiful in her smart travelling dress, while her eyes flashed as she spoke. The doctor looked at her approvingly.

"Good!" he cried. "I like a plucky woman! Go to have a good time, Nancy Ellen; but don't go for that. I do wish you would believe that there isn't a thing the matter with the little woman, she's—"

"I can go even farther than that," said Nancy Ellen, dryly. "I *know* 'there isn't a thing the matter with the little woman,' except that she wants you to look as if you were running after her. I'd be safe in wagering a thousand dollars that when she hears I'm gone, she will send for you before to-morrow evening."

"You may also wager this," he said. "If she does, I shall be very sorry, but I'm on my way to the country on an emergency call. Nancy Ellen, I wish you wouldn't!"

"Wouldn't go North, or wouldn't see what every other living soul in Hartley sees?" she asked curtly. Then she stepped inside to put on her hat and gloves.

Kate looked at the doctor in dismay. "Oh, Robert!" she said.

"I give you my word of honour, Kate," he said. "If Nancy Ellen only would be reasonable, the woman would see shortly that my wife is all the world to me. I never have been, and never shall be, untrue to her. Does that satisfy you?"

"Of course," said Kate. "I'll do all in my power to talk Nancy Ellen out of that, on this trip. Oh, if she only had children to occupy her time!"

"That's the whole trouble in a nutshell," said the doctor; "but you know there isn't a scarcity of children in the world. Never a day passes but I see half a dozen who need me, sorely. But with Nancy Ellen, *no child* will do unless she mothers it, and unfortunately, none comes to her."

"Too bad!" said Kate. "I'm so sorry!"

"Cheer her up, if you can," said the doctor.

An hour later they were speeding north, Nancy Ellen moody and distraught, Kate as frankly delighted as any child. The spring work was over; the crops were fine; Adam would surely have the premium wheat to take to the County Fair in September; he would work unceasingly for his chance with corn; he and Polly would be all right; she could see Polly waiting in the stable yard while Adam unharnessed and turned out the horse.

Kate kept watching Nancy Ellen's discontented face. At last she said: "Cheer up, child! There isn't a word of truth in it!"

"I know it," said Nancy Ellen.

"Then why take the way of all the world to start, and *keep* people talking?" asked Kate.

"I'm not doing a thing on earth but attending strictly to my own business," said Nancy Ellen.

"That's exactly the trouble," said Kate. "You're not. You let the little heifer have things all her own way. If it were my man, and I loved him as you do Robert Gray, you can stake your life I should be doing something, several things, in fact."

"This is interesting," said Nancy Ellen. "For example –?"

Kate had not given such a matter a thought. She looked from the window a minute, her lips firmly compressed. Then she spoke slowly: "Well, for one thing, I should become that woman's bosom companion. About seven times a week I should uncover her most aggravating weakness all unintentionally before the man in the case, at the same time keeping myself, strictly myself. I should keep steadily on doing and being what he first fell in love with. Lastly, since eighteen years have brought you no fulfillment of the desire of your heart, I should give it up, and content myself and delight him by taking into my heart and home a couple of the most attractive tiny babies I could find. Two are scarcely more trouble than one; you can have all the help you will accept; the children would never know the difference, if you took them as babies, and soon you wouldn't either; while Robert would be delighted. If I were you, I'd give myself something to work for besides myself, and I'd give him so much to think about at home, that charming young grass widows could go to grass!"

"I believe you would," said Nancy Ellen, wonderingly. "I believe you would!"

"You're might right, I would," said Kate. "If I were married to a man like Robert Gray, I'd fight tooth and nail before I'd let him fall below his high ideals. It's as much your job to keep him up, as it is his to keep himself. If God didn't make him a father, I would, and I'd keep him *busy* on the job, if I had to adopt sixteen."

Nancy Ellen laughed, as they went to their berths. The next morning they awakened in cool Michigan country and went speeding north among evergreen forests and clear lakes mirroring the pointed forest tops and blue sky, past slashing, splashing streams, in which they could almost see the speckled trout darting over the beds of white sand. By late afternoon they had reached their destination and were in their rooms, bathed, dressed, and ready for the dinner hour. In the evening they went walking, coming back to the hotel tired and happy. After several days they began talking to people and making friends, going out in fishing and boating parties in the morning, driving or boating in the afternoon, and attending concerts or dances at night. Kate did not dance, but she loved to see Nancy Ellen when she had a sufficiently tall, graceful partner; while, as she watched the young people and thought how innocent and happy they seemed, she asked her sister if they could not possibly arrange for Adam and Polly to go to Hartley a night or two a week that winter, and join the dancing class. Nancy Ellen was frankly delighted, so Kate cautiously skirted the school question in such a manner that she soon had Nancy Ellen asking if it could not be arranged. When that was decided, Nancy Ellen went to dance, while Kate stood on the veranda watching her. The lights from the window fell strongly on Kate. She was wearing her evening dress of smoky gray, soft fabric, over shining silk, with knots of dull blue velvet and gold lace here and there. She had dressed her hair carefully; she appeared what she was, a splendid specimen of healthy, vigorous, clean womanhood.

"Pardon me, Mrs. Holt," said a voice at her elbow, "but there's only one head in this world like yours, so this, of course, must be you."

Kate's heart leaped and stood still. She turned slowly, then held out her hand, smiling at John Jardine, but saying not a word. He took her hand, and as he gripped it tightly he studied her frankly.

"Thank God for this!" he said, fervently. "For years I've dreamed of you and hungered for the sight of your face; but you cut me off squarely, so I dared not intrude on you – only the Lord knows how delighted I am to see you here, looking like this."

Kate smiled again.

"Come away," he begged. "Come out of this. Come walk a little way with me, and tell me *who* you are, and *how* you are, and all the things I think of every day of my life, and now I must know. It's brigandage! Come, or I shall carry you!"

"Pooh! You couldn't!" laughed Kate. "Of course I'll come! And I don't own a secret. Ask anything you want to know. How good it is to see you! Your mother –?"

"At rest, years ago," he said. "She never forgave me for what I did, in the way I did it. She said it would bring disaster, and she was right. I thought it was not fair and honest not to let you know the worst. I thought I was too old, and too busy, and too flourishing, to repair neglected years at that date, but believe me, Kate, you waked me up. Try the hardest one you know, and if I can't spell it, I'll pay a thousand to your pet charity."

Kate laughed spontaneously. "Are you in earnest?" she asked.

"I am incomprehensibly, immeasurably in earnest," he said, guiding her down a narrow path to a shrub-enclosed, railed-in platform, built on the steep side of a high hill, where they faced the moon-whitened waves, rolling softly in a dancing procession across the face of the great inland sea. Here he found a seat.

"I've nothing to tell," he said. "I lost Mother, so I went on without her. I learned to spell, and a great many other things, and I'm still making money. I never forget you for a day; I never have loved and never shall love any other woman. That's all about me, in a nutshell; now go on and tell me a volume, tell me all night, about you. Heavens, woman, I wish you could see yourself, in that dress with the moon on your hair. Kate, you are the superbest thing! I always shall be mad about you. Oh, if only you could have had a little patience with me. I thought I *couldn't* learn, but of course I *could*. But, proceed! I mustn't let myself go."

Kate leaned back and looked a long time at the shining white waves and the deep blue sky, then she turned to John Jardine, and began to talk. She told him simply a few of the most presentable details of her life: how she had lost her money, then had been given her mother's farm, about the children, and how she now lived. He listened with deep interest, often interrupting to ask a question, and when she ceased talking he said half under his breath: "And you're now free! Oh, the wonder of it! You're now, free!"

Kate had that night to think about the remainder of her life. She always sincerely hoped that the moonlight did not bewitch her into leading the man beside her into saying things he seemed to take delight in saying.

She had no idea what time it was; in fact, she did not care even what Nancy Ellen thought or whether she would worry. The night was wonderful; John Jardine had now made a man of himself worthy of all consideration; being made love to by him was enchanting. She had been occupied with the stern business of daily bread for so long that to be again clothed as other women and frankly adored by such a man as John Jardine was soul satisfying. What did she care who worried or what time it was?

"But I'm keeping you here until you will be wet with these mists," John Jardine cried at last. "Forgive me, Kate, I never did have any sense where you were concerned! I'll take you back now, but you must promise me to meet me here in the morning, say at ten o'clock. I'll take you back now, if you'll agree to that."

"There's no reason why I shouldn't," said Kate.

"And you're free, free!" he repeated.

The veranda, halls, and ballroom were deserted when they returned to the hotel. As Kate entered her room, Nancy Ellen sat up in bed and stared at her sleepily, but she was laughing in high good humour. She drew her watch from under her pillow and looked at it.

"Goodness gracious, Miss!" she cried. "Do you know it's almost three o'clock?"

"I don't care in the least," said Kate, "if it's four or five. I've had a perfectly heavenly time. Don't talk to me. I'll put out the light and be quiet as soon as I get my dress off. I think likely I've ruined it."

"What's the difference?" demanded Nancy Ellen, largely. "You can ruin half a dozen a day now, if you want to."

"What do you mean?" asked Kate.

"'Mean?'" laughed Nancy Ellen. "I mean that I saw John Jardine or his ghost come up to you on the veranda, looking as if he'd eat you alive, and carry you away about nine o'clock, and you've been gone six hours and come back having had a 'perfectly heavenly time.' What should I mean! Go up head, Kate! You have earned your right to a good time. It isn't everybody who gets a second chance in this world. Tell me one thing, and I'll go to sleep in peace and leave you to moon the remainder of the night, if you like. Did he say he still loved you?"

"Still and yet," laughed Kate. "As I remember, his exact words were that he 'never had loved and never would love any other woman.' Now are you satisfied?"

Nancy Ellen sprang from the bed and ran to Kate, gathering her in her strong arms. She hugged and kissed her ecstatically. "Good! Good! Oh, you darling!" she cried. "There'll be nothing in the world you can't have! I just know he had gone on making money; he was crazy about you. Oh, Kate, this is too good! How did I ever think of coming here, and why didn't I think of it seven years ago? Kate, you must promise me you'll marry him, before I let you go."

"I'll promise to *think* about it," said Kate, trying to free herself, for despite the circumstances and the hour, her mind flew back to a thousand times when only one kind word from Nancy Ellen would have saved her endless pain. It was endless, for it was burning in her heart that instant. At the prospect of wealth, position, and power, Nancy Ellen could smother her with caresses; but poverty, pain, and disgrace she had endured alone.

"I shan't let you go till you promise," threatened Nancy Ellen. "When are you to see him again?"

"Ten, this morning," said Kate. "You better let me get to bed, or I'll look a sight."

"Then promise," said Nancy Ellen.

Kate laid firm hands on the encircling arms. "Now, look here," she said, shortly, "it's about time to stop this nonsense. There's nothing I can promise you. I must have time to think. I've got not only myself, but the children to think for. And I've only got till ten o'clock, so I better get at it."

Kate's tone made Nancy Ellen step back.

"Kate, you haven't still got that letter in your mind, have you?" she demanded.

"No!" laughed Kate, "I haven't! He offered me a thousand dollars if I could pronounce him a word he couldn't spell; and it's perfectly evident he's studied until he is exactly like anybody else. No, it's not that!"

"Then what is it? Simpleton, there WAS nothing else!" cried Nancy Ellen.

"Not so much at that time; but this is nearly twenty years later, and I have the fate of my children in my hands. I wish you'd go to bed and let me think!" said Kate.

"Yes, and the longer you think the crazier you will act," cried Nancy Ellen. "I know you! You better promise me now, and stick to it."

For answer Kate turned off the light; but she did not go to bed. She sat beside the window and she was still sitting there when dawn crept across the lake and began to lighten the room. Then she stretched herself beside Nancy Ellen, who roused and looked at her.

"You just coming to bed?" she cried in wonder.

"At least you can't complain that I didn't think," said Kate, but Nancy Ellen found no comfort in what she said, or the way she said it. In fact, she arose when Kate did, feeling distinctly sulky. As they returned to their room from breakfast, Kate laid out her hat and gloves and began to get ready to keep her appointment. Nancy Ellen could endure the suspense no longer.

"Kate," she said in her gentlest tones, "if you have no mercy on yourself, have some on your children. You've no right, positively no right, to take such a chance away from them."

"Chance for what?" asked Kate tersely.

"Education, travel, leisure, every opportunity in the world," enumerated Nancy Ellen.

Kate was handling her gloves, her forehead wrinkled, her eyes narrowed in concentration.

"That is one side of it," she said. "The other is that neither my children nor I have in our blood, breeding, or mental cosmos, the background that it takes to make one happy with money in unlimited quantities. So far as I'm concerned personally, I'm happier this minute as I am, than John Jardine's money ever could make me. I had a fierce struggle with that question long ago; since I have had nearly eight years of life I love, that is good for my soul, the struggle to leave it would be greater now. Polly would be happier and get more from life as the wife of big gangling Henry Peters, than she would as a millionaire's daughter. She'd be very suitable in a farmhouse parlour; she'd be a ridiculous little figure at a ball. As for Adam, he'd turn this down quick and hard."

"Just you try him!" cried Nancy Ellen.

"For one thing, he won't be here at ten o'clock," said Kate, "and for another, since it involves my becoming the wife of John Jardine, it isn't for Adam to decide. This decision is strictly my own. I merely mention the children, because if I married him, it would have an inevitable influence on their lives, an influence that I don't in the least covet either for them or for myself. Nancy Ellen, can't you remotely conceive of such a thing as one human being in the world who is *Satisfied that he has his share*, and who believes to the depths of his soul that no man should be allowed to amass, and to use for his personal indulgence, the amount of money that John Jardine does?"

"Yes, I can," cried Nancy Ellen, "when I see you, and the way you act! You have chance after chance, but you seem to think that life requires of you a steady job of holding your nose to the grindstone. It was rather stubby to begin with, go on and grind it clear off your face, if you like."

"All right," said Kate. "Then I'll tell you definitely that I have no particular desire to marry anybody; I like my life immensely as I'm living it. I'm free, independent, and my children are in the element to which they were born, and where they can live naturally, and spend their lives helping in the great work of feeding, clothing, and housing their fellow men. I've no desire to leave my job or take them from theirs, to start a lazy, shiftless life of self-indulgence. I don't meddle much with the Bible, but I have a profound *belief* in it, and a large *respect* for it, as the greatest book in the world, and it says: 'By the sweat of his brow shall man earn his bread,' or words to that effect. I was born a sweater, I shall just go on sweating until I die; I refuse to begin perspiring at my time of life."

"You big fool!" cried Nancy Ellen.

"Look out! You're 'in danger of Hell fire,' when you call me that!" warned Kate.

"Fire away!" cried Nancy Ellen, with tears in her eyes and voice. "When I think what you've gone through–"

Kate stared at her fixedly. "What do you know about what I've gone though?" she demanded in a cold, even voice. "Personally, I think you're not qualified to *mention* that subject; you better let it rest. Whatever it has been, it's been of such a nature that I have come out of it knowing when I have my share and when I'm well off, for me. If John Jardine wants to marry me, and will sell all he has, and come and work on the farm with me, I'll consider marrying him. To leave my life and what I love to go to Chicago with him, I do not feel called on, or inclined to do. No, I'll not marry him, and in about fifteen minutes I'll tell him so."

"And go on making a mess of your life such as you did for years," said Nancy Ellen, drying her red eyes.

"At least it was my life," said Kate. "I didn't mess things for any one else."

"Except your children," said Nancy Ellen.

"As you will," said Kate, rising. "I'll not marry John Jardine; and the sooner I tell him so and get it over, the better. Good-bye. I'll be back in half an hour."

Kate walked slowly to the observation platform, where she had been the previous evening with John Jardine; and leaning on the railing, she stood looking out over the water, and down the steep declivity, thinking how best she could word what she had to say. She was so absorbed she did not hear steps behind her or turn until a sharp voice said: "You needn't wait any longer. He's not coming!"

Kate turned and glanced at the speaker, and then around to make sure she was the person being addressed. She could see no one else. The woman was small, light haired, her face enamelled, dressed beyond all reason, and in a manner wholly out of place for morning at a summer resort in Michigan.

"If you are speaking to me, will you kindly tell me to whom you refer, and give me the message you bring?" said Kate.

"I refer to Mr. John Jardine, Mrs. Holt," said the little woman and then Kate saw that she was shaking, and gripping her hands for self-control.

"Very well," said Kate. "It will save me an unpleasant task if he doesn't come. Thank you," and she turned back to the water.

"You certainly didn't find anything unpleasant about being with him half last night," said the little woman.

Kate turned again, and looked narrowly at the speaker. Then she laughed heartily. "Well done, Jennie!" she cried. "Why, you are such a fashionable lady, such a Dolly Varden, I never saw who you were. How do you do? Won't you sit down and have a chat? It's just dawning on me that very possibly, from your dress and manner, I *should* have called you Mrs. Jardine."

"Didn't he tell you?" cried Jennie.

"He did not," said Kate. "Your name was not mentioned. He said no word about being married."

"We have been married since a few weeks after Mrs. Jardine died. I taught him the things you turned him down for not knowing; I have studied him, and waited on him, and borne his children, and *this* is my reward. What are you going to do?"

"Go back to the hotel, when I finish with this view," said Kate. "I find it almost as attractive by day as it was by night."

"Brazen!" cried Mrs. Jardine.

"Choose your words carefully," said Kate. "I was here first; since you have delivered your message, suppose you go and leave me to my view."

"Not till I get ready," said Mrs. Jardine. "Perhaps it will help you to know that I was not twenty feet from you at any time last night; and that I stood where I could have touched you, while my husband made love to you for hours."

"So?" said Kate. "I'm not at all surprised. That's exactly what I should have expected of you. But doesn't it clarify the situation any, at least for me, when I tell you that Mr. Jardine gave me no faintest hint that he was married? If you heard all we said, you surely remember that you were not mentioned?"

Mrs. Jardine sat down suddenly and gripped her little hands. Kate studied her intently. She wondered what she would look like when her hair was being washed; at this thought she smiled broadly. That made the other woman frantic.

"You can well *laugh* at me," she said. "I made the banner fool of the ages of myself when I schemed to marry him. I knew he loved you. He told me so. He told me, just as he told you last night, that he never had loved any other woman and he never would. I thought he didn't know himself as I knew him. He was so grand to his mother, I thought if I taught him, and helped him back to self-respect, and gave him children, he must, and would love me. Well, I was mistaken. He does not, and never will. Every day he thinks of you; not a night but he speaks your name. He thinks all things can be done with money–"

"So do you, Jennie," interrupted Kate. "Well, I'll show you that this *can't*!"

"Didn't you hear him exulting because you are now free?" cried Jennie. "He thinks he will give me a home, the children, a big income; then secure his freedom and marry you."

"Oh, don't talk such rot!" cried Kate. "John Jardine thinks no such thing. He wouldn't insult me by thinking I thought such a thing. That thought belongs where it sprang from, right in your little cramped, blonde brain, Jennie."

"You wouldn't? Are you sure you wouldn't?" cried Jennie, leaning forward with hands clutched closely.

"I should say not!" said Kate. "The last thing on earth I want is some other woman's husband. Now look here, Jennie, I'll tell you the plain truth. I thought last night that John Jardine was as free as I was; or I shouldn't have been here with him. I thought he was asking me again to marry him, and I was not asleep last night, thinking it over. I came here to tell him that I would not. Does that satisfy you?"

"Satisfy?" cried Jennie. "I hope no other woman lives in the kind of Hell I do."

"It's always the way," said Kate, "when people will insist on getting out of their class. You would have gotten ten times more from life as the wife of a village merchant, or a farmer, than you have as the wife of a rich man. Since you're married to him, and there are children, there's nothing for you to do but finish your job as best you can. Rest your head easy about me. I wouldn't touch John Jardine married to you; I wouldn't touch him with a ten-foot pole, divorced from you. Get that clear in your head, and do please go!"

Kate turned again to the water, but when she was sure Jennie was far away she sat down suddenly and asked of the lake: "Well, wouldn't that freeze you?"

Polly Tries her Wings

Finally Kate wandered back to the hotel and went to their room to learn if Nancy Ellen was there. She was and seemed very much perturbed. The first thing she did was to hand Kate a big white envelope, which she opened and found to be a few lines from John Jardine, explaining that he had been unexpectedly called away on some very important business. He reiterated his delight in having seen her, and hoped for the same pleasure at no very distant date. Kate read it and tossed it on the dresser. As she did so, she saw a telegram, lying opened among Nancy Ellen's toilet articles, and thought with pleasure that Robert was coming. She glanced at her sister for confirmation, and saw that she was staring from the window as if she were in doubt about something. Kate thought probably she was still upset about John Jardine, and that might as well be gotten over, so she said: "That note was not delivered promptly. It is from John Jardine. I should have had it before I left. He was called away on important business and wrote to let me know he would not be able to keep his appointment; but without his knowledge, he had a representative on the spot."

Nancy Ellen seemed interested so Kate proceeded: "You couldn't guess in a thousand years. I'll have to tell you spang! It was his wife."

"His wife!" cried Nancy Ellen. "But you said—"

"So I did," said Kate. "And so he did. Since the wife loomed on the horizon, I remembered that he said no word to me of marriage; he merely said he always had loved me and always would – "

"Merely?" scoffed Nancy Ellen. "Merely!"

"Just 'merely,'" said Kate. "He didn't lay a finger on me; he didn't ask me to marry him; he just merely met me after a long separation, and told me that he still loved me."

"The brute!" said Nancy Ellen. "He should be killed."

"I can't see it," said Kate. "He did nothing ungentlemanly. If we jumped to wrong conclusions that was not his fault. I doubt if he remembered or thought at all of his marriage. It wouldn't be much to forget. I am fresh from an interview with his wife. She's an old acquaintance of mine. I once secured her for his mother's maid. You've heard me speak of her."

"Impossible! John Jardine would not do that!" cried Nancy Ellen.

"There's a family to prove it," said Kate. "Jennie admits that she studied him, taught him, made herself indispensable to him, and a few weeks after his mother's passing, married him, after he had told her he did not love her and never could. I feel sorry for him."

"Sure! Poor defrauded creature!" said Nancy Ellen. "What about her?"

"Nothing, so far as I can see," said Kate. "By her own account she was responsible. She should have kept in her own class."

"All right. That settles Jennie!" said Nancy Ellen. "I saw you notice the telegram from Robert – now go on and settle me!"

"Is he coming?" asked Kate.

"No, he's not coming," said Nancy Ellen.

"Has he eloped with the widder?" asked Kate flippantly.

"He merely telegraphs that he thinks it would be wise for us to come home on the first train," said Nancy Ellen. "For all I can make of that, the elopement might quite as well be in your family as mine."

Kate held out her hand, Nancy Ellen laid the message in it. Kate studied it carefully; then she raised steady eyes to her sister's face.

"Do you know what I should do about this?" she asked.

"Catch the first train, of course," she said.

"Far be it from me," said Kate. "I should at once telegraph him that his message was not clear, to kindly particularize. We've only got settled. We're having a fine time; especially right now. Why should we pack up and go home? I can't think of any possibility that could arise that would make it necessary for him to send for us. Can you?"

"I can think of two things," said Nancy Ellen. "I can think of a very pretty, confiding, little cat of a woman, who is desperately infatuated with my husband; and I can think of two children fathered by George Holt, who might possibly, just possibly, have enough of his blood in their veins to be like him, given opportunity. Alone for a week, there is barely a *faint* possibility that *you* might be needed. Alone for the same week, there is the faintest possibility that *Robert* is in a situation where I could help him."

Kate drew a deep breath.

"Isn't life the most amusing thing?" she asked. "I had almost forgotten my wings. I guess we'd better take them, and fly straight home."

She arose and called the office to learn about trains, and then began packing her trunk. As she folded her dresses and stuffed them in rather carelessly she said: "I don't know why I got it into my head that I could go away and have a few days of a good time without something happening at home."

"But you are not sure anything has happened at home. This call may be for me," said Nancy Ellen.

"It *may*, but this is July," said Kate. "I've been thinking hard and fast. It's probable I can put my finger on the spot."

Nancy Ellen paused and standing erect she looked questioningly at Kate.

"The weak link in my chain at the present minute is Polly," said Kate. "I didn't pay much attention at the time, because there wasn't enough of it really to attract attention; but since I think, I can recall signs of growing discontent in Polly, lately. She fussed about the work, and resented being left in the house while I went to the fields, and she had begun looking up the road to Peters' so much that her head was slightly turned toward the north most of the time. With me away–"

"What do you think?" demanded Nancy Ellen.

"Think very likely she has decided that she'll sacrifice her chance for more schooling and to teach, for the sake of marrying a big, green country boy named Hank Peters," said Kate.

"Thereby keeping in her own class," suggested Nancy Ellen.

Kate laughed shortly. "Exactly!" she said. "I didn't aspire to anything different for her from what she has had; but I wanted her to have more education, and wait until she was older. Marriage is too hard work for a girl to begin at less than eighteen. If it is Polly, and she has gone away with Hank Peters, they've no place to go but his home; and if ever she thought I worked her too hard, she'll find out she has played most of her life, when she begins taking orders from Mrs. Amanda Peters. You know her! She never can keep a girl more than a week, and she's always wanting one. If Polly has tackled *that* job, God help her."

"Cheer up! We're in that delightful state of uncertainty where Polly may be blacking the cook stove, like a dutiful daughter; while Robert has decided that he'd like a divorce," said Nancy Ellen.

"Nancy Ellen, there's nothing in that, so far as Robert is concerned. He told me so the evening we came away," said Kate.

Nancy Ellen banged down a trunk lid and said: "Well, I am getting to the place where I don't much care whether there is or there is not."

"What a whopper!" laughed Kate. "But cheer up. This is my trouble. I feel it in my bones. Wish I knew for sure. If she's eloped, and it's all over with, we might as well stay and finish our visit. If she's married, I can't unmarry her, and I wouldn't if I could."

"How are you going to apply your philosophy to yourself?" asked Nancy Ellen.

"By letting time and Polly take their course," said Kate. "This is a place where parents are of no account whatever. They stand back until it's time to clean up the wreck, and then they get theirs – usually theirs, and several of someone's else, in the bargain."

As the train stopped at Hartley, Kate sat where she could see Robert on the platform. It was only a fleeting glance, but she thought she had never seen him look so wholesome, so vital, so much a man to be desired.

"No wonder a woman lacking in fine scruples would covet him," thought Kate. To Nancy Ellen she said hastily: "The trouble's mine. Robert's on the platform."

"Where?" demanded Nancy Ellen, peering from the window.

Kate smiled as she walked from the car and confronted Robert.

"Get it over quickly," she said. "It's Polly?"

He nodded.

"Did she remember to call on the Squire?" she asked.

"Oh, yes," said Robert. "It was at Peters', and they had the whole neighbourhood in."

Kate swayed slightly, then lifted her head, her eyes blazing. She had come, feeling not altogether guiltless, and quite prepared to overlook a youthful elopement. The insult of having her only daughter given a wedding at the home of the groom, about which the whole neighbourhood would be laughing at her, was a different matter. Slowly the high colour faded from Kate's face, as she stepped back. "Excuse me, Nancy Ellen," she said. "I didn't mean to deprive you of the chance of even speaking to Robert. I *knew* this was for me; I was over-anxious to learn what choice morsel life had in store for me now. It's one that will be bitter on my tongue to the day of my death."

"Oh, Kate, I as so sorry that if this had to happen, it happened in just that way," said Nancy Ellen, "but don't mind. They're only foolish kids!"

"Who? Mr. and Mrs. Peters, and the neighbours, who attended the wedding! Foolish kids? Oh, no!" said Kate. "Where's Adam?"

"I told him I'd bring you out," said Robert.

"Why didn't he send for you, or do something?" demanded Kate.

"I'm afraid the facts are that Polly lied to him," said Robert. "She told him that Peters were having a party, and Mrs. Peters wanted her to come early and help her with the supper. They had the Magistrate out from town and had the ceremony an hour before Adam got there. When he arrived, and found out what had happened, he told Polly and the Peters family exactly his opinion of them; and then he went home and turned on all the lights, and sat where he could be seen on the porch all evening, as a protest in evidence of his disapproval, I take it."

Slowly the colour began to creep back into Kate's face. "The good boy!" she said, in commendation.

"He called me at once, and we talked it over and I sent you the telegram; but as he said, it was done; there was no use trying to undo it. One thing will be a comfort to you. All of your family, and almost all of your friends, left as soon as Adam spoke his piece, and they found it was a wedding and not a party to which they'd been invited. It was a shabby trick of Peters."

Kate assented. "It was because I felt instinctively that Mrs. Peters had it in her to do tricks like that, that I never would have anything to do with her," said Kate, "more than to be passing civil. This is how she gets her revenge, and her hired girl, for no wages, I'll be bound! It's a shabby trick. I'm glad Adam saved me the trouble of telling her so."

Robert took Nancy Ellen home, and then drove to Bates Corners with Kate.

"In a few days now I hope we can see each other oftener," he said, on the way. "I got a car yesterday, and it doesn't seem so complicated. Any intelligent person can learn to drive in a short time. I like it so much, and I knew I'd have such constant use for it that – now this is a secret – I ordered another for Nancy Ellen, so she can drive about town, and run out here as she chooses. Will she be pleased?"

"She'll be overjoyed! That was dear of you, Robert. Only one thing in world would please her more," said Kate.

"What's that?" asked Robert.

Kate looked him in the eye, and smiled.

"Oh," he said. "But there is nothing in it!"

"Except *talk*, that worries and humiliates Nancy Ellen," said Kate.

"Kate," he said suddenly, "if you were in my shoes, what would you do?"

"The next time I got a phone call, or a note from Mrs. Southey, and she was having one of those terrible headaches, I should say: 'I'm dreadfully sorry, Mrs. Southey, but a breath of talk that might be unpleasant for you, and for my wife, has come to my ear, so I know you'll think it wiser to call Dr. Mills, who can serve you better than I. In a great rush this afternoon. Good-bye!' *that* is what I should do, Robert, and I should do it quickly, and emphatically. Then I should interest Nancy Ellen in her car for a time, and then I should keep my eyes open, and the first time I found in my practice a sound baby with a clean bill of health, and no encumbrances, I should have it dressed attractively, and bestow it on Nancy Ellen as casually as I did the car. And in the meantime, love her plenty, Robert. You can never know how she *feels* about this; and it's in no way her fault. She couldn't possibly have known; while you would have married her just the same if you had known. Isn't that so?"

"It's quite so. Kate, I think your head is level, and I'll follow your advice to the letter. Now you have 'healed my lame leg,' as the dog said in McGuffey's Third, what can I do for *this* poor dog?"

"Nothing," said Kate. "I've got to hold still, and take it. Life will do the doing. I don't want to croak, but remember my word, it will do plenty."

"We'll come often," he said as he turned to go back.

Kate slowly walked up the path, dreading to meet Adam. He evidently had been watching for her, for he came around the corner of the house, took her arm, and they walked up the steps and into the living room together. She looked at him; he looked at her. At last he said: "I'm afraid that a good deal of this is my fault, Mother."

"How so?" asked Kate, tersely.

"I guess I betrayed your trust in me," said Adam, heavily. "Of course I did all my work and attended to things; but in the evening after work was over, the very first evening on the way home we stopped to talk to Henry at the gate, and he got in and came on down. We could see Milly at their gate, and I wanted her, I wanted her so much, Mother; and it was going to be lonesome, so all of us went on there, and she came up here and we sat on the porch, and then I took her home and that left Henry and Polly together. The next night Henry took us to town for a treat, and we were all together, and the next night Milly asked us all there, and so it went. It was all as open and innocent as it could be; only Henry and Polly were in awful earnest and she was bound she wouldn't be sent to town to school–"

"Why didn't she tell me so? She never objected a word, to me," said Kate.

"Well, Mother, you are so big, and Polly was so little, and she was used to minding–"

"Yes, this looks like it," said Kate. "Well, go on!"

"That's all," said Adam. "It was only that instead of staying at home and attending to our own affairs we were somewhere every night, or Milly and Henry were here. That is where I was to blame. I'm afraid you'll never forgive me, Mother; but I didn't take good care of Sister. I left her to Henry Peters, while I tried to see how nice I could be to Milly. I didn't know what Polly and Henry were planning; honest, I didn't, Mother. I would have told Uncle Robert and sent for you if I had. I thought when I went there it was to be our little crowd like it was at York's. I was furious when I found they were married. I told Mr. and Mrs. Peters what they were, right before the company, and then I came straight home and all the family, and York's, and most of the others, came straight away. Only a few stayed to the supper. I was so angry with Polly I just pushed her away, and didn't even say good-night to her. The little silly fool! Mother, if she had told you, you would have let her stay at home this winter and got her clothing, and let her be married here, when she was old enough, wouldn't you?"

"Certainly!" said Kate. "All the world knows that. Bates all marry; and they all marry young. Don't blame yourself, Adam. If Polly had it in her system to do this, and she did, or she wouldn't have done it, the thing would have happened when I was here, and right under my nose. It was a scheme all planned and ready before I left. I know that now. Let it go! There's nothing we can do, until things begin to go *wrong*, as they always do in this kind of wedding; then we shall get our call. In the meantime, you mustn't push your sister away. She may need you sooner than you'd think; and will you just please have enough confidence in my common sense and love for you, to come to me, *first*, when you feel that there's a girl who is indispensable to your future, Adam?"

"Yes, I will," said Adam. "And it won't be long, and the girl will be Milly York."

"All right," said Kate, gravely, "whenever the time comes, let me know about it. Now see if you can find me something to eat till I lay off my hat and wash. It was a long, hot ride, and I'm tired. Since there's nothing I can do, I wish I had stayed where I was. No, I don't, either! I see joy coming over the hill for Nancy Ellen."

"Why is joy coming to Nancy Ellen?" asked the boy, pausing an instant before he started to the kitchen.

"Oh, because she's had such a very tough, uncomfortable time with life," said Kate, "that in the very nature of things joy *should* come her way."

The boy stood mystified until the expression on his face so amused Kate that she began laughing, then he understood.

"That's *why* it's coming," said Kate; "and, here's *how* it's coming. She is going to get rid of a bothersome worry that's troubling her head – and she's going to have a very splendid gift, but it's a deep secret."

"Then you'll have to whisper it," said Adam, going to her and holding a convenient ear. Kate rested her hands on his shoulder a minute, as she leaned on him, her face buried in his crisp black hair. Then she whispered the secret.

"Crickey, isn't that grand!" cried the boy, backing away to stare at her.

"Yes, it is so grand I'm going to try it ourselves," said Kate. "We've a pretty snug balance in the bank, and I think it would be great fun evenings or when we want to go to town in a hurry and the horses are tired."

Adam was slowly moving toward the kitchen, his face more of a study than before.

"Mother," he said as he reached the door, "I be hanged if I know how to take you! I thought you'd just raise Cain over what Polly has done; but you act so sane and sensible; someway it doesn't seem so bad as it did, and I feel more sorry for Polly than like going back on her. And are you truly in earnest about a car?"

"I'm going to think very seriously about it this winter, and I feel almost sure it will come true by early spring," said Kate. "But who said anything about 'going back on Polly?'"

"Oh, Mrs. York and all the neighbours said that you'd never forgive her, and that she'd never darken your door again, and things like that until I was almost crazy," answered Adam.

Kate smiled grimly. "Adam," she said, "I had seven years of that 'darken you door' business, myself. It's a mighty cold, hard proposition. It's a wonder the neighbours didn't remember that. Maybe they did, and thought I was so much of a Bates leopard that I couldn't change my spots. If they are watching me, they will find that I am not spotted; I'm sorry and humiliated over what Polly has done; but I'm not going to gnash my teeth, and tear my hair, and wail in public, or in private. I'm trying to keep my real mean spot so deep it can't be seen. If ever I get my chance, Adam, you watch me pay back Mrs. Peters. *That* is the size and location of my spot; but it's far deeper than my skin. Now go on and find me food, man, food!"

Adam sat close while Kate ate her supper, then he helped her unpack her trunk and hang away her dresses, and then they sat on the porch talking for a long time.

When at last they arose to go to bed Kate said: "Adam, about Polly: first time you see her, if she asks, tell her she left home of her own free will and accord, and in her own way, which, by the way, happens to be a Holt way; but you needn't mention that. I think by this time she has learned or soon she will learn that; and whenever she wants to come back and face me, to come right ahead. I can stand it if she can. Can you get that straight?"

Adam said he could. He got that straight and so much else that by the time he finished, Polly realized that both he and her mother had left her in the house to try to *shield* her; that if she had told what she wanted in a straightforward manner she might have had a wedding outfit prepared and been married from her home at a proper time and in a proper way, and without putting her mother to shame before the community. Polly was very much ashamed of herself by the time Adam finished. She could not find it in her heart to blame Henry; she knew he was no more to blame than she was; but she did store up a grievance against Mr. and Mrs. Peters. They were older and had had experience with the world; they might have told Polly what she should do instead of having done everything in their power to make her do what she had done, bribing, coaxing, urging, all in the direction of her inclinations.

At heart Polly was big enough to admit that she had followed her inclinations without thinking at all what the result would be. Adam never would have done what she had. Adam would have thought of his mother and his name and his honour. Poor little Polly had to admit that honour with her had always been a matter of, "Now remember," "Be careful," and like caution on the lips of her mother.

The more Polly thought, the worse she felt. The worse she felt, the more the whole Peters family tried to comfort her. She was violently homesick in a few days; but Adam had said she was to come when she "could face her mother," and Polly suddenly found that she would rather undertake to run ten miles than to face her mother, so she began a process of hiding from her. If she sat on the porch, and saw her mother coming, she ran in the house. She would go to no public place where she might meet her. For a few weeks she lived a life of working for Mrs. Peters from dawn to dark, under the stimulus of what a sweet girl she was, how splendidly she did things, how fortunate Henry was, interspersed with continual kissing, patting, and petting, all very new and unusual to Polly. By that time she was so very ill, she could not lift her head from the pillow half the day, but it was to the credit of the badly disappointed Peters family that they kept up the petting. When Polly grew better, she had no desire to go anywhere; she worked to make up for the trouble she had been during her illness, to sew every spare moment, and to do her full share of the day's work in the house of an excessively nice woman, whose work never was done, and most hopeless thing of all, never would be. Mrs. Peters' head was full of things that she meant to do three years in the future. Every night found Polly so tired she staggered to bed early as possible; every morning found her confronting the same round, which from the nature of her condition every morning was more difficult for her.

Kate and Adam followed their usual routine with only the alterations required by the absence of Polly. Kate now prepared breakfast while Adam did the feeding and milking; washed the dishes and made the beds while he hitched up; then went to the field with him. On rainy days he swept and she dusted; always they talked over and planned everything they did, in the house or afield; always they schemed, contrived, economized, and worked to attain the shortest, easiest end to any result they strove for. They were growing in physical force, they were efficient, they attended their own affairs strictly. Their work was always done on time, their place in order, their deposits at the bank frequent. As the cold days came they missed Polly, but scarcely ever mentioned her. They had more books and read and studied together, while every few evenings Adam picked up his hat and disappeared, but soon he and Milly came in together. Then they all read, popped corn, made taffy, knitted, often Kate was called away by some sewing or upstairs work she wanted to do, so that the youngsters had plenty of time alone to revel in the wonder of life's greatest secret.

To Kate's ears came the word that Polly would be a mother in the spring, that the Peters family were delighted and anxious for the child to be a girl, as they found six males sufficient for one family. Polly was looking well, feeling fine, was a famous little worker, and seldom sat on a chair because some member of the Peters family usually held her.

"I should think she would get sick of all that mushing," said Adam when he repeated these things.

"She's not like us," said Kate. "She'll take all she can get, and call for more. She's a long time coming; but I'm glad she's well and happy."

"Buncombe!" said Adam. "She isn't so very well. She's white as putty, and there are great big, dark hollows under her eyes, and she's always panting for breath like she had been running. Nearly every time I pass there I see her out scrubbing the porches, or feeding the chickens, or washing windows, or something. You bet Mrs. Peters has got a fine hired girl now, and she's smiling all over about it."

"She really has something to smile about," said Kate.

To Polly's ears went the word that Adam and her mother were having a fine time together, always together; and that they had Milly York up three times a week to spend the evening; and that Milly said that it passed her to see why Polly ran away from Mrs. Holt. She was the grandest woman alive, and if she had any running to do in her neighbourhood, she would run *to* her, and not *from* her. Whereupon Polly closed her lips firmly and looked black, but not before she had said: "Well, if Mother had done just one night a week of that entertaining for Henry and me, we wouldn't have run from her, either."

Polly said nothing until April, then Kate answered the telephone one day and a few seconds later was ringing for Adam as if she would pull down the bell. He came running and soon was on his way to Peters' with the single buggy, with instructions to drive slowly and carefully and on no account to let Polly slip getting out. The Peters family had all gone to bury an aunt in the neighbourhood, leaving Polly alone for the day; and Polly at once called up her mother, and said she was dying to see her, and if she couldn't come home for the day, she would die soon, and be glad of it. Kate knew the visit should not have been made at that time and in that way; but she knew that Polly was under a dangerous nervous strain; she herself would not go to Peters' in Mrs. Peters' absence; she did not know what else to do. As she waited for Polly she thought of many things she would say; when she saw her, she took her in her arms and almost carried her into the house, and she said nothing at all, save how glad she was to see her, and she did nothing at all, except to try with all her might to comfort and please her, for to Kate, Polly did not seem like a strong, healthy girl approaching maternity. She appeared like a very sick woman, who sorely needed attention, while a few questions made her so sure of it that she at once called Robert. He gave both of them all the comfort he could, but what he told Nancy Ellen was: "Polly has had no attention whatever. She wants me, and I'll have to go; but it's a case I'd like to side-step. I'll do all I can, but the time is short."

"Oh, Lord!" said Nancy Ellen. "Is it one more for Kate?"

"Yes," said Robert, "I am very much afraid it's 'one more for Kate.'"

One More for Kate

Polly and Kate had a long day together, while Adam was about the house much of the time. Both of them said and did everything they could think of to cheer and comfort Polly, whose spirits seemed most variable. One minute she would be laughing and planning for the summer gaily, the next she would be gloomy and depressed, and declaring she never would live through the birth of her baby. If she had appeared well, this would not have worried Kate; but she looked even sicker than she seemed to feel. She was thin while her hands were hot and tremulous. As the afternoon went on and time to go came nearer, she grew more and more despondent, until Kate proposed watching when the Peters family came home, calling them up, and telling them that Polly was there, would remain all night, and that Henry should come down.

Polly flatly vetoed the proposition, but she seemed to feel much better after it had been made. She was like herself again for a short time, and then she turned to Kate and said suddenly: "Mother, if I don't get over this, will you take my baby?"

Kate looked at Polly intently. What she saw stopped the ready answer that was on her lips. She stood thinking deeply. At last she said gently: "Why, Polly, would you want to trust a tiny baby with a woman you ran away from yourself?"

"Mother, I haven't asked you to forgive me for the light I put you in before the neighbours," said Polly, "because I knew you couldn't honestly do it, and wouldn't lie to say you did. I don't know *what* made me do that. I was *tired* staying alone at the house so much, I was *wild* about Henry, I was *bound* I wouldn't leave him and go away to school. I just thought it would settle everything easily and quickly. I never once thought of how it would make you look and feel. Honestly I didn't, Mother. You believe me, don't you?"

"Yes, I believe you," said Kate.

"It was an awful thing for me to do," said Polly. "I was foolish and crazy, and I suppose I shouldn't say it, but I certainly did have a lot of encouragement from the Peters family. They all seemed to think it would be a great joke, that it wouldn't make any difference, and all that, so I just did it. I knew I shouldn't have done it; but, Mother, you'll never know the fight I've had all my life to keep from telling stories and sneaking. I hated your everlasting: 'Now be careful,' but when I hated it most, I needed it worst; and I knew it, when I grew older. If only you had been here to say, 'Now be careful,' just once, I never would have done it; but of course I couldn't have you to keep me straight all my life. All I can say is that I'd give my life and never whimper, if I could be back home as I was this time last year, and have a chance to do things your way. But that is past, and I can't change it. What I came for to-day, and what I want to know now, is, if I go, will you take my baby?"

"Polly, you *know* the Peters family wouldn't let me have it," said Kate.

"If it's a boy, they wouldn't *want* it," said Polly. "Neither would you, for that matter. If it's a girl, they'll fight for it; but it won't do them any good. All I want to know is, *will you take it?*"

"Of course I would, Polly," said Kate.

"Since I have your word, I'll feel better," said Polly. "And Mother, you needn't be *afraid* of it. It will be all right. I have thought about it so much I have it all figured out. It's going to be a girl, and it's going to be exactly like you, and its name is going to be Katherine Eleanor. I have thought about you every hour I was awake since I have been gone; so the baby will have to be exactly like you. There won't be the taint of Grandmother in it that there is in me. You needn't be afraid. I quit sneaking forever when Adam told me what I had done to you. I have gone straight as a dart, Mother, every single minute since, Mother; truly I have!"

Kate sat down suddenly, an awful sickness in her heart.

"Why, you poor child you!" she said.

"Oh, I've been all right," said Polly. "I've been almost petted and loved to death; but Mother, there never should be the amount of work attached to living that there is in that house. It's never ending, it's intolerable. Mrs. Peters just goes until she drops, and then instead of sleeping, she lies awake planning some hard, foolish, unnecessary thing to do next. Maybe she can stand it herself, but I'm tired out. I'm going to sit down, and not budge to do another stroke until after the baby comes, and then I am going to coax Henry to rent a piece of land, and move to ourselves."

Kate took heart. "That will be fine!" she cried. "That will be the very thing. I'll ask the boys to keep their eyes open for any chance for you."

"You needn't take any bother about it," said Polly, "because that isn't what is going to happen. All I want to be sure of now is that you and Adam will take my baby. I'll see to the rest."

"How will you see to it, Polly?" asked Kate, gently.

"Well, it's already seen to, for matter of that," said Polly conclusively. "I've known for quite a while that I was sick; but I couldn't make them do anything but kiss me, and laugh at me, until I am so ill that I know better how I feel than anybody else. I got tired being laughed at, and put off about everything, so one day in Hartley, while Mother Peters was shopping, I just went in to the lawyer Grandmother always went to, and told him all about what I wanted. He has the papers made out all right and proper; so when I send for Uncle Robert, I am going to send for him, too, and soon as the baby comes I'll put in its name and sign it, and make Henry, and then if I have to go, you won't have a bit of trouble."

Kate gazed at Polly in dumb amazement. She was speechless for a time, then to break the strain she said: "My soul! Did you really, Polly? I guess there is more Bates in you than I had thought!"

"Oh, there's *some* Bates in me," said Polly. "There's enough to make me live until I sign that paper, and make Henry Peters sign it, and send Mr. Thomlins to you with it and the baby. I can do that, because I'm going to!"

Ten days later she did exactly what she had said she would. Then she turned her face to the wall and went into a convulsion out of which she never came. While the Peters family refused Kate's plea to lay Polly beside her grandmother, and laid her in their family lot, Kate, moaning dumbly, sat clasping a tiny red girl in her arms. Adam drove to Hartley to deposit one more paper, the most precious of all, in the safety deposit box.

Kate and Adam mourned too deeply to talk about it. They went about their daily rounds silently, each busy with regrets and self investigations. They watched each other carefully, were kinder than they ever had been to everyone they came in contact with; the baby they frankly adored. Kate had reared her own children with small misgivings, quite casually, in fact; but her heart was torn to the depths about this baby. Life never would be even what it had been before Polly left them, for into her going there entered an element of self-reproach and continual self-condemnation. Adam felt that if he had been less occupied with Milly York and had taken proper care of his sister, he would not have lost her. Kate had less time for recrimination, because she had the baby.

"Look for a good man to help you this summer, Adam," she said. "The baby is full of poison which can be eliminated only slowly. If I don't get it out before teething, I'll lose her, and then we never shall hear the last from the Peters family." Adam consigned the Peters family to a location he thought suitable for them on the instant. He spoke with unusual bitterness, because he had heard that the Peters family were telling that Polly had grieved herself to death, while his mother had engineered a scheme whereby she had stolen the baby. Occasionally a word drifted to Kate here and there, until she realized much of what they were saying. At first she grieved too deeply to pay any attention, but as the summer went on and the baby flourished and grew fine and strong, and she had time in the garden, she began to feel better; grief began to wear away, as it always does.

By midsummer the baby was in short clothes, sitting in a high chair, which if Miss Baby only had known it, was a throne before which knelt her two adoring subjects. Polly had said the baby would be like Kate. Its hair and colouring were like hers, but it had the brown eyes of its father, and enough of his facial lines to tone down the too generous Bates features. When the baby was five months old it was too pretty for adequate description. One baby has no business with perfect features, a mop of curly, yellow silk hair, and big brown eyes. One of the questions Kate and Adam discussed most frequently was where they would send her to college, while one they did not discuss was how sick her stomach teeth would make her. They merely lived in mortal dread of that. "Convulsion," was a word that held a terror for Kate above any other in the medical books.

The baby had a good, formal name, but no one ever used it. Adam, on first lifting the blanket, had fancied the child resembled its mother and had called her "Little Poll." The name clung to her. Kate could not call such a tiny morsel either Kate or Katherine; she liked "Little Poll," better. The baby had three regular visitors. One was her father. He was not fond of Kate; Little Poll suited him. He expressed his feeling by bringing gifts of toys, candy, and unsuitable clothes.

Kate kept these things in evidence when she saw him coming and swept them from sight when he went; for she had the good sense not to antagonize him. Nancy Ellen came almost every day, proudly driving her new car, and with the light of a new joy on her face. She never said anything to Kate, but Kate knew what had happened. Nancy Ellen came to see the baby. She brought it lovely and delicate little shoes, embroidered dresses and hoods, cloaks and blankets. One day as she sat holding it she said to Kate: "Isn't the baby a dreadful bother to you? You're not getting half your usual work done."

"No, I'm doing *unusual* work," said Kate, lightly. "Adam is hiring a man who does my work very well in the fields; there isn't money that would hire me to let any one else take my job indoors, right now."

A slow red crept into Nancy Ellen's cheeks. She had meant to be diplomatic, but diplomacy never worked well with Kate. As Nancy Ellen often said, Kate understood a sledge-hammer better. Nancy Ellen used the hammer. Her face flushed, her arms closed tightly. "Give me this baby," she demanded.

Kate looked at her in helpless amazement.

"Give it to me," repeated Nancy Ellen.

"She's a gift to me," said Kate, slowly. "One the Peters family are searching heaven and earth to find an excuse to take from me. I hear they've been to a lawyer twice, already. I wouldn't give her up to save my soul alive, for myself; for you, if I would let you have her, they would not leave you in possession a day."

"Are they really trying to get her?" asked Nancy Ellen, slowly loosening her grip.

"They are," said Kate. "They sent a lawyer to get a copy of the papers, to see if they could pick a flaw in them."

"Can they?" cried Nancy Ellen.

"God knows!" said Kate, slowly. "I *hope* not. Mr. Thomlins is the best lawyer in Hartley; he says not. He says Henry put his neck in the noose when he signed the papers. The only chance I can see for him would be to plead undue influence. When you look at her, you can't blame him for wanting her. I've two hopes. One that his mother will not want the extra work; the other that the next girl he selects will not want the baby. If I can keep them going a few months more with a teething scare, I hope they will get over wanting her."

"If they do, then may we have her?" asked Nancy Ellen.

Kate threw out her hands. "Take my eyes, or my hands, or my feet," she said; "but leave me my heart."

Nancy Ellen went soon after, and did not come again for several days. Then she began coming as usual, so that the baby soon knew her and laughed in high glee when she appeared. Dr. Gray often stopped in passing to see her; if he was in great haste, he hallooed at the gate to ask if she was all right. Kate was thankful for this, more than thankful for the telephone and car that would bring him in fifteen minutes day or night, if he were needed. But he was not needed. Little Poll throve and grew fat and rosy; for she ate measured food, slept by the clock, in a sanitary bed, and was a bathed, splendidly cared for baby. When Kate's family and friends laughed, she paid not the slightest heed.

"Laugh away," she said. "I've got something to fight with this baby; I don't propose for the battle to come and find the chances against me, because I'm unprepared."

With scrupulous care Kate watched over the child, always putting her first, the house and land afterward. One day she looked up the road and saw Henry Peters coming. She had been expecting Nancy Ellen. She had finished bathing the baby and making her especially attractive in a dainty lace ruffled dress with blue ribbons and blue shoes that her sister had brought on her latest trip. Little Poll was a wonderful picture, for her eyes were always growing bigger, her cheeks pinker, her skin fairer, her hair longer and more softly curling. At first thought Kate had been inclined to snatch off the dress and change to one of the cheap, ready-made ginghams Henry brought, but the baby was so lovely as she was, she had not the heart to spoil the picture, while Nancy Ellen might come any minute. So she began putting things in place while Little Poll sat crowing and trying to pick up a sunbeam that fell across her tray. Her father came to the door and stood looking at her. Suddenly he dropped in a chair, covered his face with his hands and began to cry, in deep, shuddering sobs. Kate stood still in wonderment. As last she seated herself before him and said gently: "Won't you tell me about it, Henry?"

Henry struggled for self-control. He looked at the baby longingly. Finally he said: "It's pretty tough to give up a baby like that, Mrs. Holt. She's my little girl. I wish God had struck my right hand with palsy, when I went to sign those papers."

"Oh, no, you don't, Henry," said Kate, suavely. "You wouldn't like to live the rest of your life a cripple. And is it any worse for me to have your girl in spite of the real desires and dictates of your heart, than it was for you to have mine? And you didn't take the intelligent care of my girl that I'm taking of yours, either. A doctor and a little right treatment at the proper time would have saved Polly to rear her own baby; but there's no use to go into that. I was waiting for Polly to come home of her own accord, as she left it; and while I waited, a poison crept into her system that took her. I never shall feel right about it; neither shall you—"

"No, I should say I won't!" said Henry emphatically. "I never thought of anything being the matter with Polly that wouldn't be all over when the baby came—"

"I know you didn't, Henry," said Kate. "I know how much you would have done, and how gladly, if you had known. There is no use going into that, we are both very much to blame; we must take our punishment. Now what is this I hear about your having been to see lawyers and trying to find a way to set aside the adoption papers you signed? Let's have a talk, and see what we can arrive at. Tell me all about it."

So Henry told Kate how he had loved Polly, how he felt guilty of her death, how he longed for and wanted her baby, how he had signed the paper which Polly put before him so unexpectedly, to humour her, because she was very ill; but he had not dreamed that she could die; how he did not feel that he should be bound by that signature now. Kate listened with the deepest sympathy, assenting to most he said until he was silent. Then she sat thinking a long time. At last she said: "Henry, if you and Polly had waited until I came home, and told me what you wanted and how you felt, I should have gotten her ready, and given you a customary wedding, and helped you to start a life that I think would have saved her to you, and to me. That is past, but the fact remains. You are hurt over giving up the baby as you have; I'm hurt over losing my daughter as I did; we are about even on the past, don't you think?"

"I suppose we are," he said, heavily.

"That being agreed," said Kate, "let us look to the future. You want the baby now, I can guess how much, by how much I want her, myself. I know *your* point of view; there are two others, one is mine, and the other is the baby's. I feel that it is only right and just that I should have this little girl to replace the one you took from me, in a way far from complimentary to me. I feel that she is mine, because Polly told me the day she came to see me how sick she had been, how she had begged for a doctor, and been kissed and told there was nothing the matter with her, when she knew she was very ill. She gave the baby to me, and at that time she had been to see a lawyer, and had her papers all made out except the signatures and dates. Mr. Thomlins can tell you that; and you know that up to that time I had not seen Polly, or had any communication with her. She simply was unnerved at the thought of trusting her baby to the care she had had."

Kate was hitting hard and straight from the shoulder. The baby, busy with her sunbeam, jabbered unnoticed.

"When Polly died as she did," continued Kate, "I knew that her baby would be full of the same poison that killed her; and that it must be eliminated before it came time to cut her worst teeth, so I undertook the work, and sleeping or waking, I have been at it ever since. Now, Henry, is there any one at your house who would have figured this out, and taken the time, pains, and done work that I have? Is there?"

"Mother raised six of us." he said defensively.

"But she didn't die of diathesis giving birth to the first of you," said Kate. "You were all big, strong boys with a perfectly sound birthright. And your mother is now a much older, wearier woman than she was then, and her hands are far too full every day, as it is. If she knew how to handle the baby as I have, and was willing to add the work to her daily round, would you be willing to have her? I have three times her strength, while I consider that I've the first right. Then there is the baby's side of the question. I have had her through the worst, hardest part of babyhood; she is accustomed to a fixed routine that you surely will concede agrees with her; she would miss me, and she would not thrive as she does with me, for her food and her hours would not be regular, while you, and your father, and the boys would tire her to death handling her. That is the start. The finish would be that she would grow up, if she survived, to take the place

Polly took at your house, while you would marry some other girl, as you *will* before a year from now. I'm dreadfully sorry to say these things to you, Henry, but you know they are the truth. If you're going to try to take the baby, I'm going to fight you to the last dollar I can raise, and the last foot of land I own. That's all. Look at the baby; think it over; and let me know what you'll do as soon as you can. I'm not asking mercy at your hands, but I do feel that I have suffered about my share."

"You needn't suffer any longer," said Henry, drying his eyes. "All you say is true; just as what I said was true; but I might as well tell you, and let one of us be happy. I saw my third lawyer yesterday, and he said the papers were unbreakable unless I could prove that the child was neglected, and not growing right, or not having proper care. Look at her! I might do some things! I did do a thing as mean as to persuade a girl to marry me without her mother's knowledge, and ruined her life thereby, but God knows I couldn't go on the witness stand and swear that that baby is not properly cared for! Mother's job is big enough; and while it doesn't seem possible now, very likely I shall marry again, as other men do; and in that event, Little Poll *would* be happier with you. I give her up. I think I came this morning to say that I was defeated; and to tell you that I'd give up if I saw that you would fight. Keep the baby, and be as happy as you can. You shan't be worried any more about her. Polly shall have this thing as she desired and planned it. Good-bye."

When he had gone Kate knelt on the floor, laid her head on the chair tray, and putting her arms around the baby she laughed and cried at the same time, while Miss Baby pulled her hair, patted her face, and plastered it with wet, uncertain kisses. Then Kate tied a little bonnet on the baby's head and taking her in her arms, she went to the field to tell Adam. It seemed to Kate that she could see responsibility slipping from his shoulders, could see him grow taller as he listened. The breath of relief he drew was long and deep.

"Fine!" he cried. "Fine! I haven't told you *half* I knew. I've been worried until I couldn't sleep."

Kate went back to the house so glad she did not realize she was touching earth at all. She fed the baby and laid her down for her morning nap, and then went out in the garden; but she was too restless to work. She walked bareheaded in the sun and was glad as she never before in her life had known how to be glad. The first thing Kate knew she was standing at the gate looking up at the noonday sky and from the depths of her heart she was crying aloud: "Praise ye the Lord, Oh my soul. Let all that is within me praise His holy name!"

For the remainder of the day Kate was unblushingly insane. She started to do a hundred things and abandoned all of them to go out and look up at the sky and to cry repeatedly: "Praise the Lord!"

If she had been asked to explain why she did this, Kate could have answered, and would have answered: "Because I *feel* like it!" She had been taught no religion as a child, she had practised no formal mode of worship as a woman. She had been straight, honest, and virtuous. She had faced life and done with small question the work that she thought fell to her hand. She had accepted joy, sorrow, shame, all in the same stoic way. Always she had felt that there was a mighty force in the universe that could as well be called God as any other name; it mattered not about the name; it was a real force, and it was there.

That day Kate exulted. She carried the baby down to the brook in the afternoon and almost shouted; she sang until she could have been heard a mile. She kept straight on praising the Lord, because expression was imperative, and that was the form of expression that seemed to come naturally to her. Without giving a thought as to how, or why, she followed her impulses and praised the Lord. The happier she grew, the more clearly she saw how uneasy and frightened she had been.

When Nancy Ellen came, she took only one glance at Kate's glorified face and asked: "What in this world has happened to you?"

Kate answered in all seriousness: "My Lord has 'shut the lions' mouths,' and they are not going to harm me."

Nancy Ellen regarded her closely. "I hope you aren't running a temperature," she said. "I'll take a shot at random. You have found out that the Peters family can't take Little Poll."

Kate laughed joyously. "Better than that, sister mine!" she cried. "I have convinced Henry that he doesn't want her himself as much as he wants me to have her, and he can speedily convert his family. He will do nothing more! He will leave me in peace with her."

"Thank God!" said Nancy Ellen.

"There you go, too!" cried Kate. "That's the very first thought that came to me, only I said, 'Praise the Lord,' which is exactly the same thing; and Nancy Ellen, since Robert has been trying to praise the Lord for twenty years, and both of us do praise Him when our time comes, wouldn't it be a good idea to open up our heads and say so, not only to ourselves and to the Lord, but to the neighbours? I'm afraid she won't understand much of it, but I think I shall find the place and read to Little Poll about Abraham and Isaac to-night, and probably about Hagar and Ishmael to-morrow night, and it wouldn't surprise me a mite to hear myself saying 'Praise the Lord,' right out loud, any time, any place. Let's gather a great big bouquet of our loveliest flowers, and go tell Mother and Polly about it."

Without a word Nancy Ellen turned toward the garden. They gathered the flowers and getting in Nancy Ellen's car drove the short distance to the church where Nancy Ellen played with the baby in the shade of a big tree while Kate arranged her flowers. Then she sat down and they talked over their lives from childhood.

"Nancy Ellen, won't you stay to supper with us?" asked Kate.

"Yes," said Nancy Ellen, rising, "I haven't had such a good time in years. I'm as glad for you as I'd be if I had such a child assured me, myself."

"You can't bring yourself –?" began Kate.

"Yes, I think so," said Nancy Ellen. "Getting things for Little Poll has broken me up so, I told Robert how I felt, and he's watching in his practice, and he's written several letters of inquiry to friends in Chicago. Any day now I may have my work cut out for me."

"Praise the Lord again!" cried Kate. "I see where you will be happier than you ever have been. Real life is just beginning for you."

Then they went home and prepared a good supper and had such a fine time they were exalted in heart and spirit. When Nancy Ellen started home, Kate took the baby and climbed in the car with her, explaining that they would go a short way and walk back. She went only as far as the Peters gate; then she bravely walked up to the porch, where Mr. Peters and some of the boys sat, and said casually: "I just thought I'd bring Little Poll up to get acquainted with her folks. Isn't she a dear?"

An hour later, as she walked back in the moonlight, Henry beside her carrying the baby, he said to her: "This is a mighty big thing, and a kind thing for you to do, Mrs. Holt. Mother has been saying scandalous things about you."

"I know," said Kate. "But never mind! She won't any more."

The remainder of the week she passed in the same uplifted mental state. She carried the baby in her arms and walked all over the farm, going often to the cemetery with fresh flowers. Sunday morning, when the work was all done, the baby dressed her prettiest, Kate slipped into one of her fresh white dresses and gathering a big bunch of flowers started again to whisper above the graves of her mother and Polly the story of her gladness, and to freshen the flowers, so that the people coming from church would see that her family were remembered. When she had finished she arose, took up the baby, and started to return across the cemetery, going behind the church, taking the path she had travelled the day she followed the minister's admonition to "take the wings of morning." She thought of that. She stood very still, thinking deeply.

"I took them," she said. "I've tried flight after flight; and I've fallen, and risen, and fallen, and got up and tried again, but never until now have I felt that I could really 'fly to the uttermost parts of the earth.' There is a rising power in me that should benefit more than myself. I guess I'll just join in."

She walked into the church as the last word of the song the congregation were singing was finished, and the minister was opening his lips to say: "Let us pray." Straight down the aisle came Kate, her bare, gold head crowned with a flash of light at each window she passed. She paused at the altar, directly facing the minister.

"Baby and I would like the privilege of praising the Lord with you," she said simply, "and we would like to do our share in keeping up this church and congregation to His honour and glory. There's some water. Can't you baptize us now?"

The minister turned to the pitcher, which always stood on his desk, filled his palm, and asked: "What is the baby's name?"

"Katherine Eleanor Peters," said Kate.

"Katherine Eleanor, I baptize thee," said the minister, and he laid his hand on the soft curls of the baby. She scattered the flowers she was holding over the altar as she reached to spat her hands in the water on her head and laughed aloud.

"What is your name?" asked the minister.

"Katherine Eleanor Holt," said Kate.

Again the minister repeated the formula, and then he raised both hands and said: "Let us pray."

The Winged Victory

Kate turned and placing the baby on the front seat, she knelt and put her arms around the little thing, but her lips only repeated the words: "Praise the Lord for this precious baby!" Her heart was filled with high resolve. She would rear the baby with such care. She would be more careful with Adam. She would make heroic effort to help him to clean, unashamed manhood. She would be a better sister to all her family. She would be friendlier, and have more patience with the neighbours. She would join in whatever effort the church was making to hold and increase its membership among the young people, and to raise funds to keep up the organization. All the time her mind was busy thinking out these fine resolves, her lips were thanking the Lord for Little Poll. Kate arose with the benediction, picked up the baby, and started down the aisle among the people she had known all her life. On every side strong hands stretched out to greet and welcome her. A daughter of Adam Bates was something new as a church member. They all knew how she could work, and what she could give if she chose; while that she had stood at the altar and been baptized, meant that something not customary with the Bates family was taking place in her heart. So they welcomed her, and praised the beauty and sweetness of the baby until Kate went out into the sunshine, her face glowing.

Slowly she walked home and as she reached the veranda, Adam took the baby.

"Been to the cemetery?" he asked.

Kate nodded and dropped into a chair.

"That's too far to walk and carry this great big woman," he said, snuggling his face in the baby's neck, while she patted his cheeks and pulled his hair. "Why didn't you tell me you wanted to go, and let me get out the car?"

Kate looked at him speculatively.

"Adam," she said, "when I started out, I meant only to take some flowers to Mother and Polly. As I came around the corner of the church to take the footpath, they were singing 'Rejoice in the Lord!' I went inside and joined. I'm going to church as often as I can after this, and I'm going to help with the work of running it."

"Well, I like that!" cried Adam, indignantly. "Why didn't you let me go with you?"

Kate sat staring down the road. She was shocked speechless. Again she had followed an impulse, without thinking of any one besides herself. Usually she could talk, but in that instant she had nothing to say. Then a carriage drew into the line of her vision, stopped at York's gate, and Mr. York alighted and swung to the ground a slim girlish figure and then helped his wife. Kate had a sudden inspiration. "But you would want to wait a little and join with Milly, wouldn't you?" she asked. "Uncle Robert always has been a church member. I think it's a fine stand for a man to take."

"Maybe that would be better," he said. "I didn't think of Milly. I only thought I'd like to have been with you and Little Poll."

"I'm sure Milly will be joining very soon, and that she'll want you with her," said Kate.

She was a very substantial woman, but for the remainder of that day she felt that she was moving with winged feet. She sang, she laughed, she was unspeakably happy. She kept saying over and over: "And a little child shall lead them." Then she would catch Little Poll, almost crushing her in her strong arms. It never occurred to Kate that she had done an unprecedented thing. She had done as her heart dictated. She did not know that she put the minister into a most uncomfortable position, when he followed her request to baptize her and the child. She had never thought of probations, and examinations, and catechisms. She had read the Bible, as was the custom, every morning before her school. In that book, when a man wanted to follow Jesus, he followed; Jesus accepted him; and that was all there was to it, with Kate.

The middle of the week Nancy Ellen came flying up the walk on winged feet, herself. She carried photographs of several small children, one of them a girl so like Little Poll that she might have been the original of the picture.

"They just came," said Nancy Ellen rather breathlessly. "I was wild for that little darling at once. I had Robert telegraph them to hold her until we could get there. We're going to start on the evening train and if her blood seems good, and her ancestors respectable, and she looks like that picture, we're going to bring her back with us. Oh, Kate, I can scarcely wait to get my fingers on her. I'm hungry for a baby all of my own."

Kate studied the picture.

"She's charming!" she said. "Oh, Nancy Ellen, this world is getting entirely too good to be true."

Nancy Ellen looked at Kate and smiled peculiarly.

"I knew you were crazy," she said, "but I never dreamed of you going such lengths. Mrs. Whistler told Robert, when she called him in about her side, Tuesday. I can't imagine a Bates joining church."

"If that is joining church, it's the easiest thing in the world," said Kate. "We just loved doing it, didn't we, Little Poll? Adam and Milly are going to come in soon, I'm almost sure. At least he is willing. I don't know what it is that I am to do, but I suppose they will give me my work soon."

"You bet they'll give you work soon, and enough," said Nancy Ellen, laughing. "But you won't mind. You'll just put it through, as you do things out here. Kate, you are making this place look fine. I used to say I'd rather die than come back here to live, but lately it has been growing so attractive, I've been here about half my time, and wished I were the other half."

Kate slipped her arm around Nancy Ellen as they walked to the gate.

"You know," said Nancy Ellen, "the *more* I study you, the *less* I know about you. Usually it's sickness, and sorrow, and losing their friends that bring people to the consolations of the church. You bore those things like a stoic. When they are all over, and you are comfortable and happy, just the joy of being sure of Little Poll has transformed you. Kate, you make me think of the 'Winged Victory,' this afternoon. If I get this darling little girl, will she make me big, and splendid, and fine, like you?"

Kate suddenly drew Nancy Ellen to her and kissed her a long, hard kiss on the lips.

"Nancy Ellen," she said, "you *are* 'big, and splendid, and fine,' or you never would be going to Chicago after this little motherless child. You haven't said a word, but I know from the joy of you and Robert during the past months that Mrs. Southey isn't troubling you any more; and I'm sure enough to put it into words that when you get your little child, she will lead you straight where mine as led me. Good-bye and good luck to you, and remember me to Robert."

Nancy Ellen stood intently studying the picture she held in her hand. Then she looked at Kate, smiling with misty eyes: "I think, Kate, I'm very close, if I am not really where you are this minute," she said. Then she started her car; but she looked back, waving and smiling until the car swerved so that Kate called after her: "Do drive carefully, Nancy Ellen!"

Kate went slowly up the walk. She stopped several times to examine the shrubs and bushes closely, to wish for rain for the flowers. She sat on the porch a few minutes talking to Little Poll, then she went inside to answer the phone.

"Kate?" cried a sharp voice.

"Yes," said Kate, recognizing a neighbour, living a few miles down the road.

"Did Nancy Ellen just leave your house?" came a breathless query.

"Yes," said Kate again.

"I just saw a car that looked like hers slip in the fresh sand at the river levee, and it went down, and two or three times over."

"O God!" said Kate. Then after an instant: "Ring the dinner bell for your men to get her out. I'll phone Robert, and come as soon as I can get there."

Kate called Dr. Gray's office. She said to the girl: "Tell the doctor that Mrs. Howe thinks she saw Nancy Ellen's car go down the river levee, and two or three times over. Have him bring what he might need to Howe's, and hurry. Rush him!"

Then she ran to her bell and rang so frantically that Adam came running. Kate was at the little garage they had built, and had the door open. She told him what she had heard, ran to get the baby, and met him at the gate. On the way she said, "You take the baby when we get there, and if I'm needed, take her back and get Milly and her mother to come stay with you. You know where her things are, and how to feed her. Don't you dare let them change any way I do. Baby knows Milly; she will be good for her and for you. You'll be careful?"

"Of course, Mother," said Adam.

He called her attention to the road.

"Look at those tracks," he said. "Was she sick? She might have been drunk, from them."

"No," said Kate, "she wasn't sick. She WAS drunk, drunken with joy. She had a picture of the most beautiful little baby girl. They were to start to Chicago after her to-night. I suspect she was driving with the picture in one hand. Oh, my God, have mercy!"

They had come to deep grooves in loose gravel, then the cut in the embankment, then they could see the wrecked car standing on the engine and lying against a big tree, near the water, while two men and a woman were carrying a limp form across the meadow toward the house. As their car stopped, Kate kissed the baby mechanically, handed her to Adam, and ran into the house where she dragged a couch to the middle of the first room she entered, found a pillow, and brought a bucket of water and a towel from the kitchen. They carried Nancy Ellen in and laid her down. Kate began unfastening clothing and trying to get the broken body in shape for the doctor to work upon; but she spread the towel over what had been a face of unusual beauty. Robert came in a few minutes, then all of them worked under his directions until he suddenly sank to the floor, burying his face in Nancy Ellen's breast; then they knew. Kate gathered her sister's feet in her arms and hid her face beside them. The neighbours silently began taking away things that had been used, while Mrs. Howe chose her whitest sheet, and laid it on a chair near Robert.

Two days later they laid Nancy Ellen beside her mother. Then they began trying to face the problem of life without her. Robert said nothing. He seemed too stunned to think. Kate wanted to tell him of her final visit with Nancy Ellen, but she could not at that time. Robert's aged mother came to him, and said she could remain as long as he wanted her, so that was a comfort to Kate, who took time to pity him, even in her blackest hour. She had some very black ones. She could have wailed, and lamented, and relinquished all she had gained, but she did not. She merely went on with life, as she always had lived it, to the best of her ability when she was so numbed with grief she scarcely knew what she was doing. She kept herself driven about the house, and when she could find no more to do, took Little Poll in her arms and went out in the fields to Adam, where she found the baby a safe place, and then cut and husked corn as usual. Every Sabbath, and often during the week, her feet carried her to the cemetery, where she sat in the deep grass and looked at those three long mounds and tried to understand life; deeper still, to fathom death.

She and her mother had agreed that there was "something." Now Kate tried as never before to understand what, and where, and why, that "something" was. Many days she would sit for an hour at a time, thinking, and at last she arrived at fixed convictions that settled matters forever with her. One day after she had arranged the fall roses she had grown, and some roadside asters she had gathered in passing, she sat in deep thought, when a car stopped on the road. Kate looked up to see Robert coming across the churchyard with his arms full of greenhouse roses. He carried a big bunch of deep red for her mother, white for Polly, and a large sheaf of warm pink for Nancy Ellen. Kate knelt up and taking her flowers, she moved them lower, and silently helped Robert place those he had brought. Then she sat where she had been, and looked at him.

Finally he asked: "Still hunting the 'why,' Kate?"

"'Why' doesn't so much matter," said Kate, "as 'where.' I'm enough of a fatalist to believe that Mother is here because she was old and worn out. Polly had a clear case of uric poison, while I'd stake my life Nancy Ellen was gloating over the picture she carried when she ran into that loose sand. In each of their cases I am satisfied as to 'why,' as well as about Father. The thing that holds me, and fascinates me, and that I have such a time being sure of, is 'where.'"

Robert glanced upward and asked: "Isn't there room enough up there, Kate?"

"Too much!" said Kate. "And what IS the soul, and *how* can it bridge the vortex lying between us and other worlds, that man never can, because of the lack of air to breathe, and support him?"

"I don't know," said Robert; "and in spite of the fact that I do know what a man *cannot* do, I still believe in the immortality of the soul."

"Oh, yes," said Kate. "If there is any such thing in science as a self-evident fact, that is one. *That* is provable."

Robert looked at her eager face. "How would you go about proving it, Kate?" he asked.

"Why, this way," said Kate, leaning to straighten and arrange the delicate velvet petalled roses with her sure, work-abused fingers. "Take the history of the world from as near dawn as we have any record, and trace it from the igloo of the northernmost Esquimo, around the globe, and down to the ice of the southern pole again, and in blackest Africa, farthest, wildest Borneo, you will never discover one single tribe of creatures, upright and belonging to the race of man, who did not come into the world with four primal instincts. They all reproduce themselves, they all make something intended for music, they all express a feeling in their hearts by the exercise we call dance, they all believe in the after life of the soul. This belief is as much a *part* of any man, ever born in any location, as his hands and his feet. Whether he believes his soul enters a cat and works back to man again after long transmigration, or goes to a Happy Hunting Ground as our Indians, makes no difference with the fact that he enters this world with belief in after life of some kind. We see material evidence in increase that man is not defeated in his desire to reproduce himself; we have advanced to something better than tom-toms and pow-wows for music and dance; these desires are fulfilled before us, now tell me why the very strongest of all, the most deeply rooted, the belief in after life, should come to nothing. Why should the others be real, and that a dream?"

"I don't think it is," said Robert.

"It's my biggest self-evident fact," said Kate, conclusively. "I never heard any one else say these things, but I think them, and they are provable. I always believed there was something; but since I saw Mother go, I know there is. She stood in full evening light, I looked straight in her face, and Robert, you know I'm no creature of fancies and delusions, I tell you I *saw her soul pass*. I saw the life go from her and go on, and on. I saw her body stand erect, long enough for me to reach her, and pick her up, after its passing. That I know."

"I shouldn't think of questioning it, Kate," said Robert. "But don't you think you are rather limiting man, when you narrow him to four primal instincts?"

"Oh, I don't know," said Kate. "Air to breathe and food to sustain are presupposed. Man *learns* to fight in self-defense, and to acquire what he covets. He learns to covet by seeing stronger men, in better locations, surpass his achievements, so if he is strong enough he goes and robs them by force. He learns the desire for the chase in food hunting; I think four are plenty to start with."

"Probably you are right," said the doctor, rising. "I must go now. Shall I take you home?"

Kate glanced at the sun and shook her head. "I can stay half an hour longer. I don't mind the walk. I need exercise to keep me in condition. Good-bye!"

As he started his car he glanced back. She was leaning over the flowers absorbed in their beauty. Kate sat looking straight before her until time to help with the evening work, and prepare supper, then she arose. She stood looking down a long time; finally she picked up a fine specimen of each of the roses and slowly dropped them on her father's grave.

"There! You may have that many," she said. "You look a little too lonely, lying here beside the others with not a single one, but if you could speak, I wonder whether you would say, 'Thank you!' or 'Take the damn weeds off me!'"

Blue Ribbon Corn

Never in her life had Kate worked harder than she did that fall; but she retained her splendid health. Everything was sheltered and housed, their implements under cover, their stock in good condition, their store-room filled, and their fruits and vegetables buried in hills and long rows in the garden. Adam had a first wheat premium at the County Fair and a second on corn, concerning which he felt abused. He thought his corn scored the highest number of points, but that the award was given another man because of Adam's having had first on wheat. In her heart Kate agreed with him; but she tried to satisfy him with the blue ribbon on wheat and keep him interested sufficiently to try for the first on corn the coming year. She began making suggestions for the possible improvement of his corn. Adam was not easily propitiated.

"Mother," he said, "you know as well as you know you're alive, that if I had failed on wheat, or had second, I would have been given *first* on my corn; my corn was the best in every way, but they thought I would swell up and burst if I had two blue ribbons. That was what ailed the judges. What encouragement is that to try again? I might grow even finer corn in the coming year than I did this, and be given no award at all, because I had two this year. It would amount to exactly the same thing."

"We'll get some more books, and see if we can study up any new wrinkles, this winter," said Kate. "Now cheer up, and go tell Milly about it. Maybe she can console you, if I can't."

"Nothing but justice will console me," said Adam. "I'm not complaining about losing the prize; I'm fighting mad because my corn, my beautiful corn, that grew and grew, and held its head so high, and waved its banners of triumph to me with every breeze, didn't get its fair show. What encouragement is there for it to try better the coming year? The crows might as well have had it, or the cutworms; while all my work is for nothing."

"You're making a big mistake," said Kate. "If your corn was the finest, it was, and the judges knew it, and you know it, and very likely the man who has the first prize, knows it. You have a clean conscience, and you know what you know. They surely can't feel right about it, or enjoy what they know. You have had the experience, you have the corn for seed; with these things to back you, clear a small strip of new land beside the woods this winter, and try what that will do for you."

Adam looked at her with wide eyes. "By jing, Mother, you are a dandy!" he said. "You just bet I'll try that next year, but don't you tell a soul; there are more than you who will let a strip be cleared, in an effort to grow blue ribbon corn. How did you come to think of it?"

"Your saying all your work had been for nothing, made me think of it," she answered. "Let them give another man the prize, when they know your corn is the best. It's their way of keeping a larger number of people interested and avoiding the appearance of partiality; this contest was too close; next year, you grow such corn, that the *corn* will force the decision in spite of the judges. Do you see?"

"I see," said Adam. "I'll try again."

After that life went on as usual. The annual Christmas party was the loveliest of all, because Kate gave it loving thought, and because all of their hearts were especially touched. As spring came on again, Kate and Adam studied over their work, planning many changes for the better, but each time they talked, when everything else was arranged, they came back to corn. More than once, each of them dreamed corn that winter while asleep, they frankly talked of it many times a day. Location, soil, fertilizers, seed, cultivation – they even studied the almanacs for a general forecast of the weather. These things brought them very close together. Also it was admitted between them, that Little Poll "grappled them with hooks of steel." They never lacked subjects for conversation. Poll always came first, corn next, and during the winter there began to be discussion of plans for Adam and Milly. Should Milly come with them, or should they build a small house on the end of the farm nearest her mother? Adam did not care, so he married Milly speedily. Kate could not make up her mind. Milly had the inclination of a bird for a personal and private nest of her own. So spring came to them.

August brought the anniversary of Nancy Ellen's death, which again saddened all of them. Then came cooler September weather, and the usual rush of preparation for winter. Kate was everywhere and enjoying her work immensely. On sturdy, tumbly legs Little Poll trotted after her or rode in state on her shoulder, when distances were too far. If Kate took her to the fields, as she did every day, she carried along the half of an old pink and white quilt, which she spread in a shaded place and filled the baby's lap with acorns, wild flowers, small brightly coloured stones, shells, and whatever she could pick up for playthings. Poll amused herself with these until the heat and air made her sleepy, then she laid herself down and slept for an hour or two. Once she had trouble with stomach teeth that brought Dr. Gray racing, and left Kate white and limp with fear. Everything else had gone finely and among helping Adam, working in her home, caring for the baby, doing whatever she could see that she thought would be of benefit to the community, and what was assigned her by church committees, Kate had a busy life. She had earned, in a degree, the leadership she exercised in her first days in Walden. Everyone liked her; but no one ever ventured to ask her for an opinion unless they truly wanted it.

Adam came from a run to Hartley for groceries one evening in late September, with a look of concern that Kate noticed on his face. He was very silent during supper and when they were on the porch as usual, he still sat as if thinking deeply. Kate knew that he would tell her what he was thinking about when he was ready but she was not in the least prepared for what he said.

"Mother, how do you feel about Uncle Robert marrying again?" he asked suddenly.

Kate was too surprised to answer. She looked at him in amazement. Instead of answering, she asked him a question: "What makes you ask that?"

"You know how that Mrs. Southey pursued him one summer. Well, she's back in Hartley, staying at the hotel right across from his office; she's dressed to beat the band, she's pretty as a picture; her car stands out in front all day, and to get to ride in it, and take meals with her, all the women are running after her. I hear she has even had Robert's old mother out for a drive. What do you think of that?"

"Think she's in love with him, of course, and trying to marry him, and that she will very probably succeed. If she has located where she is right under his eye, and lets him know that she wants him very much, he'll, no doubt, marry her."

"But what do you *think* about it?" asked Adam.

"I've had no *time* to think," said Kate. "At first blush, I'd say that I shall hate it, as badly as I could possibly hate anything that was none of my immediate business. Nancy Ellen loved him so. I never shall forget that day she first told me about him, and how loving him brought out her beauty, and made her shine and glow as if from an inner light. I was always with her most, and I loved her more than all the other girls put together. I know that Southey woman tried to take him from her one summer not long ago, and that he gave her to understand that she could not, so she went away. If she's back, it means only one thing, and I think probably she'll succeed; but you can be sure it will make me squirm properly."

"I *thought* you wouldn't like it," he said emphatically.

"Now understand me, Adam," said Kate. "I'm no fool. I didn't expect Robert to be more than human. He has no children, and he'd like a child above anything else on earth. I've known that for years, ever since it became apparent that none was coming to Nancy Ellen. I hadn't given the matter a thought, but if I had been thinking, I would have thought that as soon as was proper, he would select a strong, healthy young woman, and make her his wife. I know his mother is homesick, and wants to go back to her daughters and their children, which is natural. I haven't an objection in the world to him marrying a *proper* woman, at a proper time and place; but Oh, dear Lord, I do dread and despise to see that little Southey cat come back and catch him, because she knows how."

"Did you ever see her, Mother?"

"No, I never," said Kate, "and I hope I never shall. I know what Nancy Ellen felt, because she told me all about it that time we were up North. I'm trying with all my might to have a Christian spirit. I swallowed Mrs. Peters, and never blinked, that anybody saw; but I don't, I truly don't know from where I could muster grace to treat a woman decently, who tried to do to my sister, what I *know* Mrs. Southey tried to do to Nancy Ellen. She planned to break up my sister's home; that I know. Now that Nancy Ellen is gone, I feel to-night as if I just couldn't endure to see Mrs. Southey marry Robert."

"Bet she does it!" said Adam.

"Did you see her?" asked Kate.

"See her!" cried Adam. "I saw her half a dozen times in an hour. She's in the heart of the town, nothing to do but dress and motor. Never saw such a peach of a car. I couldn't help looking at it. Gee, I wish I could get you one like that!"

"What did you think of her looks?" asked Kate.

"Might pretty!" said Adam, promptly. "Small, but not tiny; plump, but not fat; pink, light curls, big baby blue eyes and a sort of hesitating way about her, as if she were anxious to do the right thing, but feared she might not, and wished somebody would take care of her."

Kate threw out her hands with a rough exclamation. "I get the picture!" she said. "It's a dead centre shot. *That* gets a man, every time. No man cares a picayune about a woman who can take care of herself, and help him with his job if he has a ghost of a chance at a little pink and white clinger, who will suck the life and talent out of him, like the parasite she is, while she makes him believe he is on the job, taking care of her. You can rest assured it will be settled before Christmas."

Kate had been right in her theories concerning the growing of blue ribbon corn. At the County Fair in late September Adam exhibited such heavy ears of evenly grained white and yellow corn that the blue ribbon he carried home was not an award of the judges; it was a concession to the just demands of the exhibit.

Then they began husking their annual crop. It had been one of the country's best years for corn. The long, even, golden ears they were stripping the husks from and stacking in heaps over the field might profitably have been used for seed by any farmer. They had divided the field in halves and Adam was husking one side, Kate the other. She had a big shock open and kneeling beside it she was busy stripping open the husks, and heaping up the yellow ears. Behind her the shocks stood like rows of stationed sentinels; above, the crisp October sunshine warmed the air to a delightful degree; around the field, the fence rows were filled with purple and rose coloured asters, and everywhere goldenrod, yellower than the corn, was hanging in heavy heads of pollen-spraying bloom.

On her old pink quilt Little Poll, sound asleep, was lifted from the shade of one shock to another, while Kate worked across her share of the field. As she worked she kept looking at the child. She frankly adored her, but she kept her reason and held to rigid rules in feeding, bathing, and dressing. Poll minded even a gesture or a nod.

Above, the flocking larks pierced the air with silver notes, on the fence-rows the gathering robins called to each other; high in the air the old black vulture that homed in a hollow log in Kate's woods, looked down on the spots of colour made by the pink quilt, the gold corn, the blue of Kate's dress, and her yellow head. An artist would have paused long, over the rich colour, the grouping and perspective of that picture, while the hazy fall atmosphere softened and blended the whole. Kate, herself, never had appeared or felt better. She worked rapidly, often glancing across the field to see if she was even with, or slightly in advance of

Adam. She said it would never do to let the boy get "heady," so she made a point of keeping even with him, and caring for Little Poll, "for good measure."

She was smiling as she watched him working like a machine as he ripped open husks, gave the ear a twist, tossed it aside, and reached for the next. Kate was doing the same thing, quite as automatically. She was beginning to find the afternoon sun almost hot on her bare head, so she turned until it fell on her back. Her face was flushed to coral pink, and framed in a loose border of her beautiful hair. She was smiling at the thought of how Adam was working to get ahead of her, smiling because Little Poll looked such a picture of healthy loveliness, smiling because she was so well, she felt super-abundant health rising like a stimulating tide in her body, smiling because the corn was the finest she ever had seen in a commonly cultivated field, smiling because she and Adam were of one accord about everything, smiling because the day was very beautiful, because her heart was at peace, her conscience clear.

She heard a car stop at her gate, saw a man alight and start across the yard toward the field, and knew that her visitor had seen her, and was coming to her. Kate went on husking corn and when the man swung over the fence of the field she saw that he was Robert, and instantly thought of Mrs. Southey, so she ceased to smile. "I've got a big notion to tell him what I think of him," she said to herself, even as she looked up to greet him. Instantly she saw that he had come for something.

"What is it?" she asked.

"Agatha," he said. "She's been having some severe heart attacks lately, and she just gave me a real scare."

Instantly Kate forgot everything, except Agatha, whom she cordially liked, and Robert, who appeared older, more tired, and worried than she ever had seen him. She thought Agatha had "given him a real scare," and she decided that it scarcely would have been bad enough to put lines in his face she never had noticed before, dark circles under his eyes, a look of weariness in his bearing. She doubted as she looked at him if he were really courting Mrs. Southey. Even as she thought of these things she was asking: "She's better now?"

"Yes, easier, but she suffered terribly. Adam was upset completely. Adam, 3d, and Susan and their families are away from home and won't be back for a few days unless I send for them. They went to Ohio to visit some friends. I stopped to ask if it would be possible for you to go down this evening and sleep there, so that if there did happen to be a recurrence, Adam wouldn't be alone."

"Of course," said Kate, glancing at the baby. "I'll go right away!"

"No need for that," he said, "if you'll arrange to stay with Adam to-night, as a precaution. You needn't go till bed-time. I'm going back after supper to put them in shape for the night. I'm almost sure she'll be all right now; but you know how frightened we can get about those we love."

"Yes, I know," said Kate, quietly, going straight on ripping open ear after ear of corn. Presently she wondered why he did not go. She looked up at him and met his eyes. He was studying her intently. Kate was vividly conscious in an instant of her bare wind-teased head, her husking gloves; she was not at all sure that her face was clean. She smiled at him, and picking up the sunbonnet lying beside her, she wiped her face with the skirt.

"If this sun hits too long on the same spot, it grows warm," she told him.

"Kate, I do wish you wouldn't!" he exclaimed abruptly.

Kate was too forthright for sparring.

"Why not?" she asked.

"For one thing, you are doing a man's work," he said. "For another, I hate to see you burn the loveliest hair I ever saw on the head of a woman, and coarsen your fine skin."

Kate looked down at the ear of corn she held in her hands, and considered an instant.

"There hasn't any man been around asking to relieve me of this work," she said. "I got my start in life doing a man's work, and I'm frank to say that I'd far rather do it any day, than what is usually considered a woman's. As for my looks, I never set a price on them or let them interfere with business, Robert."

"No, I know you don't," he said. "But it's a pity to spoil you."

"I don't know what's the matter with you," said Kate, patiently. She bent her head toward him. "Feel," she said, "and see if my hair isn't soft and fine. I always cover it in really burning sun; this autumn haze is good for it. My complexion is exactly as smooth and even now, as it was the day I first met you on the footlog over twenty years ago. There's one good thing about the Bates women. They wear well. None of us yet have ever faded, and frazzled out. Have you got many Hartley women, doing what you call women's work, to compare with me physically, Robert?"

"You know the answer to that," he said.

"So I do!" said Kate. "I see some of them occasionally, when business calls me that way. Now, Robert, I'm so well, I feel like running a footrace the first thing when I wake up every morning. I'm making money, I'm starting my boy in a safe, useful life; have you many year and a half babies in your practice that can beat Little Poll? I'm as happy as it's humanly possible for me to be without Mother, and Polly, and Nancy Ellen. Mother used always to say that when death struck a family it seldom stopped until it took three. That was my experience, and saving Adam and Little Poll, it took my three dearest; but the separation isn't going to be so very long. If I were you I wouldn't worry about me, Robert. There are many women in the world willing to pay for your consideration; save it for them."

"Kate, I'm sorry I said anything," he said hastily. "I wouldn't offend you purposely, you know."

Kate looked at him in surprise. "But I'm not offended," she said, snapping an ear and reaching for another. "I am merely telling you! Don't give me a thought! I'm all right! If you'll save me an hour the next time Little Poll has a tooth coming through, you'll have completely earned my gratitude. Tell Agatha I'll come as soon as I finish my evening work."

That was clearly a dismissal, for Kate glancing across the field toward Adam, saw that he had advanced to a new shock, so she began husking faster than before.

The Eleventh Hour

Robert said good-bye and started back toward his car. Kate looked after him as he reached the fence. A surge of pity for him swept up in her heart. He seemed far from happy, and he surely was very tired. Impulsive as always, she lifted her clear voice and called: "Robert!"

He paused with his foot on a rail of the fence, and turned toward her.

"Have you had any dinner?" she asked.

He seemed to be considering. "Come to think of it, I don't believe I have," he said.

"I thought you looked neglected," said Kate. "Sonny across the field is starting a shock ahead of me; I can't come, but go to the kitchen – the door is unlocked – you'll find fried chicken and some preserves and pickles in the pantry; the bread box is right there, and the milk and butter are in the spring house."

He gave Kate one long look. "Thank you," he said and leaped the fence. He stopped on the front walk and stood a minute, then he turned and went around the house. She laughed aloud. She was sending him to chicken perfectly cooked, barely cold, melon preserves, pickled cucumbers, and bread like that which had for years taken a County Fair prize each fall; butter yellow as the goldenrod lining the fences, and cream stiff enough to stand alone. Also, he would find neither germ nor mould in her pantry and spring house, while it would be a new experience for him to let him wait on himself. Kate husked away in high good humour, but she quit an hour early to be on time to go to Agatha. She explained this to Adam, when she told him that he would have to milk alone, while she bathed and dressed herself and got supper.

When she began to dress, Kate examined her hair minutely, and combed it with unusual care. If Robert was at Agatha's when she got there, she would let him see that her hair was not sunburned and ruined. To match the hair dressing, she reached back in her closet and took down her second best white dress. She was hoping that Agatha would be well enough to have a short visit. Kate worked so steadily that she seldom saw any of her brothers and sisters during the summer. In winter she spent a day with each of them, if she could possibly manage. Anyway, Agatha would like to see her appearing well, so she put on the plain snowy linen, and carefully pinning a big apron over it, she went to the kitchen. They always had a full dinner at noon and worked until dusk. Her bath had made her later than she intended to be. Dusk was deepening, evening chill was beginning to creep into the air. She closed the door, fed Little Poll and rolled her into bed; set the potatoes boiling, and began mixing the biscuit. She had them just ready to roll when steam lifted the lid of the potato pot; with the soft dough in her hand she took a step to right it. While it was in her fingers, she peered into the pot.

She did not look up on the instant the door opened, because she thought it would be Adam. When she glanced toward the door, she saw Robert standing looking at her. He had stepped inside, closed the door, and with his hand on the knob was waiting for her to see him.

"Oh! Hello!" said Kate. "I thought it was Adam. Have you been to Agatha's yet?"

"Yes. She is very much better," he said. "I only stopped to tell you that her mother happened to come out for the night, and they'll not need you."

"I'm surely glad she is better," said Kate, "but I'm rather disappointed. I've been swimming, and I'm all ready to go."

She set the pot lid in place accurately and gave her left hand a deft turn to save the dough from dripping. She glanced from it to Robert, expecting to see him open the door and disappear. Instead he stood looking at her intently. Suddenly he said: "Kate, will you marry me?"

Kate mechanically saved the dough again, as she looked at the pot an instant, then she said casually: "Sure! It would be splendid to have a doctor right in the house when Little Poll cuts her double teeth."

"Thank you!" said Robert, tersely. "No doubt that *would* be a privilege, but I decline to marry you in order to see Little Poll safely through teething. Good-night!"

He stepped outside and closed the door very completely, and somewhat pronouncedly.

Kate stood straight an instant, then realized biscuit dough was slowly creeping down her wrist. With a quick fling, she shot the mass into the scrap bucket and sinking on the chair she sat on to peel vegetables, she lifted her apron, laid her head on her knees, and gave a big gulping sob or two. Then she began to cry silently. A minute later the door opened again. That time it had to be Adam, but Kate did not care what he saw or what he thought. She cried on in perfect abandon.

Then steps crossed the room, someone knelt beside her, put an arm around her and said: "Kate, why are you crying?"

Kate lifted her head suddenly, and applied her apron skirt. "None of your business," she said to Robert's face, six inches from hers.

"Are you so anxious as all this about Little Poll's teeth?" he asked.

"Oh, *drat* Little Poll's teeth!" cried Kate, the tears rolling uninterruptedly.

"Then *why* did you say that to me?" he demanded.

"Well, you said you 'only stopped to tell me that I needn't go to Agatha's,'" she explained. "I had to say something, to get even with you!"

"Oh," said Robert, and took possession. Kate put her arms around his neck, drew his head against hers, and knew a minute of complete joy.

When Adam entered the house his mother was very busy. She was mixing more biscuit dough, she was laughing like a girl of sixteen, she snatched out one of their finest tablecloths, and put on many extra dishes for supper, while Uncle Robert, looking like a different man, was helping her. He was actually stirring the gravy, and getting the water, and setting up chairs. And he was under high tension, too. He was saying things of no moment, as if they were profound wisdom, and laughing hilariously at things that were scarcely worth a smile. Adam looked on, and marvelled and all the while his irritation grew. At last he saw a glance of understanding pass between them. He could endure it no longer.

"Oh, you might as well *say* what you think," he burst forth. "You forgot to pull down the blinds."

Both the brazen creatures laughed as if that were a fine joke. They immediately threw off all reserve. By the time the meal was finished, Adam was struggling to keep from saying the meanest things he could think of. Also, he had to go to Milly, with nothing very definite to tell. But when he came back, his mother was waiting for him. She said at once: "Adam, I'm very sorry the blind was up to-night. I wanted to talk to you, and tell you myself, that the first real love for a man that I have ever known, is in my heart to-night."

"Why, Mother!" said Adam.

"It's true," said Kate, quietly. "You see Adam, the first time I ever saw Robert Gray, I knew, and he knew, that he had made a mistake in engaging himself to Nancy Ellen; but the thing was done, she was happy, we simply realized that we would have done better together, and let it go at that. But all these years I have known that I could have made him a wife who would have come closer to his ideals than my sister, and *she* should have had the man who wanted to marry me. They would have had a wonderful time together."

"And where did my father come in?" asked Adam, quietly.

"He took advantage of my blackest hour," said Kate. "I married him when I positively didn't care what happened to me. The man I could have *loved* was married to my sister, the man I could have married and lived with in comfort to both of us was out of the question; it was in the Bates blood to marry about the time I did; I had seen only the very best of your father, and he was an attractive lover, not bad looking, not embarrassed with one single scruple – it's the way of the world. I took it. I paid for it. Only God knows how dearly I paid; but Adam, if you love me, stand by me now. Let me have this eleventh hour happiness, with no alloy. Anything I feel for your Uncle Robert has nothing in the world to do with my being your mother; with you being my son. Kiss me, and tell me you're glad, Adam."

Adam rose up and put his arms around his mother. All his resentment was gone. He was happy as he could be for his mother, and happier than he ever before had been for himself.

The following afternoon, Kate took the car and went to see Agatha instead of husking corn. She dressed with care and arrived about three o'clock, leading Poll in whitest white, with cheeks still rosy from her afternoon nap. Agatha was sitting up and delighted to see them. She said they were the first of the family who had come to visit her, and she thought they had come because she was thinking of them. Then she told Kate about her illness. She said it dated from father Bates stroke, and the dreadful days immediately following, when Adam had completely lost self-control, and she had not been able to influence him. "I think it broke my heart," she said simply. Then they talked the family over, and at last Agatha said: "Kate, what is this I hear about Robert? Have you been informed that Mrs. Southey is back in Hartley, and that she is working every possible chance and using multifarious blandishments on him?"

Kate laughed heartily and suddenly. She never had heard "blandishments" used in common conversation. As she struggled to regain self-possession Agatha spoke again.

"It's no laughing matter," she said. "The report has every ear-mark of verisimilitude. The Bates family has a way of feeling deeply. We all loved Nancy Ellen. We all suffered severely and lost something that never could be replaced when she went. Of course all of us realized that Robert would enter the bonds of matrimony again; none of us would have objected, even if he remarried soon; but all of us do object to his marrying a woman who would have broken Nancy Ellen's heart if she could; and yesterday I took advantage of my illness, and *told* him so. Then I asked him why a man of his standing and ability in this community didn't frustrate that unprincipled creature's vermiculations toward him, by marrying you, at once."

Slowly Kate sank down in her chair. Her face whitened and then grew greenish. She breathed with difficulty.

"Oh, Agatha!" was all she could say.

"I do not regret it," said Agatha. "If he is going to ruin himself, he is not going to do it without knowing that the Bates family highly disapprove of his course."

"But why drag me in?" said Kate, almost too shocked to speak at all. "Maybe he *loves* Mrs. Southey. She has let him see how she feels about him; possibly he feels the same about her."

"He does, if he weds her," said Agatha, conclusively. "Anything any one could say or do would have no effect, if he had centred his affections upon her, of that you may be very sure."

"May I?" asked Kate, dully.

"Indeed, you may!" said Agatha. "The male of the species, when he is a man of Robert's attainments and calibre, can be swerved from pursuit of the female he covets, by nothing save extinction."

"You mean," said Kate with an effort, "that if Robert asked a woman to marry him, it would mean that he loved her."

"Indubitably!" cried Agatha.

Kate laughed until she felt a little better, but she went home in a mood far different from that in which she started. Then she had been very happy, and she had intended to tell Agatha about her happiness, the very first of all. Now she was far from happy. Possibly – a thousand things, the most possible, that Robert had responded to Agatha's suggestion, and stopped and asked her that abrupt question, from an impulse as sudden and inexplicable as had possessed her when she married George Holt. Kate fervently wished she had gone to the cornfield as usual that afternoon.

"That's the way it goes," she said angrily, as she threw off her better dress and put on her every-day gingham to prepare supper. "That's the way it goes! Stay in your element, and go on with your work, and you're all right. Leave your job and go trapesing over the country, wasting your time, and you get a heartache to pay you. I might as well give up the idea that I'm ever to be happy, like anybody else. Every time I think happiness is coming my way, along comes something that knocks it higher than Gilderoy's kite. Hang the luck!"

She saw Robert pass while she was washing the dishes, and knew he was going to Agatha's, and would stop when he came back. She finished her work, put Little Poll to bed, and made herself as attractive as she knew how in her prettiest blue dress. All the time she debated whether she would say anything to him about what Agatha had said or not. She decided she would wait awhile, and watch how he acted. She thought she could soon tell. So when Robert came, she was as nearly herself as possible, but when he began to talk about being married soon, the most she would say was that she would begin to think about it at Christmas, and tell him by spring. Robert was bitterly disappointed. He was very lonely; he needed better housekeeping than his aged mother was capable of, to keep him up to a high mark in his work. Neither of them was young any longer; he could see no reason why they should not be married at once. Of the reason in Kate's mind, he had not a glimmering. But Kate had her way. She would not even talk of a time, or express an opinion as to whether she would remain on the farm, or live in Nancy Ellen's house, or sell it and build whatever she wanted for herself. Robert went away baffled, and disappointed over some intangible thing he could not understand.

For six weeks Kate tortured herself, and kept Robert from being happy. Then one morning Agatha stopped to visit with her, while Adam drove on to town. After they had exhausted farming, Little Poll's charms, and the neighbours, Agatha looked at Kate and said: "Katherine, what is this I hear about Robert coming here every day, now? It appeals to me that he must have followed my advice."

"Of course he never would have thought of coming, if you hadn't told him so," said Kate dryly.

"Now *there* you are in error," said the literal Agatha, as she smoothed down Little Poll's skirts and twisted her ringlets into formal corkscrews. "Right *there*, you are in error, my dear. The reason I told Robert to marry you was because he said to me, when he suggested going after you to stay the night with me, that he had seen you in the field when he passed, and that you were the most glorious specimen of womanhood that he ever had seen. He said you were the one to stay with me, in case there should be any trouble, because your head was always level, and your heart was big as a barrel."

"Yes, that's the reason I can't always have it with me," said Kate, looking glorified instead of glorious. "Agatha, it just happens to mean very much to me. Will you just kindly begin at the beginning, and tell me every single word Robert said to you, and you said to him, that day?"

"Why, I have informed you explicitly," said Agatha, using her handkerchief on the toe of Poll's blue shoe. "He mentioned going after you, and said what I told you, and I told him to go. He praised you so highly that when I spoke to him about the Southey woman I remembered it, so I suggested to him, as he seemed to think so well of you. It just that minute flashed into my mind; but HE made me think of it, calling you 'glorious,' and 'level headed,' and 'big hearted.' Heavens! Katherine Eleanor, what more could you ask?"

"I guess that should be enough," said Kate.

"One certainly would presume so," said Agatha.

Then Adam came, and handed Kate her mail as she stood beside his car talking to him a minute, while Agatha settled herself. As Kate closed the gate behind her, she saw a big, square white envelope among the newspapers, advertisements, and letters. She slipped it out and looked at it intently. Then she ran her finger under the flap and read the contents. She stood studying the few lines it contained, frowning deeply. "Doesn't it beat the band?" she asked of the surrounding atmosphere. She went up the walk, entered the living room, slipped the letter under the lid of the big family Bible, and walking to the telephone she called Dr. Gray's office. He answered the call in person.

"Robert, this is Kate," she said. "Would you have any deeply rooted objections to marrying me at six o'clock this evening?"

"Well, I should say not!" boomed Robert's voice, the "not" coming so forcibly Kate dodged.

"Have you got the information necessary for a license?" she asked.

"Yes," he answered.

"Then bring one, and your minister, and come at six," she said. "And Oh, yes, Robert, will it be all right with you if I stay here and keep house for Adam until he and Milly can be married and move in? Then I'll come to your house just as it is. I don't mind coming to Nancy Ellen's home, as I would another woman's."

"Surely!" he cried. "Any arrangement you make will satisfy me."

"All right, I'll expect you with the document and the minister at six, then," said Kate, and hung up the receiver.

Then she took it down again and calling Milly, asked her to bring her best white dress, and come up right away, and help her get ready to entertain a few people that evening. Then she called her sister Hannah, and asked her if she thought that in the event she, Kate, wished that evening at six o'clock to marry a very fine man, and had no preparations whatever made, her family would help her out to the extent of providing the supper. She wanted all of them, and all the children, but the arrangement had come up suddenly, and she could not possibly prepare a supper herself, for such a big family, in the length of time she had. Hannah said she was perfectly sure everyone of them would drop everything, and be tickled to pieces to bring the supper, and to come, and they would have a grand time. What did Kate want? Oh, she wanted bread, and chicken for meat, maybe some potato chips, and Angel's Food cake, and a big freezer or two of Agatha's best ice cream, and she thought possibly more butter, and coffee, than she had on hand. She had plenty of sugar, and cream, and pickles and jelly. She would have the tables all set as she did for Christmas. Then Kate rang for Adam and put a broom in his hand as he entered the back door. She met Milly with a pail of hot water and cloths to wash the glass. She went to her room and got out her best afternoon dress of dull blue with gold lace and a pink velvet rose. She shook it out and studied it. She had worn it twice on the trip North. None of them save Adam ever had seen it. She put it on, and looked at it critically. Then she called Milly and they changed the neck and sleeves a little, took a yard of width from the skirt, and behold! it became a "creation," in the very height of style. Then Kate opened her trunk, and got out the petticoat, hose, and low shoes to match it, and laid them on her bed.

Then they set the table, laid a fire ready to strike in the cook stove, saw that the gas was all right, set out the big coffee boiler, and skimmed a crock full of cream. By four o'clock, they could think of nothing else to do. Then Kate bathed and went to her room to dress. Adam and Milly were busy making themselves fine. Little Poll sat in her prettiest dress, watching her beloved "Tate," until Adam came and took her. He had been instructed to send Robert and the minister to his mother's room as soon as they came. Kate was trying to look her best, yet making haste, so that she would be ready on time. She had made no arrangements except to spread a white goatskin where she and Robert would stand at the end of the big living room near her door. Before she was fully dressed she began to hear young voices and knew that her people were coming. When she was ready Kate looked at herself and muttered: "I'll give Robert and all of them a good surprise. This is a real dress, thanks to Nancy Ellen. The poor girl! It's scarcely fair to her to marry her man in a dress she gave me; but I'd stake my life she'd rather I'd have him than any other woman."

It was an evening of surprises. At six, Adam lighted a big log, festooned with leaves and berries so that the flames roared and crackled up the chimney. The early arrivals were the young people who had hung the mantel, gas fixtures, curtain poles and draped the doors with long sprays of bittersweet, northern holly, and great branches of red spice berries, dogwood with its red leaves and berries, and scarlet and yellow oak leaves. The elders followed and piled the table with heaps of food, then trailed red vines between dishes. In a quandary as to what to wear, without knowing what was expected of him further than saying "I will," at the proper moment, Robert ended by slipping into Kate's room, dressed in white flannel. The ceremony was over at ten minutes after six. Kate was lovely, Robert was handsome, everyone was happy, the supper was a banquet. The Bates family went home, Adam disappeared with Milly, while Little Poll went to sleep.

Left to themselves, Robert took Kate in his arms and tried to tell her how much he loved her, but felt he expressed himself poorly. As she stood before him, he said: "And now, dear, tell me what changed you, and why we are married to-night instead of at Christmas, or in the spring."

"Oh, yes," said Kate, "I almost forgot! Why, I wanted you to answer a letter for me."

"Lucid!" said Robert. He seated himself beside the table. "Bring on the ink and stationary, and let me get it over."

Kate obeyed, and with the writing material, laid down the letter she had that morning received from John Jardine, telling her that his wife had died suddenly, and that as soon as he had laid her away, he was coming to exact a definite promise from her as to the future; and that he would move Heaven and earth before he would again be disappointed. Robert read the letter and laid it down, his face slowing flushing scarlet.

"You called me out here, and married me expressly to answer this?" he demanded.

"Of course!" said Kate. "I thought if you could tell him that his letter came the day I married you, it would stop his coming, and not be such a disappointment to him."

Robert pushed the letter from him violently, and arose "By – –!" he checked himself and stared at her. "Kate, you don't *mean* that!" he cried. "Tell me, you don't *mean* that!"

"Why, *sure* I do," said Kate. "It gave me a fine excuse. I was so homesick for you, and tired waiting to begin life with you. Agatha told me about her telling you the day she was ill, to marry me; and the reason I wouldn't was because I thought maybe you asked me so offhandlike, because she *told* you to, and you didn't really love me. Then this morning she was here, and we were talking, and she got round it again, and then she told me *all* you said, and I saw you did love me, and that you would have asked me if she hadn't said anything, and I wanted you so badly. Robert, ever since that day we met on the footlog, I've know that you were the only man I'd every really *want* to marry. Robert, I've never come anywhere near loving anybody else. The minute Agatha told me this morning, I began to think how I could take back what I'd been saying, how I could change, and right then Adam handed me that letter, and it gave me a fine way out, and so I called you. Sure, I married you to answer that, Robert; now go and do it."

"All right," he said. "In a minute."

Then he walked to her and took her in his arms again, but Kate could not understand why he was laughing until he shook when he kissed her.

Made in the USA
Lexington, KY
20 September 2010